I0742728

NOVEL PROBLEMS

ELIZABETH LULY

Copyright © 2024, Elizabeth Luly

Cover design © 2024, Elizabeth Luly

Cover design and illustration by Ink and Laurel

The moral rights of the author have been asserted. All rights reserved. No part of this book may be reproduced, stored in a retrieval system, stored in a database and/or transmitted or published in any form or by any means, electronic, mechanical, photocopying, recording or otherwise (other than brief quotations embodied in critical articles or reviews) without the prior written permission of the author.

This book is a work of fiction. All characters and events in this book are fictitious or are used fictitiously. Any similarity to real persons, living or dead, is purely coincidental and not intended by the author.

All brand names and product names used in this book are trademarks, registered trademarks or trade names of their respective holders. The author is not associated with any product or vendor in this book.

ISBN 978-0-6455808-5-3 (paperback)

ISBN 978-0-6455808-4-6 (ebook)

CHAPTER ONE

HANNAH

PEACE AND QUIET. At last.

I inhaled a deep breath of warm, pine-scented air as I leaned against the balcony, taking in the view. Through the dense green leaves of the oak and fir trees that surrounded my new home, I caught glimpses of the Hudson River sparkling in the sunshine.

After avoiding human contact for months, interacting with three burly and unexpectedly chatty movers had sent my anxiety—already at high levels—spiking. But now they were gone, the tension in my chest had released. Apart from the occasional boat traveling down the river at a safe distance, there were no signs of human life.

I'd choose this over our—I mean, Tania's—fancy Upper West Side apartment any day of the week.

A small blue bird with a fluffy white chest flew overhead and landed on the gutter of the roof behind me.

"Well, hello, little fellow," I murmured.

He looked me directly in the eye, tilted his head, took a gigantic poop onto one of the deck chairs, and then flew off.

"Thanks for the housewarming present," I called after

him, laughing, as he disappeared out of sight over the trees. Still chuckling, I turned my attention back to the view.

My phone rang faintly, interrupting the tranquility of the moment. I tensed. *Shit, who could that be? Tania?* My stomach flipped at the thought. We did need to talk about splitting our assets so we could finalize our divorce, but I'd hoped that could wait. Or was Barb calling for an update on my move? That would be infinitely more preferable. I frowned. *Where the hell is my phone, anyway?*

I ran inside to my tiny new living room, covered with boxes, and scanned the chaotic scene for my red phone case. *Could it have fallen into one of the boxes I was unpacking?* I'd managed to misplace my hearing aid for my left ear in the move, and its absence made it more difficult to locate sounds. My right ear, although unaffected by hearing loss, struggled on its own.

I frantically searched through the open boxes. *Not there. What did I do with it?* Surveying the room, I spotted a familiar flash of red poking out from under a pile of underwear I'd left on the coffee table. My hands shook as I threw the underwear away and disentangled a lacy black bra from my phone. I looked at the screen.

A video call from Emma. *Well, at least it isn't Tania.*

But I didn't relax. Emma was a wonderful literary agent and a close friend, but I didn't want to talk about books—specifically, my book—right now. My very much non-existent book. I sighed, took a deep breath and accepted her call.

Emma's smiling face appeared on my phone screen, framed by her long blonde hair. "Hannah! How are you doing?"

"Good, good! I just moved in. How are you?"

Emma's gaze shifted. She narrowed her eyes and gave

me a playful grin. "Ohhh! What have you been up to?" she asked.

I frowned in confusion and then realized she could see the lacy black bra I'd thrown off my phone on the armchair behind me.

I rolled my eyes, laughing. "Unpacking, Emma. Not having an orgy with my movers or wherever your mind just went."

"Sorry, sorry. This is what happens when half your clients write spicy romance. Congratulations on the move, by the way." Emma paused for a second before launching into agent mode. "Look, let me know if now isn't a good time, but I had a chat with Michael and the sales and publicity team today, and there were a few things I wanted to talk to you about."

I'd had an awkward coffee with Michael, my new editor, in Midtown Manhattan a month ago. While very serious, he seemed like a pleasant enough guy, but awkwardness was inevitable given the situation with Tania. In light of that, I'd asked that Michael and the publicity team funnel communications through Emma for now.

Emma continued. "They wanted to know if they should push the launch date for book four. The sales and publicity team would prefer to stick with March next year but if they push it back, they're talking about releasing it in February or March the year after next instead."

Panic rose in my chest. "What? Why would they push it back a whole year?"

"They've got their release schedule planned out and don't want to release too many big fantasy books in any one month to avoid cannibalizing their sales."

Shit. Maybe my publisher could wait another year, but I couldn't.

"If it's any consolation, they don't think you'll lose readers if you wait another year, especially given you've got *The Realm of Furies* releasing at the end of June."

Frowning, I rubbed my forehead with my free hand.

I had some savings in the bank, and the launch of *The Realm of Furies* would hopefully give my finances a welcome boost, but without another book release next year, there was a real risk I wouldn't be able to keep paying Barb's nursing home bills or even my own health insurance, which I'd had to procure for an eye-watering amount now that I was no longer on Tania's plan. The royalties from my earlier books wouldn't be enough, and they were slowly reducing. My throat constricted. Barb could not move back to the horrific nursing home she used to live in. I could cut back on costs, even go without health insurance, but I wasn't willing to sacrifice my beloved former nanny's comfort as well.

I pressed my lips together. I loved a lot of things about being an author, but the lack of guaranteed, predictable income was not one of them. People assumed that *The New York Times* bestselling authors would be millionaires, but that was far from the case—at least for me. Advances were paid in instalments and royalties, which only amounted to a couple of dollars per book sold, were only payable once I'd earned out the advance. After Emma took her cut and the IRS took theirs, it wasn't as lucrative as you'd think.

Before Tania and I split, it hadn't worried me. Tania owned her apartment outright, and I earned enough to pay my share of expenses and Barb's bills. And while I'd never had to rely on it, Tania's trust fund had always given me comfort. Comfort that, thanks to the prenup and our impending divorce, I didn't have anymore. Comfort Barb didn't have either.

"If we don't move the release date, you'll have to submit

the book by mid-July at the latest, which I know will be tight." Emma's voice softened. "You're dealing with a lot at the moment, so let me know if it's not realistic, and I'll manage them."

I swallowed. I hadn't been completely honest with Emma about how much progress—or lack of—I'd made on book four. It was late May now, and mid-July was only seven weeks away. Not a lot of time to write an entire 100,000-word fantasy novel. But pushing back the release date by twelve months was also not an option.

I walked back onto the deck, hoping the fresh air would help me think.

Writing had always been my escape. Having this deadline and Barb's future on the line would force me to get my butt in the chair and stop dwelling on recent events. *Assuming I can write without Tania...*

"Nope, July will be fine!" I blurted. *I wrote before Tania. I can do it again.*

"That's great. I'll let them know," Emma said, her face bright.

I sat down on the deck chair and immediately felt something damp on my ass.

"Shit!" I squealed, inwardly kicking myself.

"What's wrong?" Emma asked, concerned.

"I just sat on bird poop," I groaned.

Emma grinned. "That's what you get for abandoning me and moving to the country. Speaking of which, could you come into the city next week? The books for the pre-order promotion are ready for signing."

I closed my eyes. This call was not going well.

New York used to be my favorite place in the world. Broadway. Incredible art galleries. Amazing cocktails. Mouth-watering bagels stuffed with lox and an inch of cream cheese. But right now, you'd have to drag me kicking and screaming back there. Tania and I had been together for five years. Five years of making memories all over the city. Five years of memories I'd just fled New York to escape.

"Could we get them sent up here?" I tried to think of a good reason why I couldn't make the hour-and-a-half train trip back to the city and failed, leaving the question hanging.

Emma paused. "Let me check. I suspect, given you're one of their top-selling authors at the moment, they should be able to deliver eight hundred copies to your doorstep."

I blinked. *Surely I'd misheard.* "S-sorry, how many?"

"Eight hundred and"—Emma paused, presumably confirming the numbers—"forty-one."

"Wow, okay."

I shook my head, forgetting my troubles momentarily as the number sunk in. It still blew my mind that people wanted to read my books, let alone pre-order special signed copies.

Eight hundred and forty-one copies. Incredible, but also a logistical nightmare. I surveyed the small living room, which led into an equally small kitchen/dining room. My bedroom wasn't exactly spacious either, nor the tiny second room, which I'd planned to use as a study. There was no way eight hundred and forty-one books would fit in my new abode.

"Um, I don't think there's enough room for them here." I racked my brain, trying to think of an alternative solution that didn't involve me catching the Metro North back to Manhattan, and came up blank.

"Let me check... There might be a local bookstore or library we could deliver them to." There was another pause as Emma's manicured nails clacked on the keyboard and her eyes skimmed across the screen. "According to Google Maps, there's a café-bookstore in Sapphire Springs called Novel Gossip. Let's see if I can pull a few strings and get the books delivered there," Emma said.

I breathed out. "That would be amazing. Thanks, Emma." While venturing into Sapphire Springs wasn't part of my plan to live life as a recluse, it was infinitely preferable to stepping foot back in the city.

But my relief was short-lived as realization dawned on me. *Shit.* If I signed the books locally, I'd have to divulge my identity to at least one new person. My heart plummeted.

It's still better than going back into the city—just.

CHAPTER TWO

GEORGE

"I'M SORRY, GEORGE." Ben coughed so loudly I pulled my phone back from my ear. "I slept through all my alarms and I'm feeling terrible."

"It's not your fault. Don't worry about it. We'll manage." I eyed the growing line of customers waiting to place orders and the dirty tables that needed cleaning. Sweat pricked on my face, but there was nothing I could do. Ben was sick, and there was no one I could call on for help. I took a fortifying breath. I'd built Novel Gossip, my dream café-bookstore, from the ground up, pouring my heart and soul into it for the last three years. If required, I'd work myself to the bone to keep it going and make sure I didn't let down my customers.

Romina banged the bell, indicating a food order was ready, so I tucked the phone between my shoulder and ear and rushed into the kitchen. A breakfast burrito was wrapped up and sitting on the counter. I shot a tentative glance at Romina, who frowned as she aggressively sliced some avocado. She was clearly still in a terrible mood.

Ben cleared his throat. "Oh, by the way, a woman came

by after you left yesterday, saying she'd like to apply for the job. I told her to come back today when you're working. She seemed nice—friendly, in her thirties, a bit shy. Just moved to the area with her husband. She could be just what we need."

I handed the breakfast burrito and an iced coffee to Dan, the owner of the pub down the road, with an apologetic smile and grabbed the tongs to put the next customer's muffin in a paper bag while I processed Ben's comment.

Some tension in my chest released at the news of a potential new employee. *Hopefully she hasn't found another job already. Dippin' Donuts would snap her up in a second.* It was a shame she'd showed up after I'd left early to take Maximus, my golden retriever, to the vet for a check-up. An extra pair of hands was exactly what we needed right now. We actually needed two or three more pairs of hands, but I'd take what I could get. This time of year was always busy in Sapphire Springs, which was a popular destination for city-dwellers looking for an escape. We'd been struggling to keep up with demand since Jules resigned three weeks ago to move to Brooklyn. And now that Ben was sick, the situation was dire.

I checked the next order. Two cappuccinos to go. I needed to finish speaking to Ben before I started making them, or he wouldn't be able to hear anything over the noise.

"I hope so. That would be great!" I pulled the portafilter out of the espresso machine.

"I'm sure there was something else I was going to tell you, but it's slipped my mind. I'll text you if I think of it," Ben said, his voice weary.

"Look, rest up and take care of yourself, okay? And don't worry about us. Take as long as you need," I said.

As soon as Ben hung up, I placed my phone on the

counter, and focused my attention on getting through the backlog of coffee orders and serving the waiting customers.

It was just me on the floor today and Romina and Shane in the kitchen. Being run off my feet wasn't a bad problem to have, but if I couldn't give my customers the level of service they were used to, I worried they might take their business elsewhere. Namely, to the Dippin' Donuts chain store around the corner. While their coffee and food couldn't compete with Novel Gossip, and they didn't sell books, they were fast and cheaper. Much to my dismay, I'd already noticed a few customers walk in the door this morning, eye the long line, and then turn on their heels.

As I poured frothed milk into a couple of to-go cups, my phone lit up. I glanced over. Mom. She was probably calling about booking airfares for her visit in June. I eyed the line of waiting customers. I'd have to call her back tonight. A pang of guilt shot through me at letting her call go through to voicemail, but I had to stay focused.

"Here you go. Sorry about the delay," I said as I handed the next customer her coffees.

I took the remaining customers' orders and then set to work completing them as fast as I could.

I'd just put the finishing touches on an iced vanilla latte for one of the local teachers, Maya, and was planning to take advantage of the brief lull in new customers to rush out and clear some tables, when a loud thump made me jump. I looked up to see Rory Goldsworthy glaring at me, four dog-eared books on the counter in front of him, and I sighed. *Here we go again.*

"I want a refund," Rory barked.

Maya shook her head in sympathy as I gave her the latte, and then she sensibly made a quick escape. Rory had a reputation in Sapphire Springs for being the resident grump.

"You've obviously read the books. The spines are creased. You can't return them," I said firmly, trying not to lose my cool. This was the last thing I needed right now.

Rory's face flamed red, a stark contrast to his white hair, as he gave me a death stare. "It's within my legal rights to get a refund."

"No, Rory, it's not. Our return policy states clearly that refunds won't be given for used books. Not only that, but the refund window is thirty days, and you bought these over three months ago." A mild pain throbbed in my head. I'd barely made it through the morning coffee rush, and now I had to spend precious time—that I could have used to clear tables stacked with dirty coffee cups and plates—convincing Rory that Novel Gossip wasn't a lending library.

"I'm going to speak to my lawyer about this," Rory grumbled.

"You do that, Rory." I grabbed the cleaning spray and a cloth and beelined for the dirty tables, hoping he wouldn't follow.

I'd cleaned one table and was halfway through the second when the front door slowly opened, revealing a large man in a baseball cap walking backward, pulling a huge dolly stacked high with boxes of books. A *lot* of boxes of books. At least ten times more books than our usual delivery.

My heart sank. *Please let this not be a repeat of the time I accidentally ordered two hundred copies of a book about the Great Depression instead of two.*

I approached the man. John, our usual delivery driver, had been out sick with the flu, and this was presumably one of his replacements. "Hi, I'm George, the owner. Is all this for us?"

Please say no.

"Yep, all for Novel Gossip," the man said, smiling, looking around. His smile faltered as he took in the tables covered with dirty dishes. At least the bookstore section of Novel Gossip, which stretched from the left of the counter all the way to the back of the building, wasn't in a similar state of disarray. "Where should I offload them?"

Goddamnit. Could this day get any worse?

"Er, would you mind if I looked at the invoice first? I think there may have been a mistake. I'm sure we didn't order this many books."

He handed me the invoice, and I scanned through it. It all looked normal until the note at the end: *Special Delivery: 841 x* The Realm of Furies, *H. M. Stuart.*

My chest tightened. *Shit.* How the hell had I ordered 841 copies of *The Realm of Furies?* Yes, H. M. Stuart was one of my favorite authors, and I'd devoured an advanced reader copy of *The Realm of Furies* a few weeks ago and adored it. One perk of owning a bookstore was that publishers sent me books before they were published. But there was no way I'd be able to sell 841 copies of it in Sapphire Springs. It wasn't even meant to be released for another four or so weeks. I shook my head. The whole thing was strange.

"I'm sorry, I don't think I ordered these books." I pointed at the end note. "If I did, it was a mistake. Would you mind leaving me ten copies and taking the rest?" Even moving ten copies was optimistic.

The man's smile faded further. "No, sorry, you need to sign for them all. If there's a problem, you'll have to speak to the main office about it."

Two customers walked in. One took a seat at a table and another headed to the counter. I glanced at my watch, my heart beating faster than usual. The lunch rush would be starting soon, and I didn't have time to try to convince the delivery person to take the books back. All the books Novel Gossip stocked were returnable to the publisher, so I wasn't worried about getting stuck paying for them. It was more of a logistical issue. It'd been a squeeze fitting a café and a bookstore into this space, so we didn't have a lot of storage space for excess stock and our storage shed was completely full.

Another regular came in. I sighed. I needed to get back to work before I got even further behind. "No problem, thanks. I'll figure it out later." I looked around for somewhere to put the boxes. Most of the back wall was covered in bookshelves, but there was an empty space in one corner, in front of a heater. Given how hot it was already, there'd be no need for the heater for the next couple of months.

"Would you mind stacking the boxes on the far wall?" I pointed through the aisles of books to the back corner. He nodded, and I signed the delivery receipt. "Sorry, I'd better serve these customers. Just let me know if you need anything."

I rushed over to take the customers' orders. I'd just started making a triple shot caramel latte when another person walked through the door. I suppressed a groan. As much as I appreciated my customers' patronage, right now I needed ten uninterrupted minutes to prepare for the lunch rush.

I looked up and did a double-take as my eyes landed on the woman who'd walked in.

She was dressed for the warm weather, in a white tank top and straight-legged light-denim jeans with flat tan sandals. Dark brown, wavy, shoulder-length hair and curly bangs framed her face, and dark eyebrows accentuated her brown eyes. As she looked around, she adjusted the small chestnut-colored leather satchel that hung over one of her shoulders and then pushed her large tortoiseshell glasses up the bridge of her nose with a finger. My gaze dropped to her full pink lips that turned up a little at the ends, like she had a secret that she'd only let a lucky few in on. She had pale skin that suggested she didn't go outside a lot—or perhaps, she was just better than me at applying sunscreen. *Damn.* She was stunning.

I hadn't seen her before, and hers was not a face I'd forget. She must be a tourist. A very attractive tourist, currently staring directly at me. *Please let me not look as sweaty or flustered as I feel right now.*

CHAPTER THREE

HANNAH

THIS PLACE IS ADORABLE. Circular wooden tables, half of them occupied by patrons enjoying morning tea or brunch, took up the front of the store. A long wooden counter with an enormous shiny red espresso machine and an inviting display of cakes stood behind the tables on the right side. Behind the left of the counter stretched aisles of books. The walls were exposed red brick, except for the left wall, which was covered, floor to ceiling, with books on wooden shelves. Two comfortable-looking armchairs were arranged next to the shelves. Perfect for cozying up with a good book and a hot drink. The café smelled of coffee and baked goods, warm and comforting.

My shoulders relaxed. Apart from some early morning walks, which I'd timed and routed to avoid human contact, I hadn't left my new home since I'd moved to Sapphire Springs four days ago. I'd dreaded leaving the house this morning, but now that I'd arrived, it wasn't as bad as I'd expected. Bookstores were my happy place. And so were cafés. While completing my English Literature degree at

NYU, I worked as a server in a tiny French café, Café Mignon, in the West Village. I'd loved getting to know the regulars, serving wide-eyed tourists, and the delicious free meals were an added bonus. Although I'd left my hospitality days behind me, I still enjoyed sitting in cozy cafés by myself, sipping a good coffee, either reading, people-watching, or writing. While I wasn't in the right mindset to do that today, perhaps after I finished signing all the books, I'd grab a takeout coffee and have a quick browse of the bookshelves instead of fleeing immediately.

I sensed eyes on me and looked over to the counter. A woman stood at the espresso machine, frothing milk while she watched me. Her face broke into a warm grin as we made eye contact, revealing the hint of a dimple in her right cheek. For my first face-to-face contact since the movers left, I felt surprisingly at ease. In fact, I found myself smiling back at her.

"Feel free to grab a table anywhere you'd like, and I'll be right over," she yelled over the hiss of the espresso machine before turning her attention to the coffees she was making.

I blinked. *I've been standing here, looking around. Of course she'd assume I'm looking for a table.*

I walked toward the counter, taking the opportunity while the woman's head was down to examine her more closely. Perhaps it wasn't just her warm, relaxed demeanor that had set me at ease. The woman's brown crew-cut hairstyle and button-down shirt gave off major queer vibes. Ever since I'd developed a crush on my super-fit, short-haired yoga instructor in college, convinced she was a lesbian, only to run into her with her husband and baby at the local supermarket a few weeks later, I didn't put too much stock in my gaydar. Although, of course, the instructor might've been queer, bi, or pan. But I still found this woman's presence comforting. *I wonder how LGBTQ-friendly Sapphire Springs is? Not that it matters, given I have no plans to socialize or date.*

She handed a gigantic takeout coffee to a man in his fifties and then turned her attention back to me.

"Sorry, I thought you were here to sit down. What can get you?" Her voice was warm and friendly.

"Hi, sorry, I'm actually not here for coffee. I'm looking for George?"

Emma had emailed me to confirm the books would be delivered this morning and told me to ask for George, the owner. I hadn't seen any sign of a man working here. Perhaps he was in the kitchen or at the back of the bookstore? For the first time since I'd entered, my nerves reappeared, making my mouth dry.

I was an intensely private person. I didn't do public events, social media, or share photos of myself online, and I kept my pen name locked down to a few key people—Tania, Barb, Emma, Michael, my publicist at my publisher, and— any nerve-racking minute now—George.

"Well, you're in luck." The woman grinned again, and that dimple reappeared. "I'm George."

"Hannah," I said, my stomach erupting into butterflies at the news that this attractive woman in front of me was George.

"Nice to meet you. Are you here about—"

The café door opened, and two women walked in, laughing, drowning out the rest of George's question. *Damnit.* I still hadn't found my hearing aid, and this was exactly the type of situation where I really needed it. Background noise. Wooden floors. George standing on my left side.

I smiled and nodded—my usual response when I didn't

hear something. It seemed safe enough in this case. Surely she'd just asked if I was here to sign the books?

George's smile widened. "Oh, excellent! When would you be able to start?"

To my relief, George still seemed relaxed in my presence. I exhaled. One of the many reasons why I kept my identity secret was because I didn't want anyone to treat me differently because of who I was. But George clearly wasn't a *Realms* super fan.

"Um, right now?" I flexed my hands in anticipation of a long signing session. How long would it take to sign 841 books? A few hours? It would have to be at least that. The last time I'd signed around 200 books, it had taken me well over an hour, and by the end of it, my hand was aching. I'd never signed anywhere near 841 in one sitting before.

"Oh, wow." George's brow furrowed. "Look, I'm not sure you're really meant to start before we've done all the paperwork. We should probably do a proper interview as well. But I'm in a bit of a pickle today. Ben, who you met yesterday, is out sick. So, if you could help today, that would be amazing. It could be a trial run for both of us, and I'll pay you, of course. It's twenty-three dollars an hour, plus tips. Does that sound okay?"

I stared at her blankly. *What the hell is she talking about? Ben? Interview? Tips?*

Slowly, realization sank in. My stomach dropped. George thought I was here for a job to work at the café. *Oh god.*

And it didn't help that she was staring at me expectantly with her warm, brown eyes.

I opened my mouth as I searched for the right words to rectify this situation—and searched some more.

Someone coughed, and I looked over to see that a line of customers had formed in front of the counter waiting to order. A wave of panic swept through me, sending blood pumping through my veins and my head fuzzy.

"Yes, sure. That sounds good." I bit down hard as soon as the words left my mouth. *What the hell, Hannah? Why didn't you just tell her who you are?*

The short answer was I panicked. The long answer was that I'd always had a tendency to be a conflict-avoidant people pleaser. And there was something about George— even though I didn't know her at all—that made me want to please her. *But I'll have to tell her who I really am at some point. Those books won't sign themselves. Shit.*

"Oh, great!" George's eyes sparkled. "If you want, I can put your bag in the drawer under the counter. I keep it locked—not that I really need to. Sapphire Springs isn't exactly known for its high crime rate."

Despite the situation I'd just created, I couldn't help smiling.

"Sure." I handed my satchel over to her. "So, um, what can I do to help?" I asked when George had finished stowing my bag away.

"Well, if you wouldn't mind taking this tea over to the woman at table nine, near the window, and then clearing the dirty tables, that would be great. After the lunch rush, I'll show you how to use our ordering and payment system. Meanwhile, I'll serve these customers."

"No problem," I said, taking the tea from the counter and walking over to the table on autopilot as self-chastising thoughts churned through my mind. *You're supposed to be signing the damn books and bunkering down to start the book you've only got six weeks to write, not getting a frigging job, Hannah! Twenty-three dollars an hour isn't going to pay Barb's nursing home bills.*

The customer smiled and thanked me for the tea as I placed it next to her.

The next three hours were a blur of delivering appetizing-looking food, coffee, and cakes; cleaning tables; and sneaking glances at George. She was extremely under-staffed. Even with the two of us, we struggled to keep up with demand, but she remained calm under pressure, warmly greeting customers, whipping up coffees, and shooting orders through to the kitchen. George knew most of her customers' names and their coffee orders by heart.

The lunch rush was over, and I was carrying a pile of dirty dishes to the kitchen when George appeared at the end of the counter, smiling.

"Thank you so much for stepping in. Lunch was hectic. I don't know what I would've done without you." Her smile faded, and she raised her hand to her forehead. "Shit, I just realized—have you eaten? You should take a break. Would you like some lunch and a coffee? Choose anything on the menu. It's on the house."

I blinked. I'd been so caught up in my new role as a server that I'd forgotten to eat. But now that George had raised the subject, my hunger levels skyrocketed from zero to one hundred in seconds.

"That would be amazing, if you're sure that's okay. I'd love a grain salad and a latte." I'd been salivating over the salad all morning. Full of fresh herbs, freekeh, lentils, pome-granate seeds, currants, and slivered almonds, it was a favorite with the locals.

"Of course that's okay. One grain salad and latte coming right up. Just take a seat wherever you'd like, and I'll bring it out."

Relieved to get off my feet, I collapsed on a chair at a table near the window. While the sandals I was wearing were thankfully flat, they didn't offer much in the way of support.

Tomorrow, I'll wear my comfy flats... I ran my hand through my hair. *Tomorrow, Hannah, really? There won't be a tomorrow. You need to come clean with George, sign those damn books, and get back to writing.* I cringed. I was not looking forward to any of those things.

I chewed my lip. George didn't strike me as someone who would ever panic-agree to a career change on the spot. At best, when I confessed who I really was, she would think I was weird. And even though I hardly knew her, I didn't want that.

"Here's your latte and salad," George said a few minutes later, placing a mug and bowl in front of me.

"Thank you." I smiled gratefully at her.

"Take your time. It doesn't usually pick up again until the afternoon coffee rush, but I should be able to handle that, anyway. So let me know if you need to head off. If not, I thought I could train you on the systems, but no problem if you've got other commitments."

Yes, you do have other commitments—signing mountains of books hidden somewhere in this store. I had to tell George, but the words to explain what happened escaped me. My eyes dropped to the salad in front of me and my stomach rumbled. Maybe I'd be able to think more clearly after I'd eaten.

"Nope, that's fine. I'm free all afternoon." I inwardly sighed, frustrated at myself. The longer this went on, the more awkward it would be when I told George the truth. Typical Hannah. If I'd had enough courage to confront Tania when I'd first had suspicions about her infidelity, I wouldn't have wasted years on our relationship.

I demolished my lunch and the latte, which were both delicious, and then spent a few minutes observing the café. It was clear that someone—perhaps George—had created this place with a lot of love and thought. Each item, from the stylish wooden pepper grinders on the tables, to the wooden floating shelves, pressed tin tiles on the ceiling, and brass pendant lights, had clearly been chosen with care, creating a cohesive whole. I peered down the left side of the store, where aisles of books stretched back. I was eager to see if George's selection of books was as carefully curated as the rest of Novel Gossip's contents. The café door swung open, and a group of people entered, talking loudly and interrupting my train of thought.

I took my bowl and coffee mug back to the kitchen, where I thanked Romina, a middle-aged woman with an olive complexion and shoulder-length chestnut-brown hair who was scrubbing the stove furiously and frowning, and Shane, the gangly nineteen-year-old kitchen assistant, for the meal, and went to help George with the influx of new customers.

"Is everything okay with Romina?" I asked George as I reached into the display case to pull out a cookie.

"No," George said. Concerned, I glanced over to find her grinning. "She slightly overcooked the muffins this morning."

I laughed. "But they look incredible." The raspberry, white chocolate and macadamia muffins had been a big hit with customers.

"They are incredible. I had to sample one just to convince her not to throw out the entire tray, and I can vouch for it." George's eyes twinkled as she shook her head. "The sacrifices I have to make for this place."

"Well, if it happens again tomorrow, I'm happy to take one for the team and volunteer up my muffin-eating skills." *God, why did that sound kind of dirty?*

George laughed. "Much appreciated. But yes, Romina doesn't take cooking failures well, so Shane and I have been giving her a wide berth all day. Sorry, I should have mentioned it."

By late afternoon, the steady stream of customers had reduced to a trickle. In between serving the stragglers, George spent a few minutes walking me through the ordering and payment system, which, thankfully, was fairly intuitive.

By the time she'd finished, it was five p.m., and the café was officially closed.

"I know it's a lot to take in all at once, so don't worry if you forget it all and need me to show you again." A hint of pink flushed her cheeks, and for the first time, she looked unsure of herself. "Sorry, I just realized I'm jumping the gun. You did a great job today. I'd love to have you on board, but are you interested in joining us?"

Say no, Hannah. N. O. Two letters. One syllable. It's not that hard.

But my resolve weakened at the hopeful, golden retriever-like expression on George's face.

"Yes, that would be great!" I said quickly, and for a few seconds, George's relieved smile made everything worth it. And then the reality of my situation flooded back. *What the actual fuck, Hannah?*

"Fantastic! If you don't mind sharing your email address, I can send through the employment contract and direct deposit form to fill out. Just let me know what days

and hours you want to work, and I'll put you on the schedule. If you're okay to stay until six p.m., we could finish
closing up, and then I can give you a quick tour of the book
section?"

"Sure," I said, smiling despite how frustrated I was with
myself right now. I'd been itching to explore the aisles of
books all day. I certainly wasn't going to object to receiving
a personal tour from George.

CHAPTER FOUR

HANNAH

FORTY MINUTES LATER, we strolled down the first aisle of books. When we reached the fantasy section, I scanned the shelves, looking for my novels. Warmth filled my body as I spotted them. Two copies of each, sitting neatly together. I smiled and suddenly sensed George's eyes on me.

"Do you like reading?" George asked.

"I love it." Heat rushed to my face as the words came out louder than I intended.

George shot me a grin, clearly picking up on my enthusiasm. "That's great! We often get asked for recommendations, so that'll be really helpful. What are your favorite genres?"

"Mainly fantasy, romance, crime, thrillers, upmarket and literary fiction," I replied, hoping my reading preferences met with George's approval.

The grin on George's face widened, showcasing her dimple. *God, that dimple is cute.* "That's awesome. Nice and varied. Ben only reads sci-fi, but between the three of us, we should have most bases covered."

"What about you?" I asked, genuinely interested in George's reading habits. She seemed so down to earth. I could imagine her reading something practical, like gardening books or a biography of Jimmy Carter.

George retrieved a Neil Gaiman book that was placed out of order on the shelves and put it back where it belonged, her arm nearly brushing against me in the process. "Yeah, I love reading too. I read pretty widely, but non-fiction—science, history, biographies, that sort of thing—and fantasy are by far my favorite genres."

I smiled, pleased that I'd guessed George's predilection for non-fiction and also pleasantly surprised that fantasy was also a favorite. *I wonder if she's read my books.* My stomach fluttered at the thought. *Oh god, what if she hates them?*

"What do you like most about fantasy?" I asked, eager to keep our conversation going before I fell into a black hole of overthinking George's possible views on my books.

George furrowed her brow and paused. "Hmmm. Interesting question. I like the escapism element—being able to step into a completely different world. But I also like the freedom fantasy gives authors to explore serious issues without having to deal with the baggage and preconceived ideas that readers would have if the novel was set in the real world, if that makes sense."

"That makes complete sense," I replied, impressed by George's thoughtful response, which I thoroughly agreed with.

She broke into a smile, that hint of a dimple showing again. "Oh, and magic is pretty cool too."

I chuckled. "Yeah, magic is pretty damn cool."

We just looked at each other for a moment, smiling, and my heart bounced, sending an unexpected burst of adrenaline rushing through me. *Oh boy.* I refocused my attention on the bookshelves. I couldn't remember the last time I'd felt this kind of physical reaction to someone, and it was both exciting and slightly terrifying. But the last thing I needed right now was a new relationship.

We reached the end of the aisle and had to sidestep around boxes stacked high against the wall.

"Sorry, it's not usually this cluttered. There was an issue with our delivery this morning, and we had way too many books delivered. Eight hundred and forty-one too many books, in fact." George winced, shaking her head.

Guilt washed over me, tightening my chest. *Shit. These are my books taking up precious space in George's store.* Clearly, some wires had been crossed. Surely my publisher wouldn't have delivered the books to Novel Gossip without checking with George that it was okay? I should speak up, explain to George why she was inundated with books. But for someone whose entire living was based around words, I seemed to have a hard time stringing them together.

I opened my mouth, but before I'd formulated what to say, George chuckled. "The funny thing is, the books are H. M. Stuart's latest release, *The Realm of Furies*, which isn't even meant to be released until the end of June. Since I read an advance copy a few months ago, I've been raving about it to anyone with even a remote interest in fantasy. It's like the universe listened to me a little too well and delivered enough for almost every household in Sapphire Springs to have a copy."

"Oh no. That's a lot of books," I managed, as warmth spread across my chest at George's words, mixing with the guilt. *She likes my book.*

"It's fine. I'm sure the publisher will take them back.

But our storage shed out back is already full, so it's a little cramped in here at the moment."

George walked me through the rest of the aisles, explaining her approach to organizing the books and how special orders worked. I listened with interest. I'd spoken to booksellers in the past but had never had this behind-the-scenes insight into how bookstores actually worked.

"I should also mention that we sometimes have events in the evenings. There's no expectation that you need to work them, but if you're interested, I can usually do with extra hands, and they're a lot of fun. I've done a few board-game and paint-and-sip nights, which have been popular, and I also started a monthly book club." It was clear from George's animated tone and lit-up face that she was passionate about these gatherings. "Things have been so hectic recently I haven't had the chance to do more, but I really want Novel Gossip to be a place that brings our community together and introduces people to new ideas and interests."

I smiled. "That sounds great. I'd love to be involved, although I should let you know I have no artistic talent, so I'd have to leave that to you. I can, however, pour wine." As soon as the words were out of my mouth I remembered that by the time George held her next event, she'd know who I really was and so it was unlikely I'd have an opportunity to demonstrate my wine-pouring skills.

George chuckled. "I leave the art instruction to the experts. A local artist usually runs them. But people do get surprisingly thirsty, so I'd welcome your expert wine-pouring skills." Her eyes sparkled.

"I'm at your service," I replied, grinning.

"Excellent. And if you have any other ideas for events, let me know. I'd love to have some author talks here, but

Sapphire Springs is so small I doubt many writers would travel all this way to sell a couple of copies."

"You never know. Lots of New Yorkers like to escape to Sapphire Springs for a break. Perhaps a burned-out writer would love the excuse for a change of scene," I responded, raising my eyebrows. Surely I wasn't the only one.

"True." George looked thoughtful. "Maybe I'll reach out to some of my contacts at the publishers and ask them to see if they can entice any burned-out writers to come up here."

"But not *too* burned-out and cynical, otherwise they might not want to talk about their book," I said, grinning.

George nodded solemnly, but her lips twitched. "Right. I'll request authors with just a moderate degree of burnout."

Laughing, we headed back to the counter. It felt good to talk with George, even if it was just silly banter. Apart from my chats with Barb, it was the first time in months that I'd had a conversation with someone that wasn't about work, moving, or the divorce.

Finished with the tour, I gathered my belongings, and George walked me to the front door.

"Thanks again for stepping in on such short notice." She opened the door, flashing me a hopeful smile. "Is there any chance you're available to work the next couple of days? No problem if you can't, but Ben wasn't sounding great, and I could do with an extra set of hands."

Concern for this woman I barely knew tugged at my heart. If the next few days were anything like today, there was no way George could manage by herself. Maybe I'd work a few more days. Until Ben was better. Then I'd quit, tell George who I really was, sign the damn books, and throw myself into writing. That way, I wouldn't feel so bad about leaving George in the lurch, especially not after she'd gone to the trouble of training me.

"That's fine. I'll see you tomorrow."

DESPITE MY ACHING feet and legs—I wasn't used to standing for any stretch of time—there was an unfamiliar bounce to my step as I walked down Main Street. Leafy green maple and oak trees lined the sidewalk. While most of the quaint little shops had closed for the day, people were still taking advantage of the gorgeous weather. The outdoor seating at the local pub, Builders' Arms, was overflowing with patrons, creating a steady hum of laughter and chatter that traveled on the warm breeze, getting louder as I approached. Other townsfolk were strolling, many with dogs. A few even greeted me with smiles and nods, despite being a complete stranger. *That would never happen in New York.* I was more likely to be glared and muttered at for not walking fast enough.

I hadn't felt this cheerful, this much like my old self, in months. Was it the weather? The change of environment?

I thought back over my day. For the first time in a long time, I'd been fully absorbed in something, present in the moment, not thinking about Tania or worrying about my book or my financial situation. Just focused on the tasks in front of me. And those tasks were small and achievable, providing immediate satisfaction when I completed them. Taking coffees to a retired couple, clearing tables, mopping the floor. Perhaps one of the reasons I'd found it so hard to tell George about my pen name was because I was enjoying my time at Novel Gossip so much and I didn't want to jeopardize that. In contrast, recently when I sat down to "work,"

I just stared at a blank screen, overwhelmed by having to write an entire book when I was anything but inspired.

It hadn't always been like that. Words used to flow out of me and onto my laptop, scraps of paper, the notes app on my phone, at all hours of the day and night. But not anymore—not since I'd found out about Tania's cheating.

I took a deep breath of fresh air and smiled at a woman pushing a stroller. Maybe I'd been too hasty in deciding to lock myself away from the world. While staying in Manhattan and spending time with my New York friends— whom I'd shared with Tania—had been too painful for me, being around people today felt good. Having a job to do and purposeful interactions with the customers made it easy. And George, who seemed so genuine and relaxed, made it especially easy.

I smiled as I turned off Main Street toward my cottage. While getting a job at a café-bookstore wasn't part of my plan when I left home this morning, it might be the circuit breaker I needed to get my life back on track.

CHAPTER FIVE

GEORGE

I LOCKED the front door behind Hannah and walked to the kitchen. At the back of the kitchen, behind a nondescript door, were the stairs to my apartment. Maximus thundered down the hallway to greet me, jumping on me with gusto as I reached the top of the staircase.

"Hello, gorgeous." I rubbed his warm, golden head. "Let's get your leash and stretch our legs." After a long day of standing, all I wanted to do was collapse on the couch. But Max needed a walk, and Blake, my closest friend, was coming over in an hour with takeout, so we had to get going. I put on my headphones and called Mom back while I was getting Max ready.

"Hello?" Mom asked, her familiar voice making me smile.

"Hey, it's me. Sorry I missed your call earlier. Work was hectic. What's up?" I clipped Max's leash on and started heading toward the door to my apartment.

"Sorry, I should have known better than to call you during the day. I just wanted to let you know that I booked my flights!" Mom's excitement was clear from her voice.

"Oh great! Do you mind emailing me the details? Max and I are heading out for a walk." Max was so eager for his walk he was practically dragging me down the stairs and toward the front door of Novel Gossip.

"Yes, of course."

I opened the door and we stepped onto the sidewalk. I inhaled a lungful of fresh, late-afternoon air. It was another gorgeous, sunny day. Summer had come early to Sapphire Springs this year.

"Oh, I've been meaning to say. Did you hear Alexis is dating Sophia Landers?" Mom asked.

"Good for her." I hadn't heard that, but it wasn't terribly surprising that my attractive, famous, politician ex had found a movie star girlfriend who was also attractive and famous.

"It'll be very interesting to see if they last. I don't see how they are going to make it work with the amount of travelling Alexis does and Sophia away filming all the time."

I rolled my eyes, smiling. Alexis and I had broken up more than three years ago now, and I was well and truly over her. While I wished my ex all the best, I wasn't really interested in speculating with Mom over whether her latest relationship would last. But Mom loved a good gossip.

"Maybe they'll find a way to make it work," I said diplomatically.

"Hmmm. Maybe." Mom sounded unconvinced. "While I'll continue to vote for her, I still haven't forgiven her for the way she treated you."

I sighed. "Mom, we've been through this before. We just weren't compatible."

I'd been thrilled when Alexis Merritts ran for the House of Reps for Tampa Bay. She was young, queer, and passionate, which isn't common in Florida politics. I volunteered on her campaign, putting my tech skills to good use, and, to my surprise, we ended up getting together.

But once she won, I'd quickly discovered I wasn't cut out to be a politician's plus one. I wasn't willing to sacrifice my career to follow my partner around the country, or alternatively stay in Tampa and hardly ever see her. Not that I'd seen her much when we lived in D.C. anyway.

Mom harrumphed. "You moved for her, quit your job for her, and she didn't compromise anything." I gritted my teeth. While I'd moved on from Alexis, it was clear Mom hadn't.

"Well, it's thanks to her that your mortgage is paid off and I was able to set up Novel Gossip." I regretted the words as soon as they were out of my mouth. Trying to defend Alexis was only likely to infuriate Mom.

Mom spluttered. "You were the one who developed the app, not her. You did all the hard work, it's only fair you got paid for it."

"I know. But Alexis didn't need to sign the paperwork so I could sell it. And she did, even after I broke up with her."

I rubbed my forehead. After a long day of work, this was the last thing I felt like talking about. While I was over the break-up, I didn't want to dwell on one of the most stressful times of my life.

Mom muttered something under her breath.

Thankfully, a dog walking by began to bark loudly at Max.

"Sorry Mom, I've got to go. Love you!"

"Okay. Bye, sweetheart."

I hung up the phone and dragged Max away from the barking dog.

We walked down Main Street, Max stopping to sniff at

every cast iron lamp post and tree trunk while I smiled and nodded at locals on autopilot. Without Mom on the phone, talking about Alexis, my mind turned to Hannah. *Thank god for Hannah.* Today would've been an absolute disaster if she hadn't walked through the door, ready to start immediately.

I'd observed her all day, trying not to be too obvious. She seemed shy but attentive and on the ball, noticing customers needed a refilled water jug, running with paper towels when a customer dropped an iced latte down their t-shirt, proactively clearing tables and taking out food without me needing to ask. She was a quick learner. And judging by the way she'd emphatically said that she loved reading, she was passionate about books. I grinned. She was everything I could want.

An image of Hannah smiling at me, her eyes crinkling at the edges and white teeth framed by upturned full, pink lips, appeared in my mind. My grin widened. Even the memory of her smile was infectious. I shook myself.

Everything you could want in an EMPLOYEE, George.

The last thing I needed was a crush on Hannah. Ben had mentioned she'd moved here with her husband, so she wasn't available. And even if she was available, there was no way I'd date an employee. It was an unquestionably terrible idea.

Lost in thought, it was only when we'd almost reached the end of Main Street that I remembered to check the time.

"Crap." I looked down from my watch to Max. "No more sniffs, Max. We'd better get back, or Blake'll be waiting for us."

I tugged Max away from an apparently exquisite-smelling lamp post, and we set off up Main Street at pace. It was still warm, and the evening sun had surprising strength.

As we reached the café, I spotted a familiar figure leaning against the door, two pizza boxes and a brown paper bag by her feet.

I smiled. *Blake.*

When I'd moved to town a few years ago, I hadn't known a soul. Initially, I'd been so focused on turning my vision of a cozy café-bookstore into a reality that I'd had no time to make friends outside of the regulars I spoke to at work. A few months later, I fell off a ladder while shelving books, and Ben insisted I see the new doctor who'd just opened her practice in Sapphire Springs. Blake and I had had an immediate, but completely platonic, connection. Not only were we the only two openly queer women in Sapphire Springs of our age that we knew of, and on the more gender non-conforming side of the spectrum, but we shared a similar sense of humor and a love of hiking and good coffee. Last year Blake had started dating her childhood crush, Jenny, who had just returned to Sapphire Springs. When Jenny worked late, Blake would often come over for dinner.

"Hi. Sorry. I hope you haven't been waiting long," I said to Blake as Max and I reached her.

"Not your fault. I'm early. I grabbed pizza and salad from Michael's, and they prepared it in record time," she replied, picking up the brown paper bag before Max got to it. The smell of garlic and cheese sent my stomach rumbling.

I chuckled. Michael's was notorious for mouth-watering, traditional pizzas made excruciatingly slowly. "Maybe they've finally installed another wood-fired oven to meet the demands of pizza-obsessed Sapphire Springs."

Blake laughed. "We can only hope."

I opened the door, and we made our way up to the apartment.

"Make yourself at home," I said as I shut the door behind Blake and headed to the kitchen.

I grabbed plates, cutlery, and two pale ales from the fridge. "Are you okay to eat on the couch?" I asked Blake, walking into the living room to find she was already on it, Max curled up next to her, the pizza boxes and salad on the coffee table in front of her.

"Have I ever not been?" Blake grinned.

"Point taken." I handed Blake a beer and placed the plates and cutlery on the table. "Help yourself."

After Blake had loaded her plate, I grabbed a few slices and started making quick work of them. I'd had no time for a proper lunch break today, only devouring half a BLT bagel in the kitchen before the lunch rush began, so I was starving.

"How was your day?" Blake asked, opening the beer and taking a swig.

I filled her in on the unexpected delivery of books, Ben's illness, Romina's bad mood, Hannah's fortuitous appearance and then my call with Mom.

Blake shook her head when I'd finished. "Damn, that sounds hectic. I'm surprised you haven't already passed out from exhaustion. So, do you think you'll keep the new woman on?"

"Hannah? Yes, definitely. She's great. Assuming all her paperwork and references are fine." *They better be, or I'm screwed.* And I was already looking forward to seeing her tomorrow.

Blake furrowed her brow as she swallowed a mouthful of pizza. "I don't think I've come across her before." Blake, as the only doctor in town, took pride in knowing everyone who lived here.

"She just moved here from..." I frowned, realizing I knew very little about her. Ben hadn't mentioned where she was from, and I'd been so busy today I hadn't had a chance to ask. "Somewhere. At least, that's what Ben said. She moved here recently with her husband."

Blake's expression turned thoughtful. "If you wanted, you could invite her to come with us tomorrow night. Since Ben's sick, we have a spare ticket. If she just moved here, she might appreciate some company."

I paused. Inviting Hannah to the outdoor movie night would be a friendly gesture. I knew from experience how hard it was to make friends after a move. But, at the same time, she was an employee. Would inviting her on a social outing put her in a difficult position if she didn't want to go? I'd asked Ben without a second thought, but we'd worked together for years and I knew him well enough to know he'd say no if he didn't want to come. On first impression, Hannah struck me as the sort of person who'd agree to something she didn't want to do just to avoid hurting the other person's feelings. I didn't want to make her feel uncomfortable.

"Yeah, I'm not sure. Let me think about it."

I groaned softly, remembering that, while my legs still ached, I had to make the cake-of-the-day tonight, or my regulars would be disappointed. If I didn't get started, I'd have to stay up late to take it out of the oven.

"If you've finished eating, would you mind if I got started on baking tomorrow's cake? I was thinking of doing a miniature one for us for dessert, if you're okay staying for a while. It'll be a dark chocolate, date, and almond meringue cake with cream and berries."

Blake jumped up, a grin on her face. "I'm supportive of anything that involves me getting to eat cake. What can I do to help?"

Blake had many talents, but cooking wasn't one of them, so I set her to work clearing up dinner and then chopping the dates. There was no way I was letting her anywhere near my meringue.

We chatted while I whipped the meringue, folded it in with the nut, chocolate, and date mixture, and then put it in the oven. Once that was done, we fell back on the couch with a glass of red wine each.

"That's officially my new favorite cake," Blake groaned as she scraped her plate an hour and a half later. "I'd better move along before I fall asleep in a food coma on your couch."

I chuckled, savoring the last mouthful. The chocolate had still been slightly gooey from the oven, and the cream and berries had offset the richness of the chocolate and dates. It was pretty damn good.

Stifling a yawn as I walked back from seeing Blake out, I spotted the boxes of books piled high at the back of the store, and my heart sank. *Shit. I forgot to call the distributor about* The Realm of Furies *delivery.* I'd do it first thing tomorrow. The boxes were probably a safety hazard. Should I lug them up to my apartment so they were out of the way? That was the last thing I felt like doing after the long day, a glass of red wine, and too much cake. Desperate to change into my pajamas and fall into bed, I decided to make that tomorrow's problem.

And at least tomorrow Hannah would be back to help.

CHAPTER SIX

HANNAH

HUMMING a King Princess song I'd been singing loudly in the shower, I walked down the hill toward Main Street. There was still a spring in my step, and it couldn't all be attributed to the sensible white shoes I was wearing today or the best night's sleep I'd had in months. In fact, my legs ached from being on my feet all day yesterday, but here I was, looking forward to doing it all over again.

Too often in New York, I'd barely registered my surroundings, preoccupied with worrying about my writing, Tania, or whether subway delays would make me late. But today, I was fully present. I passed cute weatherboard cottages with front yards full of rose bushes, peonies, and nasturtiums in full bloom. Waist-height white picket fences and neatly trimmed hedges bordered the gardens. The smell of freshly cut grass carried on the breeze. It wasn't even eight a.m., but the sun was strong. Today was going to be hot.

I let out a happy sigh. This was idyllic. I'd visited Sapphire Springs a handful of times while an undergraduate at NYU and had fallen in love. I'd always thought that when the grind of New York finally wore me down, I'd retire to a small, peaceful town like Sapphire Springs. It'd just happened a lot sooner than I thought.

I'd visited here once with Tania, who'd been thoroughly unimpressed by my retirement plans. She was a New York lifer who'd have to be dragged kicking and screaming out of the city. I chuckled at the thought—Tania was always very put together and composed—and then checked myself. *Huh. That's the first time I've really thought about Tania without being overwhelmed with emotions. That's progress, Hannah!* I turned onto Main Street, smiling at a random middle-aged man walking a black Labrador, who smiled back at me.

Even the tinnitus in my left ear, which had been bothering me more since I'd lost my hearing aid, didn't seem as noticeable in Sapphire Springs. Perhaps it was because I had other, more interesting things to catch my attention. *Like one very attractive boss.*

My good mood wavered as a thought struck me. *Shit.* From what George had said, she seemed to think I was a woman who'd spoken to Ben about working at Novel Gossip. If Ben saw me, or that woman returned to the café, things could get awkward.

I kept telling myself I hadn't lied to George and that she would understand I just hadn't heard her. But the fact that I knew there'd been a misunderstanding and I hadn't corrected it made me uneasy. While Mom, a philosophy professor, and Dad, a professor of law, had not been hands-on parents, they had emphasized the importance of honesty and integrity growing up. I suspected they wouldn't approve of the situation I'd gotten myself into—not that I'd ask for their philosophical take on my predicament, anyway. They were currently vacationing in Greece and, in any event, we'd never had the kind of relationship where I felt comfortable asking their advice on anything, let alone minor moral dilemmas. And this one, in the grand scheme of moral dilemmas, was on the sillier side. Not only that, but it would involve telling them information I'd withheld from them for years.

My belly swooped as I tripped over a piece of uneven pavement, teetering for a heart-wrenching second before I righted myself. *So much for being fully present.* I was almost at Novel Gossip now and had spent most of the walk up Main Street caught in my head. But as I pushed open the door to the café, butterflies in my stomach pulled me back to reality. Would Ben be back?

To my relief, when I stepped inside, the only person I could see was George behind the counter, her back to me. I stopped for a moment, admiring her broad shoulders. *I wonder if she works out?* I did not get buff while working at Café Mignon when I was a student, but perhaps the book side of Novel Gossip required more heavy lifting. Like lifting all my damn boxes of books, which I could still see piled up at the back of the aisle. Guilt spiked in my chest at the thought.

"Hello!" George turned. Her smile lit her entire face, sending her eyes sparkling. I couldn't help but return her grin, my guilt receding into the background. "Thanks again for coming in today. Ben just texted me to say he has the flu. It doesn't sound like it's hitting him too hard, but I've told him to take it easy and stay away until all his symptoms are gone. I don't want him to infect any of our customers—or any of us, for that matter. Thank god the rest of us haven't caught it, or we'd be totally screwed."

"Oh no!" I grimaced. "I hope he's not feeling too bad." But while I meant that, I couldn't help the wave of relief that washed over me. I'd be able to keep working at the café without Ben blowing my cover for a few more days. That was, if the jobseeker who had spoken to Ben didn't reappear. As strange as it was, I wasn't ready to give up on my new career in hospitality quite yet—or for George to find out why I'd really shown up at Novel Gossip yesterday.

"It sounds like he's through the worst of it now. Hey, do you have time for me to show you how Hugo works?"

"Hugo?" I stared at George, my eyebrows raised.

She chuckled. "Sorry, I mean the espresso machine. I'm quite attached to him and couldn't resist naming him Hugo." She patted the shiny red espresso machine fondly.

Well, that's just adorable. "Sure."

"Have you had much experience making coffee?"

"Not for years, so I definitely need a refresher. And I've never used an espresso machine as magnificent as Hugo." The espresso machine at Café Mignon had been a third of the size and significantly less shiny.

George laughed. "No espresso machine is as magnificent as Hugo."

Standing only inches away from me, George walked me through the process of making a latte. The well-defined muscles on her forearms tensed as she emptied the portafilter, a small round container attached to a handle, of used coffee, refilled it with freshly ground beans and tamped them down, and then again as she twisted the portafilter into Hugo. Every motion was so strong, deliberate and smooth, flowing into each other like a carefully choreographed dance. Even the way she frothed the milk, gently lowering the pitcher as the milk turned creamy, her dark eyes fixed intently on the job at hand, sent an enjoyable shiver down my spine. Damn, who knew coffee making could be so sexy?

"Why don't you try?" George asked, turning to me once she'd finished her demonstration.

Thankfully, despite not absorbing much of the lesson (unless the lesson was about George's magnificent forearms and just how sensuous making a latte could be), muscle memory kicked in. I stumbled through the steps, acutely aware that my movements were jerky and weak compared to George's. While my technique was anything but sensuous, I produced a respectable long black on my first turn.

"Good work!" George said with approval. "Why don't you try a latte next?"

Feeling more confident, I banged the portafilter against the garbage bin to empty it, refilled it with beans, and smoothly twisted it into the espresso machine. As the golden coffee flowed into the cup waiting underneath, I filled the pitcher full of milk, put it under the steam wand and turned it on. An unpleasant screeching noise made me jump. "Oh god, it sounds like I'm murdering a cat. What am I doing wrong?"

George chuckled. "The steam wand is too low in the pitcher. You need to keep it just under the surface, lowering the pitcher as the milk expands," George explained patiently.

I lowered the pitcher down. "Shit!" I yelped as milk bubbled up, splattering Hugo's side. I turned off the steam. "Sorry, Hugo!"

"So you overcompensated a little too much." George grinned. "Do you mind if I give you a hand?"

I nodded, and she stepped closer to me, so we were almost touching, and wrapped her fingers around the pitcher. Her hand brushed mine for a second as she adjusted her grip, leaving a warm imprint that expanded over my skin.

With her other hand, she turned on the steam wand again. "So, instead of holding the pitcher by the handle, if you hold it like this, you can feel when the milk is heating up. See how the milk is expanding?" I nodded again, trying to focus on the milk swirling in front of me and not how close George was standing to me. "So now we'll slowly lower the pitcher." George gently guided the pitcher down, her hand only millimeters from mine.

An image of George standing behind me with her arms wrapped around my middle, her hands on mine, frothing milk à la the pottery scene from *Ghost* appeared without warning in my mind. Heat raced up my face.

"When it's almost too hot to touch, that's when you know it's done."

My face is too damn hot to touch. I hoped to god that George hadn't noticed.

The pitcher warmed under my hand.

"Now?" I glanced over to George, taking in the faint freckles that scattered her nose and cheeks and the flecks of golden brown in her eyes.

George was very much not a ghost. She was very real and gorgeous. She'd also pulled her hand away from the pitcher and was now nodding at me.

Ouch! Suddenly aware of a burning sensation on my fingers, I hastily released my grip and placed the pitcher on the counter.

"Is your hand okay?" George asked, concern creasing her forehead.

"Yes, it's fine," I said, ignoring the mild throbbing in my fingers.

"It's probably a little hot, but the foam looks good," George said, peering at the milk and nodding with approval. "Now you just pour it slowly and steadily into the middle of the cup. You want to try to get around a quarter to half an inch of foam on top."

I followed her instructions and thirty seconds later was staring proudly at a professional-looking latte.

"Perfect!" George said, grinning at me, her dimple on display. "I can teach you latte art another day. I haven't been bothering with it this week because it's been so busy, but it can be fun to play around with if the café is quiet."

The prospect of another one-on-one coffee making session with George sent nerves fluttering in my stomach.

"The muffins are ready!" Romina yelled from the kitchen.

"I'll go grab them," I said, hurriedly, relieved to have an excuse to get away from George and her forearms, freckles and dimple. While it was refreshing to feel attraction toward someone again, I was starting to worry that my crush on George was a distraction I didn't need right now.

CHAPTER SEVEN

HANNAH

THIRTY MINUTES LATER, I was transferring a delicious-looking cake from the kitchen fridge into the display case when an attractive woman in a colorful jumpsuit, sandals, and short brown hair walked up to the counter. In her hands was a piece of paper. My stomach dropped. *Shit, I bet this is the jobseeker George mistook me for, and my cover is about to be blown.*

I hovered nervously near the counter, pretending to wipe a stubborn mark off the display case so I could listen to their conversation. Thankfully, despite my hearing aid still missing in action, the café had just opened so the background noise was minimal.

The woman grinned at George, who was trying to fix a paper jam in the receipt printer. "Hi! Sorry, is now a bad time?"

George lifted her head and smiled. "Hey, Olivia! Nope, all good. This is always acting up. Good thing hardly anyone needs receipts. You're earlier than usual."

"Yeah, I thought I'd pop in before I open. I'm actually here for books. Everyone in my family has their birthday over the next two months, and this year I'm trying to be organized for once. I was hoping you could give me some recommendations."

I breathed out in relief. Olivia, whoever she was, wasn't the jobseeker.

"That sounds like a lot more fun than trying to fix this," George said, putting the printer on the counter and giving Olivia her full attention. "What were you thinking?"

"Maybe a biography or something similar for Blake, a fantasy novel for Dad, and a romance novel for Mom? You've probably got a better idea than me what they like. I'm giving Dave two kid-free date nights with Aunty Olivia on twin-sitting duties, so we don't need to worry about him." Olivia grimaced. "I just hope I survive the chaos of the twin tornado."

George laughed. "You might need Blake for reinforcements." Her smile widened. "I actually have the perfect idea for your dad. We both love H. M. Stuart, and I just got a whole pile of his latest release delivered. The release date isn't until the end of June, so I can't give it to you now. But if I had it wrapped and ready to go by then, would that work?"

I paused scrubbing the display case for a second. When I'd been offered my book deal, I'd insisted on using my initials and a different last name for anonymity. While Tania, who at that point was still only my editor and not my partner, was sympathetic to my request, it was not well-received by senior management at the publisher who expected authors to market their books. Tania had fought hard to convince her bosses to respect my desire for privacy, and one of the arguments she'd made was that one "benefit" of the arrangement was that many readers would assume I was a man. According to Tania, there was a bias in favor of male fantasy writers.

Tania was right. My publisher had been careful not to specify my gender and I'd been surprised at just how many people assumed H. M. Stuart was a man—including, it seemed, George. I wasn't entirely sure how I felt about that, but since I'd also assumed George was a man based on her name, I couldn't exactly be too critical. And hearing her recommend my book lit a warm glow in my chest.

"Perfect!" Olivia exclaimed.

George paused for a moment, a thoughtful expression on her face. "I think your mom would love Abby Jimenez's latest. It's got great banter, some laugh-out-loud moments, but it also explores some deeper issues."

My smile reflected in the now gleaming display case. Abby Jimenez was one of my favorite authors of straight romance too.

"That sounds just up her alley. And then I can read it once she's finished with it."

"And for Blake, let me see..." George wandered toward the non-fiction aisle, Olivia following. They returned a few minutes later, Olivia holding a grim-looking political-history book as well as Ashley Herring Blake's *Iris Kelly Doesn't Date*. That was interesting. Presumably, the political-history book was for the Blake person she'd mentioned. Was the sapphic romance for Olivia or someone else? I loved that book. I'd related so strongly to both characters—one a romance author with writer's block, and the other, an actor who had anxiety and panic attacks. Had George recommended it?

I'd stopped scrubbing the display case of non-existent marks and was now wiping the counter of invisible crumbs. While I felt guilty for being so nosy, my guilt wasn't strong enough to overcome my desire to hear the rest of their conversation. For some reason, I was keen to find out as much as I could about George.

George processed the payment, wrapped the books, and handed them to Olivia in a paper bag. "Here you go!"

"Thanks! It's so good to have this all settled now." Olivia gave George a relieved smile. "I'll be back later with the flowers and candles."

Flowers and candles? I furrowed my brow, unsettled. Were they planning a romantic night together? They would make an extremely cute couple, but I hadn't picked up on any romantic undertones in their interactions. Although, Olivia had bought a sapphic romance... A sinking sensation in my stomach signaled disappointment. I shook it off. *Don't be silly, Hannah. You hardly know George. And the last thing you need right now is a new relationship.*

A customer stood from a table as Olivia left the store, so I walked over to clear it. On my way back from dropping the dirty plates to the kitchen, I passed George standing in front of Hugo frothing milk. She turned to me and grinned. "I just sold one copy of *The Realm of Furies*. One down, only eight-hundred and forty left to go. Which reminds me, I really need to call the distributor about the delivery so I don't need to hand sell the rest!"

My stomach dropped even further at the prospect of George calling the distributor. They'd likely put her in touch with the publisher, who'd fill her in on the real reason why 841 books had been delivered to her doorstep. Would George connect the dots and work out who I was? *Probably not since she thinks H. M. Stuart is a man.*

The flowers and candles comment made sense twenty minutes later, when Olivia reappeared with a cart full of colorful bouquets and candles. I'd just delivered a coffee to a customer at a nearby table, so I rushed to help her with the door, trying not to look too pleased that Olivia's delivery was clearly for the café, rather than to woo George.

"Thank you." Olivia smiled at me.

"Hannah, this is Olivia." George materialized behind me. "She owns the flower shop down the road and supplies us with flowers for the tables. We also sell her candles. Olivia, Hannah just started working here yesterday."

Olivia dropped the cart's handle and reached out her hand. "Lovely to meet you, Hannah. I'm sorry I don't have time to chat, but I've got to rush off to open up."

I shook Olivia's hand and then helped her replace the slightly wilted white daisies with bright bunches of yellow and red zinnias while George restocked the shelf next to the counter with rustic-looking candles in brown glass jars.

"See you tonight!" Olivia said to George as she left. The unsettled feeling descended over me again. Perhaps there was something going on between them after all. *Not that I care. They both seem like lovely people. I should be happy for them.*

The next few times a woman came in by herself, my chest tightened in anticipation that she might be the real jobseeker whose position I'd taken. But as the morning rush took hold, my worries vanished, and I focused on the tasks at hand—delivering slices of cake and coffees to customers, clearing tables, helping an elderly man locate a gardening book, and, when George was swamped with making coffee, putting through orders and taking payments. I even made a few decent-looking coffees while George took a quick break to use the restroom. I didn't have any problems with the payment system, but I did struggle to hear as the café got busier, especially soft-spoken customers. I hated having to ask people to repeat themselves multiple times, some doing so with a hint of frustration in their voice. It reminded me of

Tania, who hadn't been particularly patient in those situations. *I just need to find my damn hearing aid.* Hearing aid technology had come far in the past few decades, so much so that my hearing aid was barely noticeable when I wore it. The only downside was that my hearing aid was now so small it was easy to misplace. I was sure it would turn up somewhere—hopefully sooner rather than later.

"Would you like to go for a break now, before the lunch rush starts?" George asked.

I looked at the bronze clock on the wall, surprised to see it was already 11:30 a.m. I'd eaten breakfast early today, sitting out on the back deck, enjoying my yogurt and granola, and was definitely ready for some more food.

I grabbed a pre-made bagel from the display case and took a seat at the same table I'd sat at yesterday, facing the counter. I told myself it was so I could monitor how busy the café was getting, in case George needed me to jump back in to help, and had nothing to do with being able to observe my rather attractive boss from a safe distance.

To distract myself, I scrolled through my emails as I devoured the bagel. Spam. Spam. Emma.

Hi, Hannah,

I hope you're settling in well. I wanted to check if you'll be able to sign the books this week? I need to tell the publisher when they're done so they can arrange the pick-up. They want to get them back ASAP so they can get them ready for distribution before the publication date—Friday is the absolute latest.

Many thanks,

Emma

Shit. I'd been so focused on my new job that the whole reason I'd come to Novel Gossip in the first place had taken a backseat in my mind. My heart sank. I'd been worried about Ben and the women who'd approached him for a job returning to the café and blowing my cover, but now I'd have to do it myself. Today was Wednesday, so Friday was only two days away.

The thought of confessing to George made my stomach turn. How would she react to the news? I hated the idea that she might think I'd lied to her. I also didn't want my identity as H. M. Stuart to affect the way she saw me. She seemed very down to earth, but she was also a fan of my books and that might affect our dynamic. I'd been enjoying our relaxed interactions. I didn't want that to change.

Not only that, but I'd been enjoying working at Novel Gossip. The thought of returning to my isolated existence no longer seemed as appealing as it had only yesterday morning. I sighed. Despite all that, I knew this wasn't a sustainable situation.

Someone cleared their throat, and I looked up to see George smiling at me, her adorable dimple on full display. "I made you a coffee and thought you might want to try a slice of this as well." She placed a latte and a generous slice of chocolate-almond-date cake in front of me.

"Thank you! I've been eyeing the cake all morning."

"I noticed." George grinned.

Heat shot up my face at the thought that George had seen me pining after the cake. *I hope she didn't also notice me eavesdropping on her and Olivia.* My heart warmed as I realized she'd also remembered my coffee order from yesterday. That was so thoughtful.

"If I do say so myself, it's one of my better ones."

My eyes widened. *George made it?* I'd assumed Romina made all the sweets. I watched her walk back to the counter and then stuck a forkful of cake in my mouth.

Holy shit. I closed my eyes. The cake was incredible.

Not only could George make a mean latte and give great book recommendations, but she could bake as well. If she and Olivia were dating, Olivia was one lucky woman.

I spent a few more minutes savoring the coffee and cake and then focused my mind back on the books that needed signing. I sighed. There was no getting around my predicament. I'd have to fess up to George at the end of my shift and ask if she'd mind me staying late to sign them all. I just hoped to god that my confession wouldn't make George look at me any differently. And that maybe I could keep working at Novel Gossip a little longer.

IT WAS ALMOST CLOSING TIME, and after another busy day, the café was quiet. Only one man, hunched over a laptop nursing the dregs of a cappuccino, remained.

I was stacking clean mugs, still warm from the dishwasher, on top of the coffee machine, when George spoke.

"Hannah, once you've finished with that, would you mind helping restock the shelves? I've stacked the boxes of new books we need to unpack in the kids' section. If you're not sure where any of them go, just put them aside, and I'll look at them later."

I turned to find George smiling at me. Was it my imagination, or had her gaze just jumped from my ass to my face? *Was George checking me out?* My heart leaped at the thought.

"Of course." Pleased to have an excuse to spend more time in the book aisles, I walked to the back of the bookstore and set to work. I glanced at the blurb of each book I unpacked, telling myself that it was important I familiarized myself with the new books so I could give customers recommendations, before remembering that my days at Novel Gossip were likely to be numbered. My stomach sank.

Twenty minutes later, I was kneeling on the floor, opening another box of books when George appeared, her face flushed.

"Oh my god! I just got off the phone with the distributor, and it turns out that *The Realm of Furies* delivery wasn't a mistake after all! Apparently, H. M. Stuart is staying in Sapphire Springs, and they were delivered here so he could sign them. I left work early Monday afternoon, and the publicist that was arranging the delivery spoke to Ben instead. Things have been so hectic I missed the email Ben sent me about it."

I stood, legs shaky, and braced myself. *Okay, Hannah. This is your moment to tell George who you are and what really brought you to Novel Gossip.* I took a deep breath, but before I got any further, George started speaking again, her eyes bright with excitement.

"I'm not usually one to get starstruck, but I'm really nervous about meeting him. He's such a talented writer. Have you read any of his books?" Thankfully, George was so excited she didn't stop for an answer. "He's incredible at world-building, turning classic fantasy tropes on their heads and exploring moral and ethical issues. But he somehow still manages to make them fast-paced and a lot of fun to read. And he does an amazing job at creating complex, strong characters—especially female characters."

Pride welled up in my chest at hearing George's compliments.

I must've had a strange expression on my face, because George caught my eye and then chuckled, shaking her head. "Sorry. See what I mean? I'll make a complete fool of myself around him when he comes in. I may need you for moral support—or at least to kick me if I start fangirling too hard."

I let out a nervous laugh, unsure what to say. I knew I shouldn't let this continue any further. I was just digging a deeper hole for myself the longer this went on. But after George's rave review, it felt even more awkward coming clean to her. George seemed so worried about making a good impression on H. M. Stuart that surely it would be cruel to reveal my identity immediately after she'd showered H. M. Stuart with compliments and specifically said she did not want to embarrass herself in front of "him." Perhaps I could wait to tell her tomorrow, when the memory of this conversation might have faded a little in her mind, to help dampen the humiliation. But was I grasping at excuses to put off telling her or just being reasonable? I didn't have a clue.

"The last customer has left, and I've locked the front door, so I can help put the rest of these away," George said, bending over the opened box and pulling out a handful of books.

Relieved by the change of topic, I pulled out a few more. As we worked, George told me about some books she'd enjoyed recently, her eyes sparkling.

"This is another great book, if you like high fantasy. I've got an advanced copy you're more than welcome to have if you're interested." George held up a copy of Chris Chen's latest book from the box of new releases. I opened my mouth, about to say I'd adored it too, and then slammed my mouth shut. I'd been given an advanced copy as well and had written a blurb for the book George was holding. A blurb that was now in quotes on the top left corner of the cover. Probably best not to mention I'd read it.

"I love Chris Chen," I said instead, scanning the other

books in the box to look for something that would draw the conversation away from fantasy authors, which was proving fraught. My eyes landed on a book. "Oh, and I've been looking forward to this one as well." I grabbed a copy of Alison Cochrun's latest novel. I only received fantasy books to blurb, so I had to wait like everyone else for anticipated romance reads.

George's face flickered for a second with an expression I couldn't make out. Heat rose in my cheeks as I realized, in my haste to change the subject, I might have unintention-ally signaled to her that I was queer. Not that a lot of straight people didn't read queer romance, especially the big names like Casey McQuiston, Alison Cochrun, and Ashley Herring Blake. And why did I care if George knew I was a lesbian, anyway?

"I haven't read that one yet," George said. "But I loved *Kiss Her Once for Me*. I can't remember if I mentioned this, but you get an employee discount on any books in the store."

"That sounds dangerous." I grinned, pulling the last book out of the box and placing it on the shelf.

We both stood up.

"Trust me, it is," George said, her eyes crinkling.

As we walked back to the counter, George cleared her throat. I looked over to her just in time to catch another indecipherable expression cross her face. "Hey, absolutely no pressure—you probably have plans anyway or might just want to go home and crash—but tonight, a few friends and I are going to an outdoor movie night down at Dockside Park if you're interested in coming? Ben was going to come, but he obviously can't, so we have a spare ticket you're more than welcome to have. Dinner is included."

Nerves fluttered in my belly. I hadn't socialized properly with anyone for months. I'd been getting along well with George, but that had come about organically as we worked together. The thought of being thrust into a situation where the sole purpose was to interact with strangers sent my anxiety spiking. Before the break-up with Tania, my social anxiety hadn't been this bad, but months of avoiding people had clearly exacerbated things. Would I be able to hold a conversation with George's friends? And I really should go home and workshop how to tell George I was her favorite author. But spending time with George, outdoors on a gorgeous evening, sounded a lot more appealing. If talking to her friends was a struggle, at least she'd be there too. And maybe, in a more relaxed setting outside of work, the perfect opportunity would present itself to confess to George.

"Thanks. That would be nice," I said, hoping I'd made the right call.

"Awesome. We're meeting there at eight p.m." George unlocked the drawer under the counter and handed me my bag. "Oh, and before I forget, are you happy to hold on to a spare key to the café? Just in case something happens, and I need you to open one day or lock up. Ben has a spare too."

Guilt mixed with pleasure rose in my body. George trusting me enough to share the key to Novel Gossip was touching, but it also signaled just how deep into this situation I'd already gotten myself. Would George still trust me once I told her who I really was?

CHAPTER EIGHT

GEORGE

FINALLY SATISFIED with my outfit choice—gray jeans and a plain navy tee (not an outfit that should have taken ten minutes to select)—I grabbed my keys and a light sweater, gave Max a head rub and bounded down the stairs and out into the warm evening air.

Ever since I heard H. M. Stuart would be dropping into Novel Gossip, I'd been buzzing with nervous excitement. He was notoriously private. I'd Googled him after devouring the first *Realms* book, and the bio on his publisher's website had simply said "H. M. Stuart is a New York City-based fantasy author." No social media. No author website. Nothing. It was very unusual these days for authors not to have some social media presence.

Ben had—quite rightly—assumed when the publicist called that I'd be thrilled to meet my favorite author in the flesh and had agreed to accept the delivery on my behalf. The email Ben had sent me about it, the one that had gotten lost in the mountain of unread emails that had been piling up the last few days, had mentioned that the publicist requested we keep all information regarding H. M. Stuart confidential and not make it public knowledge that H. M. Stuart was staying in Sapphire Springs. That request had only served to fuel my interest in him.

When I'd spoken to the distributor on the phone, they'd told me pick-up had been scheduled for Friday afternoon, so my encounter with my favorite author was imminent. At some point in the next two days, H. M. Stuart would be gracing Novel Gossip with his presence.

The high I got at the news had even buoyed me to invite Hannah out tonight. I'd been on the fence all day about whether it was a good idea or not, especially after the unintentionally intimate coffee-making lesson. Now, I was glad I had.

I walked down Main Street trying to think of intelligent things I could say to H. M. Stuart. I hoped he didn't turn out to be a dick. But I doubted it, based on how perceptive and empathetic his characters were.

As I reached the end of Main Street and crossed over to Dockside Park, I gave up brainstorming discussion points and drank in the scene before me instead. The evening sun was still strong enough to send sparkles over the Hudson River and light the hills on the other side with a golden glow. The grassy park was a lush green. I paused as I spotted the area that had been set up for the movie night. *Huh. This is a lot fancier than I was expecting.*

Jenny had suggested we attend and purchased tickets for us, and Blake, in typical fashion, had just told me it was an outdoor movie night with food included. She hadn't even been sure what movie was showing. For some reason, I'd assumed that we'd sit on picnic blankets, enjoying popcorn, pizza, and cheap wine. While I'd been surprised that the tickets were $80 each, this was Sapphire Springs' first outdoor movie night in living memory, and I wanted to support local initiatives, so I'd forked up the cash without giving it much thought.

Now, it was clear why the tickets were so expensive. A large screen was set up near the river. In front of it were rows of small round tables covered in crisp white tablecloths with candles in the middle. At each table two chairs sat next to each other, facing the screen. I counted four forks and four knives at each table setting. I raised my eyebrows. It looked like, instead of popcorn and pizza, we were in for a fancy four course meal. A crowd of locals milled around, chatting while waiting to be seated.

"George!" I turned to see Jenny and Blake walking up, hand in hand. Jenny, in a bright-red romper, her long blonde hair out, looked very much like the influencer she used to be. Blake wore navy chinos and a white t-shirt. They seemed happy and relaxed. I grinned. I was so glad they had found each other. Recently, seeing them together had made me think about whether I should dip my toes back in the dating pool, but work had been so busy I'd had no time to even look into it, let alone date someone.

"Hi!" I gave them both a hug. "Thanks for organizing this. It looks incredible."

Jenny smiled. "I can't wait! When I was working last night, Sam was telling me about the 1980s-themed cocktails she's created to pair with the food, and they sound amazing."

"Oh, great!" Okay, this was going to be a *lot* fancier than I'd expected. Sam, the bartender at River's Edge, Sapphire Spring's best restaurant, made a mean cocktail, and I assumed her involvement meant that River's Edge was doing the food as well.

Olivia and Amanda approached in the distance, and I waved them over.

"Wow! This is amazing. This would be a perfect date night. Next time I'll drag Peter along," Amanda exclaimed as they joined us. It was Amanda's wedding to Peter last year that had brought Jenny and Blake together.

An uneasy feeling, the source of which I couldn't place, washed over me, but I pushed it away.

"And here's Hannah," Olivia said, nodding toward Main Street.

My heart rate increased as my gaze landed on Hannah walking toward us in navy shorts that ended halfway down her thighs, a white, short-sleeved blouse, and white sneakers. Her hair, which she'd worn tied up to work today, was down. She looked stunning. *Damn. She could be a model for J. Crew.*

Hannah tucked a stray hair behind her ear as she scanned the growing crowd. As she spotted us, her face broke into a broad grin, and she strolled over. I focused on breathing slowly in an effort to regulate my pulse.

I'd just finished introducing her to everyone when the owner of River's Edge, standing next to the big screen, started speaking into a microphone. "If everyone could please take their seats, we'll be starting the event shortly. Seats are allocated. Please refer to your ticket for the seat number."

Jenny pulled the tickets out of the back pocket of her romper and began handing them out. The unease I'd ignored earlier came rushing back, and this time, the reason was clear. As Amanda had noted, the whole set-up—white tablecloths, candles, two chairs side-by-side—looked extremely date-like. All it was missing was rose petals, and it could be a Valentine's Day event. And, of course, given I was the only person who actually knew Hannah, it would make sense that we'd sit together. If it'd been Ben, I wouldn't have given it a second thought—except, perhaps, to chuckle about it with him. But with Hannah, things were different.

The last two days, whenever I had a spare moment, I'd found my eyes drifting in her direction. I'd watched her interact with customers with kindness, efficiently deliver and clear away food and drinks, and talk passionately about books, her whole face lighting up with excitement. There was no point in denying that I was attracted to her. But she was also my employee, and she was married. Two very good reasons why things could go no further. And also two reasons why being seated together under romantic date night conditions was less than ideal.

On the plus side, at least it would give me an opportunity to get to know her better. She'd sent through her paperwork last night, and there was a long, unexplained gap on her CV. The last job she'd listed had been six years ago, at a French café in the West Village. I knew people took time off work for all sorts of reasons and I didn't want to pry, especially because there'd been no red flags in the two days she'd worked with me, and quite frankly, I couldn't be too picky at this point. But it piqued my interest.

Hannah had also gotten top marks in her undergraduate English degree at NYU, graduating summa cum laude. It surprised me that, with those results and the work ethic she would have needed to achieve them, plus the student loans she would have accrued, she wasn't using her degree. I inwardly shook myself. *Um, you're not using your computer science degree either. Remember, George? Perhaps, just like you, she decided she didn't want to pursue corporate life.* Or maybe her husband was loaded or she had a trust fund, and she didn't need to work. Or she had kids and had taken time off paid work to look after them. Whatever the reason, my newest employee intrigued me.

Jenny cleared her throat. "George, this is your ticket. I figured you and Hannah would sit together."

Heat shot up my face as I reached out my hand. As anticipated, Hannah and I would be sharing an intimate table for two for the evening.

I swallowed, trying to ignore the butterflies fluttering in my stomach.

"Well, should we head over?" I asked Hannah.

"Sure," she replied.

As we turned, I thought I saw Hannah's eyes widen as she took in the scene before us.

"Do you have these movie nights often?" Hannah asked as we walked toward out table.

"No." I grinned. "In fact, this is Sapphire Spring's inaugural outdoor movie night. We're making history tonight."

Hannah's mouth twitched. "Well, I feel very privileged to be invited to this momentous occasion."

We reached our allocated tables and, without thinking, I pulled out Hannah's chair and stood behind it.

Hannah shot me an amused look, her right eyebrow quirking up.

I blinked, came to my senses and stepped away, my face burning with heat. *Good lord, George. You're worried about this feeling too much like a date, and then you suddenly go all chivalrous on her. This is not the 1950's.* What had gotten into me? Hannah was more than capable of seating herself.

Rather than sitting, Hannah stepped over and pulled my chair out with a flourish. "Madame," she said, gesturing for me to sit.

She held my gaze for a moment, her eyes twinkling, and

then we burst out laughing. The feminist in me appreciated Hannah's reaction, and I loved how she turned the whole situation into a joke.

If I could keep my uncharacteristically gallant behavior under control, perhaps the next few hours wouldn't be as awkward as I'd feared.

"THIS IS SO..." I bit down hard on my tongue, desperately searching for a word to replace *romantic*, which had almost escaped my mouth. "Cute," I landed on, wincing. Well, at least it was better than romantic.

From where we sat in Dockside Park, we had a stunning view of the sunset. The fluffy clouds were tinged red and gold, and those same vibrant colors were reflected on the Hudson River. I took a long sip of my delicious piña colada, which was going down way too quickly. It was paired with a shrimp cocktail, which was equally tasty but not very alcohol-absorbent. A pleasant, warm buzz began to spread across my body. I hadn't drunk alcohol in months. I'd been so miserable I'd been worried that booze might just make me spiral further, but on a gorgeous warm evening like tonight, in my new hometown miles away from Tania and New York, and with my new, sort-of-friend-slash-boss next to me, I was in the mood to indulge. The only gray cloud hanging over my head was the fact that I needed to tell George about my pen name at some point tonight.

"Yeah. I'm sorry, I didn't realize the seating would be

arranged like this. It's not really conducive to you getting to know everyone." George looked around. Amanda and Olivia were seated at a table to our left, while Blake and Jenny were directly behind us. I was now fairly confident that George and Olivia were not dating. If they had been, surely they would've shared a table together. That realization had, ridiculously, put me in an even better mood than I'd been in before. I'd also been thrilled that Jenny and Blake were clearly a couple and comfortable holding hands in public. That boded well for Sapphire Springs being LGBTQ+ friendly. *And maybe it supports your working hypothesis that George is queer too—queer vibes, queer books, queer friends...* I shut that train of thought down abruptly.

"If the movie doesn't finish too late, we thought we'd grab a quick drink at Builders' Arms afterwards, if you're up for it," George continued.

I nodded. "That'd be nice." Telling George who I was could wait until later into the night. For now, I just wanted to enjoy the beautiful evening. Perhaps I could do it at the pub. "Hey, I forgot to ask. Do you know what the movie is?"

George chuckled. "Sorry, no. I got all my information about this from Blake, who's notoriously bad at details. I probably should've asked Jenny. I figure, if it's terrible, we can always leave after we've finished eating."

The event organizer announced that the movie would begin once it was dark. So, George and I still had some time together, just the two of us, without a movie to distract us. Just me and my very attractive boss. I swallowed.

George nudged me. "What do you think their story is?"

She nodded her head toward a man in his forties with salt-and-pepper hair, wearing a white shirt and tan chinos, and a pretty woman in her twenties, with brown hair and a floral dress. I smiled. Making up stories about strangers was one of my favorite games. I loved that George had instigated it. I tilted my body to get a better look and accidentally brushed George's shoulder, my arm tingling where we made contact. *Focus, Hannah.*

"He's a finance bro who works on Wall Street, and she's his third wife," I said confidently. "He's been working weekends for months—probably having an affair with his soon-to-be-fourth wife—and she put her foot down and insisted they visit Sapphire Springs for a romantic getaway."

George chuckled. "That's actually Mark, who runs the ice cream parlor, and his daughter, Kim, who's home from studying law at Princeton."

I glared at her, laughing. "Hey! That's not how this game is supposed to work. You're meant to engage in wild speculation with me, not know who they really are."

George held my eye, grinning, and a small shiver ran down my spine. "I think it's more fun this way, since I know just how wrong you're getting it."

"Hmmm." I eyed George with fake disapproval. "What about that couple?" I nodded over at a sweet-looking gray-haired couple in their seventies. They'd been holding hands until the food arrived and were now chatting as they ate. "I think they were childhood sweethearts. Met on the first day of high school, fell madly in love, and got married at eighteen. Definitely have at least three kids."

George snorted. "That's Roger and Prue. They officially got together last year after a scandalous affair that got a *lot* of airtime at Novel Gossip. But they *are* madly in love and have three kids...each, with other people."

I laughed. "Ouch, strike two. I'm not doing too well at this. Are there any couples here you *don't* know?"

George paused, surveying the crowd. "Those men over there. They must be out-of-towners."

She nodded her head toward two men sitting at a table near the river, wearing Bermuda shorts and polo shirts. They were both peering at one of the men's phones.

I looked at her, smiling. "Well, what do you think? What's their story?"

"Definitely a couple. Met at Columbia, studying..." George frowned, concentrating on them as if she stared hard enough, she'd be able to see through them to their diplomas. "An MBA. They're considering buying a second home in Sapphire Springs as a weekend pad but want to spend some time here first."

"Are you serious?" I laughed, shaking my head.

"What?" George stared at me.

"Are you sure you haven't seen them before, or at least heard about them?"

"Positive. Why?"

"Because they came into Novel Gossip when you were on your lunch break today. I made them coffee to-go and had a chat. They live and work in Manhattan and are looking to buy a second home here. I don't know where they studied, but they work in finance and I wouldn't be at all surprised if it was Columbia."

George grinned, clearly very pleased with herself.

As we took turns to suggest increasingly more ridiculous stories about the people around us, I couldn't help wondering...if someone was playing the same game about us, what would they say?

I hadn't been on a date night for a long time. The last few years, Tania and I had gotten out of the swing of it. She'd often worked late—although, now I knew that hadn't always been true—and when we did go out, it was usually with our group of friends. But while I knew tonight was most definitely not a date night, it certainly reminded me of one. And a good one at that.

"What about them?" George nodded at the couple directly in front of us, who couldn't keep their hands off each other.

I squinted at them. "They met reaching for the same can of beans at the general store last week and their chemistry was explosive. They're on their third date and are hoping to get lucky tonight."

"Bah dum!" George said in a low sing-song voice. "They've been married as long as I've known them and are having a rare night out without their kids."

I laughed. "Okay, I officially suck at this game."

As we were staring at them, the couple amped up their PDA to the next level, hands going under each other's tops and kissing that involved a lot of tongue. The sun had almost disappeared behind the mountains, but it was still light enough to see exactly what was going on. We looked away to give them some privacy, exchanging amused glances. A tingle shot down my spine.

"Good lord!" George chuckled. "I mean, I want them to enjoy their date night, but the movie hasn't even started yet!" She shot me a half-grin, half-grimace. "If I'd known it was going to be quite so couple-ly I would have suggested your husband take my ticket."

"Husband?" I stared at George, confused. "I'm single. Well, separated—in the process of getting a divorce. From my soon-to-be-ex-wife." Heat rushed to my face. *Not a very subtle way of letting George I'm into women.*

George froze for a moment and then furrowed her brow.

My heart jumped into my throat as realization slammed

into me. *Shit. Had Ben mentioned to George that the woman who'd come in looking for a job was married?*

"Oh, sorry. I must've misunderstood," George said after an awkward pause.

To my relief, music started playing, and an image flashed onto the screen. What were we in for tonight?

Wet Hot American Summer.

My stomach dropped. Based on my recollection of watching this movie years ago, it was not something you wanted to watch with your gorgeous boss.

CHAPTER TEN

GEORGE

I CURSED BLAKE. If she'd told me the movie we'd be watching would be about horny teenagers, I would not have invited my new employee. My new employee, who I'd just discovered was single and interested in women.

In between enjoying the main course, beef Wellington paired with an amaretto and whiskey sour, I couldn't help stealing glances at Hannah and blushing furiously at every sexual innuendo in the movie. Thank god the sun had set so Hannah couldn't see. Although, given the heat my cheeks were letting off, I wouldn't be surprised if they were glowing in the dark. This was giving me flashbacks to the embarrassment I'd felt as a kid at any hint of sex in a movie I was watching with my parents. I knew I was being ridiculous, that Hannah and I were both adults, and sex was absolutely nothing to be ashamed of. But the romantic setting, Hannah's close proximity, her off-limits status, and possibly also the two cocktails I'd consumed in the last hour were making me particularly sensitive to any hint of sex. The fact that, before the movie started, we'd been getting along like a house on fire didn't help either.

Hannah's leg brushed against mine, sending tingles up my thigh. As much as part of me yearned to maintain that contact, I pulled my leg away.

When the credits finally began to roll, my body relaxed. *Thank god.*

I pulled my phone out of my pocket to check the time and spotted a text from Ben.

> Feeling much better today. Think I'll be back tomorrow or Friday.

I exhaled in relief. While Hannah and I had just been coping, having Ben back would make a huge difference. I also needed to give Hannah a day off soon. She was about to work her third long day in a row, and I didn't want her getting burned out. With that weight lifted off my chest, I put my phone away.

Hannah picked her satchel up off the ground, and we both stood at the same time.

"The cocktails and food were incredible," Hannah said. "Especially the beef Wellington. I don't think I've ever eaten that before, but it was delicious. I don't understand why it lost popularity after the 1980s."

I chuckled. "Agreed. There are lots of things about the '80s that deserve never to see the light of day again—mullets, slap bracelets and fast-food buffets, to name a few—but the beef Wellington is not one of them."

Hannah laughed. "I personally don't mind a good mullet. They're very practical when you think about it. They keep the hair out of your eyes, while protecting your neck from sunburn." I shot her a horrified look. "Look, I accept mullets are controversial. But I can't see why anyone would object to beef Wellington. Tender beef, melt in your mouth mushrooms, fresh herbs and buttery crisp pastry. Maybe you should put it on Novel Gossip's menu, as part of a campaign to bring back the beef Wellington," Hannah suggested. While Hannah's face was only inches from mine, I couldn't make out her facial expression in the dark. However, judging from the playful tone to her voice, she was enjoying our exchange as much as I was.

"I'll talk to Romina and see what we can do to support this important cause," I said, trying my best to keep my tone serious.

"If you do, I promise to rave about it to any customer who's willing to listen."

I grinned. "It's a deal. Perhaps together, we can turn around the fate of the beef Wellington and reinstate it to its rightful place on menus nationwide."

In the dim light, I saw Hannah swing her satchel over her shoulder. "While we're on the topic of '80s revivals, can we also bring back the fanny pack? I don't understand why they get such a bad rap. The way they hold everything securely within arms' reach is just so practical. And you don't need to worry about leaving it behind because it's attached to you at all times."

"Look, I wholeheartedly endorse reviving the fanny pack, but I think we have to be careful about overextending ourselves. There's a limit to what we can do."

"Fine! We'll just tackle one '80s trend at a time," Hannah replied.

"Hey! Do you guys want to have a quick drink at Builders' Arms?" Jenny asked from behind us.

Suddenly conscious of how close we were standing, I took a step back, nearly knocking my chair over in the process. Another burst of heat rushed to my cheeks. *Very smooth, George.*

"I'm in," I said. I turned to Hannah. "Would you like to come?"

My pulse picked up as I waited for her response.

"Sure. That sounds great," Hannah said after a pause.

I exhaled, smiling into the dark. I didn't want our night to end just yet.

"HANNAH SEEMS NICE," Blake said, leaning against the bar at Builders' Arms while we waited for Dan, the owner, to finish serving another customer. The pub was bustling with locals, including some who had attended the movie night. The male couple from Manhattan were sitting at a round high table next to one of the front windows, sipping red wine, and Roger and Prue were at a small table in the back corner, drinking what looked like whiskey neat.

I shot a look at Blake. Was her tone full of meaning, or was I just being paranoid?

"Yeah," I said, trying to keep my voice casual.

Blake glanced at me and then over at Hannah, who was sitting at one of the rustic wooden tables with Amanda, Jenny, and Olivia at the back of the pub. *Okay, that look definitely had meaning.* I was not being paranoid.

"What?" I asked.

"Nothing. Did you say she was married?"

"I did say that, but I must have misunderstood Ben. Apparently, she's single. Well, getting a divorce. From a woman."

Blake's eyebrows shot up.

Hannah's revelation about her marital status had sent a buzz of excitement mixed with confusion vibrating through my body. While the confusion was well-founded—I could have sworn Ben had said she had a husband—the excitement was not. She was an employee and so strictly off-limits when it came to dating.

"Okay, great." Blake smiled, an expression that could only be described as sly on her face.

I rolled my eyes. Blake could be infuriatingly economical with words at times. "Come on, spit it out. Why are you asking all these questions about Hannah?"

Blake grinned. "Jenny and I couldn't help noticing that you two seemed to be getting along very well. We intercepted a few lingering glances and playful looks." Blake scrunched her face into a terrible wink, which I couldn't help chuckling at. "If we hadn't known better, we'd have thought you two were on a date."

I shook my head. "There's nothing going on. The only reason it might've looked like we were on a date is because we were seated at an intimate table for two, watching a movie rated R for strong sexual content—a fact that *you* failed to warn me about." Despite my words, a small buzz of excitement rose in my chest on hearing that Blake and Jenny had sensed chemistry between us.

Blake gave an apologetic grin. "Sorry about that. We genuinely didn't know what the set-up was. But to be honest, I'm not very sorry. It looked like you two were having a great time." She paused, looking at me intently. "I don't think I've ever seen you look at someone like that before."

Hannah's laugh rang out, and I couldn't help glancing over at her. She was talking animatedly about something, her eyes sparkling. There was no denying that I was attracted to her. Not only was she gorgeous, but she was funny and sweet, and so easy to talk to. And I'd really enjoyed the rapport we'd built this evening.

"I mean, she seems great. But she's also my employee, so she's not an option. And anyway, work's so hectic at the moment, I don't have time to date."

Blake shot me another loaded look, and I regretted speaking. I should have just denied I was attracted to her and moved on, rather than listing off reasons why dating Hannah was a bad idea and signaling to Blake that I'd given the subject some thought.

Dan approached us with a warm smile, and we ordered our drinks.

"I don't think it's illegal to date an employee," Blake said when he'd gone. "When I worked in the hospital, there were plenty of relationships between senior and junior medical staff. As long as you handle it appropriately, which I'm sure you would, isn't it okay?" Blake raised an eyebrow.

"Yeah, I don't think it's illegal. But dating employees is a recipe for disaster. There's massive power imbalance, which isn't exactly a great foundation for a healthy relationship. It could also be incredibly awkward if things didn't work out. Who wants to work with their ex every day? Or what if I make a move, and it isn't reciprocated? It could expose me—and Novel Gossip—to sexual harassment claims." After working so hard to make Novel Gossip a success, I didn't want to do anything that would put it at risk.

Blake frowned. "I don't know her, but from what you've said, she's sensible, smart, and kind, so that all seems pretty unlikely to me. And while I don't know her, I do know you, and I know you'd act with integrity if you broke up and wouldn't use your power imbalance to her disadvantage."

"But even if *you* know that, Hannah might not, and that's what's important. She might not feel comfortable breaking up with me out of worry of losing her job, even if the worry is unfounded." I shook my head firmly. "No, that's a line I don't feel comfortable crossing."

Dan placed our drinks in front of us and we paid.

"I'm not trying to convince you to do anything you're not comfortable with, it just seems like a shame to discount the possibility completely if you do have a connection with her," Blake said gently.

I shook my head. "I've seen these sort of power imbalances play out in real life with my parents and then with Alexis. So maybe I am particularly sensitive about it, but it's for a good reason."

Blake tilted her head and looked at me. "Because your mom was your dad's secretary?"

I nodded. "Their relationship was so unhappy. I've always wondered if she would have left him if she wasn't reliant on him for a job or at least references."

Blake furrowed her brow. "But how does Alexis fit in? I know when you started volunteering on her campaign she was effectively your boss, but I thought by the time you broke up with her you were off the campaign and working back in tech?"

I realized that while Blake knew about my relationship with Alexis and about the app, I'd never explained how intertwined they'd been.

"That's true. But you know the app I sold, the one that let me pay off Dad's debts and buy Novel Gossip?"

"Mmmh," Blake said, clearly confused about what that had to do with my story.

"Well, because I created it to help Alexis with grassroots campaigning, when the tech company approached me with the offer to buy it, they insisted Alexis sign some paperwork giving up any rights to it."

Blake frowned. "Why?"

"Because I'd developed it while I was a volunteer on her campaign they were worried Alexis might be able to claim some rights over the app, even though I'd done all the work in my personal time."

Blake shook her head, her brow still furrowed, and took a sip of her drink.

"It was terrible timing," I continued. "Not only had I just discovered that Dad had left Mom with a mountain of debt when he died and Mom's house was at risk of being foreclosed, but I'd also just decided I needed to break-up with Alexis when I got the offer from the tech company."

Blake winced. "Shit."

"Yeah," I said, pausing to try my beer. "I knew that I had to break up with Alexis before asking her to sign the paperwork. Doing it the other way around would have felt underhanded. But with Mom's financial future on the line, I starting freaking out that Alexis would lash out in hurt or anger and refuse to sign the documents." I grimaced at the memory. I'd had such severe anxiety about the whole situation that I'd started seeing a therapist to help me work through it.

"How did she take it? I'm assuming she signed it since the app sale went through?"

I pressed my lips together in a weak smile. "Yeah, she did. She was really upset about the break-up, but she signed everything without any hesitation. But that period was one of the most stressful times of my entire life. I vowed I'd never put myself in a similar position again. I'd also hate for someone else to be in that position with me. Either way, if there is a significant power imbalance, it's not a great start to a relationship."

Blake turned to me with a softer expression on her face.

"Okay. I'll tell Jenny not to get too excited. You know how she prides herself on her match-making skills."

A twinge of disappointment vibrated through me. A part of me had hoped that Blake would find a loophole in my reasoning and convince me that dating Hannah wasn't a terrible idea.

Just then, peals of laughter rang out, and we turned to their source. Hannah, Jenny, Amanda, and Olivia were laughing uncontrollably, tears streaming down their faces.

"Looks like we're missing out on something hilarious. Should we head back?" Blake asked.

I nodded, unable to keep my eyes off Hannah as we returned to the table with our drinks. Seeing her getting along so well with my friends sent a burst of warmth rushing through me. Hannah looked up, smiling, and caught my eye. The warmth was replaced with a jolt of electricity.

Is this one of those lingering glances Blake and Jenny had intercepted? Could my attraction to her be reciprocal? Hope sparked in my chest.

I dropped my gaze, inwardly shaking myself.

Get a grip, George.

As you just explained to Blake, Hannah's off-limits. And she needs to stay that way.

CHAPTER ELEVEN

HANNAH

"ARE you sure you're okay to get home by yourself?" George asked as we stood on the pavement in front of Builders' Arms. It was past 11 p.m., but it was still comfortably warm. The old-fashioned cast-iron lamp posts that lined Main Street let off a golden glow, gently lighting George's face.

"I'll be fine. It's not very far away, and I distinctly remember someone telling me that Sapphire Springs isn't exactly known for its crime rate." I grinned.

George laughed. "True."

"Thanks again for inviting me. I had a great time. Everyone is lovely." And I meant it. I really meant it. The awkwardness over the date-like movie night had faded as the evening had worn on, possibly due to the number of drinks I'd consumed or how comfortable George just generally made me feel. I was slightly giddy, and whether it was due to the drinks or the great time I'd had, I wasn't sure. For someone who'd been ready to embrace the life of a recluse, I'd really enjoyed hanging out with George and her friends. Jenny was outgoing and optimistic. Blake initially came across somewhat reserved but had a biting sense of humor and was clearly very close to George—they'd had an intense-looking heart-to-heart about something at the bar. Amanda was direct and hilarious, and Olivia, who I'd discovered was Blake's sister, was very sweet.

And then there was George. George, looking stunning under the glow of the lamp posts, concern in her eyes. The more time I spent with her, the more I liked her. While she was warm and down-to-earth, she also had a playful side that had really shone through tonight.

Fueled either by drinks or the success of the evening, I impulsively stepped forward and gave George a hug. For a moment, I savored the heat of her body, the firmness of her upper back, the curve of her chest pressed against mine, and her smell—a faint woody scent. My body relaxed as I leaned into the hug and closed my eyes. Then, I remembered who I was hugging. My hot boss. Who had no idea I was H. M. Stuart. *What the hell are you doing, Hannah?*

My pulse racing, I detached myself, stepping back. Heat shot over my cheeks. "Well, I'd better be going. See you tomorrow!"

I managed an awkward wave and turned, walking quickly away from George.

The heat in my cheeks dissipated as I headed down Main Street. There wasn't a law against giving your boss a friendly hug. Well, at least I didn't think there was. It was fine. Some people were just huggers, and that would be totally normal for them. While I wasn't usually a hugger, at least George didn't know that.

I turned off Main Street, my mind still focused on George. I smiled as I remembered her praise for my writing, the fact that she liked the way I turned classic fantasy tropes on their heads and my strong female characters. If only I could recreate that for the book I was meant to be working on, the book I'd made absolutely no progress on. The bounce in my stride diminished. I tried to shake off the sinking feeling that thinking about the book brought on.

I also hadn't gotten any closer to telling George that I was H. M. Stuart tonight. I'd put off telling her at the start of the evening, worried I'd ruin the night, and by the time the movie was over, I felt too tipsy to handle the conversation. Shit. My stomach sank even further. *Don't start worrying about it tonight, Hannah. It's too late to do anything now and worrying won't achieve anything.*

Taking my therapist's advice, I focused on being mindful of my surroundings instead, taking in the smell of the rose bushes, the glow of the moon behind a smattering of light clouds, the soft breeze on my face.

And then it struck me. *Strong female characters.* That was one of the things George liked about my novels, and what I was missing from the outline I'd submitted to my publisher months ago. In the plot I'd sketched out, my main character, Esmae, was too passive, too lacking in agency. She needed to take charge of her own destiny, meet challenges head on, just like she had in earlier books, instead of the plot revolving around her being rescued by the two competing love interests. *Perhaps my own feelings of helplessness have rubbed off on her.* My pulse increased, my mind whirring at a million miles a second as I reimagined the plot with a new and improved kick-ass Esmae taking the lead. *Fuck yes!*

I picked up my pace, itching to get home and start typing. I hadn't felt this way about writing for a long time. When I reached my cottage, I flung open the front gate and jogged to the front door, my hands trembling as I turned the key. I dropped my bag in the hallway, raced into the living room, grabbed my laptop, and plonked myself down in the armchair.

As the words flowed out of me, my body relaxed. Finally, for the first time in months, I was in the zone.

And damn, did it feel amazing.

CHAPTER TWELVE

GEORGE

I CROUCHED in front of the mini fridges behind the counter, counting cartons of milk. It was nearly closing time, and I was taking advantage of the lull in customers to take an inventory of what I needed to order. After the movie night last night, I was looking forward to a quiet evening in.

"George."

I looked up to find Romina standing next to me behind the counter, her sensible black leather handbag slung over her shoulder. Romina would have usually left by now, but a group of tourists had ordered a late lunch just before the kitchen was due to close, and it had thrown the entire afternoon off.

"The cornbread is in the oven. I've set an alarm for twenty minutes. The pulled pork has been in the slow cooker since morning, so it's probably ready now, but I figured we might as well leave it in for a bit longer to let the flavors develop. You're okay to get them both out?"

I nodded. "Yes. That sounds great, thank you. I'm sorry you had to stay so late. The pork smells incredible." The rich smoky scent of Romina's pulled pork had been making my stomach rumble all afternoon. It would be tomorrow's lunchtime special.

"Well, I made a huge batch, so if you want some for dinner, there's plenty." Romina shifted on her feet, clearly eager to get home.

I grinned. "I will definitely take you up on that. See you tomorrow!"

I finished counting the milk and then stood, surveying the café. There were only two customers left, and they looked like they were finishing up.

I grabbed a cloth and a bottle of surface cleaner and started wiping down the tables.

Ten minutes later, both customers had paid and left. I flipped the *Open* sign on the front door to *Closed* and went to find Hannah, who'd leaped at my request to check that the bookstore section was in order. I peered down each aisle until I spotted her, head bent over a stack of books she was holding, studying one of the books intently. I smiled, warmth expanding across my chest. I loved how much she seemed to genuinely love books.

"Hannah?"

She jumped and turned to me, her eyes bright.

"Sorry. I was just going to clean Hugo and thought I'd check if you wanted anything to drink first?" I asked.

"Thanks for the offer, but I'm fine." Hannah smiled. "I've just been putting away books that were lying around, and this one caught my eye. Have you read this? It sounds fantastic." She held up the book she'd been examining. It was *The Glass Den,* a literary fiction novel by a debut author that had received a lot of buzz lately.

I shook my head. "No. I've read some great things about it, but haven't gotten around to reading it yet." I hadn't had much time for reading lately, and I really missed it. "I was actually sent an advanced reader copy of that one. Let me take a look and see if I can find it for you." Hannah sounded so excited about the book, and it seemed a shame for the advanced reader copy to go to waste.

"Oh, if it's not too hard to find it, that would be great," Hannah said.

"No, that's fine. It'll be a good opportunity for me to show you the storage shed anyway."

Hannah put down the books and followed me past the kitchen to the back door, which opened onto a small yard with a quaint-looking wooden shed in one corner.

"Oh, cute!" Hannah exclaimed.

"Unfortunately, it's not so cute inside," I said as we walked over the grass toward it.

I twisted the key and, with some difficulty, opened the door. "Hmm, the door must have shifted in the hot weather."

The door swung shut behind us. The small windows didn't provide much natural light, so I flicked the light switch and winced as it illuminated the shed.

"Sorry, it's a complete mess in here." I hadn't been in the shed for a few days, and seeing it fresh through Hannah's eyes, it was even worse than I'd remembered. Boxes were stacked precariously high. There was just enough space for the two of us to fit. Standing so close to Hannah, the memory of last night's unexpected hug came rushing back to me—Hannah's body pressed warm against mine, me inhaling her slightly floral scent, my body humming from the contact. *She's an employee, remember.*

"Wow," Hannah said, looking around. "No wonder you didn't have room for those H. M. Stuart boxes."

To my disappointment, H. M. Stuart had not shown up

at Novel Gossip today, but presumably he'd come tomorrow morning since the books were being picked up in the afternoon. My stomach fluttered with a mix of nerves and excitement at the thought.

I grimaced. "Yeah. I've been meaning to spend some time in here sorting things out. I just haven't had a chance recently." I looked around the stack of boxes and spotted the one marked *ARC*, which was thankfully within reach. I pulled the box out and started searching through it.

"Aha!" I spotted *The Glass Den* and extracted it from the box, handing it to Hannah. "Here we go! I'll be really interested to hear what you think of it."

"Oh, thanks! And I'd be happy to give you a hand in here after we close one day, if that would help?" Hannah offered with a smile.

I grinned at her. Having Hannah's company would make cleaning up the shed a lot less daunting and a lot more enjoyable. "You know, I might just take you up on the offer. Although, I think I'd need to pay you double overtime and throw in a meal as well, given the state of this shed."

Meal.

My heart jumped into my throat.

"Shit!"

"What is it? Hannah asked, eyes wide with concern.

"I was meant to get the pulled pork and cornbread out of the oven." I looked at my watch, and my stomach plummeted. "Twenty minutes ago. Romina is going to kill me."

"Oh no!" Hannah turned, twisted the door handle, and pushed to open it.

The door didn't budge.

"Damn, it's stuck," she said. She leaned her shoulder against the door and pushed again, furrowing her brow in effort. "Sorry, it's not opening. Do you want to have a try?"

Hannah moved away from the door, and I stepped up. I tried pushing the door with my hands, but it didn't move. I stepped back and rammed the door with my shoulder, throwing all my body weight behind me. Nothing. *Goddamnit.* It was suddenly feeling very warm and slightly claustrophobic in here.

I tried ramming the door with the side of my body a few more times and then stopped to catch my breath.

I turned to Hannah. "Do you have your phone on you? We could call someone for help." I'd left my phone on the counter.

Hannah shook her head. "No, sorry. I didn't bring it with me."

Damn.

My pulse racing, I tried to brainstorm a way out of here. This was not good. I'd come to terms with the fact that the cornbread was ruined, but if we didn't get out soon, I was worried that it might start burning in the oven and blanket Novel Gossip in smoke or, even worse, start a fire that might spread. *Fuck.*

Sweat pricked my face as I looked around for something I could use to lever open the door, but there were only boxes and boxes of books.

"Hey, George," Hannah said.

I turned to find her staring at one of the small square windows that lined the shed's walls, well over five feet off the ground.

"I think I could get through the window if we stacked up the boxes so I can climb up, turn around, and then drop down feet first."

I eyed the small window and frowned. There was no way I'd fit through there. But Hannah, with her slighter frame, might be able to. But the idea of Hannah potentially injuring herself in the process was not an appealing one.

"Hmm. I don't want you to hurt yourself."

"Seriously, George. It's worth a try. Otherwise, we'll be stuck here until at least morning."

That was assuming Romina or someone else would actually hear our cries for help out here, which wasn't a given. And that Novel Gossip didn't burn to the ground and take us with it.

"Let me just have a few more tries at opening the door," I said, not willing to admit defeat just yet.

I slammed my body against the door three more times without success.

"George, you're going to hurt yourself," Hannah said gently. "Come on, let me have a try with the window."

Hannah had a point. My shoulder was aching. If I injured my arm, then I'd be limited use in the café, and that would only exacerbate our staffing issues and put additional pressure on Hannah. But if Hannah hurt herself, that would be even worse.

As if she'd been reading my mind, Hannah said, "I can do it."

Hannah said those words with such conviction, I believed her. And at this point, I couldn't think of any other option.

"If you're sure..." I said. "Thank you."

We stacked boxes of books so they resembled steps leading to the window, and then Hannah stepped up them carefully. I stayed close to Hannah in case she lost balance and I had to catch her. The boxes wobbled precariously as she reached the top. My stomach lurched, and I put one hand on the boxes and the other on her arm to steady her.

"Thanks," Hannah said, smiling down at me.

Hannah opened the window, and then I held the boxes as she carefully turned around. She dangled her feet out the window and then rotated her body so she was facing me.

"Here goes!" Hannah said cheerfully as she let her body drop out the window.

I stood on a box and peered out, relieved to see Hannah had landed on her feet, apparently unharmed. *Thank god.*

She looked up at me, concern in her eyes, as she repositioned her glasses on her nose. We'd been so focused on escaping the shed, we hadn't discussed what Hannah would do once she got out.

Now that Hannah was safe, my top priority was Novel Gossip and Max, who was upstairs in my apartment. "Don't worry about me. If you can turn off the oven and take the pork off the stove, that would be amazing. Thank you!" I said.

Hannah nodded and raced into Novel Gossip, disappearing out of sight. I faintly heard the high-pitched sound of smoke alarms going off inside. *Shit.* I stuck my head out the window and inhaled. To my relief, I couldn't see or smell any smoke.

I felt so helpless, stuck in here while Hannah dealt with my mess. I examined the window more closely. Perhaps I could fit?

I waited another minute or two in the stuffy shed, jiggling my leg with nerves, and then lost my patience. *Screw it, I might as well try.*

I carefully made my way up the makeshift steps. When I reached the top, I turned my body just as Hannah had, so I was facing the floor of the shed, and tentatively began to lower myself out of the window, feet first. I slipped my legs through with relative ease.

Okay, this is promising.

And then the window frame met my butt and did *not* want to let it through. I tried wriggling and pushing without success. *Shit.* My initial instinct was right. I didn't fit.

"George?" a voice, partially muffled by my ass, said.

Heat rushed to my face. *Hannah.*

Oh god. I winced. *My ass is half hanging out the window.*

"I thought I'd give the window a try. Turns out, I don't fit!" I yelled, conscious I was facing away from Hannah, and the sound waves had my butt to contend with in order to make their way out of the shed through the window.

I tried pulling myself back into the shed, but it seemed my wriggling and pushing had gotten me well and truly wedged into the window frame. *Fuck.*

"Do you need to me to give you a boost back inside?" Hannah asked.

I cringed and then took a deep breath. As embarrassed as I felt right now, I knew I needed help.

"Yes, please!" I shouted.

I felt Hannah's arms wrap around my legs. "Okay, on the count of three. One, two...three!"

I braced my hands against the inside of the window frame and thrust myself forward while Hannah pushed up. Nothing. My heart thumped in my ears.

"Do you mind if I put my hands on your butt?" Hannah yelled after a moment of silence. "I think it might make it easier to push."

My cheeks exploded into flames. *Good lord, this is humiliating.* But Hannah's hands on my ass seemed like a better option than continuing to be stuck in the window and Hannah having to call for reinforcements. I didn't need any more witnesses to my predicament.

"Okay!" I yelled, wincing.

Warm hands pressed against my butt cheeks. *Oh god.* This was definitely crossing some employer-employee boundaries.

"One, two, three!" Hannah yelled and then pushed hard.

I pushed off the window frame with my hands, wriggling my ass and trying not to think about how this would look from Hannah's perspective, and suddenly my butt was free. I toppled forward onto the boxes, regaining my balance just in time to stop myself from falling to the ground.

"Are you okay?" Hannah asked, her voice now clear.

"Yes. Thank you," I managed to say as I made my way down the boxes, my pulse beating double-time. I could still feel the warm imprints on my butt where Hannah's hands had been.

When I reached the bottom, I took a deep breath and walked back to the window, standing on the box to peer out. I'd planned to ask Hannah if Novel Gossip was okay but she wasn't there.

A muffled noise near the door drew my attention. I turned around just in time to see the door shake and open. I exhaled in relief. Hannah was standing there, pink-cheeked and out of breath, holding a long, curved pizza cutter. My heart bounced. She looked like some gorgeous leading woman out of an action movie, coming to save the day.

I resisted the urge to fling my arms around her and hug her. I'd just had Hannah's hands on my butt, and I didn't want to cross any more employee-employer boundaries tonight. "Thank you so much! I'm so sorry about all of this. How's Novel Gossip?"

Hannah smiled. "It's fine. The kitchen is a little smoky, and the cornbread is definitely ruined, but the pulled pork looks and smells amazing. The exhaust fan was on, so that helped a lot, and I also opened a few windows to help clear the air. I don't think there will be any lasting damage."

Relief washed over me. "Oh, thank god," I said as I grabbed *The Glass Den* and walked out of the shed, taking a deep breath of fresh air. I locked the door behind me, resolving to call someone in the morning to fix it.

Hannah examined the pizza cutter. "Hopefully I haven't damaged it. It was the only thing I could find to lever the door open. I can't imagine Romina will be thrilled if it's bent."

"It looks fine from here, but I wouldn't put it past Romina's eagle eye to spot something we've missed. To be on the safe side, I'll keep pizza off the menu for now," I said, grinning. "And here's the book, by the way." I handed Hannah *The Glass Den*, which she'd left on a box in the shed.

"Thank you. After all that, I hope it lives up to the hype."

We walked back into Novel Gossip, and I sniffed the air. There was a distinctly smoky scent, mixed with the delicious, rich smell of pulled pork, but the smoke wasn't overpowering. Hopefully nothing a good airing out wouldn't fix.

The smell got stronger as we entered the kitchen. Trays of blackened cornbread muffins were sitting on the stove, under the exhaust fan, which was running at full power. Hannah had taken the pot of pulled pork off the stove. I walked over to it, opened the lid, and was nearly bowled over by the mouth-watering smell that hit me. I grabbed a spoon from the utensil rack and stirred it. *Phew.* It hadn't stuck to the bottom of the pot. In fact, it seemed to have caramelized to perfection.

"It smells incredible, doesn't it?" Hannah stepped closer to me and peered into the pot.

"Sure does." I grinned. "Hey, if you're hungry, would you like some?"

Hannah looked at me sharply, her eyes wide. "Won't Romina notice?"

I chuckled. "That's okay. She actually said it was fine to eat some." I loved that Hannah had already picked up on who the real boss in the kitchen was.

"It is a whole lot more appealing than the leftover pasta dish I was planning to eat," Hannah said.

"Come on. It's the least you deserve after climbing out that window and saving the day. And then saving my ass!" I grinned.

While the memory of Hannah's hands on my butt still made me cringe, I could see the funny side now that we were safely out of the shed, and Novel Gossip hadn't sustained any lasting damage. "I'm planning to have some too. I can steam some greens to go with it, and while unfortunately we don't have any cornbread, there's some mashed potatoes left over that I could heat up."

"You've convinced me," Hannah said, her eyes twinkling. "My sad pasta and vodka sauce leftovers can't compete with that!"

I prepared the greens, and Hannah heated up the mashed potatoes, and before long, we were sitting at one of the tables in the café, digging into the food.

"I really built up an appetite after our impromptu escape room experience," Hannah said.

I chuckled. "I'd forgotten some people pay good money to be trapped in a room and work out how to escape. That will be twenty dollars for the privilege, thank you." I held out my hand.

Hannah laughed. "The very real risk of Novel Gossip burning down added an extra level of pressure. You could probably charge a premium for that." She took another bite and groaned. "Thank goodness the pork survived. I think it's on par with last night's beef Wellington, if not better—if that's possible."

I raised my eyebrows. "Does this mean you're giving up our plan to bring back the hits of the '80s?"

"No! I'm fully committed to the cause." Hannah's lips curved upward. "But I will also be campaigning to keep pulled pork on the menu."

"You know, after last night's conversation, I half expected you to show up today wearing a fanny pack and a mullet." I put a forkful of pork in my mouth and chewed slowly, savoring the tender, juicy meat and rich smoky flavors.

"A fanny pack would be incredibly practical for work. Perhaps you should make it part of the staff uniform. But unfortunately, I don't have one just lying around. Although, you never know—I still haven't finished unpacking, so who knows what treasures I'll unearth in the process."

"Did you just move here recently, then? Or are you just one of those people, like me, who take their time to unpack?" I asked, jumping at the excuse to find out more about Hannah. "I have a bad feeling I still have one or two unopened boxes from my move here, and that was three years ago!"

Hannah laughed. "That always happens to me too. But in this case, I moved here last week, so I have an excuse."

"Hey, no judgment here," I said. "And welcome to Sapphire Springs."

"Thanks." Hannah looked around Novel Gossip, her face bright. "I really love this space. Did you set up Novel Gossip yourself or buy it like this?"

Pride welled in my chest. "I set it up. When I bought

this place, it was a rundown old restaurant that hadn't been used for years."

"Oh, wow! Well, you did an incredible job. It's such a warm, cozy space. I love the name, by the way." Hannah took another bite of pork.

"I'm glad you like it." I smiled at her, and our eyes connected for a moment. "I can't take full credit for the name. It's the Instagram handle of a Bookstagrammer I like —I did ask her permission first, though. I always thought it would be the perfect name for a café-bookstore."

"It really is. Do you like owning your own business?"

"Honestly, it's great. I get to combine two of my passions—books and food. I really feel like I'm part of the community and love the relationships I've been able to build with my regulars." I paused, realizing I'd painted a very rosy view of small business ownership. "Don't get me wrong, like most small businesses, it's not without stress— especially recently with the staffing issues I've had—so it's been an enormous relief to have you on board. But overall I love it." I grinned at Hannah. I thought I caught a strange expression cross her face, but it vanished before I had time to analyze it.

"That's great," Hannah said, smiling again. "I always thought it would be amazing to own a bookstore and be able to help people discover new books."

I nodded. "That aspect is great as well. Especially the last few years, with publishers getting so much better at publishing diverse stories, I love being able to stock books that I would have killed to have read as a child, about queer people like me living normal, happy lives. I make a point of stocking books with diverse representation generally, in the hope all our customers will be able to see themselves reflected."

Hannah nodded vigorously. "While there's still a long way to go, it's great some progress has been made. I get so furious hearing about book bans though, and unfortunately, it's in those states banning queer books that there's the most need for kids to access them." Hannah paused, her face softening. "Maybe I've just got a misconceived stereotype of Florida in my head, but I imagine that Florida probably wasn't the easiest place to grow up in the '90s as a queer kid."

"Yeah. Dunedin, where I grew up, is currently in one of the more liberal pockets of Florida, but in the '90s, it was much more conservative. It certainly wasn't the most accepting place. And I definitely didn't have any queer role models in my life."

"That must have been hard. Were your parents okay with you being queer?"

"It took a bit of adjustment. Mom and Dad decided to only have one child because Dad traveled a lot for work— well, at least that's what they told me. Perhaps I was such a handful it put them off a second kid."

Hannah laughed. "I doubt that. But as an only child myself, I can't deny I've had similar thoughts. But sorry, go on, I think I interrupted."

I grinned. "No problem. Nothing like a bit of only child solidarity. Mom had always wanted a daughter, so she was thrilled when I turned out to be a girl. Unfortunately for her, I turned out to be a bit of a disappointment in the girl department. Instead of playing with dolls or wearing dresses, I ran wild with the O'Brien brothers next door, lived in shorts and t-shirts, and cut my hair as short as Mom would allow. I also insisted on shortening my given name, Georgina, to George, which Mom was not happy about."

"That must have been difficult, especially if you knew

at the time that your mom didn't approve," Hannah said gently.

"Yeah. Dad was always a distant figure in my life, so I didn't really care what he thought. But I did feel terrible about disappointing Mom—but not terrible enough to change how I presented or who I played with. I think Mom hoped it was just a *tomboy phase* that I'd grow out of, but as I grew older and it became clear it wasn't a phase, I could tell Mom mourned the loss of having a daughter whose hair she could style, who she could share makeup tips with, and dress up for prom in a sparkling dress."

Hannah's face was soft. "That sucks. I'm sorry."

I shrugged. "It's okay. Despite all that, I never doubted that Mom loved me, no matter what. And while I'd rejected most stereotypical 'girl' pastimes, we had a shared love of cooking. According to her, I'd insisted on 'helping' her make dinner from the age of two. Most nights, we'd cook dinner together, chatting about our day. So even though we were very different, cooking brought us together."

Hannah broke into a smile. "Oh, that's so lovely. I can just imagine adorable toddler-tomboy George standing on a stool and making a complete mess of 'helping' to make a cake. Maybe if I'd had something like cooking to bond with my parents, we wouldn't have such a strained relationship. Was your mom okay when you came out?"

"I told her when I was seventeen, while I was chopping carrots for a salad to pair with the steak she was frying in a pan." I smiled at the memory. "I was incredibly nervous about how she'd react. I remember my hands shaking so much I struggled to cut the carrots into sticks the way she liked." Even though I'd told her well over a decade ago, the memory was still so strong in my mind. "I finally got up enough courage after the first carrot to tell her. I felt so sick as I watched her swallow and stare at the steak as she digested the news."

Hannah gazed at me intently, a look of concern on her face.

"But when she turned to me, she was smiling and she pulled me in for a long, warm hug. 'Do you still want to come to church?' was her only question. Mom didn't always understand me, but she was always there for me." I paused. "How about your parents? How did they take it?"

"I was so nervous telling them as well. I had put it off for months, even though they'd never shown any signs of being homophobic." Hannah gave a wry smile. "But they were fine. The whole thing felt like a bit of a letdown, really. Coming out felt like it should have been a momentous occasion, but when I finally gathered the courage to break the news to them over breakfast, they barely seemed to register it. It was like I'd just told them I'd had a good sleep. I know I can't complain, given how lucky I was that my family was so accepting, but they literally just said, 'Okay,' and then turned back to the morning papers they were reading."

"That would definitely have been a bit anti-climatic."

"Yeah. Well, that's my parents for you." Hannah shook her head, sounding defeated.

Hannah focused her attention on the almost empty plate in front of her, scraping it with her fork and put the last remnants in her mouth. She closed her eyes briefly in enjoyment.

"Would you like another serving?" I asked.

"I'm feeling so full I'd better not. But if there's any left after the lunch rush tomorrow, it'll be my first choice for lunch," Hannah replied.

I smiled, making a mental note to put some aside for Hannah to make sure she didn't miss out.

"Perfect. I'm planning to whip up another batch of cornbread tonight, so you'll be able to enjoy it with that tomorrow."

"Oh, yum! I'm happy to stay and help if you'd like."

As tempting as Hannah's offer was, she'd already had a long day, and I didn't want to tire out my only healthy front of house employee.

"Thanks for the offer, but I should be fine. Cornbread is pretty easy to make. If I do a good enough job, Romina may not even notice the difference."

Hannah chuckled. "Well, your secret is safe with me." A serious look crossed her face, and she swallowed. "Um, speaking of secrets—"

Beep. Beep. Beep.

Shit. It sounded like the smoke alarm was going off in the kitchen again.

My heart sank. *What now?*

We looked at each other wide-eyed for a second and then jumped up and raced back to the kitchen.

When we got there, I surveyed the kitchen and exhaled. While the noise from the alarm in the kitchen was ear-piercing, there was no sign of any new smoke. Hannah had a pained look on her face and was holding her hands over her ears.

"Phew!" I yelled to Hannah, who took her hands off her ears so she could hear me. "It looks like everything's fine. It must just be the sensors acting up. Why don't you head home, and I'll sort this out."

"Are you sure you don't need any help?" Hannah yelled.

"Yes!" I shouted. "I should just be able to reset it. It's really easy. No point in us both injuring our hearing being exposed to this racket."

Hannah nodded, covering her ears with her hands again, and turned to leave. As I went to get a ladder to reset the alarm, I remembered that Hannah had started to say something before the smoke alarm started sounding again. *I wonder what it could have been?* Presumably, if it was important, Hannah would tell me tomorrow.

CHAPTER THIRTEEN

HANNAH

WALKING HOME, full of delicious pulled pork, I replayed the events of the last two hours. Being trapped in the shed with George. The extremely pleasant sensation of her firm, round butt in my hands. George confirming she was queer, news that had sent butterflies excitedly swarming in my belly. Almost confessing to her that I was H. M. Stuart, only to be interrupted by the smoke alarm. It had been a long, eventful day and I should have been exhausted, especially after staying up late last night writing. But surprisingly, I wasn't.

As soon as I opened the gate to my cottage, my brain shifted gears into writing mode. I slammed my front door shut, threw my satchel on the side table and walked quickly into the study, eager to pour more words on the page.

I skipped over the sex scene—I usually found them the hardest to write—but other than that, the words kept coming so fast my fingers could barely keep up.

My bladder eventually interrupted my writing flow. Bursting to pee, I ignored it until the urge was too strong to ignore anymore. I reluctantly got up and began walking to the bathroom. *What is the time, I wonder?* I raised my arm and glanced at my wrist. *Shit.* 12:26 a.m. I needed to be at Novel Gossip by 8 a.m. Part of me wanted to keep going, to make the most of the dam that had finally broken, but I knew I'd regret it in the morning. I'd already stayed up way too late. I didn't want to be an overtired mess in front of George tomorrow.

I changed into my pajamas, took off my glasses, and flopped into bed, but I could not turn off my mind. I kept thinking of new ideas for my book and picking up the notepad I kept by the bed to write them down. I had no doubt that, tomorrow, most of my ideas would seem ridiculous, but I knew from past experience that every so often, one would be a spark of genius. My mind slowed, and I was finally drifting off to sleep when—*shit.* My eyes opened. The problem I'd been putting off dealing with all day barreled into my mind. I had to sign 841 copies of *The Realm of Furies* between now and 3pm, and I still hadn't told George who I was.

After I'd received an email from Emma this morning, reminding me the books would be picked up tomorrow afternoon, I'd promised myself I'd tell George today, but work had been so hectic, there never seemed to be a good time. I'd tried to tell George over our delectable pulled pork dinner, but just as I'd gathered the courage to speak the smoke alarm went off and George insisted I go home. I was so worried about further damaging my hearing, I'd obeyed. And now, here I was, only fourteen hours away from the books being collected, and I still hadn't come clean to her.

My stomach sank as I realized that I'd put it off so long that, even if I got up enough courage to tell George in the morning, I'd have to spend most of my shift signing books.

And there was no way George would be able to manage without me.

Shit.

And then a thought struck me.

I had a key to Novel Gossip.

It's not like you're sleeping anyway. Being tired tomorrow seemed like a better option than not getting the books signed and letting down my readers, or spending the day signing the books and letting down George.

Re-energized, I sat up, throwing the duvet off me.

Time for some late-night book signing.

THIRTY MINUTES LATER, I stood outside of Novel Gossip, looking around to make sure no one was present to witness my next move. Turning my head side to side, I felt like a cartoonish villain in a bad heist film. I'd slipped on my usual around-the-house outfit of black leggings and a black sweater without thinking. All that was missing was a black balaclava.

Unsurprisingly, Sapphire Springs was deserted at 1:30 a.m. on a Thursday night. Heart racing, I fumbled with the key George had given me. My shaky hands finally got it in the keyhole. Holding my breath, I turned the key and gently pushed open Novel Gossip's front door.

While I hadn't seen any sign of a security system, I steeled myself, convinced I'd trigger a dramatic siren or a robotic voice repeating the words "intruder alert" and bright flashing lights, immediately summoning the police and George to the scene of the crime. *Stop being so dramatic, Hannah. You're not doing anything wrong. Just using a key you've been given to sign your own books. Not exactly a crime.* But no amount of rationalizing could get rid of the feeling that I wasn't doing the right thing.

Softly closing the front door behind me, I turned on the flashlight on my phone and carefully made my way past the empty tables and chairs, down one of the book aisles to the back of the café where the boxes of books were stacked. The faint scent of Romina's pulled pork mixed with smoke still hung in the air. Novel Gossip, such a warm and vibrant place during the day, felt eerie at night, dark and deserted. I picked up my pace. When I reached the books, I stopped, staring at the pile of boxes. It looked even bigger than I'd remembered. Eight hundred and forty-one books. I swallowed.

"Okay, let's do this," I whispered, trying to psyche myself up.

I kneeled down, ripped open a box of books and pulled one out. *Damn, it looks good.* I'd seen the cover on my computer screen before, but this was the first time I'd seen a physical copy. A warm glow of pride filled my chest as I examined the front and back of the book. I hoped this feeling never got old. Seeing a story I created and poured my heart and soul into transformed into something tangible was pretty incredible.

Remembering why I was there, I shook myself. *Stop mooning over your book and get signing, Hannah!* I pulled a pen out of my pocket and immediately realized that I needed to turn on a light. There was no way I was going to be able to sign books while holding my phone up so I could see.

I clambered to my feet and walked back down the aisle to the wall behind the counter where a number of light switches were mounted. I hadn't paid any attention to them before, and they were not labelled. I tried the switch closest to me, and the front of the store was suddenly flooded with light. *Oops.* I hastily flicked the switch back and tried the next one, which lit the counter. *Nope.* The third one illuminated the book aisles. *Thank god.*

As I made my way back to the boxes, a dog barked. My chest tightened. *Shit, that sounded like it came from upstairs.* Novel Gossip was on the bottom floor of a two-story building, but I hadn't stopped to think what, or who, was above it. *Does someone live up there?* I tiptoed the rest of the way down the aisle and then settled myself kneeling on the ground. I pulled out the first book, resting it on a box while I signed the front page.

DAMNIT. I blinked my tired eyes and pressed the pen down again. No luck. My pen had run out of ink, and my back was already aching from hunching over. I stretched out my hands and counted the pile of signed books. Seventy-seven in—I checked my watch—forty-five minutes. I did rough math in my head, and my stomach sank. Surely that couldn't be right. I pulled out my phone and opened the calculator app. *Shit.* At this rate, it would take me over eight hours to sign all the books. I had to speed up. And I also needed a new pen.

Groggy, I stood, turned around, and—*fuck!*

My foot caught on a box. My heart lurched as I lost balance, teetered, and then fell. Narrowly missing the pile of signed books, I stretched out my arms just before I hit the floor, breaking my landing. I lay on the ground for a second, catching my breath. Sitting up, I surveyed the scene. To my relief, no books had been harmed. And thankfully, my wrists seemed to have survived the impact.

I walked back down the aisle, grabbed a couple of pens from behind the counter and also a handful of coffee beans. *Maybe they will help speed me up.*

Upbeat music makes me run faster. Perhaps it will help with signing as well? When I got back to my signing corner, I pulled my headphones out of my pocket, plugged them into my phone, put on Charli XCX, and shoved a few coffee beans in my mouth. They were a little bitter and grainy tasting, but combined with the music, they seemed to help.

I was onto the fourth box of books, bopping to "Speed Drive," when someone touched my shoulder.

I jumped, letting out a strangled, panicked sound somewhere between a screech and a squawk. Heart pounding, I yanked out my headphones. Grasping my pen like a weapon, I turned to see who the intruder was.

"Hannah?"

Shit.

It wasn't an intruder.

It was far worse.

It was George.

And she was holding a knife.

CHAPTER FOURTEEN

GEORGE

BLEARY-EYED AND CONFUSED, I stared at Hannah.

Max's barking had woken me about an hour ago. I'd assumed he'd heard a squirrel and was drifting back asleep when there was a loud bang, which set Max off again. While I'd thought the noise was most likely something falling over outside in the wind, after lying in bed for a while, I'd decided to walk down the stairs to investigate. It was only when I reached the bottom of the stairs and saw there was a light on that I started to take things seriously. My heart racing, I'd picked up one of the big, sharp knives from the kitchen.

Clutching the knife in one hand and my phone in the other, the last thing I'd expected was to find Hannah, hair mussed and humming to music, bent over a box of books in the back corner of the bookstore.

She was now staring at me like a deer in the headlights. Her eyes widened as they traveled down my body to the knife I was holding. I hastily put it on a bookshelf.

"What the hell are you doing?" Still recovering from the

shock of thinking Novel Gossip was being burglarized, my voice sounded uncharacteristically sharp.

Hannah's cheeks flushed. "Um...I'm signing the books."

"Why?" My brain was not computing. I stared down at the books. *The Realm of Furies.* My chest constricted in anger. *Why on earth would Hannah be defacing my stock?* I wouldn't be able to return all the books now—or sell them. *Shit.*

Hannah ran her hand through her hair, chewing on her lip. "I, uh...because I'm..."

I clenched my jaw, waiting for her to continue.

Just when I'd thought Hannah had forgotten the question, she spoke.

"Because I'm H. M. Stuart," Hannah rushed out so quickly my mind initially didn't process the words.

I stared at her blankly.

"Because you are H. M. Stuart," I repeated slowly. My eyebrows shot up as the words finally sank in. "Wait, what?"

Hannah looked flustered. "My real name is Hannah Marie Taylor. My pen name is H. M. Stuart. I wrote this book." She held up a copy of *The Realm of Furies.*

My mental gears ground slowly, still groggy from sleep. Hannah was H. M. Stuart? H. M. Stuart was Hannah? I blinked a few times and considered pinching myself to double check this wasn't a dream.

A swirl of emotions rushed through my mind. Surprise at Hannah's revelation. Hurt that Hannah hadn't told me who she was sooner. Confusion as to why Hannah had snuck into Novel Gossip in the middle of the night. Anger at the fright she'd given me. I rested my hand on the nearest bookshelf for support.

"Then what...why...why didn't you say something earlier?" I asked.

"I...It's complicated." Hannah looked up at the ceiling.

Frustration rose up my body. *How complicated can it be?*

I'd really thought that over the past three days Hannah and I had developed a genuine connection, one that was based on trust and mutual respect. So why had she gone to such great lengths to hide who she was from me?

Hannah dropped her gaze and looked at me, tears welling in her eyes. She twisted her hands together. "I'm so sorry. I really screwed up."

Some of my anger and frustration evaporated. Despite my conflicting emotions, my urge to comfort Hannah grew. I took a deep breath.

"Hey. Why don't I make us both a hot drink and you can tell me all about it?" I asked gently. Maybe there was some rational explanation. I just couldn't, for the life of me, think of what it could be.

Hannah nodded and stood up, her gaze dropping briefly to my legs.

My face heated as I suddenly became aware that I was in my boxers and a t-shirt in front of my employee who, despite her late night subterfuge, I was undeniably attracted to. The employee whose hands had been on my butt earlier tonight. The employee who had just revealed she was none other than H. M. Stuart. My favorite author, who I'd thought was a man. *God, that's embarrassing.* My brain felt like it might explode. It was the middle of the night and I was in no state to process all this new information.

I picked up the knife—I didn't want a customer to get a nasty shock tomorrow while browsing the young-adult section—and made my way back down the aisle, Hannah following.

Ten minutes later, Hannah and I were sitting face to

face across one of the tables, nursing hot chocolates, while Hannah explained from the beginning what had happened. How she'd misheard me initially due to a hearing impairment, and then found it hard to tell me why she was really there, and how surprised she'd been by just how much she enjoyed working at Novel Gossip. As she spoke, she kept jiggling her legs, tapping her index finger on the table, and averting her gaze.

"I'm so sorry. I feel terrible I misled you," Hannah concluded, her voice faltering as she made direct eye contact with me.

While feelings of anger and hurt still remained, it was clear she hadn't set out to deceive me. It seemed like she was someone who had a hard time saying no or speaking up for herself. Hannah blinked away tears, and my heart softened even further.

I reached out and squeezed her hand resting on the table. "Hey. Look, I obviously wish you'd felt comfortable telling me the truth instead of giving me a heart attack by sneaking into Novel Gossip in the middle of the night, but to be honest, it didn't turn out too badly for me." I smiled at her. "If you hadn't accepted the job and had just come in, signed the books, and left, I would have been completely screwed. Having your help over the past three days while Ben has been sick has been a godsend."

Hannah managed a weak smile. "I'm so sorry I scared you. I really should have spoken up earlier." She shook her head and laughed. "I can't believe I let it get to the point where I was breaking and entering." Her face turned serious. "I guess I should probably make an appointment to see my therapist."

I wasn't going to argue with that. Therapists had helped me through some of the most difficult periods of my life, including my break-up with Alexis. And I was relieved that Hannah realized that the whole situation had gotten out of hand, even if I still didn't understand why she'd gone to such great lengths to keep her identity secret.

My curiosity got the better of me. "If you don't mind me asking, why don't you want to people to know about your pen name?" I asked.

Hannah's eyes dropped to her mug of hot chocolate.

"It's okay if you don't want to talk about it—or want to save it for your therapist," I said. As intrigued as I was, perhaps 4 a.m. wasn't the best time to ask a question like this.

Hannah looked up and gave me a small smile. "No, it's okay. The short answer is that I'm an introvert and really don't like attention."

"Couldn't you still just tell people who you are, but not do book events and that type of thing?" I asked.

"I could. But it's not just large crowds that make me stressed. It's really any kind of special attention. It probably all tracks back to my childhood." Hannah paused for a moment, and I thought she was going to leave it at that, but then she spoke again. "When I was a kid, I spent most of my time in fantasy worlds—either those in the books I was reading or of my own creation."

I nodded. "That's probably part of the reason you're such an incredible writer." God, it felt so weird saying that. I still couldn't quite believe it was true.

"Yeah." Hannah smiled, but it didn't reach her eyes. "Unfortunately, my parents weren't so accepting of me being an introvert. They're both highly successful academics, who love public speaking and public recognition, and they expected me to follow in their footsteps. When they realized I wasn't the precocious outgoing child they'd anticipated, they took action, enrolling me in drama school and, when I was old enough, debate." Hannah shuddered. "I hated it. So much. And the more they pushed me, the more I hated it."

"That sounds awful." I frowned. Being an introvert wasn't a personality flaw that needed fixing.

"Yeah. It went on for years. They seemed to think the more I did it, the less stressed I would get about it, and their shy daughter would be transformed into some super-confident extrovert who'd go on to become a kickass attorney, politician, or something similar. But it had the opposite effect."

"I'm so sorry. Being forced to do something you weren't comfortable doing must have been terrible." I'd loved drama in high school, but I'd seen how nervous performing had made some of my friends. Thank god they didn't have parents like Hannah's pressuring them to do it.

Hannah let out a noise partway between a huff and a laugh. "The ironic thing was, I was actually good at drama. I liked getting into the heads of the characters, and I could really channel their emotions on stage. But I hated people watching me."

I nodded. "It makes sense you'd be good at it given how great you are at creating believable characters."

Hannah flushed. "When I was fourteen, I landed the role of Lady Macbeth in my school's production of *Macbeth*. About an hour before opening night, I was in the restroom, having thrown up because I was so stressed out. I was just getting ready to leave when some of the other drama kids in my year walked in, talking—about me. They were saying it was so weird how, on stage, I came across so outgoing and charismatic, but in real life, I was so shy and boring."

My heart ached for teenage Hannah. "Oh man. Kids can be so mean."

"Yeah. I'd already been extremely self-conscious about how socially awkward I was, and hearing that comment, just before I was about to go on stage and perform in front of half the school and their families, was the last straw. I had a panic attack." Hannah looked down at her mug, her face serious. "Once I was able to move again, I ran to Jackson Park, which is on the shore of Lake Michigan, close to my parent's house, and stayed there. It was late March, so not the best time of year to spend a lot of time outside in Chicago. Barb, my nanny, who knew how much I loved that place, eventually found me hiding there, freezing cold and shivering."

Hannah stirred her hot chocolate absentmindedly. "I must have looked like a mess when she found me because she took me to the hospital to make sure I didn't have hypothermia."

"Shit! Were you okay?"

"I was fine. My parents were away at the time—"

"What? So they weren't even there for opening night?" I interjected, outraged.

Hannah shook her head. "No. At least Barb let me take a few days off school and arranged for the understudy to permanently take over my role, so I had some time to recover. But it was so awful when I did go back to school, and everyone was staring at me and whispering."

I winced. "Oh shit. That's like every teenager's worst nightmare."

Hannah's lips curved slightly up. "The silver lining of the whole thing was that, when my parents did return, they let me quit drama and debate, and I could go back to being my introverted self. I don't know what Barb said to them—

she'd been trying to convince them for years not to push me so hard—but it was an enormous relief."

I let out a breath. "Thank god. Although it really sucks it had to get to that point before they were willing to back off."

"I know," Hannah said. "So while I suspect I always would have wanted to have a pen name to protect my privacy, because I am a private person, I think that whole experience made me even more sensitive about being the center of attention. I've also worried that if my fans find out who I really am, they'll be disappointed. Just like those drama kids were. Like they'd expect me to be an amazing conversationalist and incredibly interesting, even though I'm an introvert who spends most of my life escaping into imaginary worlds by myself."

"Well, from what I've seen, you're totally selling yourself short. You are anything but a disappointment." I gave Hannah's hand another squeeze.

Hannah blushed. "Thanks."

"And it also makes complete sense to me why you'd avoid the spotlight." I paused, wondering how much to share of my own experiences. "I dated someone fairly well-known a few years ago—Alexis Merritts—and I hated the public scrutiny. Being photographed at galas and other events, being asked intrusive questions about our private lives, being the subject of "Who is Alexis Merritts' girlfriend, Georgina O'Grady?" articles. And I don't even consider myself a particularly shy or introverted person."

Hannah's eyes widened. "Oh wow. That must have been really full on. How did you cope?"

"To be honest, I didn't. It was one of the reasons we split up," I replied.

"I'm sorry," Hannah said, her face soft with concern.

I shrugged. "It all worked out for the best in the end."

Hannah looked up and held my gaze. "You know, I think you might be the first person—apart from my therapist—I've told that story to."

Warmth filled my chest. "Well, thanks for sharing that with me. And your secret is safe with me," I said, remembering Hannah had said almost the exact same words in relation to the cornbread incident earlier in the evening.

Hannah smiled and this time it reached her eyes. "That's good to know."

We sat in comfortable silence for a few moments as I tried to process the events of the last hour. There'd been a lot of new information to absorb in the middle of the night, and I still couldn't get my head around it all.

Hannah finished the last of her hot chocolate, looked at her watch, and sighed. "I'd better get back to signing."

Pushing the thoughts swirling in my head aside, I focused on the tired-looking woman in front of me. "Why don't you go home and get some sleep, and come back during the day to sign once you've had some rest?"

Hannah shook her head. "There's no way I'm going to go back to sleep now." She smiled at me sheepishly. "I ate an enormous handful of coffee beans, and now I'm completely wired. I think I just need to push through at this point." The coffee beans, along with her general anxiety about the whole situation, explained her jiggling legs and tapping finger.

"Are you sure?"

Hannah nodded.

"Well, at least let me get you set up on one of the tables at the front. It'll be a lot more comfortable than hunching over boxes on the floor."

Ten minutes later, we'd carried the boxes of books to the

front of the café, and Hannah was sitting in a chair with a few pens and a glass of water on the table in front of her, the boxes stacked up on her left side.

She smiled up at me. "Thank you. This is great. I'm so sorry I woke you. You should go back to sleep now, or you'll be exhausted."

But the idea of leaving Hannah alone didn't sit right with me. "I'll just get all the boxes opened up so they're ready for you."

"I really think you should go to bed…"

I ignored Hannah and started opening the boxes and unpacking them. I placed a pile of books on Hannah's left and then collected the ones she'd signed and placed them into one of the empty boxes. I kept shooting glances at Hannah, her head bent over the books and frowning in concentration, as she carefully signed one after another. Most people, faced with a mountain of books to sign in the middle of the night, would rush through them, placing a slapdash signature on each one, but Hannah took her responsibilities seriously. A lock of wavy brown hair fell forward over her face, and I fought the urge to tuck it back behind her ear.

Warmth spread through my body. *Even at 4 a.m., I find this woman attractive.* I went to chastise myself for the thought, and then it struck me. Hannah wasn't an employee anymore. The only reason she'd been working here was because of our misunderstanding, which had now been resolved. Which meant there was no power imbalance anymore. Which meant that she was no longer off limits.

But she *was* the brilliant, bestselling author of my favorite books. The author I'd gushed over in front of Hannah and assumed was a man. Heat shot up my face at the memory.

Thankfully, Hannah was oblivious to my embarrassment, still focused on the pile of *The Realm of Furies* in front of her. I busied myself packing up another box of signed books, deciding now was not the time to work through my feelings for Hannah.

"Shit!" Hannah exclaimed forty minutes later.

I turned to find her staring horrified at the book in front of her.

"I must have lost concentration. I accidentally drew a line down the page, and then when I startled, my pen went off to the right, so it kind of turned into a giant L."

I walked behind her, bending over her shoulder to assess the situation, trying not to be too distracted by my proximity to her and her faint floral scent.

"Um, maybe you could turn it into a drawing of a book and write *Happy reading?*"

Hannah laughed. "I don't trust myself to start illustrating things. I'm terrible at drawing at the best of times, and 5 a.m. is *not* the best of times."

"Here." I grabbed an empty box and one of the spare pens and, crouching next to her, mirrored the L drawing on the box, showing her how I'd transform it into a book. "I'm sure you can do that."

Hannah studied my basic drawing. "Yeah, okay. That doesn't look too hard. I'll give it a go. It can't look worse than this."

She painstakingly copied my drawing, glancing up and down and biting her lip. I tried not to stare at her lips too closely and failed miserably. They looked so soft.

Finally, she put her pen down. "There! What do you think?" She beamed up at me.

It certainly wasn't the best book drawing I'd ever seen. But you could tell it was a book, or possibly a newspaper or magazine, which was at least something. "I think whoever gets that book will be thrilled by their one-of-a-kind, personally illustrated, signed copy."

Hannah's face brightened further. "I'm glad you think so! Hopefully that doesn't happen again. Signing these damn books is hard enough without doing illustrations as well."

I raised an eyebrow. "I don't know. It could be a fun challenge. You draw random squiggles, and I work out how to turn them into book-related drawings."

Hannah laughed. "If it wasn't five in the morning and I didn't have all these books to get through, I'd totally be up for that game. Can we take a raincheck?"

"Of course." I grinned. "Hey, before you start signing again, can I make you something? Tea, hot chocolate, coffee?"

"George, seriously. You're going to be wrecked tomorrow if you don't get some more sleep." Hannah's voice, low and gentle, tugged at my chest. My gaze met her soft brown eyes.

"I'm okay, really. I went to bed early last night, so I've had some sleep. I doubt I'd go back to sleep now anyway." Hopefully Ben would be back today, since Hannah would be in no state to work.

She narrowed her eyes. "Well, if you're sure, I would love some tea." She put down her pen and did some hand stretches.

By the time I'd brought Hannah back a tea, I needed to refresh her pile of *to be signed* books, and there was a pile of signed books to pack into boxes. For the next while, we worked in a silent production line, Hannah autographing while I packed the signed books away and brought her fresh books. All the while, I stole glances at her, trying to reconcile the fact that this gorgeous woman who I'd spent so much time with over the past three days was also a genius fantasy author, creator of worlds and complex characters. I was itching to ask Hannah so many questions, but I didn't want to disturb her while she was focused on signing the books.

"Only five more boxes. You're nearly there," I said as I finished packing another box of signed books.

"Oh, thank god!" Hannah rubbed her eyes and stretched her arms out wide.

I tore open the next box. On top of it was a piece of paper. Sleepily, I gazed at it for a few seconds before realizing what it was. Underneath the title "Personalizations," there was a table with a list of names, addresses, and, in some cases, messages. My eyes flicked down the first few rows:

Happy Birthday, Sam!

Good luck with your writing, Marj.

I looked up at Hannah, dreading breaking the news to her. "Um, so it looks like these need to be personalized."

"Oh shit." Hannah's face crumpled. "I'd completely forgotten about that."

"I wish I could help you with them, but, well, that would be forgery. But I could read them to you—that might be faster."

"Are you sure? That would be amazing."

I nodded, and as soon as Hannah had finished signing the books piled up next to her, I began reading out the personalizations. The first few were very generic, wishing people happy birthdays and anniversaries.

"Dear Jeffrey, thank you for all your support. You are my favorite reader, and I cherish you deeply. Love, HM." I stopped and snorted.

"It does not say that!" Hannah snatched the piece of paper out of my hand and stared at it, bleary eyes wide with disbelief. "Oh my god! You'd think someone would have vetted these before passing them on to me. What am I supposed to do? I know *Jeffrey* paid a premium for the personalization, but I don't feel comfortable writing that to a complete stranger, even if I'm not signing it with my real name." She let out a sound that was halfway between a groan and a chuckle.

"What about if you change the second sentence to *I cherish all my readers deeply?*" At least, that way, it's not Jeffrey-specific."

Hannah chewed on her lip, distracting me from thinking of any alternative wording, and then nodded. "Thanks. That'll do, I think. To be honest, I'm so tired right now my sympathy for Jeffrey and his personalization request is low." She picked up her pen and then looked at me with a sheepish smile on her face. "I've already forgotten what you said. Would you mind repeating it again?"

CHAPTER FIFTEEN

HANNAH

IN A HALF DREAM-LIKE STATE, I gradually became aware that the light around me had changed. The sun was rising.

I put down my pen and looked at my watch, yawning. It was just past 6 a.m., and I was half-way through the second last box of books, which thankfully did not require personalizations.

I glanced over at George, who was slumped on one of the armchairs, asleep. After reading out the last box of personalized messages to me, she'd made us both another hot chocolate and sat on the chair to drink it while I kept signing. Despite her claims that she didn't need more sleep, a minute later, she was snoring softly.

Warmth crept over my body as I watched her, eyes shut and face soft and relaxed, her chest moving slowly up and down. I'd insisted all night that she go back upstairs to bed, but she'd steadfastly refused. Instead, she'd made me hot drinks, helped unpack and pack the books, kept me awake during my hand-stretching sessions by chatting with me, and stepped in to save me on a few occasions. If it wasn't for her, I wasn't sure how I would have gotten through the night. And she'd done it all despite me breaking into Novel Gossip and revealing who I really was. While she'd initially seemed shocked, angry and more than a little confused, the shock and anger appeared to have dissipated as I'd explained how I'd gotten into the predicament. She'd been so understanding, and also opened up to me about her own experiences dating Alexis Merritts. George was so down-to-earth and self-assured, I couldn't quite imagine her being the reluctant plus one at a political gala or the center of media speculation. Although I wouldn't mind seeing how she scrubbed up in a tux...

Worried George might be cold, I grabbed the throw off the other armchair and carefully put it over her. I hovered above her for a second, admiring her face close up—her brown eyebrows, faint freckles on her nose and cheeks, and soft red lips. I fought the desire to trace my fingertips over her lips and run my hand through her short hair. She let out an adorable little snore and I smiled.

I dragged myself away from ogling George and back to the pile of books in front of me, but I couldn't help shooting glances at her as I slowly made my way through it. Exhausted, I was just packing the last of the signed books into a box when the keys jingled in the front door. I looked up and saw Romina enter.

She did a double-take when she saw me. "Hannah! What are you doing here so early?" Her eyes traveled over to George and widened further. Romina lowered her voice. "Looks like you guys had a big night."

"It's a long story," I said, eager to avoid going into any detail.

Romina raised an eyebrow but left it alone. "Well, let me know if you need anything." She bustled toward the kitchen. A few moments later, metal clanging sounds indicated that she'd started food prep for the day.

By the time I'd piled all the boxes in a corner and packed away the pens, it was 7:30 a.m., and the café was filled with the mouth-watering aroma of muffins baking. My stomach rumbled. I was looking forward to shoveling one into my face as soon as they were out of the oven.

George would usually be getting ready to open Novel Gossip, but she was still sleeping peacefully. I didn't want to disturb her—not after she'd stayed up half the night to help me.

To my surprise, now that I wasn't sitting and signing my name over and over again, I was feeling more awake. I started to get the café ready as quietly as I could, transferring the cookies from an airtight container into the display case, filling the coffee grinder with beans, and unloading the dishwasher.

I was just debating whether I should wake George when the front door opened again, and a tall, attractive man in his twenties with short black hair and dark brown skin walked in. I was about to tell him that the café wasn't open yet when I spotted a key in his hand.

He blinked and then grinned. "Hi, I'm Ben."

"I'm Hannah, Novel Gossip's newest employee." I smiled, letting out a relieved breath. I'd been so stressed about Ben reappearing and blowing my cover, but now I didn't need to worry.

"That's great! Welcome aboard." Ben grinned and then looked around. "Where's George? I messaged her earlier to let her know I'd be in."

I nodded toward the armchair, and Ben raised his eyebrows as his gaze fell on George.

"I had a bit of an emergency that she helped me with

last night. I was just thinking I should wake her before we open," I explained.

Ben's grin widened. "I'll let you do the honors, and I'll go dump this." He patted his backpack.

I walked over to George and peered at her. She looked so peaceful and relaxed. I didn't want to disturb her. But I didn't think she'd be comfortable with her customers seeing her sleeping in the café.

I placed my hand gently on George's shoulder and gave her a small shake. "George," I murmured. She turned her head, muttered something, and then slumped back into the chair.

"George," I said, louder this time, accompanied by a more vigorous shoulder shake.

George's eyes flickered open. She looked around groggily.

"It's almost eight a.m.," I said gently. Her eyes opened wide and stared at me.

"Shit!" She staggered up.

"It's okay," I said reassuringly. "Ben is back, and I've got everything ready to open."

"Oh, thank god." She focused her gaze on me. "But what are you still doing here? You should be in bed."

"I'm fine, seriously. I think I'm running on adrenaline right now, but I'm feeling good. Why don't you go take a shower, and Ben and I will hold down the fort?"

George looked at me sternly. "Seriously. Go home, Hannah."

She looks hot when she's stern. I wouldn't mind her bossing me around a little.

"I'm staying here until you've had a shower, at least," I said firmly.

"Anyone want a raspberry-and-white-chocolate muffin,

fresh out of the oven?" Ben appeared, holding a tray full of delicious-looking baked goods.

My stomach rumbled. "Yes, please!" I said, using all my willpower to resist sprinting over and grab two.

He looked us up and down and grimaced. "And a round of coffees perhaps? You two look like you need it."

Eager to avoid more looks like the one Ben had just shot me, I decided to go to the restroom to check that I didn't look too bedraggled.

"A coffee would be amazing, thank you! I'll just be a second." And with that, I hurried off to see what damage a night of frantic writing and book signing had wrought on my face and body.

As the cold water hit my face, it struck me just how lucky I was that George reacted the way she did to my breaking and entering and my revelation. It could have so easily gone the other way. And just how much stress I could have avoided the past few days if I'd told George up front who I was.

I stared at myself, face dripping wet, in the mirror.

In the manuscript I was working on, I'd decided to transform my main character Esmae from being passive and lacking in agency to taking charge of her own destiny.

I made a vow to my reflection in the mirror.

You need to take a leaf out of your own book and get better at addressing your issues head on.

CHAPTER SIXTEEN

GEORGE

FEELING SOMEWHAT REFRESHED AFTER A
LATTE, Romina's tasty muffin, and a hot shower, I walked
back into Novel Gossip. The morning rush was just starting,
and Ben was behind the counter, serving Betty and her
friend, who were ordering the cake of the day as usual.
Looking around, I spotted Hannah clearing tables and
frowned. I'd told her to go home, but she clearly hadn't
listened.

As Hannah headed toward the kitchen, carrying a tray
of empty coffee cups, she wobbled unsteadily on her feet.

"I'll take the tray. You, go home," I said, channeling my
best authoritative boss voice while I studied her face. Even
paler than usual, with dark rings under her eyes and slightly
messy hair, she still looked beautiful. Stubborn, but beautiful. "Come on, you've done enough."

"I'm fi—" Hannah swayed, and I grabbed the tray with
one hand and her shoulder with the other to keep her from
falling.

"Hannah, you're exhausted." I placed the tray on the

counter so I had two hands ready in case Hannah collapsed on the floor. "I can't let you keep working in this state. You'd be exposing me and Novel Gossip to liability." I had no idea if that was actually the case, but it sounded convincing. Hopefully it would persuade Hannah to go home.

Hannah frowned and grabbed the counter to steady herself. "Maybe I just need to take a little break. I think all those coffee beans I ate are finally wearing off."

I furrowed my brow. There was no way she was going to be able to walk or drive home in this state, but I also didn't have time to drive her. While we'd been speaking, another five customers had entered, and Ben needed help. There was only one option I could think of. *Thank god my apartment is relatively tidy at the moment.* "Why don't you lie down upstairs? I've got a spare bedroom. Ben and I have everything under control," I said gently.

Hannah hesitated. She took her hand off the counter for a moment, swayed again, and then nodded. "If you're sure that's okay, maybe a little nap would help."

"Of course." I carefully led Hannah through the kitchen, ignoring Romina's inquisitive eyes, and up the stairs to my apartment.

Max raced down the hallway to greet us. "Sorry, I forgot to mention Max. I hope you don't mind dogs."

"Not at all. Hello buddy." Hannah bent down to give Max a pat and lurched forward, nearly losing balance.

I grabbed her by the shoulders and righted her. *God, sleep deprived Hannah on a caffeine come down was kind of adorable.* "Let's get you into bed. Plenty of time to shower Max with affection later."

Holding her arm, I took her down the hallway to the spare bedroom and gently sat her on the bed. "Here you go.

Just make yourself at home. I'll leave a spare towel out for you and a change of clothes in case you want a shower."

"Thank you," Hannah managed, leaning down and pulling off her shoes.

Wanting to give her some privacy, I left her to it and walked back down to Novel Gossip, ready to start the day for a second time.

As I passed through the kitchen, I grabbed a plate of zucchini and corn fritters that was sitting on the counter and delivered it to one of our regulars. On my way back, I paused to clear a table behind Betty and her friend.

"It's a shame this place has gone downhill lately. The food and coffee are still excellent, but it takes forever to order, and a few times, I've had to move dirty dishes to another table just so I had somewhere to sit," Betty's friend muttered. "Honestly, I think I'll just start going to Dippin' Donuts like some of the others—at least they're fast."

My stomach tightened. *Shit*.

Betty frowned at her. "They're having some temporary staffing issues but I'm sure George will have things sorted soon. There's no way I'm going to Dippin' Donuts and missing out on the cake of the day." She shoveled a fork of said cake into her mouth and let out a little moan of enjoyment.

My heart warmed at Betty's words. As concerning as her friend's comments were, hopefully most of my regulars felt the same as Betty. While I assumed that Hannah would no longer want to work at Novel Gossip now her mistaken identity had been cleared up, at least Ben was back. And hopefully the woman who'd told Ben she was interested in a job would reappear soon.

I walked back into the kitchen to find Romina eating

one of the replacement cornbread muffins I'd made last night. *Oh shit.* I braced myself.

"You did a good job on the cornbread, George. A bit more sugar than I'd put in, but it works," she said, poker-faced.

I exhaled and grinned. Not much got past Romina including, it appeared, my attempt to replace the cornbread unnoticed. But Romina's comment was high praise coming from her and I was relieved she didn't ask any questions.

The rest of the day passed quickly, with Ben and I falling into our usual rhythm.

Mid-afternoon, a delivery driver came to pick up the boxes of signed books, and I let out a sigh of relief. The back of the bookstore was no longer an eyesore or tripping hazard.

While I was clearing tables after the afternoon coffee rush, I noticed a white woman, her hair pulled up in a long brown ponytail, chatting to Ben at the counter. Once I'd dropped off the dirty dishes, Ben waved me over.

"George, this is Josie. She's the person I mentioned the other day who's interested in working here."

Josie smiled and held out a hand. "Nice to meet you. Sorry it's taken me so long to come back. I got struck down with the flu. But I'm fully recovered now," she hastily added.

I made a note to warn Blake about the flu that seemed to be going around—first our delivery driver, then Ben, and now Josie.

"Great to meet you too," I said as I shook her hand and grinned.

Things were looking up. Ben was back, I had another potential employee, the mountain of boxes of *The Realm of*

Furies was gone, and I had a beautiful woman sleeping upstairs in my bed. *Your spare bed, George. Don't get too carried away.*

EXHAUSTION CRASHED over me as I locked the front door to the café and made my way back upstairs to my apartment. A disrupted night's sleep combined with a busy day on my feet had finally caught up with me. It'd been so hectic I'd had no time to process the events of the last twenty-four hours.

The spare bedroom door was open, so I cautiously peered in, unsure what the etiquette was in a situation like this. I hadn't seen Hannah leave, and Max hadn't greeted me at my front door, so I assumed they were both in there.

Warmth enveloped my body at the sight of Hannah. She was fast asleep under the covers, her dark hair strewn across the white pillow and Max snoring next to her. Smiling, I carefully closed the door and tiptoed back down the hallway to the kitchen, where I started prepping dinner.

I'd just begun sautéing the onion and garlic when floorboards creaked, and I turned to find Hannah hovering awkwardly at the kitchen entrance.

She ran her hand through her mussed hair and then tried to smooth her baggy sweater. "Sorry I passed out like that. I should give you some space and get out of here. But thanks so much for letting me crash." There was something very intimate about seeing Hannah slightly disheveled from sleep.

"Would you like to stay for dinner? I'm making tomato, basil, and burrata pasta." I smiled at her.

"Oh thanks. But I'd better not." Hannah's voice lacked conviction. She walked slowly up to the kitchen counter.

My smile widened. "Seriously, it's no problem. I made extra in case you wanted some."

"It does smell amazing," Hannah said, eyeing the pan with interest.

Banging the spoon on the pan to shake off some pasta, I turned to her. "Great. You're staying, then. Would you like a glass of pinot to go with it?"

She grinned. "Yes, please."

Thirty minutes later, Hannah let out a satisfied sigh and slumped back in the dining room chair, her plate empty. Pink had returned to her cheeks. "That was amazing. Thanks again."

"You're welcome," I replied, really meaning it. I loved feeding people, and Hannah was no exception. I'd gotten a kick out of watching her devour the pasta as I filled her in on Josie's reappearance, her books being picked up and a few of the more entertaining customer stories from today. As tired as I was, Hannah's presence re-energized me.

Before I could stop her, Hannah had stacked my empty plate and cutlery on hers and taken them to the kitchen.

"Don't worry about the dishes. I'll do them later," I said as I walked in and found Hannah already scrubbing the pan.

"It's the least I can do. And then I'll head home so you can have some time to yourself."

Hannah seemed convinced that she was a burden when quite the opposite was true. Despite my exhaustion, I'd really been enjoying her company. *H. M. Stuart's company.* God, it felt so weird even thinking that.

I grabbed a tea towel and started drying the dishes. Max, who'd wolfed down his dinner and been very disappointed to discover that our meal was vegetarian, gently pawed at my leg. I looked down to see his big, brown eyes staring up at me. Guilt washed over my body. I usually took him for a walk twice a day, but I'd missed this morning due to last night's exploits. I definitely had to take him out tonight.

"I need to take Max for a walk. We could drop you off at your place on our way?" From the employment paperwork Hannah filled out, I knew she lived on Cherry Lane. I'd feel better knowing she'd gotten home safely.

"That would be great, if it's not too much trouble," Hannah replied.

We made quick work of the dishes and then headed out with Max.

A warm breeze and the evening sun hit us as we stepped outside.

"This weather is incredible," Hannah said. "I always forget how much these longer, warmer days improve my mood."

She looked so happy, her eyes bright as she took in our surroundings. My heart bounced. Even though I'd spent most of my waking hours with Hannah over the past four days, I didn't want her to go home yet. An idea struck me. I grinned. "You know what also improves my mood?"

"What?"

"Ice cream."

Hannah laughed.

"It's true! Max and I might make a stop at Van Hoorn's Creamery. It has the best ice cream in Putnam County, possibly New York State. And the world, for that matter. Would you like to join us, or should we drop you off on the way?" I raised an eyebrow. "It's really delicious."

Hannah smiled. "How could I say no after that ringing endorsement?"

Ten minutes later, Max was tied up outside the creamery next to a water bowl while Hannah agonized over her flavor selection under the attentive gaze of the owners, Mark, and his wife, Cheryl. While the creamery was housed in a three-story Victorian building near the pier and had old-school signage and decor, the flavors were anything but old-school. I'd already selected a strawberry, balsamic, and black pepper ice cream in a cup and, having sampled a number of flavors, Hannah was debating between the red cherry and goat cheese or dark chocolate and paprika.

"Argh, I can't decide!" Hannah frowned, looking adorably serious as she weighed her options, and then her face broke into a half smile. "Screw it! I'll get both—in a cone, please."

Mark grinned. "Done. Did you two enjoy the film screening? I saw you there."

"It was a great night," I said as casually as I could muster.

I took a bite of my ice cream in hopes that it might counteract the warmth that crept up my cheeks at the memory of sitting through multiple sex scenes and gallons of sexual innuendo with Hannah. I caught Mark's gaze by accident and could have sworn there was a knowing twinkle in his eye. Perhaps it had been just as awkward for him, sitting next to his daughter, as it had been for me.

Ice creams in hand, we walked past the bandstand to the pier and leaned against the railing overlooking the Hudson. It was still light, and across the blue expanse of river, the green, tree-covered mountains were visible. The water lapped at the posts of the pier.

Hannah moaned, the sound sending my insides fizzing

and my head jerking in her direction. "This ice cream is incredible!"

"Yeah, Mark and Cheryl are really passionate about experimenting with new flavors and techniques. I'm glad it's living up to the hype." I chuckled. "Remember how you thought Mark was a finance bro who was married to his daughter?" I spooned a scoop of ice cream into my mouth, savoring the unusual flavor combination which sounded questionable but somehow worked perfectly.

Hannah laughed, shaking her head. "I couldn't have been more wrong. He is an ice-cream-making genius."

She took another lick of her ice cream, her pink tongue sliding over the chocolate. *Oh god.* A shiver of desire shot down my spine.

"If you don't mind me asking, why did you decide to move to Sapphire Springs?"

Hannah drew her gaze away from the river and looked at me. "I fell in love with this place when I was at NYU. I came out for day trips, occasionally a weekend away. It always felt like such a...tranquil escape from city life. All the gorgeous nineteenth-century buildings, being nestled in nature right next to this"—Hannah gestured to the river—"and the mountains. And everyone who lived here always seemed so happy and friendly." My heart warmed hearing that Hannah seemed to love Sapphire Springs as much as I did.

I chuckled. "You clearly didn't catch Romina on a bad cooking day or Rory Goldsworthy, ever."

Hannah grinned. "No, I got lucky. I know there are some exceptions, but don't you think people seem happier here generally than in the city? In New York, everyone seems to be in a rush—to get somewhere or to achieve something. Whereas people here seem to have more time to be in the moment and actually enjoy life."

Hannah took a long, slow lick of her ice cream, her tongue swirling to catch some drips that were making their way down the cone. *I wonder what it would be like to kiss her, for that tongue to be exploring my mouth...* I blinked. *Pull it together, George.* I tore my eyes away and focused my attention on the view of river and answering Hannah's question.

I nodded. "Even with work being so hectic lately, at least I haven't had to deal with long commutes and the other stresses of city living on top of that. And being able to take Max out in the evenings like this, being able to breath in fresh air and enjoy this incredible view without being surrounded by other people, is the perfect way to unwind." Hannah had stopped licking her ice cream for now, so it was safe for me to turn my gaze back to her. "So you'd been planning this move for a while?"

"Well, I always thought I'd end up here—or somewhere like here—eventually, but my plans were accelerated recently." Hannah's face clouded, suggesting that the reason for the acceleration wasn't a happy one. Perhaps it was the divorce she'd mentioned?

"Oh, I'm sorry," I said gently.

"It's fine." Hannah raised the cone to her mouth, parted her lips and then closed them around the ice cream. This time, I couldn't look away. "What about you? Why did you decided to move here?"

Mesmerized, I watched Hannah savor the mouthful of ice cream and then swallow it. She stared at me with a raised eyebrow, and I realized I hadn't answered her question.

"Sorry. I think I mentioned I grew up in Florida, near Tampa, but my grandma lived in Sapphire Springs, and I used to visit her at least once a year." Gran, my dad's mom, was no longer with us, but the love we'd shared for this town remained. "Like you, I fell in love with it. Compared to where I grew up, it's so quaint. I come from suburban sprawl, rows of characterless 1960's brick houses on grassy lawns in a planned community. Whereas this place just feels steeped in history."

Hannah nodded. "I know what you mean. Even while New York and Chicago—which is where I grew up—have amazing old buildings, there are also skyscrapers and so many other signs of modern life—like Times Square and all its billboards." Hannah shuddered and I grinned. I avoided Times Square like the plague every time I was in the city. "Whereas Sapphire Springs has really retained its character."

"While still having high-speed internet, running water and electricity, not to mention amazing ice cream," I said, and ate another large spoonful.

Hannah laughed. "It really is the best of both worlds."

The light was beginning to fade, but the air was still warm. "I also love the seasons here. In Florida, it's either warm, hot, or hot and humid, but in this part of the world every season is so unique. Summer's heat, fall's foliage, winter's coziness, and spring's bloom. I swear, now that I've moved here, my memories seem stronger, and I think it might be because they're linked to the changing seasons. It's almost as if the seasons mark the passing of time." I sensed Hannah's eyes on me, and heat crept up my face. I'd gotten carried away rhapsodizing about the seasons, to an extremely talented author of all people. "Sorry, that probably doesn't make any sense."

Hannah smiled. "No. I totally get it. I vividly remember

the hike I did in September two years ago in the Catskills, and I think it was because it was the first time it really felt like fall that year. The air was so cool and crisp, and the leaves were starting to change. If it hadn't been for that, the hike probably would have blended in with all the other hikes I've done over the years." Hannah paused. "By the way, have you ever considered being a writer? That was very poetic."

I chuckled, relieved that Hannah understood what I meant. "God no, I'm quite happy promoting writers and reading their books, but I can't imagine writing one." A thought struck me. "Speaking of writing, how quiet are you planning to keep your pen name in Sapphire Springs? Maintaining your privacy is clearly really important to you, but I'm just wondering if it's okay to mention it to Blake. Of course, I won't say anything if you don't want me to."

It still hadn't really sunk in that Hannah was H. M. Stuart. Each time I remembered, it took me by surprise, and I wasn't sure how I felt about it. My feelings toward Hannah were already confusing enough without her being my favorite author as well. She was so talented and success-ful. It blew my mind that she was working in my café and spending time with me outside work. Hopefully, I'd sleep well tonight, and then tomorrow, Hannah's revelation about her alter ego would all feel perfectly fine. If not, talking to Blake about it might help.

Hannah pressed her lips together in thought. I was about to tell her not to worry about it when she spoke. "If you ask Blake not to tell anyone, except Jenny, that's fine. They don't strike me as the sort of people who'll blow my cover." Hannah winced. "But if you could try to make me sound a little less weird for the whole accidentally accepting a job and breaking and entering thing, that would be great."

"Hmmm. I don't know about that." I grinned, elbowing Hannah gently in her side. "A little less weird. Is that even possible?"

"Hey!" Hannah elbowed me back, laughing, mock outrage in her voice. Our eyes locked, sending my heart bouncing.

Goddamn, she's beautiful. The sun was finally starting to set, sending a kaleidoscope of gold, pink, red, and purple hues stretching across the sky and lighting Hannah's face with a warm glow. *How do I keep getting myself into these romantic situations with her?* A little voice inside me whispered that now that I'd established she was single, interested in woman and an author rather than my employee, the barriers between us were dropping down. What would happen if I did just reach out, take her hand in mine?

I shook off the idea. *Hannah is H. M. Stuart. Is she really going to be interested in me?*

"The sun is starting to set," I said, my voice sounding more abrupt than I intended. "We should get you home before it gets dark."

Hannah nodded in agreement, demolished the last of her ice cream, and then we turned in unison, starting the trek back up Main Street toward Cherry Lane.

Chatting as we walked, we reached Cherry Lane in no time.

"Here we are," said Hannah, stopping outside a small front yard full of rose bushes and lavender a few minutes later.

Hannah turned to me. Her thick brown hair framed her face, accentuating her dark eyelashes and pink lips, which were softly lit by the fading sun. Out of nowhere, butterflies swarmed in my stomach. If we were on a date, this would be the moment when we kissed, or perhaps Hannah would invite me inside. But we weren't on a date. Although...the evening had kind of felt like it. Dinner, a stroll, ice cream by the river, watching the sunset. But unlike the movie night, the romantic elements of tonight hadn't felt awkward.

Except, perhaps, until now. I'd been staring at Hannah for more than a beat too long, and she'd been holding my gaze. Were her eyes darker than usual, or was it just the fading light? The air electrified. Everything around me disappeared. Everything except Hannah. A delicious shiver shot down my back, and my heart rate picked up pace. Every nerve in my body screamed for contact with Hannah. In a daze, I stepped forward.

And then our lips were pressing against each other. Hannah's mouth was so soft, but the kiss was not. It was hungry, hot and messy. Passionate and raw. I tightened my grip on her waist and tugged at her bottom lip with my teeth. Hannah let out a moan that sent arousal spiking through me.

Good lord, I'd forgotten how fucking amazing kissing could be.

Eventually we disentangled ourselves, and reality hit.

Shit.

I hadn't thought this through at all. Where did we go from here?

I stared at Hannah blankly. *Words, George. Say something.*

I swallowed. "I just wanted to say thanks for all your help the last few days. I seriously couldn't have managed without you." I winced at my clumsy words. *Well, at least that was something.*

An indiscernible expression flitted across Hannah's

face. *Damn.* My awkward comment had clearly not gone unnoticed.

"Um, no problem," Hannah said as she brushed the hair off her pinker-than-usual cheeks with her hand. "Now that Ben's back and you've got Josie on board, let me know what you're thinking in terms of shifts. I'm super flexible. I could even just come in for a few hours over the lunch rush, given that's when it's busiest."

I blinked, as if that would somehow help me digest Hannah's statement. "So you... You still want to work? I thought since you'd signed the books and cleared up our, um, misunderstanding about your identity, you'd want to be done?"

Hannah shifted her weight on her feet. "To be honest, I've been surprised how much I've been enjoying it. So if you need me, I'm available."

My chest tightened. Hannah was still my employee after all. *Shit. I just kissed my employee.*

I took a deep breath. There was nothing I could do about that now. It's not like I could fire her—*sorry, I got carried away and kissed you and because I have a "no dating employees" rule, your position is terminated*—or erase the kiss from our minds. And even with Josie on board, another employee would be an enormous help.

My head started thumping. I should go home and get some sleep before I did anything else stupid.

"That would be amazing," I said, hoping my voice didn't betray my confusion. "Well, if you don't mind coming in from ten to two-thirty tomorrow, that would be great. Does that sound okay to you?"

"Perfect!" Hannah replied, slightly too enthusiastically.

Before things could get even more awkward, I decided

to excuse myself. "Well, we'd better be getting home before it's too dark. See you tomorrow!"

As I walked back, I realized that I'd forgotten to bake the cake of the day. *Shit.* It was too late now. Betty would not be happy.

I took a deep breath of fresh evening air. Hopefully, tomorrow my feelings about Hannah Taylor, aka H. M. Stuart, and the kiss we'd just shared would be a lot clearer. I couldn't afford to be off my game and lose any more customers.

CHAPTER SEVENTEEN

HANNAH

"HANNAH!"

I turned, holding the dirty plates I'd just picked up from a table, to find Olivia beaming at me.

"We're going kayaking on the river this afternoon. Wanna come?"

I couldn't help darting my eyes over to George, who was serving a customer behind the counter. *Is she coming too?* I'd been sneaking glances at George all morning, replaying last night's kiss in my head. It had been unexpected and confusing but also amazing. I hadn't felt that type of heated, intense desire for anyone for a very long time. A thrill ran through me at the memory.

And then, after the kiss, everything had felt incredibly awkward.

I'd walked to work with nervous anticipation pounding through me. To my disappointment, George, although friendly as usual, seemed to be behaving like nothing had happened, just like she had after the kiss last night. Although, to be fair, so was I.

My natural impulse was to avoid awkward conversations, and the idea of sitting down with George to discuss our feelings sent my stomach flipping. But at the same time, I wanted to know what, if anything, was going on between us. However, it didn't look like I was going to find out this morning. With George focused on training Josie, and me and Ben busy with the weekend crowds, there'd been no opportunity for us to have one-on-one time together. And in any event, our workplace didn't seem like the most appropriate venue to talk about the kiss.

Not that I knew what to say about it anyway. Things were finally going well. I'd gotten those damn books signed. I was writing again, and I was excited about my new manuscript. For the first time, meeting the July deadline didn't feel completely out of reach. And if I did, Barb would be safe in her nursing home for at least another twelve months, maybe even longer if this book did well. I also loved working at Novel Gossip and my growing friendship with George and her friends reminded me that I wasn't as introverted as I often thought. I didn't want things to get complicated with George and risk blowing it all up. Did I even have time to date with everything else going on in my life? And I couldn't shake the niggling thought that if my friendship with George blew up, so would my ability to write. After all, it'd been her words that had led to my breakthrough. Last, but not least, in the string of reasons why pursuing a relationship with George seemed like a bad idea, was that I'd just come out of a long-term relationship three months ago. Jumping into something new so soon didn't seem like the smartest move.

But at the same time... George handed a customer a cookie in a paper bag, a warm smile on her face, and my stomach fluttered. Yep, I hadn't felt this type of attraction to anyone in a long time. Possibly ever.

Olivia followed my gaze and grinned, thankfully misinterpreting it. "If you want me to talk to the boss, I can. You've worked every day since you started. There has to be some kind of labor law that I can threaten George with, especially given that she's coming too. Jenny and Blake will be there as well."

I laughed. "I finish my shift at two-thirty today, same as George. Josie should be all trained up by then, so she's closing with Ben. And I'm not working tomorrow at all, so I don't think your labor lawsuit will have legs. But thanks for the offer."

Olivia clapped her hands. "Awesome! So is that a yes?"

I paused for a moment. I'd planned to spend the afternoon working on my book, and I was *not* an accomplished kayaker. In fact, I'd only done it once in my life, with Tania, and it had been an absolute disaster. We'd been in a tandem kayak, and she'd kept getting annoyed because I wasn't keeping in time with her strokes. She'd ended up insisting, with a huff, that I stop paddling altogether so she could kayak unimpeded by my ineptitude. I winced. When I looked back, there were a lot of red flags in our relationship.

But despite my writing plans and bad past experience, it was perfect weather for kayaking. It seemed a shame to spend a gorgeous warm afternoon holed up inside. I'd also enjoyed hanging out with Olivia, Jenny, and Blake at the pub after the movie night. And while I currently had no idea what was going on between George and me, I always enjoyed spending time with her. In a group setting, hopefully things wouldn't be too awkward.

"That sounds great!" I said.

I'd work on my book later. Now that Ben was back and Josie was trained, I'd have more time to write anyway. And presumably, I'd be in my own kayak, not at risk of impeding anyone else's perfect stroke.

━━━━━━

GEORGE

HANNAH PICKED up Betty's empty plate and coffee cup, saying something that made Betty laugh. I'd felt terrible there'd been no cake of the day this morning, especially after Betty rushing to my defense yesterday, but thankfully, Betty had been appeased by one of Romina's delicious muffins.

Hannah's outfit of navy shorts, white sneakers, and a white silk blouse flattered her figure and accentuated her dark eyes and hair and pink lips. My gaze lingered on her lips for a moment before I came to my senses. *Stop ogling your employee, George!*

Someone cleared their throat behind me.

"Do you want to go on your lunch break soon, George?" Ben asked. "The three of us will manage more than fine. So, actually have a proper break this time—don't just chow down a BLT in the kitchen and run back out like you have the past few weeks." Ben glared at me.

I smiled. Having Ben, Hannah, and Josie all working front of house with me was an enormous relief. Finally, it felt like my staffing issues were under control. *Another good reason not to screw things up with Hannah.*

"That would be great, thanks. I'll see if Blake is free to meet at Builders' Arms. If she is, I'll probably head off in fifteen minutes."

I shot a text off to Blake. A good night's sleep had not cleared up my confused feelings over yesterday's events, and I was desperate to talk to her about it—just not at Novel Gossip, in full sight of Hannah. My phone pinged. Blake could make it. I exhaled.

Twenty minutes later, Blake leaned back against the wall of the Builders' Arms beer garden. A warm breeze sent dappled light, filtered by the large oak tree overhead, moving in patterns across the bricks.

"No Novel Gossip this time? I wanted to see what the cake of the day was," Blake said, looking slightly disappointed.

I grimaced. "There was no cake of the day. It was my turn to make it last night, and I forgot." Romina and I shared cake-baking duties.

"That's not like you." Blake frowned, leaning forward. "Is everything okay?"

"Well, I was going to wait until our food arrived to launch into the details, but since you asked..." I gave Blake a run-down of yesterday's events, beginning with discovering Hannah signing books just before 3 a.m. and ending with last night's kiss.

Blake's eyes got wider and wider.

"So, yeah, that's why I didn't bake the cake last night. I was exhausted and also more than a bit distracted," I finished.

"How are you feeling about everything today?" Blake took a sip of her water.

I frowned. "I'd been hoping everything would be clear when I woke up this morning, but that didn't happen. I still feel weird Hannah didn't tell me who she is and that she went to such great lengths to keep it a secret from me. But at the same time, it seems like she was avoiding the topic out of anxiety rather than for any sinister purpose." After hearing about Hannah's difficult childhood, I had a good deal of sympathy for her.

Blake nodded. "And the kiss?"

"It was incredible in the moment. But afterward it was super awkward. And to make matters worse, at the time, I thought she wasn't an employee anymore, but it turns out she still is. So all my worries about there being a power imbalance still stands." I sighed. "The whole thing is a blur—I'm not even sure who instigated it. I think it was mutual, but what if I instigated it and she just went along with it out of awkwardness or because she felt she had to?" I winced at the thought.

Blake raised an eyebrow. "George, have you ever been kissed by someone you didn't want to kiss?"

I nodded.

"And what did you do?"

"Well, with the boy in seventh grade, I pushed him away. When it happened in a gay bar in Tampa, I pulled back from the woman."

"Uh-huh. So, last night, did Hannah push you away?" Blake leaned on the wooden table and stared at me.

"No."

"Did she lean into the kiss or move her lips, her tongue, her hands?"

Heat rushed to my cheeks as I remembered Hannah moaning, her hands pressed on my back, her tongue in my mouth.

Blake grinned. My body language must have given me away. "Well, I'll take that as a yes," she said.

Dan, the owner of Builders' Arms, arrived with our food, placing a burger and fries in front of me and a Caesar salad in front of Blake.

As soon as he left, Blake continued her cross-examination. "And did Hannah do anything to suggest she wasn't into it?"

I paused for a minute, thinking back. "No."

"Uh-huh. And who ended the kiss?"

"I think it ended kind of mutually. Like the kiss just came to its natural conclusion."

Blake smirked. "So, in light of all that evidence, what do you think the chances are she wasn't into the kiss?"

I shook my head, holding back a chuckle as relief washed over me. "Okay, okay, Detective Mitchell. I see your point."

Blake's smirk widened into a grin. "Hey, I'm a doctor. I like facts. But I think you're overthinking things, perhaps because of your parents' experience and what happened with Alexis. It sounds like you guys had a lovely, mutual smooch."

I snorted. "Even if you're right, Hannah is still an employee, so she's off-limits."

Blake stabbed a piece of chicken with her fork and started eating it, a thoughtful expression on her face.

I stared at her, waiting for her to swallow so she could impart whatever words of wisdom she was developing as she chewed.

"The reason you're worried about the employee thing is mainly the power imbalance, right?"

I nodded.

"But you said she's a bestselling author. Why do you think she wants to work at Novel Gossip? Maybe it's not for money. Perhaps it's more like a hobby for her—like Dad being my receptionist so he can chat with people—or maybe even research for her book? And if that's the case, maybe the power imbalance stuff isn't relevant. If things didn't work out between you, and she didn't want to work there anymore, perhaps it wouldn't be a big deal for her at all. If anything, you might need her more than she needs you, given how run off your feet you've been."

I frowned. "We don't know what her financial situation is. She could have debts to pay off or sick family to support and need the extra cash."

"Yeah, fair point." Blake furrowed her brow. "Let's say the whole power imbalance thing wasn't an issue. Would you be interested in exploring things further with her?"

"I think so. She's gorgeous, funny and I love spending time with her." I paused.

"But?" Blake asked.

"I guess my only other concerns are whether I really have enough time for a relationship at the moment and the fact Hannah is H. M. Stuart. Things have been so hectic at work lately. I've lost some customers to Dippin' Donuts because of how understaffed we've been, and I've had no time to focus on planning events."

"Well, now that you have Josie and Hannah on board, won't that solve the first problem?"

"Yeah, maybe." Blake was probably right, but I still had Betty's friend's comment ringing in my ears. "I still haven't even wrapped my head around the fact that Hannah is H. M. Stuart. It...well, the whole idea of dating my favorite author feels a bit unreal."

"Honestly, it sounds like you're overthinking this whole thing. You dated one of your favorite politicians. Why not your favorite author too?" Blake raised her eyebrow. "Seriously, what is it with you and famous people?" She chuckled.

I shifted uncomfortably in my seat. I hadn't made that connection before. But Hannah was different to Alexis. Alexis had actively sought media attention—she needed it to be elected. Hannah was the complete opposite. The Hannah Taylor I had kissed wasn't famous. Only her alter ego, H. M. Stuart, was. And given Hannah kept her pen name secret, it wasn't like I'd have to deal with the sort of unwelcome media attention I'd experienced dating Alexis.

"Yeah, maybe. Anyway, despite your forensic analysis of our kiss, I'm still not at all convinced that Hannah is interested in actually dating me."

"In that case, why don't you just talk her about last night and your worries about the power imbalance, and see what she says. Maybe she'll be able to put your mind at rest."

I sighed. "I'm sure that's the sensible course of action. My brain is just fried at the moment. I'm taking Monday off —my first day off in months—so I think I'll see how Josie goes tomorrow now I've trained her and how they cope without me on Monday. If that all goes well, then I'll be less worried about having time for a relationship, and it will also give me some time to work through the rest of my feelings." I popped a fry in my mouth, chewed, and swallowed it.

If Blake was right about Hannah's motivations for working at the café, then Hannah being H. M. Stuart could make me feel more comfortable about pursuing a relationship with her. A buzz of excitement rose in my chest.

"Well, give it some thought."

"Yeah, I will. In the meantime, I'll just keep things friendly but professional with Hannah, which shouldn't be too difficult since she's not working tomorrow. Olivia invited her kayaking this afternoon, but at least that'll be a group activity, so no risk of accidental kisses."

Blake grinned. "You once offered to chaperone me and Jenny. We can return the favor if you'd like."

I chuckled. "I should be fine. Kayaking isn't exactly the most romantic activity, especially not with my technique."

"Oh, really? I look forward to seeing it," Blake said with a laugh.

I took a bite of my burger, already feeling a lot better. Talking to Blake always helped. We hadn't solved anything, but she'd helped me work through my concerns. All I had to do now was avoid any more intimate situations with Hannah until I had time to assess the new staffing arrangements and my feelings for her. Monday was only two days away. How hard could that be?

CHAPTER EIGHTEEN

HANNAH

GEORGE WALKED out of the kitchen wearing purple flip flops, pink flamingo board shorts that ended three quarters of the way down her thighs, and a light-gray tee. Her arms and legs were tanned and strong.

I forgot the bad news I had to tell her and stared, taking this vision in. She looked so relaxed and tropical. While I'd had a hard time imagining her growing up in Florida, I could see it now. It made me feel even worse for what I was about to say.

George stopped when she saw me, an expression I couldn't pinpoint flickering across her face. "Hey! You're still here? Sorry, I didn't realize you were waiting for me."

Heat crept up my cheeks. I'd assumed we'd walk down to the kayak rental together, an assumption that sent my heart pounding each time I thought about it. That walk would be the obvious opportunity for us to talk about what happened last night.

The conflict-avoidant side of me did not want that talk to occur. Neither did the side of me that liked to have my thoughts properly gathered before embarking on a conversation like this.

But at the same time, I wanted to know what George was thinking. If she didn't want anything more to happen, then that would nip the whole thing in the bud. I could stop agonizing over what I wanted, because the decision would be made for me. And based on George's behavior today, that currently seemed like the most likely outcome. She'd been perfectly pleasant to me, but our interactions had been minimal, and I couldn't shake the feeling she was keeping her distance.

And then there was that expression that had just flickered across her face—had it been dismay? My stomach sank. She was displaying all the signs that she regretted our kiss.

I should have felt relieved. After all, George not being interested seemed like the simplest resolution—I could go back to focusing on writing, working at Novel Gossip, and enjoying spending time with George and her friends without worrying about jeopardizing it all by pursuing a relationship with George. But disappointment crept up my body at the thought.

"Oh. Sorry. I, um...I assumed we'd walk down together, but I can just head off now if you'd prefer," I said, wincing at how awkward I sounded.

"No, no. Sorry, I thought you were going to go change first, but if you're not doing that, then of course it makes sense for us to walk together." George's voice was friendly, and she was smiling, but I sensed some underlying hesitation. My chest tightened. *It's for the best, Hannah. You need to buckle down and finish that book, for both your and Barb's sakes, not strike up a romance with your boss.*

"I've got a tank top under my blouse, so I figured I'd be okay if I wore that and my shorts," I explained. I'd also swapped my glasses out for contacts—I didn't want them ending up on the bottom of the Hudson.

An uncomfortable silence fell for a moment. I shifted my weight on my feet. God, this conversation felt markedly more awkward than the easy-going discussions I was used to with George.

"Well, should we head off, then?" George asked, her voice bright.

Shit. I'd forgotten to break the bad news to her. "Um… actually, there seems to be something wrong with Hugo. I was just making a mocha when the espresso stopped running. I took the portafilter out, and there's no water coming out of this part." I pointed to where the water usually ran.

"Damn," George groaned, looking at the clock on the wall. We were meeting everyone down at the kayak rental at 3 p.m. "I'll have a quick look and see if I can fix him. If you'd prefer to just head off now, that's fine."

I paused. Was George trying to encourage me to leave now to avoid walking together? The idea of walking down alone, when George would likely only be a few minutes behind me, didn't sit right with me. I took in a deep breath and exhaled. Since the kiss last night, everything had felt off between us. While I'd been worried that pursuing something with George might throw off the new life I'd been building for myself in Sapphire Springs, this awkwardness between us was threatening to do the same thing. Working at Novel Gossip and spending time with George and her friends would be nowhere near as enjoyable if the warm, comfortable interactions I was used to having with her were replaced with these painful, confusing encounters. My throat ached at the thought. As difficult as the conversation would be, we needed to have it.

I swallowed. "That's okay, I'm happy to wait. Let me know if I can help with anything."

George was faced away from me, gently inspecting Hugo, so I couldn't see her reaction to my response.

"It might be an issue with the water pump. I'll just text everyone to let them know we're running late." George shot off a text and then opened one of the drawers under the counter, returning with a screwdriver. She began taking the coffee cups off the top of Hugo, and I jumped in to help, relieved I could contribute.

Once Hugo was cleared of cups, George opened him up and inspected his workings. While I didn't have a clue what George was doing, I was mesmerized by the intense concentration on her face as she carefully adjusted things—her lips slightly pursed, her brow furrowed, the way her arms moved, revealing lean muscles at various angles. I told myself I was standing so close to her, watching her so attentively, just in case she needed me, but the truth was I couldn't look away. *Seriously, why do I find everything this woman does sexy?*

My eyes kept finding their way to her mouth, reliving last night's kiss. Without thinking my tongue darted out, moistening my lips. I firmly pushed them together. *Good lord, Hannah. Stop salivating over your boss in public.* I looked around Novel Gossip to check no one was looking at me. Thankfully, while several people were hovering near the counter, waiting for their takeout coffee orders, they were chatting with each other or checking their phones, not watching my visceral reactions to George's hotness.

After a few minutes, George stepped back. "Okay, hopefully that'll fix it." She screwed Hugo back together, flicked the power switch on, and tried to get the water running again. It flowed out, just like normal.

"Great work!" I said, grinning with relief. "It looks like the citizens of Sapphire Springs won't need to go uncaffeinated after all."

George returned my smile and then turned to Ben, who'd been taking orders at the counter. "Are you sure you two will manage without us?"

"Of course!" Ben said as he shooed us out of the café.

As we walked down to the river, we chatted about comfortable topics, like how obnoxious Rory Goldsworthy had been this morning when he'd tried to send his brunch back for being cold because he'd been too busy watching YouTube videos on his phone to eat it when I'd delivered it steaming hot.

George didn't mention last night's kiss, and neither did I. I tried psyching myself up to raise the topic, but my confidence wavered. What would I say? *Hey, you clearly think last night's kiss was a mistake, and that's totally fine. Can we just pretend it never happened?* I swallowed. It would be much easier if George initiated the conversation. Maybe we didn't need to talk at all. I was now so sure George wasn't interested that I should just proceed on that basis. Why did I need verbal confirmation?

We arrived at the kayak rental, a rundown log shack next to the river, fifteen minutes late. Blake, Jenny, and Olivia were paddling near the shore and cheered when they saw us. Blake and Jenny were sharing a tandem kayak. Olivia was in a single.

"A high school group just came through earlier, so we've only got tandem kayaks left. Is that okay?" asked a young woman behind the counter, wearing a red *Sapphire Springs Expeditions* t-shirt.

George paused for a second, looking around almost as if she was hoping she'd spot two singles the woman had missed. My heart dropped. *Yep, there is no need for verbal confirmation.*

"That's okay by me," George said, shooting me a questioning look.

Memories of Tania complaining about my kayaking skills came rushing back, and I swallowed.

"Yep, that's fine," I replied, hoping that my kayaking game had improved in the past four years. I had gone on a rowing machine a few times since then, so that might've helped. George, with her strong legs and arms, was probably an accomplished kayaker. Growing up in Florida she likely spent half her time on the water.

"Great! I'll just have you sign the waiver and then grab life jackets and the kayak. You can either leave your phones on shore or put them into a waterproof bag."

We opted to leave them on shore, stowing them along with my satchel and George's wallet in a safe behind the counter of the rental shack, and then signed our lives away on what looked to be a very over-the-top waiver.

You agree to release, waive, and hold us harmless against any personal injury, death, or property loss arising out of or in connection with kayaking, including, without limitation, drowning, collision with other watercraft or stationary objects, overexertion, hypothermia, ingestion of polluted water, foot entrapment, dehydration, riverine fauna, and other wildlife.

"I didn't realize kayaking was so dangerous," I murmured to George as I leaned against the wooden counter, only half joking. *What the hell type of life-endangering riverine fauna lives in the Hudson River?*

A few minutes later, after giving us a brief rundown of the kayak's features, including its reclining seats, the young woman pushed our kayak—me in the front and

George in the back, both wearing blue life jackets—into the water.

The kayak looked more advanced than the colorful, fat plastic one I'd gone in last time with Tania. Hopefully that didn't mean it would be even more challenging to use, or I'd be screwed.

"Okay," I said, gripping the paddle tentatively. *How do I do this again?* I should have asked for a refresher.

I turned to George, grimacing. "Um, I probably should have said this before you agreed to share a kayak with me, but I'm not very good. I've only done it once before, and it was a long time ago."

She chuckled. "I probably also should have told you, before you agreed to share a kayak with me, that I'm a terrible kayaker."

"Really?" I laughed, relieved.

"Yep! Appalling. The last time I tried to do it, probably about five years ago, I kept going round in circles and basically didn't leave the shore. I blamed the kayak, but I'm pretty sure it was all me."

"Well, that's good. We can be terrible together," I said, grinning, already feeling more relaxed.

Olivia kayaked over to us, deploying strong, powerful strokes that sliced through the water. She made it look easy. Behind her, Blake and Jenny were bobbing in their kayak, chatting.

"So we were thinking we'd kayak up the river, past Breakback Ridge, and over to Battersby Island, which has that ruined castle on it. Sound good?" Olivia asked.

It sounded rather ambitious to me, but I didn't want to be a killjoy, so I nodded.

"Okay, folks, let's head off." Olivia powered ahead.

I tried to emulate her technique, but I didn't get the

angle of the paddle slicing into the water right and sent a big spray of water over George instead.

"Shit! Sorry about that!" I tensed, remembering Tania's criticisms. Thankfully, I'd been sitting in the back of the kayak when I'd paddled with her, but if I'd splashed water on her, she would've been furious.

But when I turned around, George was smiling, brushing drips of water off her face with her hand. *Thank god.* "That's fine. It's eighty degrees, so that was actually quite refreshing. And if you were sitting behind me, you'd be getting much worse."

I relaxed and turned back to see where everyone else was.

Olivia was now well ahead of us. Blake and Jenny were not far behind her.

Refocusing my attention on paddling, I carefully completed a few more strokes. My technique seemed to be improving, but I was doing it so tentatively I'd hardly moved us along. I glanced at George, who seemed to be experimenting unsuccessfully with different grips.

"Hey! How are you doing?"

I looked up to see Olivia floating in front of us and nearly jumped out of the kayak. *How the hell did she get back here so quickly?*

"Sorry we're so slow. We're just getting the hang of it," I said, feeling guilty that after running late, we were still holding the others up.

Olivia looked unperturbed. "Do you want me to give you a few tips? I used to kayak a lot in high school."

I said, "Yes please," at the same time George said, "That would be great." The fact that George was in the same boat as me—I grinned at my pun—made me feel slightly less self-conscious about my ineptitude.

Olivia showed us how to hold the paddles and then gave a slow-motion demonstration of how to slice the blades of the paddles through the water, providing blow-by-blow explanations that sailed right over my head.

The more we focused on trying to emulate her movements, the more uncoordinated we became. Our paddles collided, I splashed George again, and we started turning in circles.

After a few minutes of Olivia attempting different ways to teach us what looked to be a simple stroke, George spoke. "Thanks, Liv. I don't think we're going to be able to make it all the way to the island. Why don't you guys go on, and we'll practice our technique, and next time we'll be able to join you? If that's okay with you, Hannah?"

I breathed out a sigh of relief at George's suggestion. My arms were already aching from paddling, and we'd barely left the shore.

"Yes, I think that's a good idea. We don't want to hold you back," I said.

"Well, if you're sure? After this, I was thinking we could grab a drink in the beer garden at Builders' Arms if you're interested, so if you get tired of paddling we could meet you there."

"Sounds great." A vision of relaxing in a chair in the sunshine, sipping an Aperol spritz, appeared in my mind. That was very appealing right now. Perhaps we could head straight there...

Olivia raced off, leaving a trail of bubbles in her wake.

"Good lord, she's fast!" George said, followed by something I didn't catch.

"Sorry, what did you say?" I asked, turning to her so I could see her face clearly when she responded.

"I was saying why don't we just try to kayak over to

Little Pebble Point and back again, and then head to the pub? Unless you'd prefer to stay out here, of course."

George waved her hand toward a point covered in green trees. I squinted at it. It didn't look too far away—less than half a mile at a rough guess. *That should be doable...and then there will be Aperol spritz.*

"I like your plan," I said, feeling more motivated.

"If you start paddling, I'll try to sync with you."

"Sounds good, Capt'n," I said over my shoulder to George before turning back to focus on trying to recreate Olivia's technique. For the first few paddles, it felt all wrong, but without the pressure of Olivia's gaze on me, I was able to relax a little more, and suddenly something clicked. With my core engaged and my torso rotating like Olivia said, my paddle began rhythmically slicing through the water.

"Woo hoo! I think I'm getting the hang of this!"

George started paddling too, and we picked up speed. *This is more like it!* Now I understood the appeal, powering up the river, surrounded by sparkling water, blue skies, and gorgeous scenery. Maybe we could catch up to the others and go to the island after all. I felt strong and powerful and—

Whack! George's paddle smashed into mine. "Shit! I'm sorry!" George yelled.

"That's oka—"

"Oh fuck!" George exclaimed.

The kayak tipped violently to the left, sending my stomach lurching into my throat. I grabbed the side of the kayak to steady myself and then turned to see what was going on.

George leaned out of the kayak, frowning, trying to grab her paddle, which was in the water and floating quickly away from her outstretched fingers. I winced. *There's no way she'll reach it.*

George must have independently formed that conclusion, because she gave up attempting to grab her paddle, sitting back in her seat. "Goddamnit. Olivia recommended a relaxed grip, but mine was clearly a little too relaxed—I dropped it when our paddles collided. Sorry about that. That waiver didn't mention death by paddling partner!" George's cheeks were pink, whether from embarrassment or exertion I couldn't tell. Either way, she looked damn cute, all hot and flustered.

I smiled. "Don't worry about it. I'm totally fine. I'll paddle after it."

With newfound confidence, I headed toward the paddle floating in the water. *Slice, slice, slice.* It was only two feet away now. I tried to maneuver the kayak so George could reach out and grab it, but the only skill I'd mastered so far was the art of going straight ahead. Olivia's crash course on kayaking hadn't included tips on turning and stopping. In fact, every time I tried to pull the kayak closer to the paddle, it seemed to float farther away again.

After a few failed attempts, I decided to see if I could drag George's paddle back using mine.

Holding my paddle at one end, I carefully put it over George's paddle, effectively pinning it down, and started to draw it closer to me.

"Great work! You've nearly done it!" George called.

A puff of warmth expanded in my chest. *You can do this, Hannah.*

And then a gust of wind kicked up, and the kayak began to turn.

"Shit, shit, shit," I muttered under my breath as I struggled to keep my paddle over George's. I leaned out, twisting my body into an awkward position. The kayak lurched, sending my heart with it, and, in panic, I grabbed the side of the kayak again so I didn't fall in—with both hands.

"Oh no!" My gut clenched as my paddle slipped into the water. Still holding one side of the kayak, I tried to grab it, but it was already bobbing away, well out of arm's reach.

"I'm so sorry!" I looked around, hoping to spot someone who could come to our rescue, but Olivia, Blake, Jenny, and the kayak rental were all out of sight, and the only sign of life was a ferry in the distance, heading in the opposite direction. I peered down at the water. The sides of the kayak were too high for us to paddle back using our hands. My stomach sank. I'd been so close to collecting George's paddle, and now we were even worse off than before.

I peered back at George to see how she was taking it. "The expression *up shit creek without a paddle* is suddenly making a lot more sense to me," I said, grimacing.

George erupted into laughter, apparently unperturbed by the loss of both our paddles. "We'll just have to wait until someone comes past. At least we know Olivia, Blake, and Jenny will be back this way in the next hour or so." George grinned at me. "Time to lie back and relax!" She adjusted her seat down, reclined, and closed her eyes.

I chuckled, but anxiety bubbled in my stomach at the thought of being stuck out here for an hour or more. I self-soothed by gazing at George, taking advantage of her eyes being closed to admire her tanned, strong legs. The brown hairs covering them shone in the sun. My eyes traveled up her legs, past her flamingo shorts, life jacket and t-shirt to her face. She looked so peaceful, a faint smile on her lips, as she lay soaking in the sunshine. My gaze lingered on her lips. Despite all the reasons why dating George was a terrible idea, a sense of loss washed over me at the idea of not kissing those lips again.

Worried that George would open her eyes and find me gazing dreamily at her, I followed her direction and lay back, trying to relax my body and focus on my breathing.

Okay, this is quite nice. The sun was warm on my skin and sent a golden glow filtering through my eyelids. The kayak bobbed gently in the water. I let out a deep breath.

"Hey, Hannah." George paused. Her voice sounded different. Perhaps more tender than usual, or slightly tentative?

Shit, she's going to talk about the kiss.

My heart skipped a beat.

"Yes?" I said. I drew in a breath and held it, waiting for George's response.

"You mentioned your hearing loss made it hard to hear at the café. Is there anything I can do to help with that?"

I exhaled at the unexpected question.

As I considered how to respond, the sun's warmth seemed to penetrate deeper through my body. My hearing loss had happened gradually over the past few years, its cause unknown. There was a history of hearing loss in my family, so it might have had a genetic component. The only person I'd really spoken to about it was Tania, but she hadn't been very sympathetic. She'd certainly never asked if there was anything she could do to help and had grumbled every time I turned subtitles on the TV, complaining it was distracting. I think I'd known deep down that Tania's response wasn't reasonable, but it had undermined my self-confidence, making me feel guilty or nervous every time I had to ask her or anyone else to repeat something.

"Thanks for asking. I really just need to find my hearing aid." Or go and buy a new one, which I probably should do.

But the thought of forking out thousands of dollars was not appealing, especially not when I had so much financial uncertainty at the moment. Once I turned in my manuscript and *The Realm of Furies* was released and was, fingers crossed, selling well, I'd feel more comfortable about spending that kind of money. "But the main things you can do are facing me when you speak, being aware that if you're on my left side, I may have trouble hearing you, speaking clearly, and not having the background music up too loud, which you don't do anyway."

Novel Gossip's brick walls, expansive glass front windows, and wooden floors weren't great in terms of noise reduction, but they were gorgeous, and there was no way I was about to suggest George cover them up for me.

"Thank you. That's good to know. And if you don't hear me, please tell me. I'd rather that than you accidentally agreeing to something you don't want to do."

I laughed. "Yeah. Although, it turned out pretty well last time." Apart from the days of guilt and agonizing over when to tell George, which were decidedly not enjoyable. And us both nearly having a heart attack when George discovered me signing books in the middle of the night.

"Hey, I'm not complaining. It's the best miscommunication I've ever had."

My heart warmed at George's words and my body relaxed, soaking in the sunshine. Some of the general anxiety I'd been holding floated away on the warm, gentle breeze. While this wasn't how I'd anticipated my afternoon playing out, it might be exactly what I needed.

CHAPTER NINETEEN

GEORGE

WHILE BEING STRANDED on a kayak with my employee-slash-favorite-author-slash-crush was not consistent with my plan to keep a professional distance from Hannah until I'd had more time to assess the situation, it was very pleasant. Extremely pleasant.

And on the plus side, now that I was lying on the kayak, eyes closed, the sun's rays warming my skin, I couldn't see Hannah in her distractingly figure-hugging tank top that was only partially covered by the life jacket. And there was definitely no way I could kiss her without capsizing the kayak and us both ending up in the river.

It also made it easier to ask Hannah if there was anything I could do to accommodate her hearing loss—something that'd been weighing on my mind ever since she'd mentioned it on Thursday night. I'd been worried I might use the wrong words or accidentally offend her, but if I had, she'd given me no indication. It was a shame, really, that I hadn't had enough time to work out what to do about our kiss, because this would have been the perfect opportunity to raise the subject. Although, perhaps not, because if it didn't go well, then my only options would be to abandon ship or stay lying there, in awkward silence, until we were rescued. No, our current state, relaxing in the sun, enjoying the gorgeous weather and Hannah's company, was too pleasant. I didn't want to rock the boat—literally or figuratively—by bringing up the kiss. I exhaled.

"You know, I don't think I've felt this relaxed for months. Maybe years," I said. Conscious that Hannah had her eyes shut and that she'd just said it was easier to hear when she could see the speaker's face, I made an effort to project my voice and speak clearly.

"Tell me about it. Perhaps we should try getting stranded on kayaks more often."

I smiled at the warmth in Hannah's voice. "We could set up a business where we offer people a relaxing meditative experience in kayaks without paddles."

"Yesss! We could call it the Paddleless Peace Experience."

I chuckled. "Or Oarless Oasis."

Hannah laughed. "I love it! Where can I sign up?"

We spent the next twenty minutes imagining our new business, making suggestions that were more and more absurd. At one point, Hannah laughed so much I could feel the kayak shaking. *Damn, I like spending time with her.*

Finally exhausting the topic, we lay there in comfortable silence.

Well, it was initially comfortable.

The longer I lay there, the longer I had to think about Hannah and the elephant in the kayak. Our kiss.

The more I thought about it, the more I itched to know where I stood with Hannah. It wasn't in my nature to put off a conversation like this. Not only that, but my plan to wait until after my day off had been based on me keeping our interactions professional and avoiding one-on-one time with her. I hadn't factored in us being stranded in a tandem kayak in the middle of the Hudson River.

Would waiting until Tuesday to speak to Hannah really give me more comfort about my staffing concerns or clarify my feelings for Hannah? Josie had done a great job today. It seemed highly unlikely that everything would fall apart tomorrow without me, especially with Ben and Hannah working as well.

While I hadn't worked through my feelings about Hannah being H. M. Stuart, did that really matter? The important thing was what Hannah was like in real life, not her pen name or who I'd built H. M. Stuart up to be in my head. And Hannah in real life was great. Our time trapped on this kayak had only cemented that.

While my concern about how awkward it would be if the conversation went badly while we were stuck on a kayak with no way of escape was reasonable, it was now beginning to feel just as awkward not discussing it. I didn't need to have all the answers before we spoke. We could work through it together. The first thing I needed to clarify was the power imbalance situation.

"Hannah?" I asked as nonchalantly as I could. "Look, about last night"—my pulse thudded in my ears—"I got a bit carried away in the moment and, um..." My voice trailed off as I tried to think about how to best to phrase what I wanted to say. "But, um, I'm conscious that it was—or might have been—inappropriate, given I'm your boss and that I shouldn't have kissed you like that but...

Shit. I wanted to say something to make it clear I really liked her and also try to explore whether Blake's theory about the power imbalance not being a concern was right. But how could I say that in a way that wouldn't make her feel uncomfortable if my feelings weren't reciprocated or if there *was* a power imbalance?

I took another breath, about to try to explain, when Hannah spoke.

"That's fine. I totally get it. It's not like it was all you—I kissed you too—but it won't happen again," she said quickly. "Given I just got out of a long-term relationship recently, it's probably a good idea for me to not, um...start anything new, anyway...and for us just to be friends."

While Hannah's response at least indicated she'd been a willing participant, disappointment flooded through me at her words. I totally understood not wanting to jump into another relationship—I'd felt that way after Alexis and I had broken up—and this outcome was less complicated. But that did nothing to ease my disappointment. *I wonder if the recent breakup is really the reason, or if it's just an excuse to let me down gently?* I inwardly shook myself. Either way, it didn't matter. The end result was the same.

Maybe I should say something to make it clear that if, in the future, she was interested in dating again, to keep me in mind? *God, that sounds pathetic.* No, best to leave it alone.

"But you don't need to worry about the whole boss/employee thing," Hannah continued. "I don't think the usual dynamics that go along with that relationship apply here. I enjoy working at Novel Gossip, but it's more like a...hobby, not a critical stream of income or anything. I think it's helping with my writing, but I don't need it...and I'm sure I could get a similar job if I had to."

I exhaled. So Blake had been right about that. But it was no longer relevant given Hannah wasn't interested in dating.

"Dippin' Donuts would snap you up in a second," I said, trying to lighten the mood.

Hannah sucked in a dramatic breath. "I'd never join the dark side. Who do you think I am? I was thinking more like Builders' Arms or Olivia's flower shop. Not a soulless chain."

"Okay, okay. Sorry!" I smiled into the sun at the faux outrage in her voice.

Our banter hadn't helped shake my unease about how our conversation had just played out. I hadn't expressed myself very well, but now Hannah had made it clear she wasn't interested in me, it would only make things more awkward and achieve nothing if I explained my feelings for her. Hannah wanted to remain friends, and I had to respect that.

"I'm sorry about your breakup," I said. As soon as the words were out of my mouth, I started overthinking them. Was I being overly nosy, given my feelings for Hannah, or was that just the sort of thing a friend and colleague would say?

"That's okay," Hannah said, pausing for a moment. "In retrospect, it was all for the best. We didn't have the healthiest relationship. But because we were together for so long, our lives were very intertwined. We shared an apartment together, all our friends were mutual friends, so it's been an enormous change. And to make matters worse, my ex was also my editor and was cheating on me with another, much younger, author she worked with."

I winced. "Shit. That sounds tough," I said.

"Yeah," Hannah said. "It turned out the whole cheating thing was also widely known in publishing circles, including our friend group, so that was pretty humiliating."

I groaned. I knew how much Hannah valued her privacy and disliked being the center of attention. Discovering that not only was your ex cheating on you but that everyone else knew and had presumably been gossiping about it behind your back must have been awful. No wonder she wanted to leave New York. Suddenly, a thought struck me. "Oh god. Is she still your editor?"

"You sound absolutely horrified!" Hannah laughed. "No, I've got a new one. I couldn't have kept working with her after what happened."

"Oh, thank god!" I said, relieved.

"Did you always want to be a café-bookstore owner?" Hannah asked after a few moments of silence.

I chuckled. "Well, it had always been a fantasy of mine but not something I'd realistically considered. If you can believe it, I was a math and science nerd in school. I studied computer science at the University of South Florida so I could become an app developer."

"You, a nerd?" Hannah exclaimed, her voice light. "I never would have guessed from your collection of physics and American history books."

"Hey! You snooped around my bookshelves?" I asked in mock outrage.

"I was alone in your spare bedroom lined with books. I couldn't help it. It's a compulsion," Hannah protested. "So what made you change career paths?" She sounded genuinely intrigued.

"I liked being an app developer. But after a while, the work began to feel monotonous and quite isolating. The idea of opening a café, where I'd have constant interaction with people, be able to pursue my passion for cooking— which I consider a science—and books, became more and more appealing. And like you, I had a relationship break down and decided to give it a go. I've never looked back."

"Sapphire Springs, a safe haven for lesbians fleeing

breakups since 2021," Hannah said, laughing. "Sorry. I shouldn't assume you're a lesbian."

"Well, I am." I grinned.

"Me too," Hannah replied.

I opened my eyes and peered down at Hannah. She was smiling into the sun, her eyes still closed.

"Well, now I know who to call when my laptop freezes," Hannah said, her tone teasing.

I laughed. "'Have you tried turning it off and on?' will be about the extent of the tech support I can offer, I'm afraid. What about you? Did you always want to be a writer?"

"Pretty much. As I think I mentioned on Thursday night, I was one of those kids who was obsessed with reading and writing stories. My parents encouraged it but only as a hobby. They wanted me to go into academia or study law, like them. I studied English literature at NYU and did consider trying to get into academia, but my heart just wasn't in it. I didn't want to spend my life analyzing and dissecting other people's writing. I wanted to create something new myself. So, much to my parents' disappointment, after graduating, I increased my hours at the café I worked at to support myself, moved into a chaotic house full of artists and writers as roommates, and spent all my spare time working on what would become the first *Realms* book."

I frowned. While Mom had been disappointed when I decided to leave Florida, at least she'd always supported my career choices. "Did your parents change their minds about writing once that took off?"

"I didn't tell them," Hannah said after a pause.

I opened my eyes wide in surprise. "What?! Why not?"

"As you may have gathered from the whole '*I accidentally started working for you and then couldn't get up enough courage to tell you who I was'* incident, I have a tendency to shy away from difficult conversations," Hannah said sheepishly.

"But being a bestselling author is amazing and your books are incredible. Surely they'd be really proud of you."

Hannah sighed. "Honestly, I don't think so. As you can probably tell, I'm not close with my parents. Mom is a philosophy professor, and my dad is a professor of law. Growing up, they were always working—writing academic articles, going to conferences, and teaching. It was clear to me where their priorities lay, and it wasn't me. On the rare occasions they were home for dinner, instead of asking me how my day was, they'd ask me if I were a train conductor about to plow down ten people and my only option was to divert my train onto another set of tracks, in which case I'd only kill one person, what would I do?"

Good lord. Hannah's parents sounded like the worse mix of absent and controlling you could imagine. And so intense. "Yikes. That doesn't sound like a relaxing dinner table discussion."

"Yeah, especially not when you're four years old and just want to tell them about the dinosaur you drew at preschool," Hannah replied, a wry tone to her voice. "My nanny, Barb, basically raised me, and I'm still closer to her than Mom and Dad. I've called them a couple of times this year, and they haven't called me back. Honestly, I'm not sure why I even bother. Meanwhile, Barb likes to send me emails in size eighteen font, filling me in on her nursing home gossip, and we FaceTime regularly." I smiled at the warmth in Hannah's voice as she spoke about Barb. Thank god she had someone supportive in her life. "All I've gotten from my parents since Christmas was an email with their Grecce vacation itinerary. They like to send me their travel itineraries in case there is a natural disaster or something, and they need help being flown out to safety."

My heart went out to Hannah. Her parents sounded like the absolute worst, pushing her to be someone she didn't want to be and ignoring her all at the same time. It was rare for me to get angry, but rage at two people I'd never met welled up within me.

The kayak wobbled, and I peered down to see Hannah moving restlessly, her face serious but her eyes still closed. "I should have told them when I first got the book deal, but I didn't because I was convinced it would be a flop, and they'd use it as evidence that I shouldn't be a writer. And then, when it wasn't a flop, I was convinced they'd say something that would put a damper on my success. They're the sort of people who only read literary fiction and speak derisively about commercial fiction. And now it's been five years since I signed the book deal and I'm about to publish my third book, and it feels like the opportunity has well and truly passed."

I leaned back in the kayak, shutting my eyes again and taking it all in. So Hannah really wasn't kidding when she said she had trouble with difficult conversations.

"I don't know your parents, obviously, but I don't think it's ever too late to have a conversation. If you explained it to them like you did to me, surely they would understand?"

"Yeah, maybe." Hannah did not sound convinced.

"So, what do they think you do?" I asked, intrigued.

Hannah let out an embarrassed-sounding laugh. "They think I'm a kept woman. While publishing doesn't pay very well, my ex's great-grandfather was the founder of Haynes Insurance, so she had a trust fund large enough that neither of us had to work."

"Oh wow." I couldn't understand why Hannah would

prefer her parents to think she was unemployed and reliant on her wife's trust fund over being a bestselling novelist, but I didn't want to press. I knew from first-hand experience how complicated parent-child relationships could be.

"Yeah. So in addition to my hatred of attention and public speaking, and the worry over my fans finding the real Hannah Taylor a disappointment, my parents are yet another reason why I guard my identity so fiercely."

"I'm sorry." My words seemed woefully inadequate. Hannah deserved better.

"George! Hannah!" a familiar voice yelled.

My eyes shot open, and I sat up as fast as I could, dazed. In the distance, Blake and Jenny were paddling toward us.

Goddamnit! In any other situation, I would have been relieved we were finally being rescued from our paddle-less state. But despite my disappointment over how our conversation about the kiss had gone, I'd quite happily spend another few hours stranded with Hannah on the kayak in the sunshine.

I managed a weak wave.

As they got closer, I could make out Blake's and Jenny's hair plastered to their foreheads with sweat and their faces several shades pinker than usual.

"What happened?" Blake asked, out of breath. "And where are your paddles?"

"We accidentally dropped them in the water. They were last seen heading down that way." I pointed down the expanse of blue water, past Sapphire Springs, where the river wound around the tree-covered Garrison Point and disappeared from view.

Blake shook her head, chuckling. "So you've been stranded here, waiting for someone to rescue you? Good thing we turned back early and the current wasn't too strong."

"It's actually been surprisingly pleasant," I said, grinning. Based on Blake's and Jenny's exhausted appearances, we'd lucked out. A relaxing float in the sunshine with Hannah seemed infinitely preferable to a vigorous paddling session, especially given how hectic things had been recently. And at least we'd discussed our kiss, even though the outcome wasn't what I'd hoped.

Hannah, who'd also sat up, turned around and shot me a small smile. My stomach fluttered. It looked like Hannah agreed.

Blake, focused on the matter at hand—rescuing us—ignored my comment. "So, how should we do this? Should we give you one of our paddles?"

I nodded. "Yeah, that's probably the easiest option."

"Okay, I'll pass it over to you, George. Do. Not. Drop. It." Blake stared at me sternly.

I rolled my eyes and reached for the paddle, even though Blake had every right to be concerned. Thankfully, the paddle transfer went smoothly, and within minutes, we were slowly heading back toward the kayak rental shack. I finally seemed to be getting the hang of paddling, my body and the paddle working together to rhythmically slice through the water. *Huh. Maybe kayaking isn't so bad after all.*

We were only a few feet from the shore when we hit something, sending a jolt through the boat.

I frowned. "Do you know what that was?" I asked Hannah, unable to see from where I was seated.

Hannah peered over the front of the kayak. "It looks like there are some rocks."

"I think I'll just jump out then and pull the kayak onto

shore. I don't think either of us have the kayaking skills to navigate rocks—no offence—and the water looks pretty shallow here."

Hannah turned to me. "Are you sure? I can get out."

"No, it's fine. You've got sneakers on, you don't want to ruin them. At least I'm wearing flip flops."

"What did that waiver say about foot entrapment and dangerous riverine fauna?" Hannah asked. Her voice was teasing, but I thought I sensed a genuine underlying concern.

I chuckled. "Don't worry. There hasn't been a shark sighting for years."

"Sharks?" Hannah's mouth opened wide. "Maybe you shouldn't—"

Ignoring Hannah's concerns—people went swimming in the Hudson all the time—I held onto the side of the kayak and clambered out, trying not to rock the boat too much in the process. I winced as my feet and then legs hit the cold water. The bottom of the river was rocky, and the water was deeper than I'd anticipated, well above my knees. Bracing myself, I carefully waded toward the front of the kayak. As I came level with Hannah, my foot slipped on a slimy rock.

Fuck.

My gut clenched as I lost balance.

Without thinking, I grabbed the side of the kayak to stabilize myself. But the kayak, as I'd already established, was not steady.

The kayak tipped sharply toward me.

"George!" Hannah yelped as her body slammed into mine, sending me falling backward and Hannah following.

Cold water engulfed my torso as my butt hit the riverbed, my hands shooting back to brace my fall just in time to stop my head going under. A second later, Hannah landed on my lap, squealing as she made contact with the water. I wrapped my arm around her upper back to steady her.

We gazed at each other, wide-eyed, our faces only inches apart. Despite the shock of the fall, I was acutely aware of Hannah's lips only inches from mine, my hand on her warm back and her shapely butt pressing on my upper thighs. A bolt of electricity shot down my spine.

Oh boy, are we going to kiss again? Because I know for sure I want to.

"Are you guys okay?" Blake yelled from the shore, shattering the moment.

We blinked at each other and then the absurdity of the situation seemed to hit us both at the same time and we burst into laughter.

"I'll take that as a yes," Blake called.

Hannah clambered off me and stood, then held out a hand to help me up.

"I'm so sorry I landed on you. I hope it didn't hurt too much."

"I don't know why you're apologizing. I'm one hundred percent at fault for capsizing the kayak," I said as I grasped her hand and rose to my feet.

Our eyes caught for a moment, sending my heart bouncing in my chest. I gave myself a mental shake.

Hannah's made it clear she doesn't want a relationship. You need to respect that.

CHAPTER TWENTY

GEORGE

AN HOUR LATER, we were sitting in the beer garden at Builders' Arms, under a massive old oak tree in dappled sunlight, enjoying a round of drinks, and sharing a bowl of fries and a plate of nachos. The weather was so warm that our clothes had dried in no time, although a faint musty scent of river water remained. Hannah had taken her soaking wet sneakers off and left them in the sun. Olivia had joined us about fifteen minutes ago, having kayaked all the way up to Battersby Island and back again. She'd shown us photos of the crumbling castle, and we'd filled her in on being stranded in the kayak and our accidental dip in the river.

I reclined in my chair, taking it all in. Summer always lifted my mood, and today, despite still being only early June, had felt like quintessential summer. Finally, an afternoon off. And I got to spend it with some of my favorite people. My eyes lingered on Hannah, who was deep in conversation with Olivia. Hannah was rapidly becoming one of them. Our conversation about the kiss had been the only blip on an otherwise perfect day. But surely, now I knew where I stood with her, I could just move on.

"This was really fun. We should do it again soon," Jenny said during a comfortable lull in conversation.

My gaze connected with Hannah's for a moment, and she smiled at me, sending my belly fizzing. *You need to move on, George.*

"I'm always up for a kayak," Olivia said, grinning. "Is the farm next weekend?"

Jenny's eyes lit up. "Oh, yes! I'd forgotten about that. Hannah, you should come with us—if you're not busy. We're going fruit picking at Red Tractor Farm."

Hannah's eyes flicked back to me. *Is she wondering if I'm okay with her coming along?* I smiled reassuringly, just in case.

"That sounds great!" Hannah said.

"Hey, are you feeling okay?" Blake, who was sitting next to me, murmured.

"Yes...why?" I frowned. Those words didn't usually bode well for what was to come. I'd just been thinking how great I felt, but had I prematurely aged myself over the last few weeks due to stress? Or were my feelings for Hannah plastered on my face every time I looked in Hannah's direction?

"Your face is very red."

I touched my face. It was hot.

"Hmmm. Maybe I got a bit sunburned." I looked down at my legs, and the contrast between the small section of pale skin on my thighs that had been protected by my shorts when I was lying on the kayak, but was on display now that I was sitting, and the remainder of my crimson legs sent my heart sinking. "Crap. Okay, maybe I got a lot sunburned."

Goddamnit. In the rush of getting ready, I'd completely forgotten to put on sunscreen.

I peered at Hannah. She also looked more flushed than usual.

I stood. "I'm just going to head over to the general store and grab some aloe," I said to Blake.

Thankfully, the general store was close to Builders' Arms. After I'd bought the aloe, I sat on the bench outside the store and smeared it all over my legs, arms, and face. I exhaled as the cool gel gave my red skin some immediate relief.

I reentered Builders' Arms a few minutes later. As I stepped into the beer garden, I almost collided with Hannah.

"Hey! Sorry, I just slipped out to get some aloe. As you can probably tell, I got sunburned," I said, smiling at her.

"Me too," Hannah said, grimacing. "I'm kicking myself for not thinking of sunscreen. I was just going to the restroom to splash water on my face."

"Well, you're more than welcome to use this." I waved the aloe bottle around in the air like a complete dork.

The grimace vanished, replaced with a full smile. "That would be amazing. Thanks."

We stepped farther into the beer garden, next to a brick wall that was covered in green ivy so we weren't blocking the door. I handed Hannah the bottle and she started to apply it to her face and arms. Watching her rubbing the aloe into her skin was strangely mesmerizing, sending tingles vibrating through me. Sexy wasn't the first word that usually appeared in my mind when it came to green gel-like substances, but it did when Hannah was involved. I couldn't look away, which was why I noticed she'd missed a patch of delicate skin under her eyes, and on her upper chest, just below her collarbone, both of which were distinctly pink.

"You missed a bit here," I said, patting the skin under my eye with a finger. "And, um...on your chest." Helping with aloe application was the sort of thing friends did for each other, right? Maybe not bosses, but I pushed that thought away.

"Here?" Hannah asked as she smeared more aloe on her cheeks and chest, only partially covering the un-aloed patches.

"Do you want me to help? You still missed a bit."

"Sure." Hannah gave me a grateful smile and handed me the bottle.

Stepping closer, I put a dollop on my index finger and gently swiped it under both her eyes. Hannah's soft breath tickled my face. Her mouth was only inches from mine. Our eyes locked, and a thrill rushed through me. I bit my lip. *FRIENDS AND COLLEAGUES, remember. Hannah made it very clear.*

I dragged my eyes away from hers, and without think ing, they dropped to the patch of skin on her chest that she'd also missed, and then down to the soft swell of her breasts rising up from under her tank top. *Eyes up, George.* Offering to help her had been a terrible idea.

I swallowed.

"George!" Blake yelled far too loudly as she appeared out of nowhere and wrapped her arm around my shoulder. "I was wondering where you two had gone."

I flinched and turned my head to stare at Blake. It was out of character for Blake to be so loud and demonstrative. Had she downed one too many beers, or was she suffering from heatstroke?

Blake's facial expression gave nothing away, but it did bring me back down to reality.

"Well, I think that's good now," I said to Hannah, my face even hotter than before.

"What the hell was that?" I whispered to Blake as we made our way back to our table.

Blake frowned. "You told me to chaperone you to make sure you didn't do anything with Hannah."

"Um, I'm pretty sure I said I *didn't* need you to chaperone." Although, it was probably for the best Blake had interrupted us.

Blake shrugged. "Well, you definitely said you wanted to keep things 'friendly but professional' with her."

"I was just applying aloe on her sunburn," I said, wincing at the defensive tone in my voice.

Blake's eyebrows rose. "George, you were standing inches away from her, staring at her boobs, and licking your lips. That did not scream 'friendly but professional' to me."

I groaned softly. I couldn't argue with that. My feelings toward Hannah were anything but professional. I sat back in my chair in the dappled sunlight, took a sip of beer, and shut my eyes for a moment. I had to focus on what I did have—sunshine, good food and drink, and the company of my friends—and accept that was all Hannah and I could be. Friends.

CHAPTER TWENTY-ONE

HANNAH

"HERE YOU GO," George said, as she placed a smoked salmon quiche and side salad in front of me with a smile.

"Thank you! I was salivating over this one all shift. It looks incredible." I smiled back up at George, my gaze following her as she returned to making coffees on Hugo.

It had been seven days since our eventful kayaking trip. Seven days since we'd decided to be just friends. And in those seven days, I'd been replaying our conversation over and over in my head.

When George had apologized for kissing me, saying it was inappropriate, disappointment had flooded through me. All I'd heard was that she thought the kiss was a mistake, and I'd instinctively gone into self-protection mode, blurting out that it was best if we just stayed friends. But as I analyzed our conversation afterward, I couldn't shake the feeling that George had been about to say something else, and I had cut her off. She'd never actually *said* it was a mistake or that she wasn't attracted to me. It was possible her only concern with the kiss was that she was my boss.

But instead of giving her space to talk through her concerns with me, I'd panicked and effectively shut the entire conversation down with my comment.

I sighed. At least things hadn't felt too awkward between us—the easy, fun rapport we'd had on the kayak was still there. George had joined me for lunch after my shift twice, and last night, I'd met up with George, Olivia, Blake, and Jenny for a drink at Frankie's. But I couldn't escape the nagging sensation that I'd screwed up our conversation on the kayak.

I took a bite of the quiche, which tasted just as good as it looked—crisp, buttery pastry and a creamy salmon filling—and let out a small groan of appreciation. After working from 10 a.m. to 2 p.m., I was starving, and this was exactly what I needed. I pulled my phone out of my pocket and saw I'd just missed a FaceTime call from Barb. She'd emailed me last week, asking if I was free for a chat, and I'd forgotten I'd told her she could call me any time after my shift ended.

The café was quiet, in a post-lunch lull, and I was sitting at a table in the corner, away from the other customers. Calling Barb back wouldn't be too disruptive, so I pulled on my noise-canceling headphones, dialed her number, and then balanced my phone against one of Olivia's candles so it pointed toward me. Barb's chin appeared on the screen, wobbled, and then her entire lovely wrinkled face appeared, framed by short curly gray hair, a broad smile on her face.

"Hannah! How are you, sweetheart?"

Barb's voice filled me with warmth.

"I'm good! Just finished my shift. I'm still at the café, eating my lunch. Hopefully it's not too noisy. Can you hear me okay?"

"Loud and clear, my girl." Barb narrowed her eyes at me. "I hope you're not overdoing it with all this waitressing and your writing."

I smiled. Barb had always been the biggest supporter of my writing, patiently listening to me telling her stories as a child, helping me transcribe them onto paper, which I illustrated, and which we stapled together like books.

"I'm only working at the café for three or four hours at the most, and so far, the writing and the waitressing seem to complement each other pretty well. I write for a couple of hours in the morning, and then head down here to work. Writing is so solitary it's nice to have some human interaction and get myself out of my head for a while. And then when I get home, usually after having a delicious lunch here"—I lifted my plate so Barb could see the quiche—"I'm ready to start writing again." For the last week, I'd often written until bedtime, only stopping for a quick meal, which I'd usually eat on the deck. I loved spending time out there, surrounded by nature.

"Oh, can you show me the café?" Barb asked, her blue eyes flashing with interest.

I grinned, lifting the phone up and slowly circling it around. "There's the bookstore section—it's not huge, but it has a great selection—and there's the counter. The kitchen is behind there. And here are all the tables... And the view out the windows." I placed the phone back on the table in front of me.

"It looks lovely. Very cozy," Barb said.

"It really is. You'll have to come and visit me."

"That would be wonderful. And was that George I spotted behind the counter?" Barb's eyes twinkled.

I pressed my lips together to conceal my smile. Had she really wanted a tour of Novel Gossip, or had she just been after a glimpse of George? I hadn't told Barb about my feelings for George, but she'd always been very perceptive when it came to these things.

"Yes, that was George."

"She's very handsome," Barb said approvingly.

I laughed. "Anyway, enough about me. How are you?"

Barb launched into an update of the latest gossip at her aged care facility. There was a new, very attractive physical therapist who some of her friends were trying to set up with their daughters. Susan's three-year-old grandson had gone missing on a visit yesterday but was found in the kitchen, trying to convince the staff to give him "chippies." And Barb had gotten into a very heated discussion with another resident, Bruce, about gerrymandering.

As Barb spoke and I laughed along, my chest filled with warmth. She was the energetic, positive Barb I'd known most of my life. It had been a very different story a few years ago, after she'd fallen and fractured her hip. After having a hip replacement, she'd struggled to manage on her own and had to move out of the apartment she'd lived in for decades into an aged care facility nearby. She'd hated the tasteless food, the way some staff treated her as if she was a child, and her small, dark and musty room. The place was run down and understaffed, and Barb had been completely miserable. I could tell something was wrong, but she hadn't confided in me. It was only when I went to visit her that it became clear. The nursing home I'd moved her to was well-resourced, her room bright and airy, overlooking a gorgeous garden, and the food—while not at Novel Gossip standards—wasn't too bad at all. It also had excellent rehabilitation services, which had resulted in her mobility significantly improving. And it was horrendously expensive.

Thank god I'd gotten my writing mojo back. If I kept up

at my current pace—yesterday, I'd written eight thousand words, a personal best—I'd meet the July deadline easily. And the risk of me not being able to afford Barb's nursing home bills anytime soon would reduce substantially.

"I'd better go. I've got to get ready for my session with the new PT." Barb winked, and I laughed. "But Hannah, I'm so glad to hear you're enjoying your new life. You know how proud I am of you, don't you, love? Pursuing the career you wanted, even when your parents weren't supportive, moving to New York all by yourself—and then again to Sapphire Springs. You've always had the courage to do what makes you happy, and that's really something. A lot of people don't."

"Thanks for saying that. I love you. Talk to you soon."

We hung up, Barb's words still echoing in my brain. I'd never considered myself a particularly brave person. I'd shied away from confronting Tania about her suspected infidelity, avoided telling my parents for years about my writing career, and, most recently, gotten myself into a very awkward situation because I couldn't bring myself to tell George that I was H. M. Stuart. But while I wasn't good at confronting people head on, I was willing to put myself on the line in other ways to follow my dreams.

Now that I'd finally moved to the town I'd wanted to live in for years, started writing again, and made new friends, what were my dreams now?

I gazed at George standing behind the counter, speaking to a customer who was buying a stack of books, and knew the answer immediately.

I wanted a partner. Someone to share my life with, someone who I connected with on a deep emotional, intellectual, and physical level. I wanted a relationship where we cared for and supported each other, but also had a lot of fun together.

George grinned, her dimple making an appearance, as she handed the books, now carefully stacked in a bag, to the customer, and my heart stuttered.

I hadn't been this attracted to anyone else in years, and George was kind, funny, and intelligent—all the things I'd realized I really valued in a relationship. The more time I spent with her, whether it was working, on our lunch breaks, or hanging out with her friends, the more I appreciated her.

And the more I doubted whether my concerns about dating her had been valid. I'd worried that if we started dating, and then things went badly, that I could lose the life I'd started to make here—my growing friendship with George and her friends, Novel Gossip, even perhaps my writing mojo. But the more I got to know George, the less this seemed like a valid concern. George was warm-hearted and reasonable. I couldn't imagine her being vindictive if the relationship ended. We'd already been through a few bumps in our short friendship—the whole *me not telling her I was H. M. Stuart* thing and, more recently, the kiss—and both times she'd dealt with them with understanding and kindness. Her concern about the fact that she was my boss also indicated that she was someone with a strong sense of ethics and fairness. And while I hadn't stayed friends with any of my exes, it wasn't like it was unheard of.

I took another bite of my quiche, chewing it as I worked through my reservations.

While my concerns about starting a new relationship only months after Tania and I split up seemed sensible, it was so hard to find people you connected with. Was it smart to dismiss a potential partner just because it wasn't the ideal time to strike up a new relationship?

And while Tania's and my relationship had officially only ended three months ago, the real ending had happened long before then. We'd stopped going on date nights years ago, our sex life had been pretty much non-existent, and with Tania "working late" and on weekends, we'd been more like roommates who worked together and shared mutual friends than lovers. While I was devastated when I discovered she'd cheated on me, a lot of the emotional pain I went through was facing the fact that our relationship had not been good for a while, and I had to move on, with the massive life upheaval that would bring. And that everyone but me seemed to know about her cheating.

So maybe I wasn't really rushing into something too fast. There was also a risk that if I didn't grab this opportunity, someone else might come along and snap George up.

George reached for a coffee cup on top of Hugo, saying something to Ben that made him laugh as she made a coffee, and I couldn't help smiling as my insides fizzed.

There was no doubt that what I wanted was George.

And while it was quite possible she didn't want me, because I'd shut down the conversation on the kayak I didn't know for sure. My stomach churned at the thought of reopening the conversation. It could be extremely awkward if George wasn't interested—would she think I couldn't take no for an answer? *You were just telling yourself what a great person George is, Hannah. She'll understand, even if the answer is no.*

And if I didn't do anything, nothing would happen. George would assume, quite reasonably, that what I'd said on the kayak reflected what I wanted and respect my wishes. I pressed my lips together. I had to channel some of my character Esmae's energy, who was currently challenging her evil brother for the throne, and tackle this head on. I just needed to find a good time to do it, and now, in public at the café, was definitely not the right time.

I stood, lifting up my plate to take it back to the kitchen, suddenly eager to get home. Talking to Barb had given me additional motivation to keep writing, and I was also eager to channel the nervous energy, that'd built up from thinking about George, into something productive.

"Hey, I can take that back for you. I'm heading there now anyway," George said, stepping out from the side of the counter with her hand out.

"Thanks!" I grinned at her. Our eyes connected and my heart fluttered.

"I've been meaning to ask. Do you need a lift to fruit picking tomorrow? I could pick you up around three if that works for you?"

"That would be amazing if it's not too much trouble," I said. *The car trip could be the perfect opportunity to talk to George about us.*

Walking home down the streets lined with leafy green trees, I decided to stop worrying about what I'd say to George tomorrow and focus my energy on planning what I'd write when I got home. Maybe I should try to tackle the pesky sex scene I'd skipped over the other day. To avoid losing momentum, I'd just written "[insert hot sex scene here]" and kept going, in the hope inspiration would strike at a later date. I didn't have high hopes this would occur. Sex scenes were always a challenge for me, and the ones I'd written previously had been criticized by some for being wooden and lacking in chemistry.

Since today seemed to be all about deciding to tackle

difficult things head on, I resolved to give the sex scene another red hot go this afternoon.

I unlatched my front gate and strode with purpose toward the front door of my cottage.

Today, I'll write a steamy sex scene, and tomorrow, I'll put my heart on the line with George.

CHAPTER TWENTY-TWO

I NERVOUSLY CHECKED MY WATCH. George should be here any minute. I took a few deep breaths. Sex scene writing yesterday had not been successful. I'd ended up abandoning it after thirty minutes of staring blankly at the screen and instead focused on confronting evil brothers and dragons. Hopefully today's discussion with George would go better.

I peered out the window to look for any sign of George's car. Nothing.

Butterflies swarmed in my abdomen. Restless, I got out of the chair and paced up and down my small study until I heard a car pull up outside. *Here goes.*

I grabbed my bag and walked out the front door. My heart bounced as I confirmed that it was, indeed, George in her beat-up blue Ford Fiesta out on the road, and then it sank as I made out another figure sitting next to her. Olivia. *Damnit.*

George turned to me as I jumped into the backseat. "Hey," she said, voice low, the dimple showing on her right cheek. A thrill ran down my spine. She grinned and held up a bottle of sunscreen. "Do you need any of this?"

An image of George massaging sunscreen over my body appeared without warning in my mind, leaving me short of breath. I collected myself and shook my head.

"No thanks. I learned my lesson after our kayaking adventure and am well and truly smothered in sunscreen."

As much as I wanted George's hands all over my body, I had to tell her how I felt first in order for there to be any chance of that happening. Unfortunately, with Olivia in the car, now was not the moment.

The car trip went quickly, and before long, George was pulling into Red Tractor Farm, marked by a large red sign next to the main road out of town.

We met Jenny, Blake, and Amanda at the farmhouse where we picked up green buckets and then followed a wooden arrow sign with *Fruit Picking* written on it down a dirt path.

"This place is great!" I said, taking in the rustic farmhouse with a shining red tractor parked nearby, green fields, and scarecrows. I inhaled the sweet scent of flowers and grass. As we walked, we passed other wooden signs pointing in the direction of the *Petting Zoo, Christmas Trees, Hayride, Flower Farm, Corn Maze,* and *Pumpkin Patch*. "It seems like they do everything here!"

"We should definitely come back in the fall," Jenny said. "They go all out on the fall festivities. There's a hayride, pumpkin patch, apple cannon and amazing apple fritters." She shot Blake a beaming smile which made me think there was a story there. I made a note to ask George about it later.

"They're also my main supplier of flowers for my shop,"

Olivia chimed in. "And an absolute pleasure to work with. I don't know what I'd do without them."

"It seems like everyone in Sapphire Springs is a pleasure to work with," I said, smiling, and then felt my cheeks warm as I wondered how George would interpret the comment.

The blue sky was dotted with wisps of clouds, and there was a gentle breeze. My chest expanded as we strolled along the dirt lane, chatting and laughing. I'd always dreamed of having a group of friends like this.

George was walking in front of me and I couldn't help admiring her butt in her charcoal shorts and the way her white t-shirt clung to her broad shoulders. The memory of my hands pressing against her butt cheeks while she was stuck in the shed window came rushing back. *Damn.* If our talk goes well, maybe I'll be able to run my hands over them again. I bit my lip. *Let's not get ahead of ourselves.*

A few minutes later, the orchard, full of rows of leafy green apple and cherry trees, came into sight. "The strawberries are over there," Olivia said, pointing to a field to the south. "But I'm thinking we should start with the cherries, as they'll probably last better than the strawberries once they're picked."

The apples weren't ripe yet, but the cherries, in gleaming dark-red clusters against the vibrant green leaves, were ready for picking. My stomach rumbled. I loved cherries.

"Do you know what the etiquette is about sampling a few as we pick?" I whispered to George.

"It's one hundred percent illegal. But don't worry, I won't call the cops," George replied with a wink.

"Should we work in pairs?" Amanda asked. "It looks like most of the fruit is higher up in the tree, so it might be easiest if one person goes up the tree and the other person stays on the ground to collect the cherries and help support the ladder if need be." She eyed the rustic wooden ladders—some leaning against the trees and others lying on the ground under the trees—with trepidation. They did look a little rickety.

"I'm surprised we weren't required to sign another waiver, relinquishing all our rights in the event of fruit-picking-related injuries," I murmured to George, who chuckled.

"Who knows what other dangers are lurking in this cherry orchard," George whispered close to my ear. Her soft breath on my cheek sent my pulse racing.

"Pairs sound good to me!" Jenny said, turning to Blake with a cheeky grin. "You can go up the tree first."

"Gee, thanks," Blake responded, sounding less than thrilled.

I suddenly became ridiculously nervous. George and I were standing right next to each other, so it made sense that we'd pair off together, but I didn't want to assume. Memories of waiting to be picked by some boy I wasn't interested in at high school dances, all the while wishing Sadie Charlesworth, my long-standing teen crush, would snap me up, came rushing back. I mentally shook myself. It really wasn't the same at all. In this case, all my potential cherry-picking companions were lovely, unlike some of the boys I'd gone to school with. But George was my preferred one. I swallowed. *Time to take action, Hannah. You're not in high school anymore.*

"Would you like to pick with me?" I asked George as casually as I could muster. I winced. Good lord, I sounded like a nervous schoolgirl.

If George heard a quiver in my voice, she didn't let on. She turned to me and grinned. "That sounds great. I'm hoping we'll get enough so I can make cherry preserves and a cherry pie for the café. By my calculations, we'll need at least three buckets' worth of cherries, so we'll have to pick fast if we want to get strawberries as well. Are you up for the challenge?" She raised an eyebrow, a playful smile dancing on her face.

The buckets were big. *Perfect. Lots of opportunity for one-on-one time with George to talk to her about my feelings.*

"Challenge accepted." I reached out my hand and shook George's, enjoying the soft warmth of her skin against mine. *Am I holding on for too long?* I quickly dropped her hand, heat prickling my cheeks.

"I'm happy to go up the ladder first," I said, staring longingly at a bunch of juicy cherries on a tree a few feet away from me.

George chuckled.

"What?" I asked.

"You volunteering to go first on the ladder wouldn't have anything to do with wanting to sample a few cherries, would it?"

"Excuse me! How dare you!" I said with mock indignation. "My offer was driven by pure selflessness. I'm risking my life on a rickety ladder to get cherries for your pie. The least you could do is show some gratitude."

"Thank you *so* much," George said, her dimple appearing in full force. My stomach fluttered. "Well, let's get to it, then. Not a moment to waste!" She clapped her hands and beelined toward a tree in the middle of the orchard.

I walked swiftly to catch up with her. *Should I raise the topic now? George seemed like she was in a rush to get started, so perhaps not.* Or was I just making excuses to put the conversation off?

I'd almost reached George when a noise made me jump.

Loud grunts and snorts filled the air. I twisted my head, trying to identify the source of the sound. George looked similarly confused.

I jogged a few feet to where George was standing. "Where the hell is that coming from? It sounds like there's a herd of pigs on the loose. Did you jinx us by joking about the dangers lurking in this orchard?"

"Surely we'd be able to see them if there was." George stepped toward a tree. "It sounds like the noise is coming from up in the trees. Pigs don't climb trees...do they?" George stared tentatively up the trunk, as if worried a pig might fall out and land on her.

"I'm no expert on pigs, but surely not. Don't they have short, stubby little legs? That doesn't seem conducive to tree-climbing."

George, who'd been examining the tree, suddenly turned to me and grinned. "Okay, we don't need to worry about being accosted by feral pigs. I found out what's causing the noise." She beckoned me over until I was under the tree, and pointed up. There was a black, box-shaped object attached to the tree. "It's a speaker. They must be blasting pig noises to scare off birds or something, I guess. How bizarre."

The speaker emitted an extra-loud snort, and I jumped again. "Good lord! Let's find a tree away from the speakers. It's not exactly the ideal soundtrack for a relaxing afternoon of cherry picking." *Or for the sort of conversation I'm hoping to have with George.*

We found a tree a safe distance from the speakers and positioned the ladder under a branch dripping with cherries. Over the faint snorting of pigs, I could hear the others laughing in the distance, but I couldn't see them. For the first time today, we were alone. Now was my chance to have that relationship talk. I swallowed.

"Are you having second thoughts about going up the tree? I'm happy to do it if you want," George said gently, clearly picking up that something was bothering me.

"No, no. It's fine." I stared up at the gleaming red fruit, my mouth watering, and decided that potentially awkward discussions with George could wait until I'd sampled a few cherries. I'd had an early lunch today, and it was probably best not to have the talk on an empty stomach, especially not when there was such delicious fruit to fill it.

I climbed the ladder and looked around. It was lovely up here, surrounded by green leaves and red cherries. I reached for the nearest bunch, pulling them off one by one. Reaching down, I gently dropped them in the bucket George was holding up high, saving one to try.

I popped it in my mouth as I scanned the branches for the next cluster to pick. Sweet, rich juices rushed over my taste buds. *Mmmm.* Delicious. But now I was stuck with a cherry pit. If I was by myself, I would have just spat it on the ground, but I wasn't, and spitting in front of your crush did not seem like a surefire way to woo them. I cursed the lack of pockets in my shorts as I looked around for somewhere to put it. Maybe there'd be a little hole in the tree trunk I could squirrel it away in. But there was no obvious pit storage location. *Damnit.* I was out of luck. I'd just need to spit it discreetly, far away from where George was standing so she didn't notice. I carefully aimed at the other side of the tree from George and ejected the pit undetected.

I moved to the next bunch of cherries and put another one in my mouth as I placed the rest in the bucket. I knew I couldn't keep up this *one-for-me-the-rest-for-the-bucket* approach much longer, but hot damn, the cherries were good. I spat the cherry pit again. My stomach dropped as the pit bounced off one of the branches and ricocheted backward, toward George. A strangled yelp left my mouth. George looked up at me just as the cherry pit plummeted directly into her face. I winced. *Oh god.*

"Shit! I'm so sorry," I exclaimed as the cherry pit bounced off her cheek and onto the ground. "Are you okay?" I tensed, waiting for George's reaction. George erupted into laughter.

My muscles eased. *Thank god George has a sense of humor.*

After what felt like at least a minute, George stopped laughing. "I mean, aggressive pig recordings and projectile cherry pits aren't exactly what I had in mind when I agreed to go cherry picking," she said, staring up at me,. "But I'm completely unharmed by that tiny pit."

I decided not to sample any more cherries for the time being and, instead, focused on the task at hand: picking enough cherries so George could make the preserves and pie.

After ten minutes, all the bunches within easy reach had been picked. One large, particularly juicy-looking bunch of cherries was just outside my comfortable arm span. While the sensible approach would have been to step down the ladder and reposition it, I was eager for a few more minutes to recover from the cherry pit incident before I had to face George. *Maybe if I leaned out and held the branch in front of me for support, I could grab it...*

I reached out, grasping the branch in front of me. My insides twisted as the branch bowed under my weight. *Shit.* I lost my balance, and for a heart-stopping moment, I thought I was going to fall. I grabbed a studier branch just in time and took a deep breath, trying to keep the panic at bay.

"Everything okay up there?" George peered up at me, concern on her face. I was leaning at an almost forty-five-degree angle, my feet on the ladder but most of my weight supported by the branch I'd just grabbed.

I tried to transfer my balance to get into an upright position on the ladder, but I couldn't do it. *Damn.*

I looked back down at George. "I think I'm stuck." I grimaced.

"What about if I shuffle the ladder so it's closer to your head. Do you think that would help?"

Anxiety flooded my brain, making it difficult to think straight. "I think so."

My arms aching, I focused on holding onto the branch while George carefully shifted the ladder closer to me.

"Shit. I can't move the ladder any further. There's a branch in the way. Hold on a second, I'm coming up," George said.

Oh god, I hope the ladder can hold us both.

The ladder wobbled underneath my feet and then a warm arm wrapped around the side of my waist.

"Okay, I'm holding onto a branch. On the count of three, I'll try pulling you up and you try shifting your weight back on the ladder. Are you ready?" George asked.

"Yes," I said. My arm felt like it might give way at any minute.

"One, two, three!"

I pushed off the branch with my hands and George's arm yanked my waist up. The ladder shook ominously, sending my heart shooting into my throat. But George's grasp was firm around my waist, and as she pulled me up, my weight transferred back onto the ladder. Almost upright, I grabbed another branch to steady myself and take the load off George, and then stood straight on the ladder. *Phew.*

"Are you okay?" George asked, standing one rung below me, her arm still around my waist and her body pressing against mine. *God, that feels nice.*

I exhaled a shaky breath. "Yes. But I think I might need a break for a moment."

"Let me get down first." George scrambled down the ladder, and then held it in place.

Relief washed over me when I finally landed on solid ground.

"I'm sorry about that," I said to George, my face hot. "I spotted a particularly juicy bunch of cherries out of my reach and got a little ambitious." I frowned as I remembered my mission. "Damnit! I should've picked them once I'd stabilized." I stared up into the tree, not convinced I wanted to retread my steps up the ladder so soon after my near-topple.

George grinned. "Hey. If you want to have a break from picking, I can go and retrieve that 'juicy' bunch for you." George raised her eyebrows at me, and despite not having fully recovered from the ordeal of being stuck in a cherry tree, I laughed.

"If you're sure you're not concussed after that pit hit your head, then I'm happy to stay on bucket duties for now. And thanks for saving me, by the way."

"Well, I wasn't about to leave you hanging." George's eyes twinkled.

I rolled my eyes and stifled a giggle.

And with that parting remark, she hightailed it up the ladder and got picking.

"HEY! George, Hannah! We're going to move on to the strawberries!" Jenny yelled.

Thank god. My arms ached from holding the now very full bucket up high to collect the cherries George had picked. Strawberries were close to the ground. Less opportunity for unfortunate incidents. Not that any had occurred since George had climbed the ladder.

Cherry picking, at least the way we were doing it with one person up a tree and the other underneath them, was also not conducive to having serious discussions. It was, however, conducive to checking out the person up the tree's calves, and George, I'd decided, had very nice calves—strong, tanned, shapely. When she shifted her weight, her muscles rippled. Those calves began their descent down the ladder, and within thirty seconds, George appeared on the ground next to me.

She eyed the almost-overflowing bucket. "I think we've got plenty now. Should we join the others?"

I nodded, and we picked up the buckets—three full of cherries, two empty ones for the strawberries—and walked over to the strawberry fields, where we spotted Jenny and Blake partway down a row of strawberry plants. Amanda and Olivia were nowhere to be seen. Perhaps they were still picking cherries, or had given up and gone to the farm café for refreshments.

Jenny popped a strawberry in Blake's mouth, and George let out a sound halfway between a groan and a chuckle. "Why don't we make a start over there, give the love birds some space?"

I nodded, and we wandered over to the spot George had suggested, a safe distance from Jenny and Blake.

"Have they been dating long?" I asked as I kneeled next

to a strawberry plant and began to pick the ripe fruit, inhaling the sweet, earthy fragrance.

"Since fall." George chuckled as she crouched opposite me on the other side of the strawberry plant. "Don't get me wrong. I'm thrilled for them, and it's cute how into each other they are, but I like to keep my distance when they're in that mood."

Was now a good time to bring up our relationship? The topic was dating, so it might be an opportunity to segue to us. Or was it weird if I brought us up immediately after discussing two people who were clearly madly in love with each other? I stared at George, who was delicately pulling a strawberry off a plant.

Tania had given me feedback on my last novel, which had a romantic subplot, that readers hated when love interests didn't communicate. I'd taken her feedback without objection, but this experience reminded me just how damn hard communicating could be, especially when you weren't sure how the other person felt, and you were potentially putting yourself out there for rejection. And looking back, Tania and I hadn't exactly been the best communicators either. We still weren't. We were well overdue for a conversation about how to divide our shared assets—a conversation that I'd been putting off. But George was different, and I wanted to learn from my mistakes.

I looked down at the plant in front of me and picked another strawberry. "I imagine it must be hard dating in a small town like Sapphire Springs as a queer person. I'm assuming it's a fairly small dating pool. It's so nice that Blake and Jenny found each other." I looked up at George. Our eyes connected, and my heart stuttered.

I'm so glad I found you too. The words were so loud in

my head that, for a moment, I panicked, thinking I'd said them out loud. But it was true. It'd only been two weeks since I'd met George, but in that time, my life had improved drastically. I was writing again and actually enjoying it. I was social again and also enjoying it. I felt more like myself than I had in years.

My eyes lowered to George's dimple, which was peeking through, and then her soft lips.

Focus on the strawberries, Hannah. A strawberry field was way too public a setting for another make-out session, even if I was getting vibes George might be into it. A thrill rushed through me at the thought.

I dropped my eyes to the ground and pulled off another juicy, red strawberry, imagining George and me sharing it in a romantic, strawberry-scented montage. I internally shook myself. One of the drawbacks of being an author was an overactive imagination.

I thought I could feel George's eyes on me, studying my face, but I didn't dare look up.

My stomach churned. This was the moment. We were alone and relaxed, without pig recordings or friends close by to disturb us. *You can do this, Hannah.*

I slowly lifted my eyes to find George focusing on the strawberry plant in front of her. I took a deep breath. *Here goes. Possible rejection incoming.*

"Hey, George," I said. George looked up at me expectantly, and I swallowed. "I feel like I didn't handle the conversation we started on the kayak, about us, very well. And that maybe I cut you off before you'd finished what you'd been planning to say." Everything—stomach, chest, throat—felt tight. But I had to keep going. I cleared my throat. "I know I said I had some reservations about starting a new relationship after just coming out of a long-term one. But I've been thinking about it more, and in reality, my past relationship was over long ago. Look, I, um...really like you, and if you're interested, I'm down to give it a go. But of course, it's totally okay if you're not." The words spilled out of me, too fast and jumbled. It was definitely not a romantic speech worthy of my novels—*"down to give it a go." Really, Hannah?*—but at least I'd said it.

Holding my breath and not moving, I studied George's face for her reaction. She was smiling, a gorgeous, tender smile that sent sparks shooting down my spine. That was a good sign, right? She started to lean in over the strawberry plant. Also promising.

"Hannah?" Her voice was low and gentle.

"Mmmm?" I said, trying to not get my hopes up.

George's gaze was intense.

"I'm trying to kiss you, but if I lean in any farther, I'm going to capsize into this strawberry plant. Can you meet me halfway?"

"Oh shit! Sorry." I laughed. With her words, all my worries about the strawberry field being too public a setting for any PDA flew away on the wind.

Maintaining contact with George's warm, brown eyes, I leaned in, excitement fizzing in my chest. I closed my eyes as our lips met. George tasted faintly of cherries, her mouth soft and warm. I moaned. *Damn.* I didn't think I could like cherries any more than I already did, but this was heaven. The kiss started off slow and gentle but quickly intensified, causing me to lose my balance. To avoid squashing the strawberry plant, I grabbed George's waist to steady myself, and she wobbled, nearly toppling backward.

"Sorry!" I murmured.

"Don't apologize." George's breath was warm on my face. She kissed me gently. "This wasn't"—another kiss—"the most sensible"—and another—"position to kiss you in." George pulled back softly. "I just couldn't help myself. And in case you hadn't gathered, I'm 'down to give it a go' too."

CHAPTER TWENTY-THREE

HANNAH

I LEANED against the kitchen counter watching George transfer the pastry dough onto the floured countertop. It had been two hours since we'd kissed over the strawberry plants, and this was not how I'd anticipated things would play out once we got back to George's apartment.

Mesmerized by the way George's hands worked the dough, an excited shiver of anticipation shot through my nervous system. We'd finally had the talk and agreed to "give it a go"—I cringed again at the memory of my clumsy wording—and now, except for Max who was snoozing on the couch, we were alone in George's apartment. I wanted those strong hands on me. My eyes drifted up George's forearms to the t-shirt that concealed her upper torso, and then down the curve of her back. And I wanted to explore her body desperately. I was *not* in the mood for baking a damn pie.

"I thought inviting me back to help bake the pie was just a ploy to have a bit more privacy?" I asked.

George smirked. "It was. All part of my evil plan to get some alone time with you."

"Well, all this baking is sending me very mixed messages," I said, walking over to George and placing my hand on the small of her back.

George dropped the dough on the counter and turned to me. Looking deep into my eyes, she leaned in and gave me a slow, sensual kiss. *Fuck.* I opened my mouth to deepen the kiss, but she pulled back.

"Is my message clear now?" George asked, her eyes twinkling. "But I do need to get the dough and filling made and put it in the fridge to chill first if cherry pie is going to be on the menu tomorrow, so we'll both just have to exercise some self-control."

The heat from George's body, her warm sweet breath on my face, and her soft lips so close to mine, was almost unbearable. Heat pooled in my core. I wrapped my arms around her back and pulled her in for another kiss.

"Uh-uh," George said, chuckling as she shook her head and gently disentangled herself from my grasp, leaving flour dusting my skin. "Self-control, remember?" She stared at me sternly, narrowing her eyes, and then returned to kneading the dough.

I groaned dramatically and slumped back against the counter, even more turned on than I was before.

"I guess I don't want to have to explain to Betty that I'm the reason there's no cake of the day," I said grudgingly. "Can I do anything to help?"

"Well, since you're such an expert at pitting cherries"—George grinned—"you can wash and pit four and a half cups of them."

I eyed the bag of freshly picked cherries and then looked back at George. "Okay. But while I might be an expert at pitting cherries with my mouth, I'm not so sure how to do it in a more, um...hygienic manner. Is there a special technique?"

"Hmmm," George responded, holding my gaze. She stepped closer to me again, sending a thrill of anticipation down my spine. *Self-control is overrated.*

"Yes, maybe save the mouth work—for now, at least," she said, her eyes lingering on my lips.

Instead of leaning toward me as I'd hoped, George bent down, opened a drawer, and pulled out a metal utensil. "You can use one of these."

George handed it to me slowly, like she was intentionally drawing out my torture.

I snatched it out of her palm, determined to pit those damn cherries as fast as I could.

I'd never been so focused in the kitchen in my entire life. A woman on a mission, I made quick work of the cherries. Once I was done George mixed them in with the other filling ingredients she'd prepped.

"Okay, that should do it." George dipped a spoon in the mixture and tasted it. "Yep, I think that's good. You wanna try it?"

I nodded, and she dipped another spoon in and carefully lifted it to my mouth.

I leaned in to taste it, opening my mouth, and she pulled the spoon away, a cheeky smile on her face.

"You...are such a damn tease, George O'Grady," I said, shaking my head.

She laughed and moved the spoon back toward me. I closed my eyes as cherries, with a hint of lemon and almond extract, exploded in my mouth. "Oh shit, that's incredible."

"That's just a taste of things to come," George murmured near my ear, her hot breath sending my nerve endings tingling. "You, wait there."

George put the cherry mixture in the fridge, washed her hands, and turned to me.

Her eyes were so intense they took my breath away. Everything around us seemed to fade. *Oh shit.* Desire and nervous anticipation flooded my body, sending my stomach somersaulting.

George stepped toward me, wrapped her arms around my waist, and pulled me to her.

"I think that's enough waiting," she murmured, delicately brushing my cheek with her fingers. "Goddamn, Hannah," she said, her voice husky. "You are so fucking gorgeous."

My breath hitched in my throat. "You are..." I struggled to put into words just how attractive I found George in every way, so I decided to show her instead, leaning forward and kissing her slowly and with purpose. I slipped my hands under her t-shirt so I could feel her warm, smooth back. George let out a low moan that vibrated through me, shooting heat directly to my core. Our kiss turned hungry, verging on desperate. George's hands slid under my top and caressed my back.

"Can I take off your shirt?" George asked between kisses.

"Mmmhmm," I hummed into her mouth, not wanting to break our kiss unless absolutely necessary. I briefly pulled back and took off my glasses so George could yank my top over my head.

"Yours too?" I asked breathlessly, tugging at her t-shirt, itching to feel more of George's bare skin against mine. She nodded, and I peeled off her t-shirt, my hands trembling in eagerness. Underneath, she was wearing a plain black sports bra, which emphasized her strong, sexy shoulders. I threw her top on the floor, and we pressed our bodies and lips together again. I reveled in the skin-on-skin contact. George felt strong, sturdy and incredibly sexy and my body pulsed with excitement at the thought of exploring her even more.

George pulled back for a second, her dark eyes glancing behind me.

"Is everything okay?" I asked.

She grinned, pulling me back into her. "Yes, I was just thinking it would be hot if you sat up there"—she nodded at the kitchen counter—"but as much as I'd love to be one of those buff romance novel love interests who can effortlessly lift you onto the countertop, I think I'd need to significantly amp up my gym routine before I'm up to the challenge."

I laughed. *That would be hot.* I stepped back, placing each hand on the counter behind me. "I think if you give me a boost, I'll be able to get up."

George placed her hands around my hips and lifted as I pushed up.

"There! Not super graceful, but at least it worked!" I said, smiling down at George, who was now an inch or two shorter than me. This position gave me a distractingly excellent view of her cleavage.

She stepped in between my legs, wrapped her arms around my waist, and we continued kissing. My hands roamed over her shoulders and upper back, finally getting to explore the part of her body I'd been lusting after for some time. I ran my fingers through her short hair, gently tugging it, and George moaned again.

"Can I?" George murmured, reaching around me so her hands were on the clasp of my bra.

"Yes," I said, biting my lip.

George unclipped my bra and flung it off. Her gaze lingered on my breasts before she pulled her bra over her head and stepped back between my legs, giving me another intense kiss.

"Is there anywhere you don't like to be touched?" I asked, taking the opportunity to admire George's round, firm-looking breasts and her dark-mauve nipples. My hands itched to caress them.

"No. You?" George rasped.

"No," I said, moving my hands down to cup her breasts, reveling in their heaviness. I bit my lip as I traced my fingers over her pebbled areolae and circled them around her nipples.

George trailed her hot mouth down my neck, making me giddy with need.

"Fuck," I whimpered.

George kept going until her mouth was on one of my nipples. I groaned with pleasure as she circled her tongue around it and then sucked it gently. I grasped her hair with my fingers as she moved to my other breast, giving it the same treatment.

My entire body vibrated with desire. While George continued her attention on my breasts, her hand glided down and unbuttoned my shorts. Her fingers slipped in between my shorts and my panties and I tightened my grip on her hair.

"Mmmm, you're so wet," George murmured.

She circled her fingers around my clit, her mouth still on my breasts, and all my nerve endings started firing at full speed.

"That feels incredible," I said, tugging her hair with more force than I'd intended as my arousal skyrocketed to intergalactic levels. George moaned again.

George's fingers slipped under the top of my panties

and then paused as she looked up at me, eyebrows raised in a silent question.

I nodded, biting my lip, and George dipped her fingers farther into my wetness and then back to my clit. The direct contact sent my whole body trembling. To steady myself, I moved my left hand to the counter. George kept going, increasing the speed and pressure of her fingers circling my clit and sucking harder on my right nipple.

Time lost all meaning as pleasure took hold, and then suddenly, I was leaning back on both hands to support my body as an intense orgasm rushed through me, making me arch my back and cry out in pleasure.

As the aftershocks subsided, I leaned forward, placing a hand on each of George's pink cheeks. She looked up at me, flushed and smiling, and my heart leaped. *Damn. I really like this woman. A lot.*

"That. Was. Amazing," I said, my breath still ragged as I gazed down at her. "Now, can you help me down so I can, um...do things to you?" Not the smoothest proposition, but with George, I was comfortable not being completely smooth.

George grinned, raising an eyebrow. "Do things to me? What sort of things?"

"Help me down, and you'll find out," I replied, a teasing tone to my voice.

George wrapped her hands around my waist and helped lower me to the floor.

I leaned in for another kiss, caressing George's upper body, enjoying the extra reach I had now that I was back on solid ground. "Since I'm shorter than you, I don't think you on the counter is going to work. Are you okay with the bed?"

George nodded, grinning, and I grabbed her hand and

tugged her toward the bedroom. Max got off the bed as soon as we entered, wisely making a quick exit, and I focused my attention back on the gorgeous woman next to me.

"Mmmm," I said appreciatively as I took in George's body, so strong and sexy. I stepped closer so our breasts touched, the soft warmth of the contact sending a shiver of desire through me. I kissed her softly again before jumping onto the bed and holding out my hand. "Come here, you. And shorts off, please."

George grinned, shaking her head, but obeyed, throwing off her shorts so that her plain black briefs were the only item of clothing remaining on her body. She grabbed my hand and jumped onto the bed with me. We faced each other, kneeling on the mattress, our thighs touching, and wrapped our arms around each other, pulling tight. I breathed in George's familiar, faintly woody, scent, melting at the sensation of our naked bodies pressed together. Being this close to George felt incredible. Intimate, comforting, and hot all at the same time. I lifted my head and began trailing kisses along George's collarbone, slowly making my way up her neck. When I reached her earlobe, I gently teased it with my teeth. George moaned, and I did it again, this time applying more pressure. She moaned louder. Encouraged, I continued my attention on her ear, lifting my hands to gently tug at her hair. George gripped me tighter.

"Can we take these off?" I murmured into her ear, tugging at her briefs.

"Yes," she responded breathlessly, and we both scrambled to take off our only remaining item of clothing.

My eyes hungrily dipped to the dark brown curls between George's legs as she tugged her underwear over her left foot. I bit my lip.

As soon as George was back on her knees, I pulled her

closer again. She grabbed my butt and groaned softly into my ear, the warmth of her breath setting my nerve endings tingling. "You drive me wild," she murmured before shifting her head to kiss me.

Deep and passionate, our kisses combined with George's words sent me dizzy with need. Continuing our hungry kisses, I caressed her left breast with my hand, my thumb running over her hard nipple. She let out a hum of enjoyment, which I took as a sign to double down on my approach, moving my other hand to give her right breast the same attention.

"Fuck, Hannah," George begged, panting in between kisses.

I trailed a hand down to her curls, cupping it between her legs. "Okay?"

"Yes," George groaned, and I dipped my fingers into her wetness, determined to make George groan even louder. Circling her clit with one hand and her nipple with the other, it wasn't long before my wish was granted.

"Oh fuck," George let out a guttural moan, our kisses now messy. George's hands roamed over my body, grabbing my butt and then my hair.

I shifted my hand so my thumb focused on her clit while two fingers teased her entrance and then dipped into her, over and over again.

"Do you wanna lie down?" I gasped, frustrated that our position didn't allow for deeper penetration. George lay back on the bed, and I scrambled between her legs, letting my tongue take over for my thumb and my fingers going deeper inside her. She smelled and tasted incredible. *I can't believe I'm actually doing this.*

George gripped my hair, and I increased my pace,

paying close attention to her moans to gauge what pressure and speed she liked most. *Fuck, this is hot.*

Finally, her muscles contracted around my fingers, and she writhed on the bed, muttering curses as she came. I continued, relishing the enjoyment I was bringing her, feeling like I might almost come again simply from bringing George pleasure, until she cried out, "Enough!" while laughing.

From between her legs, I looked up, taking in her slightly dopey, smiling face, and a rush of happiness shot over me.

"Come here, you," she said with affection. I clambered up to her, wiped my face, and gave her a long, soft kiss before lying down next to her and resting my head on her chest. We lay there for a few minutes in silence, George gently caressing my back while I listened to her heart beating. It felt so right, so natural, so comfortable. Even though it was only early evening, my eyelids were heavy, my body completely relaxed. This was where I was meant to be, who I was meant to be with.

A beeping sound broke me out of my reverie.

George jolted. "Shit, I better get the pie into the oven, and then we should really think about dinner."

I LET OUT A SATISFIED SIGH. Sex, a delicious Vietnamese chicken salad for dinner, more sex, and now snuggling with George in her bed was a pretty perfect way to spend the evening. But instead of being ready to nod off to sleep, our activities had sparked something in me—something I was very eager to get down on paper.

"George?"

"Yes?" she responded.

"I know this is weird, but would you mind if I borrowed your laptop to do some writing?" While I sometimes wrote on my phone, it was currently low on battery, and I was bursting to get the words down as quickly as possible.

"Are you serious? But it's so nice and cozy just lying here." To my relief, George didn't sound annoyed—just sleepy and a little surprised.

"I know. I'm sorry. I'm loving this too. But inspiration just hit me, and I know from past experience that if I don't get it down now, it might fade away."

George chuckled. "That's okay. I accept that artists must make sacrifices for their work, including ending one of the best spooning sessions ever when inspiration hits." She unwrapped her arms from around my waist, pushed herself up, and swung her legs over the side of the mattress.

A wave of guilt swept over me. "Don't worry about getting up. Just tell me where it is, and I can find it."

"No, it's fine. I need to put the pie away anyway. It should've cooled by now."

I followed her into the spare room, where she opened her laptop, entered her password, and set it up on the desk. "There you go. Can I get you anything? Tea, coffee, hot chocolate?"

I smiled, George's offer bringing back memories of the night she'd discovered me signing 841 copies of *The Realm of Furies* at Novel Gossip. "No, you should go back to bed. I'll be in when I've got this down."

Forty minutes later, I flopped back against George's desk chair. The words "[insert hot sex scene here]" in my manuscript had been replaced with the steamiest scene I'd ever written. And it had flowed out of me painlessly. No one could complain this one was wooden or lacking in chemistry. I chuckled to myself. While I had some regrets over not telling my parents about my success as an author, at least they'd never read this chapter.

I shut the laptop and snuck back into George's room, reclaiming my position next to her and wrapping my arms around her warm body. What a perfect day. I was just drifting off to sleep when Max, who was now lying at the foot of the bed, began snoring loudly. I rolled onto my right side so my ear with unimpaired hearing was pressed against the pillow. With just my left ear exposed, the snores weren't nearly as intense, and I relaxed into the warmth of George's body.

CHAPTER TWENTY-FOUR

HANNAH

"GOOD MORNING! How did your writing go last night?" George, who'd been putting something away in the fridge, shut the door. She walked up to where I was standing at the entrance to the kitchen, a giant smile on her face, and kissed my forehead.

"It went really well. I think you might be my muse." I wrapped my arms around her waist and looked up at her beaming face.

"Oh, really? Exactly what type of scene were you writing?" George's eyes narrowed suspiciously.

I giggled. "No comment." I was pretty sure when George read the book, she'd be able to work out exactly what scene I'd been writing, as I'd liberally incorporated last night's events.

There was a faint bang from downstairs.

"That must be the carpenters," George said. "Can we please revisit this conversation later today? I've got to head down to the café. But there's a pot of coffee on the stove, bread on the counter, and cereal and spreads in the cupboard. I've put an extra towel and toothbrush for you in the bathroom, and if you want to borrow any of my clothes, feel free. Just help yourself, and if you have any questions, you know where to find me." George kissed me gently on the lips, gave Max a head rub, and started to make her way toward the front door.

"Oh," she said, turning. "And I should check. Are you okay if I tell the café crew that we're dating?"

A warm glow lit my belly at George's use of the term *dating*, closely followed by surprise as her question sank in.

"Today?" I asked. It was exactly the sort of awkward conversation I'd put off until there was a pressing need to disclose the information.

"Unless you have any objections, that was my plan. I think it's better to just get it over and done with before people start gossiping or feel like we're trying to hide something."

I stood in silence, thinking it through. While my gut reaction was to delay as long as possible, George's reasoning was sensible. From what I'd overheard in Novel Gossip, Sapphire Springs's gossip grapevine was just as bad as the rumor mills in the small-town cozy mystery and romance novels I loved. Word we were dating would almost certainly spread like wildfire as soon as we were spotted in public, making any displays of affection, so it made sense for George to get out in front of it and control the message. And while we were moving quickly, I felt serious enough about George already that I wasn't worried about things fizzling out before they'd even begun.

"If you don't feel comfortable, that's okay, Hannah." George stepped back toward me, her eyes soft.

"No, no," I said, shaking my head and smiling. "That's fine. I think it's a good idea. I'll see you downstairs in a little bit."

I watched George leave with some regret, memories of last night flooding back. In a perfect world, I'd drag George back into bed, and we'd spend the day there. But we were adults with responsibilities, and today, those responsibilities involved us both working at the café. I poured myself some coffee, made toast with raspberry jam, and curled up on the couch next to Max to enjoy it. More bangs sounded from downstairs, and I wondered what the carpenters George had mentioned were up to. I hadn't noticed anything in need of repair.

Once I'd finished eating, I investigated George's wardrobe. The large quantity of button-down short-sleeve shirts and chinos made me chuckle. I couldn't go downstairs wearing them, or the café staff would immediately get suspicious before George had the chance to debrief them. I found a plain black t-shirt and charcoal-gray pants and decided they would do. They were slightly too baggy, and I had to roll up the bottom of the pants, but given loose-fitting clothing was in right now, no one would likely notice. At least the outfit didn't scream, *"George and I slept together last night, and now I'm wearing her clothes."* Although, Romina would already be in the kitchen, so the chances of her not noticing me exiting George's staircase were low. I frowned. Hmmm. Hopefully George was planning to talk to her early.

When I got out of the shower, George had messaged me.

Hope you've found everything okay. Romina is in a terrible mood this morning because the hollandaise sauce didn't emulsify, so I haven't told her about us yet. If you want to avoid her, there's a fire escape out the back room window you can use (but it's also okay if you just want to use the normal stairs!).

I smiled. Given Romina's tendency for taking cooking failures extremely personally, I didn't blame George for wanting to wait until she'd calmed down. I was also relieved there was an escape route that didn't involve coming face to face with Romina in a bad mood.

The banging downstairs intensified. Itching to find out what was going on, I threw on George's clothes, ran a comb through my hair, and went to the back room. Thankfully, the fire escape didn't look anywhere near as rickety as the ones attached to my old apartment building in Manhattan, and I made it down without a hitch. I'd been planning to enter Novel Gossip through the back door, but I spotted a gate that let out onto the cobblestone lane behind the café and decided that way was safer to stay under the radar. Knowing my luck, Ben would arrive early, or Romina would leave the kitchen and notice me sneaking in the back. I went through the gate, walked back around to Main Street, and then let myself in through the front door.

The source of the noise was immediately clear. Floating wooden shelves were being installed on the exposed brick wall of the café that wasn't already covered in bookshelves. Some of the shelves were long, others short, and they were being placed at different points up the wall, giving that section of Novel Gossip a cozy, eclectic vibe.

George, who was directing the carpenters on where to install the next shelf, turned around and grinned when she saw me.

I walked over to her and admired the shelves up close. "They look great! What are you planning to put on them?"

"Books, mainly. I might use the lower shelf for storing communal magazines, local flyers, that sort of thing. After talking to you, I realized just how noisy it can get here, so I looked into ways to reduce sound, and it turns out, happily, books can help. Since we can always do with more book-shelves, it seemed like a win-win solution. And I've ordered a rug for the armchair area and some rubber caps to put on the chair legs to stop them from scraping so loudly on the floor, which should hopefully help as well."

Warmth flooded my body. "Oh, wow. That's incredible, George."

I still hadn't found my damn hearing aid. I'd basically accepted that I needed to just buy a new one, but in between working at the café, writing, and spending time with George and her friends, I hadn't had a chance yet. But even with a hearing aid, I knew I'd still find the background noise at Novel Gossip a challenge. The fact that George had gone out of her way, and invested money, in trying to improve things for me and other people who were hard of hearing meant a lot.

"It's not much, but hopefully it will make it easier for you to hear things—and also for my patrons too. As the name Novel Gossip suggests, I want this to be a place where someone can enjoy a book by themselves or meet up with friends or family to chat, and if it's too noisy, doing either of those things will be challenging."

I resisted the urge to wrap my arms around George and beamed at her instead.

Her eyes dropped from my face to my body and lingered there for a moment. "My clothes look good on you," she murmured, sending my body humming with desire. *Damnit.* I hadn't thought about how challenging working with George while dating her might be, when all I wanted to do was to jump back into bed and continue what we'd started last night.

Eager for a distraction, I offered to get Hugo ready for the day. However, as I switched him on, checked the water levels, and made sure the steam wands were working, I couldn't help thinking about George. George had done so much for me, welcoming me into her café and friend group, giving up sleep to help me sign 841 books, inspiring me to write again, and now this. I wanted to do something to show her how grateful I was, to repay some of her kindness. But what?

In between helping George clean up after the carpenters left, serving customers once the café opened, and hoping that there was a slice of cherry pie left by the time I went on my lunch break, I spent the morning brainstorming ideas. In the early afternoon, a woman in her mid-seventies came in asking for fantasy recommendations for her teenage grandson. I leaped at the chance to assist and walked her to the fantasy section, where my eyes landed on a title by Chris Chen, and an idea hit me. Not only would the first book in Chris Chen's series be perfect for her grandson, but Chris Chen themself could be the perfect thing for George...

I'd never met Chris, but they lived in New York, and we'd exchanged multiple emails, raving about each other's work. They'd been very appreciative that I'd blurbed their book, which had come out recently, and I knew they were still in publicity mode for it, so perhaps they'd be willing to travel to Sapphire Springs to do an event at Novel Gossip. If Chris said yes, I'd have to deal with revealing my identity to yet another new person, but I was willing to push myself out of my comfort zone if it meant doing something nice for George. The first spare moment I had, I would email them.

GEORGE

"SHIT!" I muttered under my breath as my foot caught a backpack lying on the floor near a customer's chair, causing my heart to leap into my throat as I nearly lost balance. I steadied myself, apologized to the customer and started walking back to the kitchen.

Working with Hannah had been distracting before we'd gotten together. Now, with memories of last night swirling in my brain—Hannah topless on the countertop, arching her back in pleasure, Hannah's warm, naked body pressed against mine on the bed and then waves of orgasm washing over me—it was even more difficult to keep my mind on work. I'd already given two customers the wrong coffee order and now I'd almost tripped over holding a stack of dirty plates due to a flashback of me caressing Hannah's breasts. But while it worried me that my concerns our relationship might impact Novel Gossip may not have been completely unfounded, my feelings toward Hannah were far too strong for me to entertain any genuine doubts about us. Last night had been incredible and I had absolutely no regrets.

I glanced over at the newly installed floating wooden shelves and smiled. I also had no regrets about the shelves either, especially after seeing Hannah's reaction to them.

I made it back to the kitchen unscathed and left the dirty plates on the counter. Romina and Shane were busy cooking, Romina's face still set in a scowl. Now was definitely not a good time to talk to them about me and Hannah. I felt uncharacteristically nervous about how the team would react to the news. Not because we were a same-sex couple—I had no concerns about that. But they might be justifiably concerned our relationship could affect the team dynamics or feel it was inappropriate, given I was her boss. And some of the information that had persuaded me that I wasn't overstepping an ethical boundary—such as Hannah being a best-selling novelist who didn't actually need to work in a café—I couldn't share with the team. With Josie on board and Hannah still working most days, my staffing issues had finally been resolved. I just hoped this news didn't disrupt the team's equilibrium.

There was a lull in customers mid-afternoon. Romina and Shane had finished prepping for tomorrow and were cleaning the kitchen. Thankfully, Romina's mood had improved as the day wore on, so it seemed like an opportune time to call a team meeting. Josie wasn't working today, but I'd speak to her tomorrow. Hannah had already left. She'd offered to stay for the talk for moral support, but I got the strong impression she was dreading it, so I told her it was probably better she didn't attend, as the rest of the team might feel more comfortable airing concerns or asking questions if she wasn't there. The look of relief that splashed across her face when I said that convinced me I'd made the right decision.

"Ben, do you mind coming into the kitchen for a moment?" My hands were clammy, despite the air conditioning.

Ben followed me into the kitchen, and I cleared my throat.

"So, there's something I wanted to tell you," I said.

Romina continued scrubbing the stovetop, but I didn't take it personally. She liked to keep moving. Ben and Shane leaned back against one of the kitchen counters, Ben eyeing me with interest, Shane staring at his feet.

I took a deep breath. "Um, so I just wanted to let you know that Hannah and I have started dating. This won't affect anything at work—we'll keep it very professional—but I thought I should tell you all, given how fast gossip moves in this town. Does anyone have any questions?"

Romina, who'd moved on to wiping down the range-hood, snorted. "Is that it? You don't think we noticed she was wearing your clothes this morning? And how the two of you have been gazing at each other since Hannah started?"

I chuckled uncomfortably, dismay that we'd apparently been so obvious mixing with amusement at Romina's reaction. Trust Romina to tell it like it was. But at least she didn't appear to have any objections.

I glanced over at Shane. His expression betrayed no emotion. He looked at his watch, clearly eager to finish his shift. I guessed it wasn't surprising that a teenage boy wasn't too concerned with ethical issues or interested in his boss's love life. My gaze continued to Ben, who was smirking.

"Ben?"

"Well, all I can say is thank god, because it's been, quite frankly, painful watching the two of you acting all googly eyes over each other for the last two weeks without doing anything about it."

I laughed, taking his feedback as a stamp of approval, and my shoulders relaxed. That hadn't gone too badly at all. Any remaining concerns I had about the perceived power imbalance between me and Hannah evaporated.

CHAPTER TWENTY-FIVE

GEORGE

"I'LL JUST CHANGE out of my work clothes. Make yourself at home."

Hannah hung her bag on a hook next to the front door and disappeared into a room on the left. We'd officially been dating for a week now and it was my first time inside Hannah's house, so my curiosity was high. Holding the paper bag of takeout we'd picked up from Pok Pok on the way over here, I commenced some light snooping. *Well, she did tell me to make myself at home...*

I peered in the room opposite—a study. *This must be where the magic happens.* An antique wooden desk looked out over the cottage garden in the front yard, a laptop, notepad, and pen on top.

I still hadn't quite come to terms with Hannah being my favorite author. Thinking about it brought on *pinch me, this is kind of amazing* feelings mixed with a slight sense of unease. I'd shrugged it off, telling myself it'd take some time to get used to, especially since I knew Hannah only as Hannah, not H. M. Stuart, first.

A large bookcase covered the wall behind the desk. I wandered over, unable to resist examining its contents. Books about writing craft. A *lot* of fantasy books. But also an eclectic collection of other genres, from romance and thrillers to literary fiction and non-fiction books about gender theory and feminism. I smiled in approval.

Eager to get a feel for the rest of the house before Hannah returned, I dragged myself away from the bookshelves and continued my journey. The next room down was a small bathroom. I kept going and walked into a modest kitchen/dining area at the back of the house. The kitchen was, in my opinion, woefully inadequate. Occupying only one wall of the room, it had very limited counter and storage space and a small oven that looked sub-par. But the view from the large window of lush green trees and glimpses of the Hudson was anything but. I placed the takeout bag on the counter and stepped closer to the glass.

"The view is my favorite thing about this house," Hannah said behind me. "Being able to just walk onto my deck and breathe fresh air and be surrounded by nature is incredible. I didn't realize what I was missing out on until I moved here."

"It's pretty spectacular, but then, so is this view." I turned, grinning as I gazed at her. She'd changed into jeans and a white shirt, but even in the plain outfit, she glowed.

Hannah, smiling, rolled her eyes. "Should we crack open the wine? We could eat on the deck and enjoy the view some more."

"That sounds perfect given the week we've had."

The last week had been hectic. With the warmer weather there'd been an influx of tourists, which meant we'd been slammed at work. And outside work, Hannah and I couldn't keep our hands off each other which, while highly enjoyable, meant neither of us was getting as much sleep as usual. I also hadn't had any time to plan the July and August events calendar for Novel Gossip—something I'd promised myself I'd do this week. While I loved spending every spare minute with Hannah, my lack of progress on the events calendar reminded me of my initial reservations about embarking on a relationship with her. As amazing as it was, was it going to be at the expense of Novel Gossip?

I pushed down the thought as we pulled out plates and wine glasses and loaded up on pad thai, pad see ew, and stir-fried veggies, accompanied by a generous glass of dry Riesling each.

We'd vowed that, tonight, we would have a relaxing, no sex evening and go to bed at a decent hour. The plan had made perfect sense this morning when we both had to have extra coffee to counteract the effects of yet another late night of getting lost in each other's bodies. But my exhaustion was no match for my attraction to Hannah, and looking at her now, a wave of arousal washed over me. I inwardly shook myself. *Not tonight, George.*

Hannah led me into the next room, a cozy living room with a large glass sliding door leading out onto the back deck. The walls were lined with even more books. My gaze lingered on them for a moment, but the fragrant smell of lemongrass, galangal, and garlic trumped my desire to examine the bookshelves, and I followed Hannah out onto the deck. Hannah placed her food and wine on an aged round wooden table, and we sat down on rickety wooden chairs.

I took a gulp of wine, letting my body relax into the

chair, which was surprisingly comfortable despite its appearance. It was another perfect summer evening—warm enough to wear shorts and a t-shirt without being oppressively hot. And being out here, with Hannah, surrounded by fir and oak trees, was incredibly peaceful. I exhaled. After a busy week, this was exactly what I needed. I loved my apartment, but it couldn't offer me this type of escape.

"This is gorgeous," I said, smiling at Hannah, who looked as relaxed as I felt.

We wolfed down the food, chatting about the new books that'd been delivered today and two of our regulars, Jasper and Maya, who'd just gotten engaged. Jenny had practically danced into Novel Gossip to tell us the news. She was taking full credit for getting them together at Amanda's wedding last year.

We watched the birds fly away and the sky slowly change color as the sun began to set. I couldn't remember feeling this at ease with someone I'd only just started dating. With Alexis, it had taken me a couple months to be my true self around her. I'd been so in awe of her public persona it had been hard to see past that. But even though Hannah was my favorite author, she was also just...Hannah. Warm, funny, kind, interested in people and ideas. Even Mom, who'd had reservations about Alexis, would surely love Hannah. Which reminded me...

"Hey, by the way, my mom is coming to visit at the end of June. She'll be staying with me and will almost certainly hang around the café quite a bit, so while I know it is kind of early for a *meet the parents* situation, I'd love for you to meet her."

"Of course," Hannah said, smiling. While her smile looked genuine, she shifted on her chair, and I couldn't shake the feeling she was worried about something.

The sky was almost dark by the time we'd finished our food and wine.

Once we'd washed the dishes, we collapsed on the couch.

"In light of our vow, do you feel like watching something?" Hannah asked.

While I was tempted to make a bad joke about screwing the vow to see how Hannah would react, I restrained myself. *It's just one night, George. You can do it.* "What do you feel like?" I asked.

"*Drag Race?* I haven't seen the latest season yet. Or for something completely different, I heard the Beckham documentary is good." Hannah grinned. "I have to warn you, my viewing preferences are not super highbrow."

"No judgment here. I binged an entire season of *The Real Housewives of Beverly Hills* when that bad snowstorm in January shut everything down. Let's start with *Drag Race.*"

We were ten minutes in when Hannah looked at me, slightly warily. I paused the show, concerned.

"Is everything okay?"

"Um, would you mind turning on the subtitles if it's not too annoying for you? I'm just struggling to hear everything."

"Of course." I flicked on the closed captions and relaxed back onto the couch, wondering why Hannah had seemed nervous about asking me the question. I frowned. Maybe she didn't feel as comfortable with me as I did with her. I hoped not.

"Thank you." She snuggled in next to me, and I focused on enjoying Hannah's body pressed against mine and the queens' antics on *Drag Race,* pushing aside my concerns.

After two episodes, we decided to call it a night and began getting ready for bed.

Like the rest of her house, Hannah's bedroom was small, just big enough for a queen-sized bed, two small side tables, and a dresser. There were no bookshelves to distract me as I tried not to watch Hannah change into her pajamas. Hannah turned to me, looking adorable in red silk shorts and a matching short-sleeve button-down bed shirt. An image of unbuttoning her top slowly appeared in my mind. I shook it off. *Maybe you should take a cold shower.*

"George."

I focused on her face, and my heart dropped when I realized she was chewing on her lip. She looked nervous again. What was going on?

"Yes?" I pulled on my boxers.

"Remember how you said you were interested in having more author events at Novel Gossip?"

My body relaxed. This line of conversation was intriguing but didn't sound too concerning. Although, it did bring on a twinge of guilt about my failure to organize any events this week.

"Yes?" I tilted my head, putting on my best encouraging expression to try to put Hannah at ease.

"Well... I hope you don't mind—I didn't want to tell you in case they said no—but I reached out to Chris Chen to ask if they'd be interested in doing one at Novel Gossip."

I froze. *Hannah knows Chris Chen and invited them to Novel Gossip?*

"They said they could come Thursday if that would work? They can do afternoon or evening. I know that's soon, but their schedule is pretty full with book launch activities. Would you be interested?"

"Are you fucking serious?" I stared at Hannah in shock.

"Yes. Is that okay?"

My heart ached at the nervous waver in her voice. I walked over to her and wrapped my arms around her waist. "Of course it's okay. It's incredible! Chris Chen is my second-favorite author—after you, of course." I ran my thumb down Hannah's cheek and kissed her. "And Thursday is perfect. It gives us enough time to get organized and get the word out."

"Okay, good." Hannah smiled at me.

My chest expanded as I gazed into Hannah's eyes. Goddamn, she was wonderful. I'd just been worrying about my lack of events, and she'd organized one for me. But Hannah's reticence at raising certain topics of conversation with me was concerning. I desperately wanted Hannah to feel as comfortable with me as I did with her and to be able to talk to me about issues that were bothering her.

"Hey, babe. Is everything okay?" I asked, my voice low. "I got the impression you were nervous when you asked me to turn the subtitles on earlier and again just then when you told me the amazing news about Chris. You know you can ask or tell me anything, right?"

Hannah gave me a soft, slightly ashamed smile. "I know. I'm sorry." She exhaled. "I usually feel so comfortable with you, but I clearly still have some hang-ups from living with Tania. She used to complain about me putting the subtitles on because she found it distracting. And there were a few times when I tried to do something special for her but totally missed the mark. And she wasn't afraid of letting me know." Hannah sighed. "Sorry, I know you're not Tania, but I think I've still got some residual anxiety hardwired in from that relationship that'll take a while to disappear."

I smiled back at her, relieved, and then leaned closer to her, tucking a stray hair behind her ear.

"I get it. These things take time to get over. And now that I understand where it's coming from, hopefully it will make things easier for both of us," I said.

"Damn, George O'Grady. Could you get any more perfect?" Hannah asked softly.

She took off her glasses, placed them on the side table, and turned back to me.

I leaned in, kissing her again, my hands finding their way under her silk pajama top and caressing the bare skin of her back. Our kisses deepened in intensity, our mouths hungry for more.

"If we keep this up, some vows are going to be broken tonight," I mumbled in between kisses.

Hannah gently pushed me down on the bed, straddling me. She bent over, her lips tracing my jawline to my earlobe. She gently tugged at it with her teeth, her warm breath sending electricity shooting down my body.

"Well, in the scheme of vows that could be broken, I think this is one of the better ones. That is, if you're feeling up for it, of course," Hannah murmured near my ear.

"I am always up for it," I said, my breath ragged, as I flipped her on her back and kissed her collarbone, my hands running over her soft, warm skin. All my exhaustion had vanished, replaced with pulsing desire.

"How do you feel about toys?" Hannah panted.

I grinned. I loved that Hannah felt comfortable enough with me to raise the topic. "I feel very positively about toys. What were you thinking?"

"Well, I have a selection...in the gray box under my bed."

I rolled off Hannah and flung myself over the side of the bed, just managing to keep my lower body balanced on the sheets. I peered under the bed, spotting the box just a few inches away. I gave it an excited yank and nearly fell off the mattress.

Feeling like a kid opening presents on Christmas morning, my body buzzed with anticipation as to what would be in Hannah's sex toy box.

After my near fall, I carefully pulled the box, which was promisingly heavy, onto the bed and opened the lid. Hannah lay on her side, a tentative smile on her face as she watched me explore its contents.

Dildos in various sizes and colors, a harness, and a number of vibrators, ranging from small bullet and suction models to a gigantic magic wand, handcuffs, silk ties, a blindfold, and feathers. *Wow.* I was not expecting such a collection. I took a deep breath, trying not to get too excited at the thought of trying out all the toys with Hannah.

Something at the bottom of the box caught my attention. "Um, Hannah, what's this for?" I pulled out a small, curved piece of rose-gold plastic with a very thin tube and a tiny cone-shaped bit of silicon at the end, inspecting it curiously. Was the cone thing the world's tiniest vibrator? I frowned. It didn't look very appealing or easy to control, with miniature switches that would be difficult to maneuver while in the throes of passion.

"Oh my god!" Hannah yelled, snatching it out of my hand and staring at it with wide eyes. I jumped, nearly losing balance and toppling into the box. "How the hell did that get in there?"

All sorts of random explanations ran through my head. It was for an unusual kink that Hannah was ashamed of. One of her toys had broken, and this was a missing part.

"Um, what exactly is it?"

"It's my hearing aid," Hannah said, grinning. "It won't

give you an orgasm, but it'll help me hear yours even louder —once I recharge it, that is."

I straddled her, picking the hearing aid out of her hand and placing it on the side table, and then leaned down so my face was only inches from hers. "Well, in that case, I'll just have to focus on making *you* come tonight—so loudly the whole damn town will hear it."

CHAPTER TWENTY-SIX

HANNAH

I WALKED toward Novel Gossip's front door, fiddling with my hearing aid, checking it was working even though there was no reason to think it wasn't. I'd finally gotten used to wearing it again. The first few days, I'd been very conscious of my hair brushing against the microphone and how loud certain sounds, like my fingers typing on the keyboard and birds chirping, were. But touching it was a nervous habit.

Ouch. Pain shot up my leg as I walked into a chair. Usually, I could navigate Novel Gossip on autopilot, but we'd rearranged the tables and chairs so they were facing a raised platform with two armchairs and a small round table under the newly installed floating shelves, and I was more than a little preoccupied.

When I'd reached out to Chris, I'd convinced myself that I'd be fine meeting them in person as H. M. Stuart. It was worth it to do something nice for George. But now that the moment was imminent, nausea rocked my stomach. I'd be a disappointment. I'd clam up, get all flustered, and not be able to hold a conversation. Anything that came out of my mouth would be awkward and weird. Meanwhile, Chris would be everything I was not. To calm myself, I silently walked through the conversation topics I'd brainstormed earlier, since it was inevitable that Chris and I would talk tonight. At least George would be by my side most of the evening.

I looked out of the window. George had picked Chris up from the train station, dropped their luggage at Willow Inn, a gorgeous bed and breakfast near the river, and had just pulled up in front of Novel Gossip.

As George and Chris began walking toward Novel Gossip, I took a deep breath, plastered a smile on my face and opened the front door.

My fears were completely unfounded. A few inches taller than me, in their late twenties with short black hair, black jeans, heavy black boots, and a black t-shirt with a funky cut, Chris's look screamed *cool writer from NYC* vibes. But while their outfit was intimidatingly cool, Chris themself was anything but. They were warm, friendly, and also a little bit awkward in a way that put me immediately at ease. When George excused herself to help finish setting up the café for the event, I was relieved that I didn't find it a struggle to make conversation with Chris at all. We covered some publishing news—a few big editors had recently changed publishing houses, and we bemoaned that a small New York press had been acquired by one of the *Big Five* publishers. In more positive news, Cobble Hill Books, a beloved independent Brooklyn bookstore had managed to evade closure after their landlord threatened to almost double their rent. Heartwarmingly, the local community had banded together and pressured the landlord into renewing their lease with only a modest rent increase.

"No problem if you don't feel like talking about it—I

totally understand—but if you do…how's your current book going?" Chris asked with an open smile.

"If you'd asked me a month ago, I would've probably curled up into a ball, but I actually sent off the first sixty thousand words to my editor this morning, and I'm on track to finish it in the next week or so, which is a huge relief." It had felt amazing this morning to hit *send* on that email.

"Oh that's awesome! Your editor is Tania Haynes, isn't it? What's she like? She sounds super intimidating. I saw her speak at an industry event a few weeks ago, and she seemed like a real gun. But not someone you'd want to get on the bad side of."

Surprised at just how little the mention of Tania's name affected me, I smiled. Chris knew my first name was Hannah, but my real last name hadn't come up, so even if they knew that Hannah Taylor was in the process of divorcing Tania after discovering she was sleeping with a very talented twenty-three-year-old romantasy author, whom Tania also worked with, they probably hadn't made the connection.

"She's a very talented editor," I said diplomatically. And it was true—she was. It felt good to be able to see Tania more objectively, not colored by hurt and emotions. Tania was ten years older than me, confident, whip smart and one of the best editors in the business. And she'd been one of the first people who'd seen the promise in my writing. Looking back, it wasn't surprising that I'd fallen for her, ice queen vibes and all. "But I've actually changed editors. I'm now with Michael Burrows. The current book I'm working on is our first together, so it's very early days."

While I'd been able to talk about Tania without my anxiety rearing its head, my throat tightened at the reminder that Michael might currently be reading the first part of my manuscript. I was confident that it was some of my best work, but what if Michael disagreed? What if he didn't share my vision for the book or wasn't able to provide the sort of constructive feedback I needed to make it even better? For all Tania's failings, she'd been instrumental in elevating my manuscripts so they reached their full potential. Could Michael do the same?

"Oh wow, changing editors must be hard. But I've heard good things about Michael." I appreciated that Chris didn't ask what was behind the change. "And your latest book is launching next week, isn't it? Are you going to do an event here as well? It's a great venue."

I blinked at Chris. I'd been so swept up in finishing my current book, spending time with George, and the rest of my new life in Sapphire Springs that the release date for *The Realm of Furies* had crept up on me. But they were right—it was next week. One benefit of being a reclusive author was that I wasn't required to do much in the weeks leading up to my book's release. It was in stark contrast to Chris, who was in the midst of a busy schedule of publicity events and media interviews for their latest release.

"Yeah, it's releasing Tuesday, but I'm not having a launch event," I said. My stomach fluttered with nerves. Hopefully it was as well-received as my last *Realms* book. I didn't want to think about what would happen if it bombed.

"Oh, of course. Sorry, I forgot you keep a low profile," Chris said.

I changed the conversation topic onto Chris's latest release, which I raved about. I'd just realized that this had been a poor choice of topic, as Chris looked as awkward as I usually felt when people said positive things about my books, when George walked over to us.

"The audience should start arriving in the next few

minutes, so if you want to use the restroom or would like a drink or something to eat before we start, just let me know."

Chris ran their hand through their hair. "Okay, thanks. Where is the restroom?"

George gave Chris directions and turned to me as they disappeared down the hall behind the kitchen.

"How are you doing?" George put a hand on my lower back. "It looks like you aren't short on conversation." I'd confided in George about my nerves earlier.

"Surprisingly good. Chris is great and way less intimidating in person than they were in my imagination." I smiled and gave George a quick kiss on the cheek.

"Ha! That's the way I felt about you too." George gave me a squeeze. "Remember how stressed out I was about the prospect of meeting H. M. Stuart?"

"Little did you know you'd already met 'him'." I laughed at the memory. It felt like months rather than weeks ago.

George squeezed my hand. "Hey, thanks again for organizing this. I think it's going to be a really good night."

The first of our guests started to trickle in. Within fifteen minutes, the rows of seats were nearly full. The time we'd spent putting flyers up around Main Street and in neighboring towns had paid off. I jumped behind the counter to serve drinks while Chris and George, who was tonight's interviewer, took their seats on the stage.

Watching Chris, so poised and impressive, answering each of George's questions thoughtfully and clearly, I couldn't help feeling a little envious. I wished that I had the confidence required to get up in front of a crowd and talk about my books. But even the thought made my insides clench. As much as I'd like to be like that, I wasn't. And, when it came down to it, I was perfectly content with my quiet, under-the-radar, existence in Sapphire Springs.

My gaze drifted to George, enthusiastically asking Chris another question, and my chest filled with warmth. I still found it hard to believe just how well things had worked out. An amazing girlfriend, a new job and friends I loved. My manuscript was nearly done, and unless *The Realm of Furies* flopped next week, Barb's future was hopefully secure, at least for now.

CHAPTER TWENTY-SEVEN

GEORGE

MAX and I both bounded down the hallway to greet Hannah.

"Hey, babe." I kissed her. "How did your writing go?"

"Good! I've only got a couple of chapters to review, and then I'm done." Hannah grinned and wrapped her hands around my neck, drawing me in for another kiss.

I placed my hands on her hips, savoring the sensation of her soft lips on mine. Hannah hadn't been scheduled to work today, so I hadn't seen her since she'd left my apartment this morning, and I'd missed her all day. I knew when Mom arrived tomorrow afternoon, I wouldn't be able to spend as much time with Hannah as I was used to, and I was already bracing myself for it.

But despite my apprehension, I was excited for Mom to meet Hannah. Mom had had mixed feelings about Alexis, but I was confident she'd love Hannah. How could she not?

"That's awesome. Writing a whole book, a fantasy book at that, in basically a month is an enormous achievement," I said. "I can't wait to read it. You know, if you do want an extra set of eyes on it before you send the rest off to your editor..."

Hannah glared at me, shaking her head, but her lips were twitching. "How many times do I have to tell you that until I get edits back from Michael and have fixed the manuscript up, you're not reading it? As much as I value your feedback, I also want you to read a half-decent book."

I held up my hands in mock defeat. "Fine, fine. I'll wait. It was worth a try."

The glare softened, and she clapped her hands. "Okay, should we get this strawberry tart started? I'm assuming we'll need to chill the dough."

"Spot on, chef." I laughed, impressed at how quickly Hannah was picking up baking. We'd started making the cake of the day together on the evenings it was my turn, and I hoped this would become a tradition. There was something so relaxing about us both being in the kitchen, working together to create something. Sometimes we'd just chat about random news articles or books we'd read, but my favorite was when we'd talk about the chapter Hannah was currently writing, and I'd help brainstorm plot points. Creative multitasking, in the best way possible. It was pretty incredible to know I was contributing to the development of my favorite series, even if the author wouldn't let me read her drafts.

"What time is your mom coming tomorrow?" Hannah asked as she sifted flour for the pastry dough.

An uncertain note in her voice made me look up at her. She was biting her lip, which by now I knew meant she was either nervous or she wanted to kiss me. Given the context, it was safe to assume this one signaled nerves.

"Her train should arrive by six. How are you feeling

about meeting her? I know it's a bit weird this early in a relationship, but I think you'll get along well."

Hannah smiled weakly. "No, I'm sure it will be really nice. I just don't have a great track record with parents. As you know, I'm not exactly close to my own. And Tania's parents were extremely wealthy New York socialites who I had very little in common with." She grimaced. "I never knew what to say to them. I always suspected they thought Tania could have done better than me."

I bent over and kissed her forehead. "If they thought that, they were sorely wrong."

"Hmmm," Hannah said, clearly unconvinced.

I pulled back a few inches and held her gaze. "Hey, it'll be fine. To be honest, I don't think you'll have a lot in common with my mom either—she's not a big reader, loves gossip, and has terrible taste in television." I chuckled, thinking of her obsession with *The Bold and the Beautiful*.

"Well, our tastes aren't exactly highbrow either," Hannah said smiling.

"True. But she's a good person and excels at small talk, so you won't need to worry about awkward silences. I think you'll like her, even if she is very different from us." I wrapped my arms around her waist and smiled at her. "Perhaps I'll get you two to bake a cake for a bonding experience, just like how Mom and I used to bond over cooking when I was a kid."

Hannah's face softened. "Okay, sign me up for a bonding baking session. At least it's not kayaking or cherry picking—all things we've established I don't excel at. The last thing I want to do is make a bad first impression in front of your mom."

"I don't think that's possible," I said, pulling my arms tighter around her. "Hey, I know it's not the best timing with Mom coming, but I was thinking we should do something tomorrow to celebrate the launch of *The Realm of Furies* and also the fact that your new book is almost done."

"Oh, you don't need to worry. You'll be busy with your mom and everything."

"Hannah," I said gently. "I want to celebrate your successes. I know you like to keep things low-key, so I wasn't planning anything too extravagant. Perhaps we could finish work a little earlier than usual, and have a glass of champagne down at Rivers' Edge before Mom arrives?"

Hannah's face broke into a warm smile. "That sounds amazing. It's a date."

I grinned. "Excellent. Now, let's get to work on that strawberry tart. If we make good time, we might be able to fit in a few other activities tonight."

I leaned in, giving Hannah a slow, sensual kiss so she had no doubt as to the type of activities I had in mind.

HANNAH

"HAVE YOU SEEN MY PHONE?"

The strawberry tart was cooked, we'd enjoyed a mouth-watering pesto pasta dish George had whipped up, and we were getting ready for bed and the other "activities" George had alluded to.

George, squeezing toothpaste on her toothbrush, looked at my reflection in the bathroom mirror and frowned. "I think the last time I saw it was in the kitchen?"

I wandered out to the kitchen, enjoying the lingering scent of strawberries and freshly cooked pastry, and found my phone under a dish towel on the countertop. I must have flung it there after washing up a couple of hours ago.

On autopilot, I tapped the screen, not expecting to see any notifications.

I frowned. Six missed calls and twenty-three unread messages. My chest tightened. *What the...?*

Oh god, I hope something hasn't gone wrong with the book launch tomorrow. Or Barb? Or Mom and Dad?

I had two missed calls from my parents, one from my agent, Emma, and three from "friends" from New York who I hadn't heard from in months. It was such a random selection of people. *Why the hell did they all decide to call me today?*

I clicked on my messages, hoping they'd shed more light on what was going on.

My stomach plummeted as I scrolled through the messages, most of which were from New York friends or acquaintances.

> I can't believe you never told us! I love your books. We should catch up. I'd love to hear how you are doing xxx Mel

> Hannah! I just saw the article! How have you managed to keep this a secret from us all this time? Do you want to grab a drink next week? x Dana

My heart started pounding. What the hell was this article?

Hands shaking, I Googled my name and clicked on the top news article, titled "Best-selling author H. M. Stuart's real identity revealed."

Reclusive author H. M. Stuart took the fantasy world by storm four years ago with the publication of the first book in her Realms *series,* The Realm of Thunder. *Since then, her novels have been climbing the NYT best sellers list, and interest in the author's identity has grown. A day before the publication of her fourth book, it has been revealed that H. M. Stuart is the pen name of Hannah Taylor, graduate of NYU's English Literature program and daughter of Professor Douglas Taylor and Professor Genevieve Taylor of Chicago University. Ms. Taylor filed for divorce from her wife, editor Tania Haynes, in March. Divorce proceedings have not yet been finalized...*

A photo of me accompanied the article. *It has been revealed?* Bile rose in my throat.

As it sank in that my carefully guarded identity was no longer private, my throat constricted. *Shit. Shit. Shit.*

Tears welled in my eyes and I let out a strangled sob, my mind racing.

Who the hell had revealed my identity? Possibilities raced through my mind. Tania? Surely not. She had her failings, but she wasn't vindictive—at least, I didn't think so.

I'd gone for so long without anyone finding out. Could it have been someone who'd learned my identity recently? My new editor, Michael? I didn't know him very well, so that was possible. Chris? I couldn't imagine them betraying my confidence. George or Blake? I shook my head firmly, annoyed at myself for even considering the possibility. No, they would never do this.

My hands still trembling, I checked my emails to see if they could provide any further insight into what the hell had happened. An email from my parents asking me to call them. And another from Michael from earlier today. Hoping it might shed some light on what was going on, I clicked it.

Hi, Hannah,

I've read the first part of the manuscript you sent through. Would you be free to meet up to discuss? There's lots to talk about. I'm in the office Tuesday to Thursday.

Thanks,

Michael

Fuck. That didn't sound good. If Michael wanted an extensive rewrite—or worse, if he wanted me to start again—we might miss the deadline to have it ready for publication in March of next year. And if that happened, then Barb's future at her nursing home would be in peril. While George paid above minimum wage, even if I worked full-time at Novel Gossip, I wouldn't be able to bring in enough to pay the bills. *Shit.*

First my identity being leaked, and now this. My chest tightened further as a stabbing pain took hold, and suddenly, I was gasping for air. I tried to regulate my breathing, doing my best to inhale slowly, hold, and then breathe out, just like my therapist had taught me, but it didn't work. I sunk to the kitchen floor, wheezing. Pins and needles pricked my face.

"Hannah?" George called. Footsteps followed. "Shit! Are you okay? What's wrong?"

George crouched down beside me, studying my face with concern. "Do you need me to call Blake or an ambulance?"

I shook my head. "No," I managed to say, my voice strangled. "Panic attack."

"Would it help if I held you?" George's voice was calm and low.

I nodded, and she sat next to me, wrapping her arms around me. Focusing on the warmth of her body, her comfortingly familiar woody scent, this time mixed with baked goods, the pain in my chest subsided, and my breathing and heart rate started to drop. I still didn't feel like myself, but at least I could breathe.

"Do you want to talk about it?" George asked after a few minutes.

Feeling like I'd burst into tears if I explained what had happened, I pulled up the news article instead and gave it to George.

George's brow furrowed as she scanned it. "Oh shit!"

"I've got a whole heap of messages and missed calls from people who saw the article, including my parents," I said, my voice wavering.

"I'm so sorry, Hannah," George said, handing my phone back to me.

"And to make matters worse, I also got an email from my editor about the first part of the manuscript I sent him that sounds really ominous. He wants to meet in person because there is 'lots to talk about.' He must hate it." Tears pricked my eyes.

"Hey, we don't know that—"

My phone, still on silent, lit up with a call from Tania. *Just what I need right now.*

We both stared at it. I was in no state to speak to her, so I let it go to voicemail.

"Is there anything I can do to help?" George asked once Tania's name had disappeared.

I shook my head. "I don't think so."

Thoughts tumbled incoherently through my mind as I struggled to process what had happened and the implications. My carefully guarded pseudonym was now public and had already attracted the type of attention I'd been so desperate to avoid. My parents knew. Someone had betrayed my trust. And my new editor hated my manuscript.

My immediate instinct was to withdraw—to ignore the calls and emails, give up on my manuscript, and hide away in George's apartment for the foreseeable future, with only George and Max for company. But even in my distressed state, I knew that wasn't a real solution. It wouldn't help me in the long run, and giving up on my manuscript sure as hell wouldn't help Barb.

Perhaps my lawyers could take down the article. Maybe we could even sue for breach of privacy or something? I sighed. I had to accept that the ship had already sailed. Even if we took down the article, the news would have spread, and it would be impossible to undo that.

The most practical course of action, rather than burning money on legal fees, was probably to sit down with Emma and my publicist to work out how best to limit the exposure. The three of us, all in the same room, could surely come up with some ideas on how to mitigate the damage. While I didn't love the idea of returning to Manhattan, getting this addressed effectively and making sure my publisher took this seriously trumped those concerns. A teleconference didn't have the same weight as showing up to a formal business meeting.

I could also kill two birds with one stone and meet with Michael as well. Meeting face to face might make it easier to convince him why my manuscript wasn't as bad as he thought. If he didn't see it, then—and my stomach flipped at the thought—I'd have to try to get Tania back as an editor. She'd understand my manuscript, and as awkward as working with her again would be, that would be preferable to scrapping it and having to start again or trying to convince my publisher to find me a new editor. I didn't have time to do either. And if I had to go begging to Tania, persuading your ex to work with you after she cheated on you and you ditched her definitely seemed like the sort of conversation you needed to have in person. I winced at the thought.

George and I sat in silence on the kitchen floor for a few minutes as my mind raced, George stroking my hair. I was desperate to get on top of the situation, to regain some control over this part of my life that had suddenly gone off the rails, and going back to the city to confront my problems seemed like the best way forward. I'd channel my character Esmae and fight for my privacy, my manuscript, and Barb.

"George," I said, my voice croaky.

"Yes?"

George looked at me with such concern and care that guilt spiked in my throat. I inhaled shakily and then let out a breath. As much as I hated the thought of leaving George, I needed to face my issues head on.

"I'm really sorry, but I think I need to go to New York to try to sort this all out. Will you be okay without me for a few days?"

"Of course," George said, her voice low and full of understanding. "Take as long as you need."

CHAPTER TWENTY-EIGHT

HANNAH

I ARRIVED in Manhattan late morning, after a torturous train ride during which I scrolled through the growing number of news articles and social media posts about me, ignored the influx of messages from acquaintances who were suddenly very eager to reconnect, obsessed about who could have revealed my identity, and set up meetings with Michael today and my publicist and Emma tomorrow. I'd been disappointed they couldn't meet with me sooner, but in fairness to them it was incredibly short notice. On the plus side, the article had been out for over sixteen hours, and no one in Sapphire Springs appeared to have seen it or the ensuing media coverage. Or if they did, they apparently didn't care, as I hadn't received messages from my new friends. But that one piece of good news didn't do anything to relieve the heavy, tight feeling in my stomach and chest or the gray cloud that had been hanging over me since last night.

I'd been hoping my hotel room would be ready early so I could crawl into bed and try to sleep, but it wasn't. Standing in the hotel lobby, I glanced at my phone to check the time, ignoring the new notifications that had appeared since I'd looked last. I was meeting Michael at 2 p.m., which left me with almost three hours to kill. Since hiding in my room wasn't an option, I decided to jump on the subway and have lunch at one of my favorite cafés in the West Village, an Australian-run joint with delicious, fresh food and coffee that was almost as good as George's. My appetite was non-existent, but I needed to eat something, and at least going to the Village would keep me busy. I left my suitcase at the hotel, and to reduce the risk of being recognized— more photos of me had been appearing online, including a particularly unflattering one of me frowning at a fundraising gala with Tania—I put on a cap and sunglasses and headed out.

I WALKED down the dirty stairs to the subway station and was hit with a rush of dank, hot air as a train flew past. *I have not missed this at all.* A giant rat scurried away as I walked down the platform. *At ALL.* Thankfully, it wasn't long before a B train appeared, and fifteen minutes later, I was in the West Village, strolling down the leafy green streets lined with red-bricked apartment buildings, brownstones, cafés, bars, and restaurants. I hadn't thought about it when I'd decided to come down here, but the Village held a lot of Tania-related memories for me. We'd had our first date at an Italian restaurant I'd just passed, sitting on the sidewalk, and our first kiss was at Cubbyhole, a tiny, colorful queer bar that was a New York institution. Our wedding rings had been made by a jeweler on Bleeker Street. But to my surprise, these memories weren't painful anymore. They were part of my life that felt very much in the past, almost as if they'd happened to a different person.

A cute white picket fence marking the café's claim to the sidewalk and blue awnings signaled that I'd reached my destination. I was early enough that there wasn't a wait for a table, and I managed to grab one outside. Fighting the urge to check my phone again, I focused on the menu instead, deciding on an avocado smash and a latte.

While I waited for my order to arrive, I mentally prepared for my meeting with Michael.

I was very much open to constructive criticism—thoughtful feedback I could take onboard and use to make my manuscript even better. But based on the email he'd sent me, I was convinced Michael was going to rip it to shreds or tell me I needed to ditch the whole thing. My pulse increased as I brainstormed possible criticisms Michael might have and how I could respond. I needed to be prepared to advocate for myself and my manuscript. I started to go down a rabbit hole, imagining biting comments Michael could make and decided that this line of thought was counterproductive. Much better to focus on positive things: George, my new friends, and life in Sapphire Springs. I smiled, already feeling lighter.

My life really had done a 180 since I'd met George. I'd been so unhappy when I left New York, still devastated by the breakup, lonely and struggling with writer's block, and now my life in Sapphire Springs was everything I could have dreamed of. And it was all thanks to George. If I hadn't walked into Novel Gossip that day and spoken to George, I wouldn't have an almost-completed manuscript, an amazing new group of friends, or the strong connection I now felt to the Sapphire Springs community. I also wouldn't have a supportive girlfriend, who in the past twelve hours alone had comforted me through my panic attack, made me pancakes for breakfast to celebrate release day, and drove me to the station. Honestly, it all felt too good to be true.

Was it too good to be true?

A sense of unease grew inside me. I took a deep breath. *Hannah, you're just going through a rough twenty-four hours. Now is not the time to start overanalyzing things and manufacturing problems where there aren't any.* But rationalizing my worries didn't make them go away. Being back in New York had brought with it memories of my relationship with Tania, and while they were no longer painful, they had reminded me of the problems we had. And one of the many problems was that I'd become too reliant on Tania. Like George, she'd been the more extroverted of the two of us, and I'd basically adopted her friend group. And then, when I discovered Tania was cheating on me, my life had imploded. I'd lost my ability to write and my friends. Was I falling into exactly the same trap?

All my new friends, and my job, I had because of George. She'd sparked my passion for my current manuscript, inspired the spicy scenes, and helped me work through issues when I was stuck. Was that really healthy? If we broke up, would I go back to being a friendless, unemployed author with writer's block, stressing about how to pay Barb's and my bills?

I sighed. I was pretty sure this whole train of thought was because of my anxiety, but the worries suddenly felt very real. Perhaps I should pull back from George to protect myself. We had been moving very quickly.

My latte arrived. Since thoughts of George and Sapphire Springs didn't seem to be alleviating my anxiety either, I tried to follow my therapist's advice and practice mindfulness instead, focusing on the smooth, slightly nutty flavor of the latte and the warm sensation as it flowed down my throat. For a moment, it seemed to be working, but then my phone pinged, and my concentration shattered, replaced with a swirl of theories about who could have messaged me. My parents, Tania, a media outlet... The hypotheticals felt worse than not knowing, so I picked up my phone. To my relief, it was a message from Chris.

> Hey, I just saw that article. I'm so sorry. That's really shitty. If you need to chat at all, just let me know. Chris.

I managed a weak smile. Chris was one of the few friends who I'd made independently of Tania and George. Maybe talking to another author about what was going on would help. *Unless they were the source of the leak...* I shook my head. While I didn't know Chris well, they seemed so warm and genuine. I couldn't believe that they would have divulged my identity. I wasn't even sure they knew my real last name. I shot off a text, letting them know I was going to be in New York for a couple of days and asking if they were free to meet. Chris responded quickly, inviting me to an event for their latest release in Cobble Hill at 5 p.m. tomorrow and suggesting we grab a drink afterward.

Feeling slightly more cheerful, I eyed the smashed avocado toast that had arrived. My appetite was still dampened, but it looked like a damn good avocado toast. That observation was verified as soon as I bit into it. The creamy avocado offset the tangy goat cheese perfectly, and the heirloom tomatoes and micro herbs added bursts of flavor. It was exactly what I needed. Substantial, healthy, and comforting.

Just as I was about to get up and pay, another notification lit up my phone. My heart rate increased as I saw it was a message from George.

> Hey, gorgeous, I just wanted to let you know that I'm thinking of you and hope you're doing okay. If you want to talk, just call me. I don't care what time it is. Good luck for your meeting with Michael xoxo

My eyes filled with tears, which I blinked away hurriedly. George was so damn sweet. Not only that, but her text was a timely reminder that she was not Tania. Maybe I was too dependent on her—something I needed to consider more—but if I was going to put all my eggs in one basket, George would be my top pick for holding it.

> Thanks babe. I miss you. I'll text you after the meeting to let you know how it goes and maybe we can talk tonight xoxo

IT DIDN'T dawn on me until I was on the subway heading uptown that there was a risk I'd run into Tania while I was in New York. She worked in the same office as Michael and my publicist, after all—the office I was about to meet Michael at for our meeting.

I'd suddenly found it difficult to swallow, a sensation that was still present as I waited for Michael in the lobby of the building. I touched my hearing aid to make sure it was working and then looked around the lobby. *Please don't run into Tania. Please don't run into Tania.* Despite feeling like I'd finally moved on from her, I didn't want to see her, especially not in my current state. She'd almost certainly say something cutting that left me feeling even worse about myself. And we still hadn't spoken about formally dividing up our assets—a conversation that I didn't currently have the mental capacity to deal with. I also couldn't shake the thought that perhaps she'd been the one to reveal my identity. It didn't seem in keeping with her character, but perhaps there was a motive hidden somewhere in there.

My phone vibrated, and I pulled it out to see who was calling. My parents. I sighed and put the phone back in my satchel. They'd probably heard the news about my pen name and my divorce and were calling to express their disappointment. Now was definitely not the time.

I spotted Michael, with his neatly cut, dark brown hair and thick, black-rimmed glasses, approaching through a security gate from the elevator bays. I walked toward him, half relieved that I didn't need to wait exposed in the lobby anymore, a sitting duck for Tania to see, and half a bundle of nerves that I was finally about to hear Michael's thoughts.

"Hi, Hannah." Michael shook my hand, barely managing a smile. Anxiety bubbled up, causing the lump in my throat to expand even further.

"Hi," I managed.

For a moment, there was an awkward silence as we stood in the lobby. I assumed Michael was going to take me up to a soulless meeting room in my publisher's office, perhaps one with a screen so he could give a PowerPoint presentation about all the things wrong with my manuscript.

"Would you like to grab a coffee? The café around the corner is decent," he said instead. His tone and expression were so neutral it was impossible to get any idea of what he was thinking.

"Um, sure," I responded, taken aback. A café didn't

seem like the most professional place to rip your author to shreds.

As we walked out of the lobby and around the corner to a light and airy coffee shop full of Scandinavian furniture, we made stilted small talk about the weather. Settling ourselves at a table near the window, I was relieved the café was quiet—less people to witness my humiliation.

I ordered a decaf, conscious from past experience that too much coffee could increase my anxiety. Given where my anxiety was currently at, I didn't want to risk it.

"Thanks for coming to meet me in person, especially after what's happened in the past twenty-four hours. I'm sorry you've had to go through it." Michael's neutral delivery didn't match his apologetic words. "I won't be at your meeting tomorrow with the publicity team and Emma, but I've asked them to give me an update afterward. I wanted to also let you know that we're launching an internal investigation to ensure the leak didn't come from us, as we take the confidentiality of our authors very seriously."

"Oh. Uh, thank you," I said, surprised. It hadn't crossed my mind that they'd do something like that. Did they have a reason to think the leak had been an inside job? Now that I was with Michael again, I couldn't imagine it had come from him. He was so serious and reserved, and what would he have had to gain from making my identity public?

Continuing in the same tone, it took me a few seconds to work out that he'd changed subjects. "I also wanted to let you know that we're really happy with how *The Realm of Furies* launch is going so far. It's had some excellent early reviews, strong pre-orders, and a good amount of interest from bookstores."

"Oh, that's great to hear, thanks," I said, relief washing

over me. Hopefully if sales continued, I'd earn out the advance quickly and start receiving royalties.

"Thanks for sending me your partial manuscript." He pulled out a notebook and a stack of paper, which I immediately recognized as the first part of my manuscript, and my stomach turned. *Here goes.* I braced myself.

Michael looked down at his notes and then stared intently at me, a solemn expression on his face.

"I obviously haven't read the entire novel"—*Okay, good, at least he is acknowledging this up front*—"but based on what I have read"—I took a deep, fortifying breath—"I think this is, by far, your best work yet. You've always been a talented writer, Hannah, but you've really taken this to the next level."

I stared at him, struggling to process his words. He looked like he'd just told me my cat had died and his tone was as flat as a pancake, but his words...his words were something else. A wave of relief, verging on elation, flooded over me.

"Oh, wow! I thought, based on your email, that you hated it."

Michael frowned. "No." He shook his head. "I'm really excited to read the rest of it." And while I'd never seen anyone "really excited" while remaining as outwardly composed as Michael, I believed him.

Forty-five minutes later, after he'd finished earnestly going through all the things he loved about the manuscript and giving me a few thoughtful suggestions for improvement, my view of my new editor had been completely overturned. He *got* the book. And most of his suggestions would make it even better. Not only that, but his approach seemed collaborative. Tania had often *told* me how to fix my books, whereas Michael made it clear that his comments were just ideas that I could take or leave. I could get used to his deadpan delivery if this was the payoff. A faint buzz of excitement vibrated through me. Perhaps changing editors hadn't been such a bad thing after all. Getting a fresh perspective might improve my books and my writing. I was already looking forward to weaving in some of Michael's suggestions.

Walking back to the hotel to check in, I reread the email Michael sent me last night. How had I gotten it all so wrong? Looking at it again, without being in full-blown panic mode, the email was neutral. I'd clearly read way too much into his staid writing style. I also hadn't been very accepting or understanding that Michael might just have a communication style that was different than what I was used to. Perhaps he was socially anxious like me, neurodiverse, or just a serious guy. I sighed. I hated when my anxiety got to this level. I kept telling myself that it would pass, like it had before, but when my anxiety was high, it was hard to believe it. And unfortunately the initial trigger for my anxiety, the revelation of my author identity, was still a very real problem I had to deal with.

I changed direction, heading up Sixth Avenue toward Central Park to extend my walk. Exercise usually helped when my anxiety got to be too much, as did sleep and eating well. Constantly looking at my phone did *not* help, but I'd noticed I had two new messages when I was checking my email, and curiosity got the better of me.

> Hi, Hannah. George told us about the article. I'm so sorry. If there is anything I can do, please let me know xxx Olivia

We're thinking of you. If you need a girls'
night out at Frankie's to burn off some
steam, just LMK xo Jenny

I smiled. Olivia and Jenny reaching out independently to check in on me was unexpected but welcome. Unlike the messages I'd received from some of my New York friends and acquaintances, it didn't feel like there was any hidden agenda or a sudden new interest in me because they'd discovered I was H. M. Stuart. They seemed to actually care. A pang of longing for Sapphire Springs, for my friends, for George, hit me again. I just needed to get through tomorrow's meetings, and if everything went to plan, I'd be back there the following day. And by the time I returned, hopefully I would have contained the unwanted publicity situation as best I could and gotten my anxiety under control.

CHAPTER TWENTY-NINE

GEORGE

MOM and I sat at my small dining table while we ate dinner, and Mom filled me in on the latest Dunedin gossip, her familiar gray bob bouncing up and down as she spoke. Mom always looked put together, and even after spending the day travelling, today was no exception. She was wearing ironed navy slacks and a floral blouse and her face was covered in carefully applied make-up.

I pushed the salmon I'd cooked around on the plate. I hadn't been able to shake the sense of unease that had settled in my stomach as I saw Hannah off this morning. I'd never seen Hannah so distraught, and it killed me that I couldn't do anything to help, especially now she was fifty miles away. If she was here, at least I could have made sure she was eating, offered physical comfort, and otherwise supported her in whatever way I could.

Instead of finishing work early to celebrate Hannah's release day as planned, I'd finished work as usual and then headed down to the station to pick up Mom. Before Hannah had left this morning, I'd made her pancakes as a special treat, but Hannah was, understandably, so preoccupied with the events of the last twenty-four hours that the festivities fell flat. I'd driven her to the station and sent her off with the warmest, most comforting hug I could muster. I was already, pathetically, missing her. At least, according to the text Hannah had sent me, it sounded like the meeting with her editor had gone much better than expected.

Work had been so busy I hadn't had much time to dwell on it until now. Ben had left on a four-day trip to Fire Island this morning, so it'd just been me and Josie working front of house, and we'd been flat-out busy for the entire shift. When Hannah had asked if she could go last night, I'd told her that me, Ben, and Josie would be fine, but Ben's vacation had slipped my mind. I would have told Hannah to go anyway, so perhaps it was for the best that I hadn't remembered so I could respond to Hannah truthfully and without adding to her stress, but it was terrible timing. With summer break just starting, the café was busier than ever, and there were more customers than two of us could handle. And tomorrow Josie was going to be away as well—she had a specialist appointment in the city, which would take up most of the day. I wasn't sure how I was going to cope by myself. A pang of guilt that I wouldn't be able to spend as much time with Mom as I'd planned shot through me.

"You're not hungry?" Mom asked, staring at my half-eaten plate of food.

My guilt increased as I realized I'd been worrying about Hannah, work, and not being able to give Mom enough attention, so much so that I'd zoned out on Mom.

"No. I ate a big lunch. If you're not too tired from all the travel, how do you feel about giving me a hand with an apple-cinnamon tea cake?"

"Of course," Mom said, smiling as she stood and rolled up the sleeves of her blouse. "I thought you'd never ask."

We cleaned up after dinner and then set to work on baking.

Mom paused peeling the apples and glanced at me. "So, when am I going to meet Hannah? I'd been hoping she'd join us for dinner tonight. You've sounded so happy since the two of you got together. I'm really looking forward to getting to know her."

My heart sank. I'd been really looking forward to them meeting as well. But I wasn't sure how long Hannah would stay in New York for. There was a chance she'd miss Mom altogether.

I measured out the baking powder and tipped it into the mixing bowl. "Unfortunately, she had to go to New York for a work thing, and we're not sure how long it's going to take. But hopefully, she'll be back before you leave. She's really excited to meet you too."

"Oh, that's a shame." Mom frowned. "Just a second, why does she need to go to New York for work? Are you thinking of expanding into the city or something?"

Whoops. I'd been careful not to tell anyone but Blake about Hannah's alter ego as H. M. Stuart, and that included Mom. All Mom knew was that Hannah worked at Novel Gossip with me, and given Mom's reading tastes leaned toward "women's" fiction and cozy mysteries, it wasn't surprising she'd missed the news articles and social media posts about Hannah's pen name. But now that it was public knowledge, I thought I'd better fill her in. I'd rather it come from me than a Novel Gossip patron.

"Um, no. In addition to working at Novel Gossip, Hannah writes fantasy novels. She writes under a pen name and kept her real identity quiet, but it was disclosed without her consent yesterday. She's gone to New York so she can meet with her publisher and agent and work out what to do. Her books are pretty popular, so there'd been a lot of speculation about who she was, and now her identity has been revealed, a lot of attention is on her."

I hadn't had much time to look at the news or social media today, but I'd seen enough to know that X and Threads were both full of posts about Hannah, some people going into full detective mode to try to find out more about her.

I stirred the sugar into the mixing bowl, glancing at Mom, who was unusually quiet.

"So, she's famous too?" Mom asked, putting down the knife and looking at me.

My stomach sank. I immediately knew what Mom was getting at. Mom had liked Alexis as a person, liked Alexis as a politician, but hadn't been a fan of Alexis as a partner for me. She'd felt that Alexis's career took priority over our relationship and that I had to make all the compromises so we could be together. Now that I thought about it, it made sense that Mom would have been thrilled to hear that Hannah fit so well into my life—same town, same job, same friends—and was now less than thrilled to hear that Hannah actually had a whole other, highly successful career that had the potential to overshadow mine.

"Well, only in certain circles. Nothing like Alexis. And very reluctantly. She was guarding her identity because she doesn't like the attention."

"Are you going to be able to manage okay at the café without her?" Mom asked, her face serious.

I wasn't sure if I was being overly sensitive or if this was a pointed question, the subtext being that Hannah had left me in the lurch. Mom knew I'd struggled with staffing recently and had only just gotten things under control. I debated how to answer. My first reaction was to go on the defensive, to tell Mom it'd be fine. If Mom had been back in Florida, that would have worked. But Mom was here, in Sapphire Springs, and if she spent any time in the café, she'd quickly work out that having both Hannah and Ben away was a struggle. And tomorrow was going to be a nightmare with Josie away as well.

"You know, I'm really happy to help out in the café. It'd be nice to meet your regulars and learn a few new things," Mom said gently.

Mom must have seen straight through me. The way I was breaking the eggs into the bowl, my facial expression, or my silence must have given me away.

"Hannah checked with me if it was okay before she left. She didn't realize Ben was away this week, and I'd totally forgotten about it too," I said.

I turned over Mom's proposition in my mind. Having an extra set of hands while Hannah was away would be a huge help, especially tomorrow. But I wasn't so sure about that extra set of hands being Mom's. She had no hospitality experience, and after years of retirement, I wasn't sure how she'd manage being back in a fast-paced work environment. It could all end in disaster. But on the other hand, I'd been worrying I wouldn't be able to spend much time with her, so her suggestion would kill two birds with one stone—I could work *and* hang out with her. It wouldn't exactly be quality time, not with how hectic the café had been recently, but perhaps it'd be like when we cooked together and would bring us closer. It would certainly give her a better understanding of my day-to-day life.

Hoping I wouldn't live to regret it, I wrapped an arm

around Mom and gave her a squeeze. "If you're sure about helping out at the café, that would be great."

With any luck, Hannah would be back before I knew it. While work was hard without her, it was even more difficult worrying about what she was going through. After the cake was in the oven, I'd call her to check she was managing okay.

CHAPTER THIRTY

HANNAH

WHILE MY MEETING with Michael yesterday had helped alleviate some of my worries, I'd still woken at 5 a.m., my mind whirring with everything that had happened in the past few days. Thinking about the information I'd so carefully protected being out there in the world, against my will, made me feel ill. I couldn't stop mulling over who could have exposed my identity, mentally listing everyone who knew about my pseudonym and any motives they might have for revealing it. Each time I thought of George and Blake, I quickly skipped over them, not willing to even contemplate that they might have been involved.

My gut twisted with nerves as I walked back to my publisher's office building to meet with Emma and the publicity team for our midday meeting.

"Excuse me!" A woman in her twenties, wearing loose jeans and a cropped red t-shirt, walked toward me, holding her phone.

My whole body tensed. *Oh shit. Had she recognized me?* I braced myself.

"Do you know where the Rockefeller Center is?" she asked. "My phone just died."

Breathing out, I gave her some quick directions and wished her luck, feeling like an idiot.

I was relieved to see Emma's familiar face in the lobby, but we barely had time to greet each other before my publicist, Rosie, appeared and we followed her into an elevator.

"It's good to see you both," she said smiling, after she'd pushed the button for the thirty-fifth floor. "And thanks again for signing all those pre-orders, Hannah. Some of them were accidentally delivered a day or two early, but it's been good from a publicity perspective. I saw one fan did a TikTok about the drawing of a book you did next to your signature. That was such a cute idea."

Despite my nerves, I couldn't help smiling at the memory of the book George had helped me draw after my pen had slipped that night at Novel Gossip. I was glad the recipient had appreciated it.

The elevator doors opened and Rosie ushered us into a small meeting room overlooking Broadway.

After exchanging pleasantries with Rosie's boss, Lucy, who was waiting for us in the room, we took our seats.

Lucy leaned forward, furrowing her brow. "First, I just wanted to say how sorry we are about your identity being made public." Her face relaxed, and her tone brightened as she continued. "But on the plus side, the timing couldn't have been more perfect from a publicity perspective with *The Realm of Furies* just being released. It's really helped increase interest in the book. We've had a lot of media reach out to us, asking if you'd be available for interviews, and Emma has been fielding similar requests. I know this wasn't how you wanted things to play out, but agreeing to some of these requests would be amazing publicity for *The Realm of*

Furies." Lucy's eyes flashed with excitement. "I mean, we're talking *Good Morning America, NPR, The New York Times*...opportunities most authors would kill for. Now that everyone knows who you are, you don't have a lot to lose. I've printed out a list of media offers and put stars next to the ones I think we should definitely accept. Just let me know which ones you're comfortable with, and we can set them up."

I stared at her, lost for words. The whole point of this meeting was to talk about how best to protect my privacy, not to completely blow it up. What the hell was Lucy thinking?

Maybe without Tania—who was so highly regarded—going in to fight for me anymore, the publicity team thought they could get away with this.

I frowned as a thought struck me. Had Lucy or Rosie leaked my identity? As Lucy had just said, the timing had been perfect from a publicity perspective. Anger welled in my stomach at the thought. I took a deep breath in an attempt to calm myself. I had no proof it had been them and I didn't want to derail the meeting with unsubstantiated accusations. Better to wait until the outcome of the internal investigation Michael mentioned.

Emma shot me a concerned look. "Do you want me to speak?"

I shook my head. "No, it's okay. I've got it."

I looked Lucy squarely in the face. "Lucy, I'm not going to do any interviews. My identity may be out there now, but I still want to keep a low profile. Agreeing to these would just attract more attention, which is exactly what I'm trying to avoid. I set up this meeting to talk about how to minimize the fallout from my privacy being breached, not capitalize on it. I know you want *The Realm of Furies* to do well, and so do I, but I'm not willing to sacrifice my privacy to achieve it. In any event, I understand that pre-orders and interest from booksellers was strong even before my identity was leaked, so clearly *The Realm of Furies* can speak for itself." I kept my voice steady and polite but assertive.

Lucy made one more attempt at trying to convince me to at least do the *Good Morning America* appearance, but being on national television was literally my worst nightmare, so I didn't have any trouble rejecting the suggestion forcefully and changing the topic to focus on my key area of concern, which was the exact opposite of Lucy's: how to reduce attention on me.

By the end of the meeting, we had a standard response for Emma and my publisher to use when turning down interview requests, and Lucy had reluctantly agreed that her team wouldn't engage with any social media posts about my identity or provide any further information about me. My official author bio would continue to only mention my pen name.

Michael was leaning against a wall, waiting, as we exited the meeting room. *Huh. I wonder what he's doing here.* "Hannah and Emma, do you have a few minutes? I wanted to talk to you about the leak."

I swallowed, my mind racing. Did Michael know who it was? *Shit.* If he did, that probably meant it was an inside job. Maybe it had been Tania? Or Lucy or Rosie? Or was Michael about to confess himself? As usual, Michael's facial expression gave nothing away.

Michael waited for Lucy and Rosie to leave the room and then led Emma and me back in, gesturing for us to sit.

Once we were seated, he cleared his throat.

"So, we discovered the source of the leak." Michael shifted on his seat.

I stared at him expectantly, willing him to go on.

He cleared his throat again and then tugged at his collar. *Okay, he's definitely uncomfortable about something.*

"So, who was it?" I blurted out, the suspense killing me.

"It was, uh…you." Michael grimaced.

I blinked. *What?*

"Me?" I squeaked, confusion swirling though my mind. *How could it have been me?*

"Um, yes. One of our assistants called the journalist who broke the story. They were tipped off by a video on TikTok from a reader who'd pre-ordered *The Realm of Furies* and had been confused to discover that it been signed by H. M. Taylor rather than H. M. Stuart. The journalist Googled your real name, saw your degree and *The New York Times* wedding announcement about you and Tania getting married, and put two and two together."

Blood drained from my face, and I grasped the table for support as Michael's comments sunk in.

Shit. I'd been so tired the night that I'd signed all the books at Novel Gossip, it wasn't surprising I'd made a mistake. I wondered how many books I'd mistakenly signed using my legal name. I winced.

"Oh my god," I murmured.

"Are you okay?" Emma asked softly, putting a hand on my arm.

"I feel so stupid," I said, heat rising again up my cheeks. I'd been suspecting everyone else of being at fault. I never stopped to consider it could be me. If I hadn't put off telling George who I really was and had signed the books as planned on the first day I arrived at Novel Gossip, I was sure I would never have made that mistake. Talk about karma.

"Hey, everyone makes mistakes," Emma said, patting my back.

I turned to Michael. "I'm so sorry about wasting your time with the investigation."

"That's fine. It was no problem at all," he responded.

I walked out of the office with Emma and Michael in a daze.

Once Emma and I were alone in the elevator, Emma turned to me, eyes wide. "Are you sure you're okay?"

"I'm really annoyed at myself. I protected my real name for so many years, so the fact that I blew it all up with a silly mistake is..." I trailed off, lost for words.

"Hey, don't be too hard on yourself. You've gone through a lot recently," Emma said, gently.

I gave her a weak smile. "On the plus side, at least the whole thing was a mistake, and not malicious, and I can stop wondering who was behind it."

My attempt to put a positive spin on the news must not have been convincing, because Emma eyed me with concern. "Why don't we grab lunch?" she asked.

I glanced at my watch. All I wanted was to call George and tell her what had happened. But it was just past 1 p.m., and she'd still be deep in the lunch rush.

"That would be great," I replied, grateful for some company after Michael's bombshell news. Hopefully Emma's presence would stop me from spiraling into self-admonition.

CHAPTER THIRTY-ONE

GEORGE

"GEORGE?" I finished pouring milk into a takeout cup and looked up to find Mom grimacing. "I accidentally typed in the wrong numbers and charged Mrs. Seabourne four hundred dollars for her cappuccino instead of four dollars. Can you fix it?"

I took a deep breath and nodded. As much as I appreciated Mom helping out while my staff were away, day one of working together was off to a shaky start. A tray of cookies had already been dropped on the ground when Mom was placing them in the display case, and two people had received the wrong orders.

"No problem. I'll put through a refund. Do you mind taking the eggs and bacon over to Mr. Goldsworthy in the corner?" I tilted my head in the direction of Rory Goldsworthy, pushing down my guilt at asking Mom to interact with one of my most difficult customers.

I processed the refund for Mrs. Seabourne and made her coffee, keeping an eye on Mom and Rory in case I had to intervene. To my surprise, they seemed to be chatting. I blinked. *And laughing?*

After handing Mrs. Seabourne her takeout cup, I ignored the tables that needed clearing and checked my phone instead. I'd spoken to Hannah last night, and while she'd sounded a little more upbeat after the meeting with her editor, I was worried about her. She had the meeting with her agent and publicist today, so I was keeping an eye on my phone in case she called. At least, if all went to plan, she thought she'd be back in Sapphire Springs tomorrow. My chest lightened at the thought. I couldn't wait to see her.

Mom's comments about Hannah being famous and drawing similarities between her and Alexis had tugged at me uncomfortably while we'd made the cake last night. The media attention Hannah was getting as a result of her real name being made public and her absence was dredging up some unwelcome memories of Alexis.

At least speaking to Hannah before I went to sleep had eased my worries. While Hannah had understandably been preoccupied with the major events that were going on in her life, she was still...Hannah. She'd still asked me to say hi to Mom, and pass on her apologies again, and to give Max a head rub for her, as well as asked how my day was. Needless to say, I hadn't told her how hectic things were with both her and Ben away and how Mom was stepping in to help out. I didn't want to add to her stress. When we'd said goodnight, her voice had hitched telling me how much she missed me and couldn't wait to come back home to Sapphire Springs.

"George, did you want to take your break now? It's quiet, so I should be fine on my own. You need to eat to keep your energy up," Mom said, reappearing next to me.

I surveyed the café. Everything seemed under control. The lunch rush would start soon, and if I didn't eat now, then I likely wouldn't get a chance until after 2 p.m.

"Okay, I'll have a quick bite, and then we can swap. But if you need help with anything, just let me know, and if anyone needs an espresso, I'll jump up and make it."

I grabbed a pre-made BLT bagel and took a seat at a table facing the counter so I could keep an eye on things. It wasn't that I didn't trust Mom, but getting up to speed at the café was a steep learning curve.

Almost as soon as I'd taken the first bite of my bagel, Rory approached the counter, holding some books. He put them in front of Mom and started talking. My eyes narrowed. I should have sat closer to the counter so I could hear what they were saying. *Oh no, he's not...* I suddenly recognized those books. They were the same ones he'd tried to return a few weeks ago. My jaw clenched. He must have waited until I was away from the counter to try to take advantage of Mom. I pushed back my chair, about to stand, when Mom firmly slid the books back to Rory, speaking to him with a stern expression on her face. Rory frowned and reluctantly picked up the pile of paperbacks. But instead of stomping off in disgust, he leaned in, a smile on his face, and started talking to Mom. To my relief, after a few minutes, he paid for his meal and left without making a scene threatening legal action like last time.

Despite my concerns, Mom managed fine while I wolfed down my lunch. At one point, she got a little distracted, chatting to the book club, a group of five ladies in their sixties who met at Novel Gossip once a week, and didn't notice a customer was waiting to order until they rang the bell on the countertop, but other than that, it was completely uneventful.

Once I'd finished eating, I went back behind the counter and took advantage of the café being quiet to make us both coffees.

Mom leaned on the counter, dusting some cocoa powder off her shirt, while I frothed the milk. "You know what? I'm really enjoying this, George. It's so nice chatting with people and bringing them delicious food. The book club even invited me to their meet-ups whenever I'm in town. Maybe I should look into getting a part-time job at a café when I get home. It's not like I need the money, but it would be a nice way to connect with more people and add some structure to my day."

I laughed. "Why not?" I bit back saying that was exactly what Hannah did, in case it gave Mom additional reason to think that Hannah wasn't as committed to me and my career as Mom thought she should be. "I saw you had a run-in with Rory. I hope he wasn't too much of a pain." I poured the milk into our coffee mugs, handed Mom one, and took a large gulp of mine.

"Oh no. He asked me out on a date," Mom replied casually.

I almost spat out my coffee. "He...what? Did you say yes?" An image of Rory as my stepfather sent chills shooting down my spine.

"God no," Mom laughed, shaking her head. "He seems like a real curmudgeon. But it's nice to know I've still got it."

I burst out laughing, immediately wishing Hannah was here so I could share the latest update on our most difficult customer with her.

CHAPTER THIRTY-TWO

HANNAH

A WELCOME BREEZE of fresh air hit me as I walked out of the Bergen Street subway station and headed down a residential street full of gorgeous brownstones and leafy green oak trees toward Court Street. I took a deep breath. Not only did it feel good to get out of the subway, which was never pleasant during summer, but it was also nice to get out of Manhattan. Brooklyn was only a bridge away, but it felt like a completely different world.

Now that I'd had time to process Michael's revelation, my mood had lightened significantly. While I was still kicking myself about signing the wrong name in the pre-order book, it was a huge relief to get to the bottom of it and discover there had been no sinister motivations behind the whole thing. And while the publicity meeting with Rosie and Lucy had not started as planned, I was happy that by the end we had a plan to help minimize interest in me.

I turned onto Court Street and was soon standing outside Cobble Hill Books. A pang of homesickness for Novel Gossip hit me as I peered through the large windows into the bookstore. Thank god the local community had rallied to save it. It was *almost* as cute and cozy as Novel Gossip. And damn, would I give anything for George to be there, behind the counter, her face lighting up like it usually did when I walked in to start my shift.

My lunch with Emma had gone longer than expected. Not only was there a lot to debrief on, given the events of the past few days, but we hadn't caught up properly for months. I'd tried giving George a call after we'd finished, but she hadn't responded, probably busy either working or entertaining her mom.

I shot off a text to George, letting her know I was about to go to Chris's talk and wouldn't be available for the next couple of hours, and then pushed open the door to the bookstore. The chairs lined up in rows were almost full, so I pulled off my hat and sunglasses, walked in, and took a seat at the back, giving Chris, who was seated at the front, a small wave on my way. They waved back, smiling, and a few audience members' heads turned to look at me.

As I sat, it struck me that, for someone wanting to avoid the spotlight, going to a fellow fantasy author's event while there was significant media attention on me was probably a terrible idea. This adorable bookstore was full of devoted fantasy readers, many of whom had probably read my books and seen the recent articles or social media posts. My stomach turned, and I looked down to avoid any eye contact.

I got through the interview and audience Q&A without anyone recognizing me, but as I stood to hide amongst the bookshelves until Chris had finished signing, a young man approached, his face flushed.

"Excuse me. Um...sorry to bother you, but are you H. M. Stuart?"

I tensed and considered denying it, but lying didn't sit right with me.

"Yes," I said, trying for a smile. A group of people nearby must have overheard, as they turned to look and then edged closer to me.

I spent the next twenty minutes making small talk with a number of the attendees. While they were all lovely and only had positive things to say about my books, the experience just affirmed my decision to push back on my publicity team earlier today. My small-talk skills had improved, probably as a result of working at Novel Gossip, but I still hated being the center of attention and found the whole experience excruciatingly awkward. I liked talking to people when we were on an even playing field. When they saw me first and foremost as a successful fantasy author, that made things difficult. While I worried that perhaps I was being selfish, I reminded myself that I preferred to give back to my fans in ways that did not make me uncomfortable, like signing 841 pre-order books, writing free bonus scenes, and responding to emails I received from readers. I also worried that I was stealing the limelight from Chris, but each time I looked over at them, they were busy signing books in front of a long line of people. At least it looked like I didn't need to worry about that.

As soon as I could, I excused myself to go to the restroom and sat on the toilet seat, scrolling through my Instagram feed—which consisted of photos of a few friends, a lot of cute dogs, and my favorite female comedians—until I felt more relaxed.

I took a deep breath and steeled myself to go back into the bookstore.

"There you are! Are you ready for that drink?" Chris

asked as soon as I exited the restroom. "Please say yes." Desperation tinged their voice.

I chuckled. "Sure am. Did you have somewhere in mind?"

Chris nodded, and we walked down Court Street to Congress, a small bar known for its cocktails. We ordered drinks from the friendly bartender and then grabbed a seat at a table in the corner.

Chris took a long swig of their old fashioned and leaned back with a satisfied sigh. "These events really take it out of me. I can't wait for them all to be over so I can squirrel back into my cave and get back to what I actually enjoy—writing."

I looked at Chris, surprised. "I don't know how you do events. I'd find them incredibly stressful. But you're so good at public speaking. Your answers are always clear, you weave in funny anecdotes, and you come across as so genuine and warm. Both times I've seen you, you've had the audience enthralled." I sipped my gimlet, the refreshing lime and gin combination going down very easily.

Chris grimaced. "That's very kind of you to say, but I find them nerve-wracking. I spent weeks doing practice interviews, rehearsing those anecdotes, and I still feel like I'm about to vomit before they start. I wish I could be as brave as you and just refuse to do them altogether."

I looked at them, startled. "Um, I don't think avoiding public speaking is exactly brave. If anything, it's the opposite."

"I don't see it that way. In this industry, there's so much pressure on authors to sell their books—to constantly be on social media, have a website, do interviews and events. Publishers expect it, and most authors I know feel like they have to do it, even though they'd often prefer to be writing their next book. The fact that you were able to draw some firm boundaries and push back on those expectations seems pretty brave to me."

Huh. I'd never thought about it in that way before. It had always felt like a personal failing that I wasn't willing to put myself out there publicly. But when I looked back to those initial discussions I'd had, first with Emma and then with Tania and other representatives from my publisher when they offered me a book deal, there had been a lot of pressure from all concerned for me to do all the things Chris had just described. But I'd held steadfast to my position that it was my job to write the books and my publisher's job to sell them.

I frowned. "You know, I'm not sure I could have convinced them on my own. I think having Tania on my side made a huge difference. She had, and still has, a lot of influence at the publishing house and really fought for me." Tania and I hadn't been together when I signed the contract —we'd started dating shortly after—but she'd seen how important privacy was to me. Tania was by no means perfect, but she'd had some good qualities as well.

"Maybe I should see if I can switch editors," Chris said, a joking glint in their eye.

"Well, she might have an opening since she's lost one of her authors recently," I said, smiling. "And she is an excellent editor."

ON THE SUBWAY ride home I checked my phone. Two text messages. One from George, letting me know she was free tonight if I still wanted to talk. I grinned. I couldn't wait to get back to the hotel and call her. And one from Tania. My heart rate picked up as I clicked on it.

> Hi, I heard you're in New York. We need to talk about dividing our assets, and I'd prefer if we could come to an amicable agreement rather than getting our lawyers involved. Are you free tomorrow to meet up and discuss? T

I shut my eyes. Despite feeling like I'd well and truly moved on from Tania, I did not want to talk to her about dividing up our assets. There were some things, like the painting of our dog, Henry, who had passed away a few years ago, that I knew we'd both want, and the idea of having to hash those issues out made my stomach turn. Maybe once the media attention had calmed down and I was back in Sapphire Springs, I'd feel more prepared for that conversation.

As soon as I got back to the hotel room, I pulled off my shoes, changed into my pajamas, and FaceTimed George. Seeing her smiling face, as she sat propped up against the head of her bed, and hearing her voice sent a warm rush through me. Max was snoring somewhere nearby. I wished I could teleport myself next to her and nuzzle into her chest.

"Hi, gorgeous. How are you doing?" George asked.

Leaning back on the pillows on my hotel bed, I filled her in on the publicity meeting. Tears welled in my eyes as I told George that I was the source of the leak.

"I know it really sucks, but try not to be too hard on yourself about signing the wrong name," George said gently.

"It's hard not to since I brought it all on myself,' I said, blinking.

"I wouldn't say that. You were going through a huge upheaval which was caused by something outside your control—Tania cheating on you. You were dealing with a divorce, moving, writer's block, financial stress and worry about Barb. You need to cut yourself some slack."

I swallowed and nodded.

"You know, for someone who doesn't like difficult conversations, it sounds like you did a pretty amazing job today. Standing up to your publicity team like that couldn't have been easy," George said.

I managed a weak smile. "Chris said something similar to me today—that I was 'brave' for refusing to do any publicity when there was so much pressure on authors to do it. I'd always felt it was a character flaw on my part. I was too shy, too introverted, too socially awkward."

"I don't see that as a character flaw at all. It's just who you are. Surely a lot of authors would be the same. What are the chances, really, that people who love spending most of their time in imaginary worlds are also going to be extroverts who love the limelight?"

"True. Although, I was lucky to have Tania on my side, advocating for me, when I pushed back on all the publicity originally."

"Even still, it doesn't detract from the fact that it was a difficult conversation, but you stood firm. And you spoke to Michael about the book, even when you thought he was going to rip it to shreds."

I laughed softly. "I'm so glad I did that, or I would have spent days worrying about what he was going to say, when I didn't need to at all."

George paused again. "Hey, Hannah. Why do you think you found those conversations easier to have than some of the other conversations you've struggled with?" Her voice was low and thoughtful.

There was silence while I turned George's question

over in my mind, thinking of all the conversations I'd agonized over and delayed. Telling George and my parents I was H. M. Stuart, confronting Tania about her infidelity, and now, talking to her about finalizing the financial side of our divorce.

"Looking back, I wonder if it all stemmed from my parents. They were so distant and unapproachable that I found it really hard to talk to them. And when I did get up enough courage, they were so often dismissive. Whether it was about my desire to be a writer or my desire not to do drama and debate."

George furrowed her brow. "That would have been really tough. Kids need to be able to feel comfortable speaking to their parents."

"Yeah." I gave George a small smile. "I think the conversations I struggle with the most are the more personal ones, because there's more potential for me to get hurt or hurt others." I shifted in the bed, trying to find the best words to express my feelings.

"Like with you and my parents, I was worried revealing I'm H. M. Stuart might make you think I was weird or see me differently, and result in my parents saying hurtful things about my career. And I've been putting off speaking to Tania about the division of our assets, and again, it's very personal, especially when it comes to things like furniture or artwork that we both love. Whereas with the publisher, it's business." I pressed my lips together, still trying to work through my thoughts. "Although, having said that I was very nervous about talking to Michael yesterday. Getting negative feedback on my work is pretty personal, and I was also worried about what it would mean financially if I had to do a total rewrite."

"Well, that makes it even more awesome that you did it, then."

I smiled. "I think the events of the last few months made me realize that there's rarely any benefit in delaying the inevitable. All it does is give me more time to stress about the whole thing—like I did when I first met you and spent days agonizing over when and how to tell you I was H. M. Stuart. With Michael, I knew that if I could muster up the courage to speak to him, instead of spending days anticipating his concerns, sending myself into even more of an anxiety spiral with what-ifs, I'd find out exactly what his problem was. And once I was armed with that information, I could at least take steps to deal with it—whether it was revising my book or something more drastic. So maybe I am getting better at having difficult conversations."

"That's great. And it makes sense about it being more challenging when it's personal," George said gently. "When Alexis and I were breaking up, I saw a therapist for a while, and they really helped me with how to address some conversations I had to have with Alexis. I've got a worksheet she sent me somewhere with some tips that I'll try to dig up."

"That would be awesome." The fact that George had struggled with similar problems was oddly comforting. She seemed so good at addressing issues head on now that it gave me hope to hear that it really was something I could work on and improve.

"My therapist also emphasized that all I could control was how I handled my side of the conversation. I couldn't control how the other person reacted to what I said. I had to let go of my worries about how Alexis would react and instead focus on breaking up with her in the kindest way possible. It was kind of liberating to hear that."

I nodded thoughtfully. "That is a good way of looking at it."

The more I thought about it, the more it dawned on me that I probably didn't have a lot to lose by having the conversations with my parents and Tania. With my parents, my feelings were already hurt after years of them not supporting my writing career or making an effort to be close to me. Could they really do much to hurt me further? And with Tania, she currently had all the assets that were up for discussion in her possession. Unless she refused to give me anything, which was highly unlikely, speaking to her could only improve my position. Resolve washed over me. Instead of continuing to avoid facing Tania and my parents, I should just get it over with.

"Tania messaged me to see if I could meet with her tomorrow to talk about dividing our assets. Would you mind if I stayed an extra night to try to get it sorted? And while I'm at it, I should probably call my parents too." My pulse quickened at the thought, but I also felt relief that I'd finally decided to take action.

George smiled softly. "Of course that's fine. And if you want me to help you practice some role-playing, just let me know." George's face broke into a cheeky grin.

I smiled. "Role-playing, eh? I can think of much better role-playing options than you pretending to be my ex or my parents..."

"Oh, really? Care to share?" George asked, her tone playful.

"Let's wait until I'm back." My voice turned serious. "But George, thanks so much for talking to me about all this stuff. I really appreciate it," I said, my voice wavering. *God, George is great.* I felt almost overwhelmed by how strong my feelings were for her. I cleared my throat. "Anyway, that's enough of my news. How's your mom's visit going?"

CHAPTER THIRTY-THREE

HANNAH

AS I TOOK a shower and dressed for the day, I reflected on last night's conversation with George. It had given me a new way of seeing things and had been immensely comforting at the time, but this morning, a niggling voice in the back of my head kept asking whether this was another example of me becoming too reliant on George.

If I depended on George for emotional support, writing inspiration, and her friendship circle, and then we broke up... My throat constricted at the thought, making it hard to swallow. The thought of losing George was unbearable, I didn't know how I'd cope with losing everything else too.

No. I took a deep breath in an attempt to keep my anxiety at bay.

If I was becoming too reliant on George, then I should do something about it. Rather than depending on George to help me work through my problems, I could get a professional involved. Once I'd finished putting on my pants and t-shirt, I pulled up my therapist's booking page. She was usually booked out for weeks, but she must have had a last-minute cancellation as there was an appointment available later in the afternoon. *I might as well take advantage of being here and see her face to face.* I pounced on it before someone else snapped it up. A therapy appointment was long overdue. While it was healthy to be open with your partner about your struggles, it wasn't healthy to expect them to fix them for you. That was something I had to do myself—ideally with a trained professional.

Speaking of trained professionals, George had sent me the worksheet from her therapist, listing various techniques for having difficult conversations.

Once I'd finished getting ready, I sat on my hotel bed and read through it again. All the tips made perfect sense when I read them, but they weren't things I necessarily would have thought of myself. Things like expressing my perspective using "I" statements, such as "I feel" rather than directing "You" statements at the other person to avoid sounding too accusatory. Actively listening and paraphrasing to make sure I understood the other person's point of view. Trying to remain respectful and calm, even when I didn't agree with what the other person was saying.

I was reading the worksheet for a third time, considering how I could put it into practice with Tania and my parents, when my phone vibrated. It was Tania.

I'd texted her after I'd finished speaking to George last night, asking if she was free to discuss our asset split. I took in a deep breath as I read her message. It was really happening.

> I can meet you at 8:30 a.m. at Jean-Jacques, if it's not too late notice?

I checked my phone. It was just after 7:30 a.m. Plenty of time to catch the subway up to my old local French café by 8:30 a.m. In fact, it'd only take about twenty minutes, leaving me with time to burn.

Assuming my parents were back from Greece—which they should be, according to their itinerary—they'd both be awake and likely reading the news at their dining table by now. I might as well get my conversation with them over and done with too. I wasn't sure which one I was dreading the most, speaking to Tania or my parents, but tackling them both, one after another, didn't seem like the worst idea. Then I could tell myself it'd all be over in two hours.

I made a coffee using the Keurig in my room and took a long swig. With the much-needed stimulant in my system, I inhaled a deep breath and video-called my parents.

It rang multiple times, and I was almost about to give up when my parents' ceiling appeared on my phone, followed by my dad's nostrils.

"Hello?" I said.

"Who is it?" Mom asked, irritation clear in her voice.

"Hannah," Dad replied.

Mom must have grabbed Dad's iPad because the ceiling disappeared and was replaced with most of Mom's face, frowning at me. "We've been trying to get a hold of you."

My immediate reaction was to want to point out that they didn't have a great track record of returning my calls either, but I took a deep breath instead. *Stay calm and respectful, and practice active listening.* "Not being able to speak to me must have been frustrating. I'm sorry. I've had a lot going on the past few days. How was your vacation?"

"Fine," Mom snapped. "But the last thing we needed was to get back home to discover that not only are you and Tania getting a divorce but you've published four *fantasy* novels"—she emphasized the word fantasy—"which you failed to tell us about. It was humiliating receiving the news from a friend who read an article about it. Not only that, but it has overshadowed the publication of your father's latest book." Mom swung the camera over to Dad, who pressed his lips together, his face serious. He said nothing.

I resisted the urge to shake my head. *Good lord.* It wasn't like I'd revealed my identity on purpose to undermine my father. And surely there wouldn't be much cross-over in readership between my *fantasy* novels and Dad's academic literature?

"Honestly, I thought we raised you better than this," Mom concluded.

I took another deep breath and bit back a snarky comment about how it had been Barb, not them, who'd raised me. Instead, for the first time in my life, I told my parents how I felt, trying to use all the skills in the worksheet. I explained how I'd felt they hadn't approved of my writing dreams, why I hadn't been comfortable telling them when I'd finally gotten a book deal, and how, when my books took off, I didn't want to share the news with them because I was worried they'd only throw cold water on my success. And with Tania...well, I'd tried phoning them a few times since we separated, and they hadn't returned my calls, and it wasn't the sort of thing you just texted about.

"Well, we've been busy," Mom said defensively, and I sighed. They were always busy. That appeared to be my parents' only response to what I'd said, so there wasn't a lot of opportunity for me to practice my active listening skills. I asked Dad about his book, and we spent a few more minutes engaging in superficial chit-chat before we hung up. I stared at my blank phone screen. It had gone about as well as I'd expected. There'd been no come-to-Jesus moment where we all realized the error of our ways and vowed to be closer, but it felt good that I'd been open and honest with them. I'd said my piece, made them aware of how their words and actions impacted me, and I couldn't control how they responded. What I could control was who I chose to have in my life. Like George.

One down, one to go.

I checked the time on my phone. While I still had time to spare, I might as well start making my way up to Jean-Jacques.

The subway trip passed uneventfully. It was a strange sensation getting out at 79th Street station, with its cramped staircase and arched skylights. *I used to come here twice a day.* I crossed Broadway and walked down 73rd Street until I arrived at Jean-Jacques's red, white and blue striped awning.

Paul, the owner of the café, who was placing a vase of flowers on one of the front tables, looked up as I walked in. "Hannah! We haven't seen you in a while!" he exclaimed. "How have you been?"

"Really well. Thanks, Paul," I replied, smiling. Three months ago, I couldn't have fathomed that I'd be saying that and actually meaning it, especially not immediately before meeting Tania for the talk I'd been avoiding for just as long.

"Hannah." I turned to see Tania just behind me.

She had the same short, dark brown bob, the same black-rimmed glasses, and was wearing her usual shirt and custom-tailored pantsuit—today it was a white shirt paired with a navy suit and brown Oxford shoes. Even in her flat footwear, Tania was a few inches taller than me. She held herself with the same self-assurance I used to find so attractive. She looked so familiar, but at the same time, she felt like a stranger. Any connection between us had disappeared. Paul had disappeared as well. I didn't blame him.

"Hi," I said. We stood awkwardly, staring at each

other. *Shit. I'd prepared for our talk, but not this initial reunion part. What is the etiquette here?* I didn't want to hug her. But a handshake felt too formal and business-like.

"Should we get a table?" Tania asked briskly, raising an eyebrow.

"Sure," I said, leading the way toward a table by the window. Previously, Tania's curt tone would have put me on edge, but it was empowering to realize that I no longer cared what she thought of me, and as a result, her ability to hurt my feelings had weakened substantially. Despite that breakthrough, my chest was still tight with nervousness about how our conversation would go.

We took a seat and studied the menu in silence, even though we both knew it by heart and always ordered the same thing—a croissant with strawberry jam. Jean-Jacques was an institution—an institution that didn't see the need to ever change the menu.

Paul reappeared, standing next to the table, darting his eyes between Tania and me as if he was worried we'd make a scene in the middle of Jean-Jacques's usually peaceful morning service, and he'd be forced to eject us. He'd clearly heard about the divorce, or noticed my absence for the last few months and put two and two together. "Would you like the usual?"

Tania nodded. I opened my mouth to agree, but a desire to try something new washed over me. "You know what, I think I'll try the croque monsieur today. And a decaf latte." I handed the menu back to Paul with a smile.

For some reason, my decision to mix up my order gave me a confidence boost.

"Thanks for agreeing to meet me on such short notice. And I'm sorry that I haven't gotten in touch earlier," I said, hoping my opening made it clear to Tania that I was ready for a calm and reasonable conversation.

"That's okay." Tania pressed her lips together. "How things ended couldn't have been easy for you."

I smiled. "It all worked out for the best." And I really meant it. If Tania hadn't cheated on me, then I'd likely still be living here in an unhappy marriage. My new life in Sapphire Springs was a thousand times better.

"Really?" Tania studied me closely, clearly unable to keep the note of surprise out of her voice. "Well, that's good."

"I've got the list of assets you sent me on my laptop. I was thinking I could pull it out, and we could go through them one by one? If there are things we both want, perhaps we can make a separate list of them, and then at the end try to divide them up fairly?"

Tania glanced at her watch. "Yes. Let's get moving," she said, her voice business-like.

We spent the next forty minutes working our way through the list while we ate breakfast. The croque monsieur was to die for and, in my opinion, significantly more delicious than the jam croissant. By the time we'd reached the end of the list, there were only a few items—including the painting of our dog, Henry, and a mid-century modern armchair we'd bought at a vintage store—that we both loved.

We ordered another round of coffees and then dived into the most challenging part of our meeting—how to divide up the objects we both wanted.

We went through item by item, speaking about what each one meant to us. A few times, Tania's tone turned biting as she argued for the objects she wanted, but I kept calm, and eventually, we reached what felt like a fair and reasonable compromise, even if we both weren't getting everything we wanted.

After a few minutes of polite small talk, Tania stood. "Well, I'd better get to work. Good to see you, Hannah." She pressed her lips into a weak smile. "Send me your address, and I'll have it all delivered."

She took a step and then turned to me. I steeled myself for a biting final remark.

"Oh, and Hannah. You seem...different. More assertive. It looks good on you."

I blinked as she turned around and headed toward the door. I didn't need Tania's approval anymore, but the fact that she'd noticed a change in me was strangely satisfying, even if it also felt slightly condescending.

After saying goodbye to Paul, I walked back to the station. A weight had been lifted from my chest. It was just past 9 a.m., and I'd already managed to knock off two conversations that had been hanging over my head for months or, in my parents' case, years. Energized, I called my lawyer to see if she could fit me in after my therapist session this afternoon to update my will. Since I was accomplishing goals today, I might as well cross another task off my list. I'd been meaning to remove Tania from my will for months, and it needed to be signed and witnessed in person, so today seemed like the perfect opportunity.

On the subway back to my hotel, I mindlessly scrolled on Instagram, pausing at a gorgeous photo of a beach at sunset. *When George hires another staff member, I wonder if she'd be interested in a beach vacation. We could get a cute Airbnb, read books while lounging on the sand, even practice our kayaking skills...* I smiled at the thought, looking at the photo more closely, and did a double-take when I realized

Ben had posted it late last night, and the location was Fire Island.

My heart plummeted. *Shit.*

I clicked on his account and went to his stories, where there was a photo of five men, one of them him, at a pool, also on Fire Island. If Ben was at Fire Island, then George was seriously understaffed. George and I had struggled when I'd first started at Novel Gossip with just the two of us working front of house, and the café would be even busier this week with summer break commencing. George and Josie would be completely under water without either Ben or me to help. *That's the last thing George needs while her mom is visiting.* Guilt washed over me.

As soon as I got back to the hotel, I packed my bags. If I hurried, I could make it back to Sapphire Springs before the lunch rush. After checking out, I walked as fast as I could to Grand Central, where I bought a ticket for the next Hudson Line train, which was leaving in ten minutes. I considered calling or texting George to let her know I was on my way back, but I didn't want to distract her. She'd have enough on her plate opening Novel Gossip.

Instead, while I waited for the train, I canceled my therapist and lawyer appointments this afternoon. This time, I wasn't putting them off out of fear of a difficult conversation. I was putting it off so I could be there for George. And that was more than enough of a reason.

CHAPTER THIRTY-FOUR

GEORGE

I TOOK a large gulp of coffee, hoping it would counteract my terrible night's sleep. I'd had a vivid dream that Alexis had won the presidency, and I was at her victory speech, standing behind her on the stage with a smile plastered on my face, desperately wishing I didn't have hundreds of eyes and cameras pointed at me. My happiness for Alexis was mixed with horror that I was about to become First Lady and that I'd have to sell Novel Gossip to focus on my new role. But when I'd turned to Alexis, it was Hannah, instead, standing behind the podium, looking radiant as she announced she was going on a world-wide book tour for twelve months—a book tour she'd failed to mention to me. I'd woken with a start at the news and then taken two hours to get back to bed. I kept telling myself that Hannah wasn't like Alexis and that Novel Gossip was going to be just fine, but I couldn't help wondering if the dream was a sign my subconscious wasn't completely convinced.

"What time will Hannah be arriving back?" Mom's voice cut through my thoughts as I sat in the armchair, cupping my mug with my hands. "If you need me to look after the café while you go pick her up, that's fine with me. I think I'm really getting the hang of things."

I smiled at Mom, who was eating cereal on the couch, Max curled up next to her. By the time we closed the café yesterday, Mom had well and truly found her feet. If she'd been a paid employee, my only complaint would have been that she spent too much time chatting with customers. And I had offered to pay her—an offer she'd firmly refused.

"You are. If you keep this up, I'll be enlisting your services every time you visit," I said. Mom grinned with pride. "But to answer your question, Hannah's going to stay another day. Something came up that she needs to deal with."

Disappointment flitted across Mom's face. "Oh, that's a shame. Alexis used to do this sort of thing all the time too—"

"Mom!" I cut her off abruptly, unable to keep the frustration out of my voice. "Hannah is not Alexis."

I clenched my teeth. Alexis had often had to extend her work trips or cancel our plans at the last minute because of a political crisis or an unexpected media interview or a networking event had arisen, but this was different. While Mom only had my best interests at heart, her making these comparisons was not helpful. Deep down, I knew that Mom's concerns about Hannah were baseless, but her words still triggered a flicker of doubt in my mind and unearthed latent insecurities.

"Well, I Googled her last night, and she certainly has a lot of media attention at the moment," Mom replied defensively.

"Yes, and she didn't ask for any of it," I snapped, guilt sweeping over me immediately. "Mom, I know you mean well, but I don't want to talk about this right now. You haven't even met Hannah yet, so I'd appreciate it if you didn't make assumptions about her. Let's change the topic." I smiled at her, pushing my annoyance aside. "So, how many dates do you think you'll be asked out on today?"

"IT LOOKS like your mom is really enjoying herself," Blake said, grinning over the counter as I made her a coffee. I glanced up to see Mom befriending another patron.

I chuckled. "Yeah, she's actually been a huge help the last few days."

"Have you heard from Hannah?"

I looked up, checking that no other customers were waiting in line. Thankfully, we were in a quiet spell. "Yeah, it sounds like things have been going about as well as they could, and she's decided to stay an extra day to try to sort out some divorce stuff with her ex."

I hit the pitcher of frothed milk on the counter to break up some larger bubbles that had formed.

Blake grimaced. "That doesn't sound fun. Are you holding up okay?"

I poured the frothed milk into a mug. "Yes. I'm not worried about her ex or anything like that..."

"I feel there's a 'but' coming."

I paused, collecting my thoughts. "You remember how, before we started dating, I was worried about our relationship being imbalanced because I was her boss?" Blake nodded. "Well, all the events of the last few days have brought home just how successful Hannah is, and while I think that's amazing and she deserves it, I guess I've had this underlying worry that perhaps our relationship is imbalanced, just not in the way I originally thought. It's not helping that Mom keeps trying to draw parallels between

Hannah and Alexis. It's also been a real struggle having her gone, which has made me think again about the impact our relationship might have on Novel Gossip."

Blake pressed her lips together thoughtfully. "I don't think a relationship is ever going to be perfectly equal. Jenny did so much for me when we first got together, and now she's working hard building up her business, and I've been doing more around the house, looking after the pets and that sort of thing, to take the load off her. Those kinds of swings and roundabouts are quite different from what you described with Alexis, which was basically you making all the sacrifices without any sign she'd be willing to do the same for you, to the extent that you were completely miserable. From an outsider's perspective, at least, it doesn't seem like that's the case with you and Hannah."

I nodded, thinking over all the times Hannah had stepped in to help me. Hannah had initially kept working at the café because she felt bad leaving me in the lurch, baked multiple cakes of the day with me, saved Novel Gossip from burning down and organized Chris Chen's talk, which I could tell had caused her anxiety. I smiled. It was definitely swings and roundabouts with us. And Hannah had checked with me first, asking if it was okay for her to go to New York, so it really wasn't fair to treat her absence as evidence that our relationship might damage Novel Gossip or that she didn't value me. My employees also needed to be able to take time off. I just had to stop letting Mom get to me.

I exhaled. I couldn't wait for Hannah to be back in Sapphire Springs tomorrow. *Unless something else delays her.* I pushed down the thought. For now, my priority was to finish making Blake's double-shot latte.

An hour later, I was making yet another coffee when someone walked through the door. As usual, I lifted my head to greet them and did a double-take, my heart skyrocketing.

I blinked.

Just like the very first time I'd set eyes on her, Hannah stood near the front door, dressed in brown sandals, wide-legged navy pants, and a white t-shirt, looking absolutely gorgeous. But this time, she was staring at me and smiling.

My face broke into a grin so broad my cheek muscles ached. *What the hell is she doing here?* It took every ounce of self-control not to throw down the milk jug, run over, and take her in my arms, but I'd almost finished this latte and the customer who'd ordered it had been looking at their watch and sighing. In any event, having a reunion make-out session in the middle of my café was probably not the most professional look. Surely she'd walk over here any minute.

But Hannah spotted a recently vacated table that hadn't been cleared yet and, instead, beelined toward it and started stacking the plates. *Goddamnit. I want her here, now.*

Mom, who'd just picked up a food order from the kitchen and was about to deliver it to a table, stopped next to me, frowning.

"Why is that customer clearing tables, honey? Should I tell her to stop?"

I laughed. "That's not a customer. It's Hannah, Mom." I poured the frothed milk into the latte, forcing myself to focus on the coffee rather than the fact that Hannah was now walking toward us.

"Oh!" Mom watched her silently for a moment. "Well, I guess I'd better deliver this to Mr. Jackson, and then you can properly introduce us."

I handed over the triple-shot caramel latte just as Hannah came around behind the counter, balancing a stack of plates and coffee cups. She was still smiling and her eyes were glowing. *Screw being professional.*

I walked toward her, grabbed the plates, put them on the counter, and then wrapped my arms around her waist. I kissed her, closing my eyes and reveling in her soft lips and her familiar scent. *Damn, I'd missed this.*

Before I got too carried away, I pulled back, opening my eyes and looking intently at her. "What are you doing back early? I thought you were going to be at least another day. Is everything okay?"

"I saw Ben's post from Fire Island on Instagram. I can't believe you didn't tell me he was away this week. How have you coped?"

I grinned. "I found another staff member."

"You did?" Hannah's eyes widened.

"Hannah, meet the newest staff member of Novel Gossip: my mom, Helen." I pulled away and gently turned Hannah around as Mom walked back behind the counter.

Hannah froze for a moment before stepping forward and enveloping Mom in a warm embrace. "It's so nice to finally meet you. I'm so sorry I wasn't here when you arrived and you've been roped into working."

Mom raised her eyebrows as she looked at me over Hannah's shoulder and tentatively placed her arms around Hannah. After a few moments, Mom took a step back and looked at Hannah. "Well, you're here now," Mom said with a half-smile. "And, you know, I actually don't mind working here at all."

"Yeah, it's not too bad. Although, the boss is a real taskmaster," Hannah responded, her eyes twinkling as she turned to look at me.

Mom laughed, and I breathed out, relieved that their initial interaction seemed to be going smoothly.

"She's already made friends with all the regulars and has been invited out on a date by Rory Goldsworthy!" I said, excited to finally share the latter with Hannah.

"What?!" Hannah's eyebrows leaped up.

"Don't worry. I turned him down," Mom assured her.

Hannah let out a peal of laughter. Our eyes connected, and all I wanted to do was lift her into my arms and carry her up the staircase and into the privacy of my apartment in a fit of Herculean strength I definitely didn't have.

A cough brought me back down to earth. I turned to find a line had formed in front of the counter. Hannah jumped into action, taking orders and processing payments while I made the coffees, and Mom and Josie ferried food out from the kitchen and took orders from customers at tables.

"George, is this what I think it is?" Hannah asked behind me, half an hour later.

I turned from the counter to find her beaming at me, holding a plate of beef Wellington, Dauphinoise Potatoes and green beans that she'd just picked up from the kitchen.

I grinned. "Yes. Romina made it as a special on Tuesday, but it's been so popular I'm planning to add it to the menu." I didn't mention that it had been a special I'd asked Romina to make for Hannah to celebrate *The Realm of Furies* release.

"Oh my god!" Hannah exclaimed.

"Don't worry, I've already asked Romina to make sure there is one set aside for you for lunch."

"You are the best, George O'Grady," Hannah murmured in my ear, surreptitiously placing her hand on my butt and giving it a squeeze as she walked past me to deliver the food.

With the four of us working, everything ran like a well-oiled machine. After the lunch rush was over, I waylaid Mom, who was carrying plates back to the kitchen. "Mom, why don't you take the rest of the afternoon off and relax? You're on vacation, after all."

"No, no. I'm happy to stay and help," Mom protested.

Hannah, standing nearby, turned. "Why don't both of you finish up early so you can spend some quality time with each other? Josie and I will manage fine without you."

Part of me didn't want to leave Hannah, but I also wanted to make sure Mom enjoyed her stay here, and so far, all she'd really done was work and help me cook. It would be nice to take her for a walk down Main Street, go to the antique store she loved, and perhaps grab an ice cream from the creamery and walk along the waterfront. Mom's face brightened at Hannah's suggestion, making the decision easier.

"Are you sure?" I asked.

Hannah nodded emphatically. "Positive. Go on! Go and have some fun! You two deserve a break after the last few days."

MOM and I had a lovely afternoon doing all the things I'd planned, although I couldn't help feeling guilty that I was itching to get home and see Hannah the entire time we were out. By the time we returned to Novel Gossip, Josie had left, and Hannah had almost finished mopping, her hair falling over her face as she scrubbed a stubborn mark in front of the counter. *How the hell does she even manage to make mopping hot?*

"Mom, why don't you go upstairs. I'll help finish up down here," I said, unable to take my eyes off Hannah.

Hannah looked up, her face breaking into a contagious smile. *Damn, it is good to have her back.*

"Here, let me." I held my hand out for the mop.

"I can do it," Hannah protested, but I shook my head.

"I know you can," I said, "but I want to."

Our hands brushed as she gave me the handle, and even though it was brief, a thrill shot through my spine. *Time for that later*. The floor wouldn't mop itself.

I took over the last section of the floor, making quick work of it, and then we headed upstairs together. I was itching to have a proper conversation with Hannah, but with Mom staying, our privacy was seriously lacking. Thankfully, as soon as we entered the apartment, Mom excused herself to take a shower.

As soon as she was out of sight, I wrapped my arms around Hannah again, enveloping her in a bear hug. "I missed you," I murmured into her hair.

"Me too. I know it was only two days, but it felt like an eternity."

"It really did." I pulled back so I could see her face, my arms still around her, and regaled her with a few highlights from the past few days of working with my mother.

"I'm so sorry," she managed to say, trying to bite back laughter. "I would never have left if I'd realized you were so understaffed."

"Well, I'm glad you did. Not only did Mom discover her new calling of working in a café, but it sounds like you managed to sort out a lot of things." I could have stayed like this, face to face with Hannah, for hours, but I was conscious that we'd be eating late if we didn't put the marinara sauce on to simmer soon. "Are you okay if I start making dinner?"

"Of course." Hannah nodded and walked with me to the kitchen. "What can I do to help?"

I passed Hannah garlic and onion to chop while I got out the saucepan and searched for the cans of tomatoes.

"I guess you didn't get a chance to speak to Tania or your parents today?" I asked as I opened the can. Hannah had arrived back at the café before noon, which meant she'd have had very little time in New York this morning.

Hannah's face broke into a grin. "Actually, I did both!"

I did a double-take. "You did?"

"I was very efficient—spoke to my parents at seven-thirty this morning and Tania at eight-thirty," Hannah said.

"Wow! That must have been an intense couple of hours." My face softened. "How did it all go?"

As Hannah chopped the alliums, she filled me in on the conversation with her parents. My heart ached hearing their reaction. They sounded awful.

"I'm so sorry it didn't go well."

Hannah gave a small smile. "Well, in some ways it did. My side of the conversation went well. I kept my cool and told them how I felt. Even though their response was disappointing, it felt good to finally be open and honest with them. As your therapist said, you can't control how people react."

My chest swelled with pride. "I'm so glad to hear that, babe. And how did things go with Tania?"

"That went better. We worked out the asset split, and while the conversation was definitely awkward, we got through it without things getting nasty."

Hannah tipped the garlic and onion into the saucepan. They sizzled as they made contact with the hot oil.

She turned around to me, her smile broadening. "It's such a relief to have both of those conversations behind me.

And while I can't control how my parents react, I can control who I surround myself with." She stepped toward me, holding my gaze. "And there's one person in particular I want to surround myself with as much as they'll let me."

"Oh, really?" I grinned. "And who might that be?"

Hannah wrapped her arms around my neck and kissed me gently before pulling back.

"Who do you think?" She smiled, her eyes crinkling, sending warmth rushing from my chest to my extremities.

"Well, I don't think you'll be hearing any objections from that person." I leaned in and kissed her again. "I would quite happily spend twenty-four seven with you."

As our kiss deepened and I slipped my hands under her top to caress the soft skin of her back, I was hit with a heady rush of endorphins.

Damn, I love this woman.

CHAPTER THIRTY-FIVE

HANNAH

GEORGE SHUT the door to her bedroom and turned to me, gripping my hips and pulling me to her. She kissed me on the lips slowly, deeply, firmly. It had been a long day, starting with the call with my parents early this morning, but thanks to the stunning woman in front of me I was suddenly wide awake.

Returning the kiss with gusto, I closed my eyes, relishing the soft, wet warmth of George's mouth. "I missed you...this...so much."

"Me too," George replied, her voice husky.

While I enjoyed the sensation of her body and mouth pressed against mine, it wasn't enough. I slid my hands under the back of her shorts, feeling the warm, soft curve of her ass, and then ran them up her strong back, rubbing my fingers in patterns over her skin.

"Mmm," George moaned softly. She deftly undid my bra and then tugged my t-shirt and bra up and off before doing the same to hers. George's eyes were dark and heavy-lidded as they lingered on my breasts. The sight of her half-naked, a sensual mix of strength and curves, combined with the obvious hunger in her eyes, sent desire gnawing low in my core.

"What about your mom?" I murmured, conscious she was just down the hallway from us.

"She won't hear a thing. If she's not asleep already, she'll have her headphones in and be listening to sleep stories."

Relieved, I stepped forward, pressing my body against hers. As much as I enjoyed the view of George topless, I was desperate to remove the space between us. There had been far too much of that in the past few days.

"You are so fucking sexy," she growled, nuzzling into my neck before trailing hot, wet kisses to my collarbone.

A moan escaped my lips as I caressed her back with my hands. "What do you feel like doing?" I murmured.

"I want to watch you come," George said, her voice low. "How do you feel about using the strap-on?"

I bit my lip, excitement pulsing through me. We hadn't used a strap-on together yet.

"That sounds amazing."

George jogged over to the side table next to her bed, opened the drawer, and pulled out a black harness and a purple, medium-sized dildo. She held it up, and looked at me, raising an eyebrow in question.

I nodded, my body humming in anticipation. George yanked off her pants and hopped into the harness, pushing the dildo through the O-ring, and then adjusting the straps so the harness was fastened around her hips and thighs. While George was busy doing that, I took the opportunity to remove my underwear.

George grinned, walking toward me. "Now, where were we?"

I put my hands on her ass and pulled her to me,

enjoying the pressure of the dildo pressing against me, and gave her a long, lingering kiss.

"Ah yes," she murmured, deepening the kiss as she slowly walked me backward.

When the backs of my thighs hit the mattress, I clambered onto the bed, grabbing George's hand and pulling her down with me. I rolled on top of her, legs straddling her waist, and leaned down to kiss her gorgeous mouth, running my hands over her firm biceps. *Damn, she's hot.*

George slid her hand between my legs. I lifted my hips slightly to give her access, desperate for her touch. I moaned as her fingers, slick with my wetness, circled my clit.

"God, that feels so good," I said before leaning in to kiss her again, closing my eyes to focus on the incredible sensations.

After a few minutes of George's skillful fingers teasing my clit, I was well and truly ready for more. Desire pulsed through my body, making it difficult to think straight.

"I want you inside me," I gasped, raising my hips up farther.

George, continuing to work her magic on my clit with one hand, used her other hand to turn on the vibrator nestled in the harness so that it pressed against her and then grabbed the dildo, positioning it upright for me. I slid onto it, closing my eyes as it filled me.

"Fuck, that feels incredible," I said.

I opened my eyes, and our gazes locked, sending a rush of endorphins through my body. The connection I felt with George was like nothing I'd felt before. It was intense, loving, and deep, and I couldn't get enough of it.

"You are so goddamn amazing, Hannah Taylor," George growled, her voice low.

"You're pretty fucking incredible too, George O'Grady," I replied breathlessly.

We slowly rocked our hips in unison, maintaining eye contact as our breathing became more labored. I picked up pace, and George followed suit, increasing the momentum of her hips and the pressure and speed of her fingers on my clit.

I gripped her hair, tugging, and George moaned.

"I'm so close," I whimpered, my thighs trembling.

"Me too," George said, her voice hoarse, as she pumped her hips and worked her hand harder.

Explosions surged through me. As the orgasm engulfed my body, George came as well, throwing her head back against the pillow and gasping as she continued to thrust into me, sending the last waves of pleasure washing over me. It was so intimate, coming together, knowing that we were both experiencing the same out-of-body experience.

"Fuck," George said, pulling me close for a kiss. "That was..."

"Phenomenal," I finished with a smile, my muscles continuing to twitch from the powerful orgasm.

Ten minutes later, my heart rate back to normal and my body relaxed, I lay on my side in bed, gazing into George's warm brown eyes only inches from mine. I let out a happy sigh. She gently lifted her hand and tucked a lock of hair behind my ear.

"How are you feeling now about your identity being disclosed?" George's voice was low and sympathetic.

"Honestly, still not great." I made a face.

"I'm sorry, babe," George said, stroking my hair.

"As much as I appreciate my readers, I really don't want to be a public figure. And after years of carefully guarding my identity, it kinda sucks that now when you Google H.

M. Stuart, my real name immediately pops up." I pressed my lips together. "But in some ways, it hasn't been as bad as I thought. Except for being recognized at Chris's book event in Brooklyn, I haven't had anyone approach me. And the event was full of fantasy readers, and it was the day after my identity was leaked, so it probably wasn't that surprising."

"That's good. It shouldn't be too difficult to avoid fantasy book events in Sapphire Springs, especially since we're the only people who would organize them," George said, her dimple on display.

"True." I smiled at George. "And it was reassuring that no one mentioned anything about it in the café today. I have a good feeling that it's not going to impact much, if at all, on my life in Sapphire Springs. And since I've pushed back on doing any further publicity, hopefully we've contained the damage as best we can."

"If anyone bothers you about it at the café, just let me know, and I'll set them straight," George said, her tone serious.

I smiled, imagining George sternly telling off a customer who dared to ask for my autograph. "I appreciate the offer, but I'm sure I'd be able to cope myself." I paused. "And while it has been kind of shitty, there have been some silver linings."

"Like Mom finding her calling?" George chuckled.

I laughed. "Well, that. But it also led to me building up confidence to speak to my parents and Tania. And it's been a bit of a wake-up call that I need to get back to therapy. My anxiety has felt a little out of control the last few days."

George wriggled closer to me and put a hand on my waist. "I'm sorry to hear that. Let me know if there is anything I can do to help."

George's presence was so comforting and grounding it

reminded me of the worries I'd had about our relationship while I was in New York. Was the fact that I was feeling so much better about everything now that I was back in Sapphire Springs evidence that I was too reliant on George? Maybe I should just practice my newfound skills at difficult conversations and talk to her about my worries. Before I had a chance to chicken out, I took a deep breath and went for it.

"After Tania and I broke up, I realized that I'd become way too dependent on her. We worked and lived together. I really relied on her for my social life—all my friends were originally her friends, and we were living in an apartment she'd bought. It also felt like she'd been so fundamental in my writing process that I couldn't write without her. So, when our relationship fell apart, it seemed as if I'd lost everything—my home, my friends, and my writing. Sorry, I know that sounds really dramatic." I gave George a weak smile.

"No, it makes sense," George said.

I swallowed, shifting my body on the bed to get even closer to George. "And I guess I've been starting to worry if I'm falling into the same trap with you. I feel like I already rely on you so much for support, both emotionally and with my writing, and we obviously work together. I've also managed to infiltrate your friend group. While I love how supportive you are, I want to make sure I'm not relying on you to an unhealthy extent. So I've been thinking about ways I can avoid that happening."

I bit my lip and stared at George, trying to gauge her reaction, leaving my words out there as almost a question. George looked at me with soft eyes, as if she was carefully considering my concerns.

She reached out and brushed a stray strand of hair

behind my ear. "Hey, that makes sense too. For what it's worth, if we ever broke up, your job here would be safe—although, as you said yourself, you don't need to work at Novel Gossip. I'm also confident that Blake, Jenny, Olivia, and Amanda would all want to continue to be your friend. They really like you. And while you sometimes bounce ideas off me, the writing is all you. Having said all that, I don't think there's anything wrong with relying on your partner for love and support."

I smiled, my body sinking into the mattress. Everything George had just said was exactly what I'd tried telling myself. But somehow, hearing it from her was a lot more convincing. And I kind of loved that she'd just used the words *partner* and *love* in the context of our relationship, albeit in a roundabout way. But still, it sounded so...official. And serious. Which was how I felt about her too.

"But I also don't want to minimize your concerns. Especially when we work together, it makes sense that you'd want to have some parts of your life that are separate from me." George's eyes twinkled. "You know, the book club is always looking for new blood. We could schedule your shifts to make sure you're available. Or according to some flyers that were dropped off downstairs this morning, there's a regular kayaking meet-up on Wednesday evenings and Saturday mornings you could attend."

I snorted. "Ha ha! But point taken." I furrowed my brow, thinking about possible options. "I'm pretty sure I saw a flyer for a hiking group, which might be more my scene—and more conducive to conversation than kayaking."

George grinned. "That sounds perfect. And thanks for sharing that, by the way."

"Do you have anything like that that would be helpful for me to know about?"

George paused for a moment. "Yeah. I think my hang-up is about a different type of relationship imbalance: where one person's career or interests constantly take priority over the other's, or where there is a significant power disparity. And I'm pretty sure that all tracks back to my parents and Alexis."

"Oh, that's good to know," I said, wondering if George had any concerns like that about our relationship.

"Yeah. Mom was Dad's secretary—that's how they met—and since their marriage wasn't very happy, I always wondered whether the fact that she was dependent on him for her livelihood might have stopped her from leaving him. And with Alexis, our relationship was unequal on quite a few levels, which caused me some grief at the time."

"That must have been difficult." I bit my lip. "Can you please let me know if you ever feel like something like that is affecting our relationship? When I'm working toward a deadline, I might sometimes hole up in my study, but my relationships trump work." My parents had always put work first, and I wasn't about to follow in their footsteps.

George nodded.

I wriggled forward so our noses were almost touching and kissed George softly on the lips.

George returned the kiss and then smiled. "Good, so my nightmare that you committed to a twelve-month international book tour without talking to me about it first is unlikely to come true?"

I laughed. "I'd say more than unlikely. Impossible. I can't think of anything worse. I'm not going anywhere—except, perhaps, to the city every now and again, and to Chicago to visit Barb a couple times a year."

"I'm glad to hear it." George pulled me in for another kiss. "I'm not going anywhere either."

CHAPTER THIRTY-SIX

GEORGE

"HOW WAS the rest of the afternoon?" I sat on the couch, massaging Hannah's feet as Mom took yet another fortunately timed shower. I was beginning to think she was purposefully taking them so Hannah and I could have some alone time, because I could have sworn she usually showered in the morning, and typically only once a day.

"Good!" Hannah grinned. "I scored myself an invite to the book club next week."

I looked up sharply from Hannah's feet. "Really?"

Hannah laughed. "Yes. I know you suggested it as a joke, but the more I thought about it, the more I liked the idea. It'll be nice to talk about books from a reader's perspective. And just because they're all a lot older than me doesn't mean we can't be friends. I mean, you get on really well with your mom, and she's in her sixties. And Barb is in her eighties, and she's one of my closest friends."

"Well, in that case, I love it," I said.

"Here, let's swap. You were on your feet all day. At least I had the morning off." Hannah pulled her feet off my lap and gestured for me to put mine on hers. Hannah had again insisted that Mom and I stop working after the lunch rush, so we'd driven to the open-air sculpture park and spent the afternoon walking around it.

"How did it go?" I worried for a moment that Hannah wouldn't know what I meant, but she knew immediately what I was referring to.

"The therapy session was really good. I've already booked another three for the next few weeks."

"That's great, babe." I stifled a moan as Hannah massaged the heel of my left foot, sending warm tingles up my leg.

I felt so proud of the progress she was making. And our conversation last night felt cathartic. We'd both confessed our major relationship insecurities and met each other with support and understanding. Any doubts I'd had about Hannah in the past few days had completely evaporated. She'd cut her trip short to make sure I was okay and was clearly invested in her life in Sapphire Springs. I couldn't see her abandoning me to court publicity and fame as Mom had implied.

Which reminded me. While Mom and Hannah had been getting along well, they hadn't had a chance to get to properly know each other yet. I still sensed Mom had some reservations about Hannah, but I was convinced that if they spent time together, just the two of them, they'd hit it off, and any worries Mom had would fade away.

"Hey, are you still up for a bonding baking session with Mom? I thought tonight could be a good opportunity since the cake I have planned is fairly simple—my blueberry-lemon cake. But no pressure if you're not. I know there's been a lot going on in the past few days."

Hannah smiled at me as she focused her attention on

my arch, sending off another wave of pleasurable sensations. "Yes, of course."

"Excellent," I said. Now all I needed was to get Mom onboard.

After Mom was out of the shower and we'd finished dinner, I enacted my scheme.

"I really need to take Max on a walk tonight. Would you two mind getting started on the cake of the day while I'm out?" I fought the urge to wink at Hannah.

"Why don't you two go out with Max, and I'll take care of the cake?" Mom asked, clearly trying to be helpful. My heart sank.

I racked my brain for a reason why that would be a terrible idea.

Thankfully, Hannah stepped in. "That's okay. I'd love to do it with you, Helen, if you don't mind." She smiled shyly at Mom.

"Excellent! Well, we'll be off. See you in a bit!" I grabbed Max's leash and my keys off the hall table and headed downstairs before Mom had a chance to respond.

I spent the next hour walking Max down Main Street, along the river, and then up through a warren of smaller residential streets, extending our route much longer than usual. While I'd felt confident in my plan when I'd left, as we walked, I couldn't help wondering if it could backfire. I knew how much Mom cared about me. Was there any chance she might voice her concerns directly to Hannah with the misguided view that she was protecting me? I picked up my pace at the thought.

"Let's head home, little fella," I said to Max, who pricked up his ears, clearly tired of our marathon trundle.

As we walked up the stairs to my apartment, I heard a clatter of metal and some raised voices. *Shit, shit, shit!* My pulse pounded in my ears. Surely it hadn't gone so badly it'd devolved into a shouting and pan-throwing match?

I ran up the rest of the stairs, sweating more than I had all through my walk.

My hands shook as I opened the apartment door and then raced to the kitchen.

I paused at the kitchen entrance and let out a deep breath. Mom and Hannah were standing side by side at the sink, Hannah washing the dishes and Mom drying them as they chatted. Two of my favorite people in the world seemed to be getting along just fine. But the noises I'd heard on the stairs had been concerning.

"Is everything okay in here? I heard some loud noises as I was coming in."

"Everything is excellent." Mom turned, smiling at me. "The cake is in the oven, we've nearly finished washing up, and your lovely girlfriend was just telling me about your kayaking incident, which made me laugh so hard I dropped a pan on my foot. Good thing I was wearing my shoes, or it really would have hurt."

I leaned back against the kitchen counter, warmth filling my chest. It seemed like my scheme to bring Mom and Hannah together hadn't been a half-baked plan after all.

CHAPTER THIRTY-SEVEN

HANNAH

AS THE LOCAL fire trucks drove down Main Street, lights flashing, George flipped the sign on Novel Gossip's front door to *Closed* and grabbed my hand.

"It's your first Fourth of July in Sapphire Springs. Let's make it a memorable one!" she said with a grin as she tugged me to the edge of the sidewalk to watch the Fourth of July parade.

George had decided to close Novel Gossip early so we could enjoy the festivities. It was a shame George's mom had left yesterday, as I was sure Helen would have loved the celebrations. George had been spot-on about her mom. While we didn't have a lot in common, we'd still gotten along very well. And we did have one, very important, thing in common—George.

As the fire trucks drove out of view, fifteen bagpipe players and drummers marched by, cheered on by locals who lined the streets. Various community groups followed: the local Lions Club, the Scouts and the group that ran the community garden. A random teenager walked by with two alpacas. Every so often, I'd recognize one of our regulars from the café and give them an encouraging yell.

George glanced at her watch. "I'd better go get Max ready for the pet parade. You're more than welcome to stay and watch if you want."

"Are you sure?" I was fairly confident George could manage Max and was excited to see who would appear next in the parade. Not only was I getting a kick out of seeing our regulars in a completely different context, learning more about them in the process (who would have thought that Mrs. Harding was a bagpipe player?) but I was also enjoying the real community feel of the festivities. The Thanksgiving and Pride parades I'd been to in New York had been massive, well-oiled, commercialized affairs full of floats promoting businesses and overwhelming crowds. You would never have seen two random alpacas or a minibus packed full of residents from the local retirement home waving American flags.

An excited sniffing at my knees ten minutes later caught my attention, and I looked down to see Max, his golden hair freshly brushed and shining in the sunlight, wearing a tiny red sequin hat on his head and a red-white-and-blue bandana around his neck. On his red harness, George had attached the white and blue cardboard stars we'd cut out on the floor of her living room last night.

"Aww, who's a gorgeous boy." I gave Max a pat, careful not to damage his outfit. I'd become very attached to Max during the past few weeks. He was intelligent, gentle, and affectionate—not unlike his owner. Although, thankfully, his owner didn't drool or snore as much. I smiled to myself. The term *golden retriever* was often used by romance readers to describe love interests who were kind, loyal, loving, and reliable, which fit George perfectly. It seemed appropriate that she had a golden retriever of her own. My smile widened as I realized another romance term for George's personality was a *cinnamon roll*—also perfect given George's baking skills. *I bet she makes a mean cinnamon roll.* I looked over at George, my chest full of love. While I hadn't told George yet how I felt, I planned to. I was just waiting for the right time.

"I also got something for you. To celebrate your first Fourth of July at Sapphire Springs," George said, grinning.

It took me a moment to realize what George was handing me. It was a fanny pack, decorated in sequins depicting the American flag.

I burst into laughter. "Oh my god!"

There was something inside. I unzipped it to find a travel-sized bottle of sunscreen, lip balm and hand sanitizer.

"This is amazing, thank you," I said, leaning into give George a kiss.

"Don't feel you have to wear it. I just saw it when I was buying Max's hat and couldn't resist getting it for you." George said, as I wrapped it around my waist and clipped it on.

"Nope, I love it," I said, peering down to admire it. I pulled my phone out of the satchel I had been wearing and transferred it to my fanny pack. "I'll drop my bag inside, since I've got this much more practical and very patriotic fanny pack to carry my belongings now."

I ran back into Novel Gossip and left my satchel on one of the café's tables, and then went back out to join George and Max.

"I don't think the hat is going to last long," George said, just as Max rubbed his head against the lamppost, dislodging his hat in the process. "Yep, okay, I'll just carry that until we're down at the waterfront."

We walked along Main Street in time with a group of cheerleaders from the local high school dressed in blue-and-white Lycra tops and matching skirts or shorts, shiny blue pom poms waving wildly. I'd never been the cheerleading type, but their enthusiasm was contagious, and my step had a decided bounce to it.

Dockside Park was buzzing with energy when we arrived. Lines had formed in front of food and drink stalls, kids were screaming with glee as they launched themselves into the air on colorful jumping castles, and a bluegrass band was playing from a stage on the opposite side of the park. Groups of locals sat on picnic blankets or folding chairs, listening to the music. The scent of barbecued meats and hot fries hung in the air. I spotted even more Novel Gossip regulars, many of whom said hi or gave us a wave in acknowledgement. On the other side of the park, the Hudson River sparkled in the sunlight, a deep blue reflecting the almost cloudless sky.

"Wow, this is amazing!" I said, taking it all in. There'd never been anything like this growing up in Chicago or on the Upper West Side. This level of community spirit was completely foreign to me, but I absolutely loved it.

George grinned. "It's one of my favorite days of the year." She tugged at Max's leash to stop him from going after a toddler holding a half-eaten hot dog, tomato sauce smeared all over her face. "Now, where is the pet p—"

"Hey! Are you guys heading to the pet parade?" Jenny walked into our line of sight, holding an extremely handsome golden-brown toy poodle—her dog, Walter. A white wig and navy tricorn hat adorned his head, which was framed by white ruffles around his collar. A tiny waistcoat with a small Declaration of Independence attached to it completed the outfit.

George nodded, and Jenny showed us the way while I gushed over how cute Walter looked. As much as I loved Max to bits, there was no way he was winning the competition with Walter in contention. We arrived at a small stage near a large oak tree where a number of pets and their owners had gathered. Unsurprisingly, there were a lot of dogs, but other animals were featured as well, some much more surprising. The two alpacas we'd seen earlier in the parade were now wearing matching red hats with white stars and large American flags attached to their backs. A turtle had blue and red tinsel on its shell, a white hat perched on top. An undecorated green-and-yellow parrot sat preening in a bird cage.

The sun's rays were still strong, so we stood under a tree, chatting with Jenny, and were soon joined by Blake, who'd decided not to involve her cat in the competition but had come to cheer on Walter. Max quickly fell asleep, snoring at our feet.

The MC started calling pets and their owners to walk across the stage in front of the three judges.

George knelt down next to Max and gave him a pat. "Okay, Max, it could be our turn any minute. Let's get this hat on you, big fella, before they call you up." Max snorted but didn't rouse.

I gazed down at George. "Your dog seems to sleep as soundly as you do," I said, smiling.

Our eyes locked, and George grinned back at me, sending a jolt of happiness coursing through my veins. George's impressive ability to sleep through Max's snoring and her mom puttering loudly around the kitchen in the mornings had been the subject of some gentle teasing from me over the past few days.

George chuckled and gave him a gentle shake.

"C'mon, Max." He opened one eye and glared at her before closing it again.

"Maybe he's just waiting for the official announcement," I offered.

George got to her feet, shaking her head. "Yeah, maybe." She didn't sound convinced.

The MC announced Walter's name, and Walter, accompanied by Jenny, marched in a very stately manner onto the stage, unfazed by clapping from the onlookers.

"Wow, he's a pro," I murmured to George.

"Yeah, Jenny used to dress him up all the time for social media, so he's used to it," George said as she watched them.

Stevie, the parrot, was called up next, now wearing a little red-white-and-blue frilly collar around its neck. Stevie perched on its owner's hand, singing "America the Beautiful." I turned down my hearing aid temporarily. As impressive as Stevie's vocal range was, she—or he, I wasn't sure—was a little screechy.

Two alpacas followed Stevie, and then Max was called.

"Max, it's your time to shine," George said. But Max was in a deep sleep, twitching as though he was dreaming about chasing squirrels. "Max!" I patted his head and then tugged gently on his lead.

George tried to push his butt up. Nothing.

We looked at each other, shaking our heads. At this point, if Max had been my dog, I would have given up. But George was clearly keen to give Max his minute of glory. She bent at the knees and enveloped Max in a bear hug. I held Max's lead as George carried him toward the stage, wobbling up the stairs and depositing him at the top.

"Come on, Max!" George said encouragingly.

Awake now, Max stood at the edge of the stage and stared at her, unimpressed.

I tugged gently on the lead without any success. Conscious that we had about fifty people's eyes on us, I looked around for inspiration and spotted a man walking past, digging into a German sausage with mustard.

"I'll go halves with you on a sausage if you come with me. See, sausage!" I pointed at the man.

Max sprang up, giving my arm a vigorous yank, and bounded across the stage, in pursuit of the unsuspecting sausage eater, his hat falling off his head in the process. George rushed to help me, and I briefly registered some applause and laughter as we wrestled Max back under control.

"I'm sorry," I said to George as we did a walk of shame back to Jenny, Blake, and Walter. "I didn't think my bribe would be so effective."

George laughed. "It certainly worked. You got him across the stage, although he was moving so quickly I suspect all the judges saw was a flash of gold. But I think we both know he never had a hope of winning anyway," she said with a twinkle in her eye.

"Well, it was certainly a dramatic return to the stage after a fifteen-year plus absence."

George's face clouded. "Oh shit, I didn't even think about your history, babe. I hope it wasn't too upsetting.

I smiled. "It's fine. It was very different being up there with you and Max. And we all know who the center of attention was just then, and it wasn't me." I looked fondly down at Max.

When we reached the others, George wrapped her arm around me and gave me a squeeze. Max collapsed back onto the ground and snored all the way through Walter receiving first place.

After the awards had been handed out, we made our

way to a red-and-white striped tent where the pie contest was about be held. After winning the contest for the past two years, George had been appointed to the judging panel. Based on the number of pies on the long banquet tables, the pie contest was very popular.

George's eyes widened as she took in the amount of food before her.

"It looks like I'm going to be here a while. Rather than watch me gorge on pies, do you want to go wander around and come back in half an hour?"

Two hours later, George, Blake, Jenny, Olivia, Amanda, and I were relaxing on two tartan picnic rugs, a blues band playing in the background. I was devouring a German sausage, which I'd been craving ever since the pet parade incident, while George, who'd sworn she'd never eat again after the pie winners were announced, had almost finished a serving of barbecue ribs and cornbread. I grinned at her, fingers sticky with barbecue sauce, as she devoured them with relish.

I washed down the last bite of sausage with a gulp of cider and leaned back on my arms, letting my body relax. Since dogs and fireworks didn't mix, we'd dropped Walter and Max back at home. Now it was evening, the strength had faded from the sun's rays.

"How are you doing, gorgeous?" George asked, wrapping an arm around me.

"Good. Perfect, actually," I said, turning my head to smile at her.

Today had been perfect. I'd sent the rest of my manuscript off to Michael this morning, FaceTimed Barb to fill her in on recent events and let her know that George and I were planning to visit in August, worked a shift at Novel Gossip, and then spent the rest of the day enjoying the

Fourth of July celebrations. And now, here I was, lounging outside with George and my friends on a beautiful summer evening.

As we sat together on the picnic rug, another stunning yellow, red, and purple sunset appeared and faded, and then the fireworks, launched from a barge on the river, propelled bursts of vibrant colors into the night's sky. Star bursts, circles, and showers of light exploded around us, and I couldn't help squealing with glee. I snuggled closer into George. A perfect ending to a perfect day.

The words that I'd been wanting to say for some time now suddenly became too urgent not to express.

"Hey, George," I murmured.

"Mmm?" George hummed softly in my ear.

I looked up at her. A mixture of nerves and adrenaline rushed through me at the thought of what I was about to say.

I took a deep breath, and then let the words come out. "I love you."

Her face burst into a smile as bright as the fireworks we'd just watched and any worries I'd had about how George would react vanished.

"I love you too," she said, giving me slow, tender kiss.

I melted into the kiss, savoring her soft lips on mine. *An even more perfect ending to an already perfect day.*

As George and I walked home, hand in hand, George leaned close to my ear. "When we get home, I'm keen to give you an intimate pyrotechnics show with a hopefully explosive finale," she murmured.

My heart full, I laughed, tilting my head up to kiss her again. "Don't you need a license for that? But I'm not at all averse to ending the night with a bang."

EPILOGUE
HANNAH

TEN MONTHS LATER

"OH, I'VE MISSED THIS."

"Me too." I closed my eyes, enjoying the gentle bobbing of the water and the sun's warmth on my skin.

It was the first warm day in early May, so we'd leaped at the chance to go kayaking.

Last summer, after I handed in my book to Michael for edits and George found two more employees to work at Novel Gossip, we'd finally had more time to spend together outside work. And one of our favorite things to do as a couple was to rent a kayak, paddle until we were just out of sight of Sapphire Springs, and then lie back and lounge in the sunshine, just as we were doing now, relaxing and chatting—and covered in sunscreen, of course. All our friends thought we'd become kayaking enthusiasts, and Olivia had even suggested we do an overnight kayaking trip. Little did they know that minimal actual kayaking was involved in our excursions.

We lay there for a few minutes in silence as the sun soaked into my bones.

"Hey, Hannah?" George asked. There was something in her voice that would have made me sit up and look at her if I hadn't been so damn comfortable.

"Yeah?"

"I was wondering..." George paused, and it reminded me of that awkward conversation we'd had on a kayak about our first kiss eleven months ago. I frowned. It was unlike George to sound hesitant.

The kayak wobbled. I opened my eyes and found myself looking at George, who was now seated in the kayak, gazing down at me, her face upside down. I blinked. That was unexpected.

She put a hand on my shoulder. "Would you be interested in moving in together? I know your lease is up soon, and we spend pretty much every night together."

Oh. Now I understood. I'd been thinking about this for a while. I wanted to live with George. A lot. I couldn't imagine my life without her, and on the rare occasion we did spend a night apart, I missed her.

But as much as I liked George's apartment—mainly because it was *George's* apartment—I didn't want to live there. I'd made a point of ensuring we spent at least a few days a week at my little cottage.

I smiled up at her. "I would love to move in with you, but I'm worried that I'll struggle. Not with living with you," I said hurriedly, "but just with your apartment. Well, not the apartment, really, more the location. I like your apartment, but I really love living in nature, being able to walk out onto my deck and only see trees, grass, and flashes of the Hudson. And I like having some separation between work and home if I can—at least with one of my jobs. But you own your place, whereas I'm just renting, so I know it makes sense for me to move in with you. Not to mention how convenient it is, being so close to work." Twelve months ago, I would have shied away from this conversation. Pride that I was now able to express myself to George welled up in me.

George stroked my head, beaming down at me. "I thought you'd feel that way. And I was actually thinking we could find our own place together. Something similar to your current house, just with a bit more space so we can have visitors and you can still have a proper study for your writing."

I furrowed my brow. "Are you sure? I don't want you to leave your apartment just for me."

George continued to caress my head gently. "I'm sure. And it's not just for you. It's for us. I think getting our own place, together, is important. Max would love some outdoor space to run around in, and I'd really like a bit more work/life separation as well."

George's words filled me with comfort.

"What would you do with your apartment? It seems like a waste for it to just sit there."

"I spoke to Ben, and he's interested in renting it. I did warn him about the work/life separation thing, but he's still super excited. It's twice the size of his current place, and I'm offering him a discount on the basis that he will effectively be adding an extra level of security to Novel Gossip. You know, just in case anyone decides to break in to sign hundreds of books in the middle of the night or something."

I laughed. "Who in their right mind would do something so ridiculous?"

"Who indeed?" George grinned fondly at me and then leaned down and kissed me on the head, sending the kayak on another wobble that threatened to tip us into the water.

I squealed. "George! It might be a warm day for early May, but the water will still be freezing! Please don't capsize us."

George chuckled. "Okay, no more kisses until we are out of the kayak. But you still haven't answered my question. What do you think? Do you want to move in together?"

I smiled back up at George. "I'm oar-ficially on board to find a home that floats both our boats."

George rolled her eyes, laughing at me. "That was oar-ful."

"But in all seriousness, I would absolutely love to move in with you."

I relaxed back into the kayak, gazing up at George.

It was hard to believe that it had been less than a year ago that I'd met her. We'd faced some novel problems along the way, but we'd gotten through them, supporting each other and—at least in my case—learning a lot in the process. My love for George pulsed through my veins as I studied her face.

"You know what, screw it! Come back down here and give me a kiss!" And with that, I reached up, cupped George's face in my hands, and gently pulled my gorgeous girlfriend toward me, ignoring the ominous wobble the kayak made.

Thank you so much for reading **Novel Problems**.

If you enjoyed it, I would really appreciate if you could leave a review on Amazon, Goodreads or share your thoughts on social media.

If you'd like to receive a bonus scene for **Novel Problems** and hear when future books in the Sapphire Springs series are published, please sign up to my newsletter: https://elizabethluly.com/newsletter-sign-up.

If you haven't read Jenny and Blake's love story yet (**Not Just Gal Pals**) you can find it here: https://mybook.to/NotJustGalPals.

Thanks again,

Liz

AUTHOR'S NOTE

Like Hannah, in the past few years, I have experienced unexplained hearing loss in my left ear. Also, like Hannah, I have a hearing aid that I frequently misplace! Hannah's experience in the book with hearing loss is based on my own. However, I would like to emphasize that everyone's experience with hearing loss is different, so my experience/Hannah's experience are in no way representative of all.

In case it's helpful, below are some tips for communicating with people who are hard of hearing that resonate with me:

1. Attract the person's attention before beginning a conversation (e.g., say the person's name or use a gesture to get their attention).

2. Where possible, find a quiet area free of background noise to have a conversation.

3. Maintain eye contact with the person, face them directly, and avoid covering your mouth with your hands or other objects if possible. Lip reading and facial expressions assist with communication.

4. Speak clearly, and slow down if necessary. While speaking slightly louder can sometimes help, shouting can be counterproductive as it can distort words and make lip reading harder.

5. Consider rephrasing instead of repeating if the person is finding it difficult to hear you.

6. Some people, like me, may have one ear that is better at hearing than the other. If you are aware of this (e.g., in my case, it's the ear without the hearing aid), then try to situate yourself to be on that side of the person.

7. Be patient and understanding. Interacting with those who are hard of hearing can be frustrating, but please try to be considerate. I find it terribly frustrating when I can't hear and have to ask someone to repeat themselves, but it's not due to a lack of trying!

ACKNOWLEDGMENTS

Many thanks to my family for their ongoing support and encouragement, in particular Mum for reading it twice, once when very jet-lagged!

Thank you to Lauren for your thoughtful comments and Jenn Lockwood for your excellent proofreading (any typos that slipped through are almost certainly due to me making some last-minute changes after Jenn's review!).

To my amazing beta readers, your helpful feedback and supportive comments meant the world to me.

A huge thank you to Sam at Ink & Laurel for bringing Hannah and George to life through your fantastic cover design.

Amy, thanks again for letting me use your Instagram handle, @novelgossip, as the name of George's cafe.

Thank you also to Annie Metcalf at Magers & Quinn Booksellers in Minneapolis, who provided very helpful information about book signings, and Mary of @maryanher-library and @diversifyyourshelves, who provided invaluable feedback that enabled me to find a German translator for this book.

And to everyone else who provided feedback and support along the way, thank you.

ABOUT THE AUTHOR

Elizabeth Luly lives with her wife, toddler, and Schnoodle in Melbourne, Australia, in a home overflowing with books. She loves (in no particular order) rom coms, coffee, dogs and traveling.

Sign up for her newsletter and stay up to date on her book news: www.elizabethluly.com.

And find her here:

Website: www.elizabethluly.com
Facebook: www.facebook.com/elizabethlulyauthor
Instagram: www.instagram.com/elizabethlulyauthor
Goodreads: https://www.goodreads.com/author/show/ 22986218.Elizabeth_Luly

ALSO BY ELIZABETH LULY

SAPPHIRE SPRINGS SERIES

Not Just Gal Pals (Book 1)

A grumpy/sunshine sapphic fall romance featuring Blake, Sapphire Spring's local doctor, and Jenny, an influencer fleeing a social media scandal.

Novel Problems (Book 2)

A feel-good sapphic summer romance between George, the golden retriever owner of the cafe-bookstore Novel Gossip, and Hannah, a secretive fantasy author who has a lot of novel problems.

OTHER

From LA to London, With Love

A Koru-award winning M/F celebrity romance set in London, featuring Sophie Shah, a bisexual single-mom-by-choice, Chris Trent, a humiliated movie star, and a cast of queer characters.